CONFINEMENT

Katharine McMahon

CONFINEMENT

Flamingo
An Imprint of HarperCollins*Publishers*

Flamingo
An Imprint of HarperCollins*Publishers*
77−85 Fulham Palace Road,
Hammersmith, London W6 8JB

Published by Flamingo 1998
1 3 5 7 9 8 6 4 2

A catalogue record for this book is
available from the British Library

ISBN 0 00 225632 0

Set in Postscript Monotype Spectrum by
Rowland Phototypesetting Ltd,
Bury St Edmunds, Suffolk

Printed and bound in Great Britain by
Caledonian International Book Manufacturing Ltd, Glasgow

Acknowledgements

With special thanks to Mary Portas, Martin Rainsford, Kate and Hugh St John and Gill Woods for helping me out with research and ideas.

To Queen's College, London and North London Collegiate School for giving me access to archives.

To Gillian Avery for her book: *The Best Type of Girl*, and to Mark Lucas and Mandy Kirkby for their advice and encouragement.

For Jenny, Charlotte
and Jacob

1

Sarah and Mrs Beckett spoke in whispers. The entrance hall was dotted with rival pairs of mothers and daughters and it wouldn't do to be overheard.

At the back of the hall was a graceful staircase of white marble. Every ten minutes or so a woman in a maroon knitted suit would come down with a girl who'd been interviewed and swap her for the next on the list. Mrs Beckett, afraid of being accidentally forgotten, insisted on edging closer to the staircase every time there was a gap. After half an hour she and Sarah were actually on the best seat of all, a wooden bench nearest the bottom step.

Sarah felt the pressure of her mother's bony elbow in her ribs. 'Your shoe.'

'What? What's the matter with my shoe?'

'Ssssh. Wipe it. Here.'

A handkerchief was passed tensely across and Sarah obediently rubbed away at the toe of her tan lace-up. Mrs Beckett smiled blindly out into the hall. 'Hurry up.'

Afterwards Sarah sat up, flushed. The drama had been followed with intense interest, she realized, though everyone pretended not to have noticed. Nerves hummed in the warm, dusty air.

'Who do you think that is?' she asked, her voice unexpectedly loud and high. 'I'll have a look.'

'Sarah!'

But Sarah marched boldly across to a portrait hanging in the central panel of the back wall. A young woman in a blue gown returned her gaze from prominent grey eyes. Shining brown hair was parted above a stern brow and the jaw did not suggest a kind or tolerant nature.

'Elizabeth Hardemon. Headmistress, Priors Heath 1856—1901,

read a little plaque set in the ornate frame:

Presented to the school in 1907 by Revd Martin Hardemon.

'Sarah Beckett.'

The woman in maroon was back.

'Here. Here,' called Mrs Beckett leaping up and raising her hand. Sarah stepped forward, feeling herself strong in the spotlight of her own life.

'Don't forget to mention the Brownies,' hissed her mother.

'Come with me, dear.'

Sarah's feet were now actually on those beautiful white steps and her hand skimmed the polished rail. Below sat Mrs Beckett in her best green mac, the insistent tug of her ambition dragging at her daughter's shoulders. Sarah concentrated on the delicious click of the maroon woman's heels on the bare marble and the way her hair was pinned into a perfect roll at the back. At the first turn of the stairs was a landing on which fell jewelled pools of light from a high stained-glass window. Sarah ran her hand through the beams and saw her fingers dappled.

'I like that,' she said, but the secretary didn't pause.

Upstairs there was a broad corridor with creaking wooden boards. Sarah had to sit on a chair opposite a white door bearing the words *Miss Simon, Headmistress.* Her hands were clammy, her woollen gym-slip hot under her thighs. Now at last she was nervous because for the first time it mattered to her whether she succeeded or not. The portrait of Elizabeth Hardemon, the white staircase and the stained glass had shown her how different Priors Heath School for Girls might be to Becksmith

Primary's tarmacked playground, wire fences and corridors with brown-tiled walls.

The door opened and a golden-haired girl came out, actually shaking the Head's hand as she left. I couldn't manage that, thought Sarah, and felt the burden of all the things she had never done.

'I'll be with you in a minute, dear,' said the Head who went mysteriously back into her room and closed the door. Sarah guessed that she was making notes on the last candidate. What possible chance had she against such perfection?

After a very short time Sarah was summoned. Miss Simon's study was a marvel of floral chintz and flowers in vases, not at all resembling the little green-painted room occupied by Mr Turner, Head of Becksmith Primary. Sarah was ushered to a seat by a gas fire and Miss Simon sat opposite looking rather like Aunty Win, although Miss Simon didn't wear a hat.

There followed a comfortable chat in which Miss Simon asked Sarah lots of easy questions about herself. 'What are you reading at the moment?'

'Well, my mother and I have just finished *Jane Eyre*. I read to her when she's ironing and sometimes we alternate pages. Next we'll try *The Mill on the Floss*.'

'And what did you like about *Jane Eyre*?'

'Oh, the bit when Blanche Ingrams visits, and you know Mr Rochester really loves Jane all along. And of course the beginning when Jane was at school and Helen Burns was ill.'

'Why do you suppose that part appealed to you?'

'Because I like reading about schools and Helen is so good. I don't think anyone would cry over me like that. Not that I would ever want them to,' she added hurriedly, 'not that I would ever want to give them the trouble.'

'I see. Now what about your own school? Do you enjoy school, Sarah?'

'Oh yes. I'm an only child so I like having all the people around me.'

3

'What are your favourite lessons?'

'History. I love history.'

'Why's that, do you think?'

'Well, you know those books we have, with the pictures of cavemen and women and the fires? I always want to know what's happening behind, inside the cave.'

'And how do you occupy your spare time when you're not reading?'

'Brownies,' said Sarah triumphantly. 'Though I'm getting too old and I can't say I like knots.' She remembered belatedly that her mother had warned her never to say what she didn't like doing, so she changed the subject to elocution classes.

After Sarah had read aloud an extract from *Through the Looking Glass*, Miss Simon indicated that the interview was over. It was actually quite easy to shake hands and Sarah walked dreamily back along the passage with the memory of the Head's dry, cool fingers pressing her own hot palm. She could hardly bear to go down the stairs in case she should never come back again. Glancing up at the stained-glass window she saw that it depicted three running, laughing girls in long frocks with white roses round their feet, holding out a scroll which read '*FIAT LUX*'.

Please, please, please, she prayed, let me belong to somewhere this old.

As soon as they were out of the double doors and down the steps on to the forecourt of Priors Heath Mrs Beckett whispered loudly: 'How did it go? What did she say?'

'She liked my reading aloud. I told her about *Jane Eyre*.'

Mrs Beckett looked pleased and her compressed lips relaxed. 'What did you say exactly?'

'I said I read to you while you did the ironing.'

'Sarah, you didn't. You didn't mention my ironing! Miss Simon wouldn't want to hear about my ironing.'

'Oh, never mind, it doesn't matter.' Sarah quickened her pace. They were passing the wall of a brewery which gave off a sickly aroma of malt. She knew that this interrogation would continue throughout the walk into the town centre and the bus ride back to Hillingdon. 'I said that my favourite subject was history.'

'Sarah, you hardly do any history at Becksmith. Whyever didn't you concentrate on your English?'

'History was fine.'

'I hope she didn't ask any arithmetic questions.'

'Of course not. Anyway, I must have done all right in the maths test, mustn't I, or I wouldn't have got this far?'

'Sarah, I'm sure lots of girls did very well in the test. There's no need to boast.'

'I wasn't boasting, I was just saying . . .'

'I know. Dear old Sarah, you've done so well. Come on, let's go and have tea in a shop. You deserve it after that ordeal. Daddy said we should.' The moment of tension was over. Mrs Beckett had established that her child had not been showing off, at least not deliberately. Faringford town centre was unknown to them, being some fifteen miles from home, but it had a proper high street with several tempting little cafés. Mother and daughter linked arms in joyous anticipation of the wonderful treat of tea out.

Nine months later Sarah was studying history in a classroom on the top floor of the New Building at Priors Heath School for Girls, Faringford, Hertfordshire. She had graduated from cavemen to Saxons and was grappling with a page of questions set by the formidable Miss Stone who wore a sack-shaped pinafore over a checked shirt.

During their first lesson at the beginning of September Miss Stone had terrified Sarah by her strictness. 'Girls, I don't care what anyone else in this school expects from you. I demand one hundred per cent and I cannot stand halfheartedness. I will not tolerate sloppy work or lame excuses for homework not being done. You are bright girls, or so we've been told. Your brains give you privilege. Do not abuse or waste them.'

Afterwards groups of girls wearing new navy-blue tunics and knitted cardigans had stood about in the quad doubled up with hilarity at the squat fierceness of Miss Stone. But Sarah had felt as if she had just emerged from an ice-cold shower. I will please her, she thought, I will make her notice me. She matters.

8. *Describe a typical Saxon dwelling.* In the picture two girls with immensely long plaits did some weaving outside a neat little hut. The next drawing showed their living accommodation with skins tossed over a plank bed. It must have been dark and smoky, Sarah decided, with spiders and rats probably, unless they had cats. I wonder if cats had been tamed by then?

She had just written a neat number 8 in the margin when a scrap of minutely folded paper landed full square on the fresh ink and made a faint smudge. Sarah's head jolted up but everyone else seemed to be writing busily. She unfolded the note.

Sarah Beckett. Do you want to come to my birthday outing on Saturday? Imogen.

All speculation about Saxon domesticity went flying from Sarah's head. An invitation from Imogen Taylor? But they weren't friends. Surely Imogen was barely conscious that Sarah existed? She dared a glance at Imogen who sat three rows away with her long thin legs splayed in the aisle and her angular shoulder in its grubby white shirt turned away. Sarah's heart beat faster and her cheeks were hot.

After the lesson Imogen dived for the door and stalked off, bound no doubt for some unlawful break-time activity. Sarah scurried in her wake.

'Sarah,' called Claire Tomkins, 'aren't you coming to the dining room? It's Tuesday. Chelsea buns.' But Sarah had no time to explain where she was going.

In the short time that the girls had been at Priors Heath Imogen Taylor had established herself as a wild card. She wore her new uniform with panache, the knot of her tie almost invisible, her skirt hitched to knicker-level. Witty and impudent, she kept to the line of acceptable behaviour by a whisker, accumulating a following of reprobates as surely as a magnet will attract iron filings. Sarah had watched Imogen with wistful, alarmed eyes, absorbing the quality of her fine cheek-bones, white skin and thin, unruly body. Her own friends like Claire tended to be calm and sensible, 'good workers' as the teachers said.

She caught up with Imogen on the stairs and felt dwarfish and awkward elbowing along behind her.

'This birthday. Do you mean it?'

'Of course.'

'Will Caroline be there?'

'No.'

'Will Fiona?'

'No.'

'Will Laura?'

'No one else. Just you.'

'It's very nice of you.'

'Yep.' By now they had crossed the crowded quadrangle. Behind them was the red-brick New Building dating from the 1920s when Priors Heath School for Girls had undergone a major expansion. Ahead was the eighteenth-century Old House where Sarah had been interviewed and to the left was a high wall with an arched entrance to the rose garden, a haven for staff and prefects and absolutely out of bounds to anyone in the lower school. 'I'm meeting Laura in the garden,' said Imogen. 'Coming?'

'Oh no. No.' Sarah hung back, scared of such insubordination. Imogen tossed her hair from her forehead and was gone, leaving Sarah in the quad which seemed suddenly dull and chill because emptied of Imogen.

Sarah's peace of mind was destroyed. Priors Heath had hitherto been a manageable place, orderly, industrious, cheerful, all qualities she was used to at home. The girls had sifted themselves into little groups and Sarah had a special friend,

Claire, who was also on a scholarship and lived in the same north-west London suburb as Sarah, though her family's semi-detached house was much bigger and had a garage. They travelled by bus together through the farmland of the Green Belt to the town of Faringford where they got off at the stop outside Boots. From there they walked past the brewery to Priors Heath which stood back from the road in a wide forecourt where the senior teachers parked their cars. Junior girls were never allowed to use the main entrance through the double doors of the Old House. Instead they were herded down a narrow passage which came out in the quadrangle. To the left of this alleyway was a wooden fence protecting them from Ryder Street and the mysterious, shouting den of iniquity beyond, which was Ryder Street Secondary Modern.

Throughout the hour-long journey to school Claire gave minute details of her family's domestic arrangements and in particular the activities of her brilliant older brother Stephen. On the way home the girls would discuss their teachers and class-mates. Sarah felt affection and gratitude for Claire but was sometimes a little stifled. Certainly it was not possible to discuss Imogen's birthday party with her as she would undoubtedly disapprove, or at least ask many awkward questions.

For the rest of the week Sarah wallowed in her secret glory, though once the event had been arranged Imogen treated her exactly as before, with a complete disregard for her existence.

The pride of Sarah's parents when they understood that she had been invited to Imogen Taylor's was profound, as they could tell from the posh address that already Sarah was rubbing shoulders with the rich and the noble. There was a considerable argument about what Sarah should wear. Mrs Beckett spent an entire episode of *The Archers* ironing Sarah's best red corduroy dress though Sarah knew the frock would be totally wrong. 'Please can we go to Dorothy Perkins in the morning? I need something short. And some stocking tights.'

She was wasting her breath. A birthday treat demanded a best dress.

Straight after lunch on Saturday Sarah and her parents set out in the car for Hampstead. The drive was a terrible ordeal for Mr Beckett who hated traffic and unknown roads. Of course they were nearly an hour early and had to park round the corner and go for a cold, gritty walk on the Heath. Then they all stood awe-struck on the pavement outside Imogen's high white house until Sarah plucked up the courage to climb the five steps to the front door.

After lifting the heavy iron knocker she looked back to her parents. There they were in their best macs, proud and nervous. Suddenly she wanted to return with them, home to 16, Heskwith Close, Hillingdon, where she might make a chocolate cake with her mother or play jacks on the garden path while her father painted the French windows. But it was too late. Light footsteps could be heard from within the house and Imogen, wearing a short black skirt and yellow skinny-rib jumper, flung wide the door.

The hall of Imogen's house was cold, large and empty with big black and white floor tiles and a huge piece of dark furniture on which lay a man's hat with a brim. It smelt mothbally, as if under-used, and so did Imogen's parents who were very tall. But despite their size the family was dwarfed by high-ceilinged rooms filled with unlovely antiques. There had once been another child, Lawrence, but he had left home to pursue a vague offer of work with a record company in the States. The only signs of him were a closed door on the first floor and a couple of unclaimed football boots in the cloakroom. In the vast, white lounge, called 'the drawing room' by Mrs Taylor, was a photograph of a schoolboy with dark curly hair and intense blue eyes.

Mrs Taylor, unlike most mothers, had a career. She was a lawyer and wore a smart tailored suit in a strong green colour. She had big glasses and her hair was cut in a springy, short style which suggested great determination. Imogen's father was a chemist and had at some stage made a fortune with a pharmaceutical company. Despite his Anglicized name he retained a strong Polish accent and his square, close-shaven head and sad eyes bore witness to a haunting past. Music, as alien to Sarah as a grey wind blowing from a distant sea, flowed from beneath the door of his vast study. 'Mahler,' drawled Imogen. 'He's obsessed by Mahler.' In every room were books in foreign languages, neatly shelved and obviously well read. Mr Taylor always held a book, his finger between its pages to retain his place. Whenever he spoke to Sarah in his soft, elaborate English, he seemed to her to be dragging his attention from some lofty area of learning which she could never reach.

The adult Taylors didn't know how to perform the necessary rituals of their daughter's birthday. Instead of the statutory sausages on sticks and ham sandwiches there was the unheard-of luxury of food from containers. A chicken dinner in foil cases was drawn from the oven and for pudding there was a pink, shop-bought cake. 'My mother never cooks,' explained Imogen and Sarah thought of her own mother in her cotton apron, churning out scones, victoria sponges and a flow of nourishing main meals.

After tea Sarah and the Taylors stood awkwardly to attention whilst Imogen lit her twelve candles and blew them out. 'Happy Birthday' was not sung.

The birthday treat was a visit to the theatre to see *Kiss Me Kate*. They went into town by car, which was extraordinary. Why not go by Underground? The Taylors' car was very wide and had soft squashy seats which made Sarah car-sick. She lay back in her corner with clenched teeth rehearsing the horror of asking to stop so she could be sick in a gutter.

Questions were fired at the girls from across the front seats. 'Who lived in that house with the blue plaque? ... What does Number 1, London, mean to you? ... When was the Battle of Waterloo?' Sarah adopted a knowing smile and kept quiet.

Imogen responded sullenly. Please, please, please could we get there soon, Sarah prayed.

Her pleasure in the musical was marred by residual nausea and the discomfort of being with the Taylors. Imogen sighed and shifted restlessly in her seat. Mr Taylor, who had probably chosen the show because of its instructive Shakespearian connections, could not enjoy it himself but was at pains to ensure that his daughter's guest did. He peered repeatedly round his wife's back to see whether or not Sarah was smiling. Mrs Taylor was rigid with irritation. Her shoulders twitched and her foot tapped but not in time to the music.

Afterwards Sarah wrote a careful thank you note to Mr and Mrs Taylor which she handed to Imogen at school on Monday. 'You needn't have bothered,' said Imogen and crammed the note into her bag. All day Sarah kept peeping at her to see if there would be any recognition of their new intimacy but there was none so with some relief she returned to the safe orbit of Claire Tomkins. And then in English that afternoon it was announced that Sarah Beckett had been chosen from the whole year to do the reading at the Christmas carol service. She was so thrilled by the honour that any lingering hurt caused by Imogen's coldness almost disappeared.

In the Wyatt Hall, which had a gallery on three sides for the sixth form, were rows of metal and canvas seats the colour of decaying mushrooms. The junior-school children sat on the left nearest the stage, the rest were ranked by age. Readers had to sit apart near the steep wooden steps leading up on to the platform. Because she was the youngest reader, Sarah was first. She and her mother had practised the extract from Isaiah so often that she could have recited the whole thing by heart. Her ears sang with elation and dread.

After 'Once in Royal David's City' the school sank down with a clatter of chair on chair and a crescendo of coughs. Sarah, bolt upright, climbed the steps. In front of her was the table where the Head and deputies sat. To her left was a shimmering meadow of pink faces.

'The people that walked in darkness have seen a great light: they that dwell in the land of the shadow of death, upon them hath the light shined . . .'

Her voice was cool, clipped and strong. She felt the yellow lamps above the stage warm on her head and became courageous enough to glance out occasionally. Was that Imogen's pale head? Did Imogen think she had done well?

Afterwards there was no applause of course, just a reverent silence. Sarah took her time walking off the stage for this was a precious moment of glory. But she was descending into a big problem. That morning Mrs Beckett had said: 'You really must invite Imogen Taylor back, Sarah. They gave you that lovely trip to the theatre. She'll think you're not grateful. Ask her to tea on Saturday.'

But how terrible, first to have to issue the invitation which would in all probability be bluntly refused, and then perhaps to have Imogen witness Sarah's home life. But the deed could not be avoided. Sarah knew that her mother would never be happy until the debt of hospitality had been paid.

So that the humiliation of rejection would at least go unwitnessed Sarah tried to pass a note discreetly along the bench in Physics. Unfortunately it had to go via Claire, who disapproved of note-passing, and then Laura Harding, the golden-haired paragon whom Sarah had admired on the day of her interview. Laura had a deceptive coy innocence which allowed her to open the note as if by mistake and read it. She gave Sarah a knowing smirk and handed it on. Imogen seemed to ignore it completely.

But after lunch she brushed past Sarah in the quad. 'Yeah. OK. What time?'

Sarah blurted out three o'clock and her address.

'You were the best reader,' added Imogen.

*　　*　　*

By two forty-five on Saturday afternoon ham sandwiches, scones, celery, orange cake and flapjack were arranged on the best cloth embroidered by Grandma in her youth. 'I think Imogen might prefer something else, like salad,' Sarah said, gazing in despair at the seersucker serviettes rolled into their wooden rings. Imogen's casual sophistication threatened to engulf the entire contents of 16, Heskwith Close.

Sarah was clammy with dread. The whole of Saturday had been spent in agonized speculation. How could she possibly amuse Imogen for four hours or so? What would Imogen think of this tiny house with its green moquette settee in the room her mother called the lounge, and the garden laid to lawn and vegetable patch? Perched on the gold quilted bedspread recently bought from Brentford Nylons Sarah surveyed her bedroom with newly critical eyes. Even the shelves of books were suddenly unsatisfactory. All the favourites beloved by first her mother and then herself were so winsome and irrelevant: *Heidi*, *What Katy Did*, *Little Women*. The *Sue Barton, Staff Nurse* books now seemed cheaply romantic; the Everyman Classics: Brontë, Dickens, Austen, most of which had not yet been tackled, hopelessly pretentious.

The doorbell rang and there was Imogen, glamorous and easy in a red jumper and black, tight trousers. Mrs Beckett peered past her to the pavement. 'Have your mum and dad gone already?'

'Oh, I came by bus.'

'Did you? My goodness. Clever girl.' Mrs Beckett, cheery but nervous, had set her hair and wore her second-best crimplene two-piece. 'Harry,' she called. 'Harry, Sarah's friend is here.'

Out came Mr Beckett, rumpled from his Saturday afternoon sit down with a cup of tea. 'Hello there.' He was still carrying the *Daily Telegraph*, which he now folded briskly. 'I was just off outside to light a bonfire. See you later then.' In the garage he would pull on his long woollen socks and wellingtons, and out he would go into the grey, cold garden, which was his weekend world. Lucky Dad, thought Sarah.

'Now then, what are you two girls going to do?' asked Mrs Beckett. 'I thought we'd have tea at five.'

'Would you like to see my room?' said Sarah and Imogen shrugged, a gesture which she had perfected at school for the benefit of weak teachers. It was a slow lift of one shoulder and then a heavy drop as if even the shrug itself was too much effort. Poor Miss Shaw, who wore brown and taught Latin, had once run out of the classroom in tears because of this shrug. She had tried to tell Imogen off for doing a crossword during the lesson.

Climbing the stairs, however slowly, could hardly be expected to last more than thirty seconds, thought Sarah in desperation. If she had been with Claire they would have galloped up and curled on the bed to play Coppit, or perhaps dressed up in Mrs Beckett's cast-off dirndls and pointed shoes. Any such mundane and childish activity seemed impossible with Imogen.

'There's the bathroom and that's my parents' room and this is a tiny boxroom, really small, see, which is the spare room, and this is my room.' Her father had decorated the walls with a gold and white floral paper that Sarah had loved only three months previously. The furniture they had bought at a local second-hand shop had been painted white and displayed Sarah's collections of china ornaments and foreign dolls. There was a little sheepskin rug by the bed. Sarah shrank at the memory of Imogen's vast room with its rich red carpet and muddle of exotic objects and posters, draped with swirly scarves.

'It's nice,' said Imogen.

Her quick eye missed nothing. She wanted to know where everything had come from. When Sarah spoke of aunts, cousins and grandmothers she was interrogated about their jobs, ages and marital status. Imogen was intrigued by the thought of the great-aunts, Win and Victoria, who shared a dark house in Acton and by Uncle Charlie who lived alone in a twelfth-floor flat in Hounslow.

When the rows of knick-knacks had been exhausted she pulled book after book off the shelf and read the fly leaves. 'Have you read this? Is it good? What's it about? Would I like it? Could I borrow it?' She stood in the bay window facing the road and looked out at the nearly identical houses opposite. In the back garden of one grew a pair of waving poplar trees, their tops, bared of leaves, visible above the orangey-red roofs. 'It's a good view,' she said.

She wanted to examine every inch of the house. Mrs Beckett was in the living room cutting out a skirt for Sarah. Imogen knelt beside her and picked up the tissue pattern, scrutinizing the little printed directions and signs. 'I could never do this,' she said, so Mrs Beckett showed her how easy it was to pin a dart.

'Do you want to see the garden now?' asked Sarah, who was bored.

They stood shivering by the bonfire which Mr Beckett had stacked with his usual care so that it burned cleanly, the crackling flames almost liquid in their clarity. Imogen's cheeks were thin and angular in the fading afternoon light, her eyes peaceful, her hands like glowing flowers. She smiled at Sarah across the bonfire so that Sarah felt an instant of pure joy.

'Can I help you?' Imogen asked Mr Beckett and he let her fork damp cabbage stalks on to the fire. He wore a felt cap low on his forehead and Sarah loved him for his gentle courtesy.

At tea Imogen handled Mrs Beckett's best pink and gold china tea service as if it were priceless porcelain. She ate more than anyone but was very quiet, responding politely but briefly to Mrs Beckett's questions.

'Where do you plan to spend Christmas, Imogen?'

'At home, as usual.'

'Sarah tells me you have a brother in the music business. What exactly does he do?'

'He plays bass guitar. We don't hear from him often. I wish we did but he's so in demand.'

'He must be much older than you.'

'He is. Ten years. I think I was a bit of a mistake.'

Mrs Beckett looked uncomfortable. 'You must miss your brother.'

'Oh, I do. It's so brilliant when he's home. He takes me out or plays games with me and doesn't mind me around at all, unlike some people's brothers.'

'Oh well, I expect he'll be home for Christmas.'

'I hope so. We haven't heard from him for ages.' There was a bleakness about Imogen as she said this which was deeply at odds with Mrs Beckett's snug little dining room.

'And how do you find Priors Heath? Sarah's very happy there.'

'I could never like school,' replied Imogen.

'Oh, what a shame. Why not?'

'I'm no good at sitting still. And I'm not clever like Sarah.'

'Oh, Sarah's hopeless at maths,' exclaimed Mrs Beckett. 'She tells me you're especially good at physics. How wonderful to understand science. Nobody in this family can manage figures.'

'Let's hope my clients have a little more faith in me than you,' said Mr Beckett, smiling and winking at Imogen. 'My job is to deal with insurance claims. I spend all day working with figures.'

When the washing-up was done, dutifully dried by Imogen and Sarah, they played Scrabble and Mrs Beckett got out the Quality Street. Imogen's hair swung forward in a fine blonde curtain as she set ponderous Mr Beckett up with a triple word score. She is lovely, thought Sarah. She is.

At seven-thirty the spell was broken by the arrival of Mrs Taylor who stood in the porch frigid and irritated in a grey coat and high boots. She wouldn't come in. 'We're going out to dinner,' she explained. 'Hurry up, Imogen, I did ask you to be ready.' Imogen was transformed at once into the brittle child Sarah knew at Priors Heath. She scarcely said goodbye but whisked out into the night with a clatter of heavy heels on the paved front path.

'See you on Monday,' called Sarah but the only reply was the slamming of a car door.

This friendship with Imogen Taylor was for Sarah both a source of excitement and a great trial. Sarah was most comfortable when she was teamed up with Claire Tomkins who was conscientious, friendly and co-operative. Like Claire, Sarah basked in the warmth of teacher approval and suffered if she was reprimanded. She soon had a reputation for being one of the brightest in the class and other girls measured themselves against her. She was neat and pretty with glossy hair and dark expressive eyes and could run fast. At the end of the first year her report was glowing. *Sarah is an excellent all-rounder*, concluded her form teacher. *It has been a pleasure to see her becoming a popular and diligent member of the school.*

But beneath the surface Sarah was leading a secret life, emotional and dangerous, bound to Imogen Taylor. Most of the time they barely spoke at school. Imogen scraped her way from one crisis to the next, her days punctuated by reproaches about forgotten homework, lost books and unacceptable behaviour. Everyone knew she was very bright but that she simply couldn't be bothered to put any effort into schoolwork. She spent most of her time with lazy, moneyed girls who smoked in the loos at lunch-time and whose conversation was punctuated by audacious swear words and sexual innuendo. After school they mooched off to buy cans of drink, paint their nails and listen to rock music.

Once, hurt by weeks of neglect, Sarah approached Imogen. 'You never speak to me any more,' she said, trying to laugh.

'You mean you never speak to me,' responded Imogen sharply.

Then suddenly, after days of not bothering, Imogen would

take up with Sarah again and Sarah would follow, mesmerized. How could she refuse Imogen anything when to do so might earn that dismissive shrug? In any case, to hurt Imogen, to be disliked by her would be unbearable. At weekends they would alternate visits to each other's homes, adapting their behaviour without prior discussion, slipping from one role to another, depending on where they were.

At Imogen's they roamed the great, unloved house, trying on make-up, reading magazines and cooking themselves terrifyingly grown-up suppers of steak and chips. Once Imogen played a record sent by Lawrence of a band called The Masters in which his name was mentioned as 'bass'. The sound the group made was a noisy blur to Sarah but she liked the accompanying photograph of a thin tall man in tight red loons and a striped tank top. His face was white and angular, like Imogen's, his hair a cloud of dark curls. 'He might be coming home soon,' said Imogen.

She showed Sarah Lawrence's bedroom. Sarah realized that Imogen must have copied her brother's style for his dark grey walls were covered with posters of rock stars: Lennon, Mick Jagger and Dylan. There were mountains of books stacked in piles, text books, novels and magazines with sophisticated, dull covers. On the bed was some kind of African striped blanket.

'He could have done anything,' said Imogen. 'He was brilliant at school. My mother's furious he didn't do law. She really wanted him to. But Lawrence is his own person, you see. You can't force him.' She closed his bedroom door carefully and they tiptoed away, as if from a shrine.

Afternoons with Sarah's family were a great contrast to the wide-open hours the girls spent in Hampstead. They went shopping with Mrs Beckett or helped with chores such as clearing out the shed. Imogen invested these mundane activities with glamour. She was energetic, enthusiastic and humorous. Once she asked Mr Beckett if she could try on his wellingtons and work clothes and the family watched helpless with laughter as she lumbered down the path in his size ten and a half boots, cap over one eye, long overcoat to the ground. Then she hung the coat back on the hook in the garage with touching respect.

In the evenings the girls sometimes read poetry into Sarah's reel-to-reel tape recorder, a gift on her thirteenth birthday.

Sarah loved these poetry sessions. Each would choose a poem, practise it aloud and then recite it into the microphone. While Imogen was reading her face was thoughtful and serene, with the sharp, sardonic glare gone from her eyes. She had a deep, sonorous voice and the knack of choosing poems that lingered for days in Sarah's head.

> '*Do you remember an Inn,*
> *Miranda,*
> *Do you remember an Inn?*'

Her head wagged a little on the fast, dancing section: '*Snapping of a clapper to the spin, Out and in . . .*', but when she reached: '*And the Ting, Tong, Tang of the Guitar,*' Imogen's voice slowed and Sarah knew she was remembering Lawrence.

The poem Sarah best liked Imogen to read was by Robert Frost and ended:

> '. . . *But I have promises to keep,*
> *And miles to go before I sleep,*
> *And miles to go before I sleep.*'

Then Sarah knew that the brash, rushing Imogen of Priors Heath was not the true girl, but one who understood the emotions of longing and love. *Promises to keep*, was, Sarah thought, some kind of profound covenant to herself.

Sarah always chose complicated poetry that was difficult to read well because she never got over the desire to impress Imogen, or to convey a secret, yearning message that might betray the true depth of her soul.

> '*I wonder by my troth, what thou, and I*
> *Did, till we loved? . . .*'

With love poems Sarah always ran into difficulties because when she said them aloud in front of Imogen they sounded soppy, even though before she had thought them beautiful.

> *'Woman much missed, how you call to me, call to me,*
> *Saying that now you are not as you were*
> *When you had changed from the one who was all to me . . .'*

After the readings they would rewind the tape, listen to their recorded voices and shriek with embarrassment. Then the game was over and they'd lie on Sarah's bed talking about Priors Heath. Imogen was critical and astute about people at school but quick to acknowledge talent. And they'd discuss long-term plans. Imogen was going to America the minute she could to join Lawrence. Then she would study sociology, an ambition Sarah didn't mention to her parents who put many of the world's ills down to the money spent by the state on social workers. Sarah said she would teach history though Imogen always rocked with laughter when she heard this. 'I can't imagine anyone, ever, wanting to teach. Let alone history.'

2

January 1849

Bess Hardemon arrived at Priors Heath School for the Daughters of Clergy on a damp and blustery evening in late January. As she climbed out of the carriage a gust of wind thrust her skirts against her knees and flung back a door at the top of a shallow flight of steps to reveal a wavering light. A maid appeared, carrying a lamp and a bulging carpet bag. Behind her came a much larger woman, her arm thrust firmly through the elbow of a tiny female whom she forced into the empty carriage. Bess glimpsed bewildered eyes under a crooked bonnet before the door was slammed and the carriage waved away. The muscular crunch of the horses' hooves made a poignant contrast to the frailty of the lone passenger.

'Bring her to my parlour,' ordered the fat woman and scurried inside. Bess was left to haul her own belongings up to the porch where the servant waited with the lamp, tapping her foot. The door was slammed and two heavy bolts drawn.

'Follow me if you like,' said the girl, setting off across a cavernous hallway and beneath a staircase into the tunnel of a low corridor.

Bess set down her bags and stood still in the extreme darkness. There was no sound but the maid's distant footfall and the beat of the wind against shuttered windows. Somewhere above, dozens of girls lay sleeping but down here there was no hint of their presence. With a deep sigh Bess closed her eyes and folded her gloved hands, drawing herself up for a new struggle.

After a few minutes the door under the stairs was flung open and the maid reappeared, outrage in her small, sullen eyes. 'I said follow me.'

Bess spoke very low. 'What is your name?'

'Annie Laidlaw.' The girl's lower lip was tight with defiance.

'Will you take my bags now, Annie, or come back for them later?'

Annie's heavy eyelids drooped as she considered her options. After a moment she cleared her throat. 'I'll bring them later.'

'Thank you.' At last Bess stepped forward. 'Now, perhaps you'll take me to see the Headmistress.'

Not another word was said as they walked rapidly along the passage and up a steep, narrow flight of stairs, emerging at last on to an uncarpeted corridor where their shadows rose and fell in the candle-light like mournful ghosts. Annie knocked on one of a series of closed doors, pushed it open and departed, the set of her shoulders proclaiming that she was highly affronted.

In the Headmistress's parlour Bess was greeted by the whiff of candle-wax and unwashed female flesh. The fat woman was now seated before the fire, a closely inscribed account ledger open on her knee. 'We expected you earlier,' she said in a voice muffled by many chins. 'Miss Porter was getting very agitated.' Scraps of dull hair emerged from an unstarched cap and her mouth was heavy-lipped and bitter. 'I am Miss Simms, Headmistress of Priors Heath. There is a list of your duties.' She pointed triumphantly to a grubby page on the table beside her.

When Bess didn't move Miss Simms jerked the sheet of paper with a plump, mittened hand. 'We're up at six in the morning,' she added, flustered by Bess's silence, 'so I expect you'll want to study this and then get to bed.'

Bess calmly removed her bonnet and gloves, stepped forward

and extended one small hand. 'We haven't been introduced. I am Elizabeth Hardemon. No doubt Reverend Carnegie has given you details of my experience in other schools.'

'Yes, yes.'

'I believe there are seventy-two pupils on roll at present.'

'Sixty-nine. Three left suddenly.'

'You and I are the only teaching staff?'

'Of course, and I hope you'll pull your weight. Miss Porter has been in a very bad way for months. I've been doing the work of two women. Fortunately Reverend Carnegie knows he can lean on me. Entirely.'

'Miss Porter was the woman who left in the carriage just now?'

'The Board had kept her on out of charity. Reverend Carnegie is all kindness.'

Bess, having met Reverend Carnegie, had her doubts about this last statement. 'Is the Reverend often in school?'

'Oh, very often.' Miss Simms smiled with wolfish affection. 'His dedication is a model, as I frequently tell the girls. He takes an interest in every aspect of the life of the pupils. And the staff.'

'I see. Miss Simms, I have been on the road since dawn. Where might I find supper?'

'No supper. The kitchens are locked at seven.' But after a nervous glance at Bess Miss Simms added, 'Unless Annie can find you something. If she's still up.' She extended a podgy hand to the bell-pull and then returned to her figures, her expression blurring into confusion. Miss Simms was obviously someone for whom numbers, once on the page, acquired a mystical life of their own.

In another few minutes Bess was alone in a little room beside the girls' dormitories on the second floor. The cold was intense. She unpacked with quick, precise movements, quelling violent fits of shivering. Two matted blankets covered the bed and she wrapped herself in these to eat an unappetizing supper of bread and jam, listening to the wind and frequent coughs from the next room.

Afterwards she pulled the blankets tight round her shoulders and stood at the window, her forehead pressed to the freezing glass. Bare branches swayed in a garden below and further away, in the town perhaps, three tiny lights shone. There was not a hill to be seen, only a flat, comfortless landscape of buildings and trees. 'Heaven help me,' she murmured and flung herself on the bed in a tight ball with the blankets over her head to form a stifling tent.

The interview, such as it was, for the position of assistant mistress at the Priors Heath School for the Daughters of Clergy in the town of Faringford, Hertfordshire, had taken place in the tasteful London drawing room of Mrs Penhaligon, a keen member of the Board. Bess had been offered tea in a wafer-thin cup and watched from gimlet eyes as she drank it. I presume that if I handle my teacup well I shall be appointed, she thought.

The Chairman of the Board and founder of Priors Heath, Reverend Thomas Carnegie, was also present, though he at first had said little, choosing to remain at the window, hands folded behind him, face obscured.

Tired of the limitations of a dame school near her home in Derbyshire Bess had travelled to London to stay with her older brother Gerald and his new wife Laetitia to look for a better position. Gerald, a clergyman acquaintance of Reverend Carnegie, had told her about the post at Priors Heath. 'Carnegie is well intentioned but grim. His school is said to be repressive and archaic in its practices. Yet he has influence and is not without resources. Think of what you might achieve, Bess, in the position of assistant mistress.'

Already, in Mrs Penhaligon's hushed drawing room, Bess had her doubts.

'You are very young, Miss Hardemon,' pronounced Mrs

Penhaligon, whose vowels were polished to reflect her noble birth, 'but, I judge, not inexperienced. You come with a glowing testimonial from your previous school and the list of subjects you offer is extensive. Arithmetic, Mathematics, Ancient, Modern and Church History – of course we won't require you to teach that, Reverend Carnegie covers all aspects of theology at Priors Heath – Geography, English grammar and composition, French, Latin. Most impressive.'

'Do you know German or Greek?' demanded Carnegie suddenly.

'A little. But most schools have no space in the curriculum for those subjects.'

Mrs Penhaligon waited with a deferential smile in case the Reverend chose to speak again, then said: 'It further states in your testimonial that your discipline is exceptional. Punctuality, excellent. Health, robust. Well, all seems to be in order.'

Reverend Carnegie again intervened. 'Miss Hardemon. I aim to provide the pupils of Priors Heath with an education which will enable them to lead diligent, meek and respectable lives. The philosophy of the school is applied with rigour, its rules strictly enforced. The staff are expected to follow without question the strictures of the Board. I presume you agree to this?'

Bess returned his flinty gaze fearlessly. Carnegie was perhaps thirty-five years old, tall and slender with regular features and thick, golden hair. His toneless voice was at odds with his rare physical beauty but not with the impersonal chill of his eye. 'Reverend Carnegie, I believe that I have a vocation to teach. When my brother told me about your school I knew it was my duty to apply. I will bring to the position all the dedication and energy I have always given my work.'

'Excellent,' murmured Mrs Penhaligon, glancing anxiously at Carnegie for approval.

'You are twenty-one years old,' continued Carnegie, perhaps aware that Bess had not given him the undertaking he required.

'This is your third position in as many years. Do you lack tenacity?'

'No, I lack funds,' replied Bess smoothly and saw Mrs Penhaligon wince. 'I have two younger brothers whose education must be paid for. My father, as you know, is rector of a remote, rural parish. The school in Buxton paid me barely twenty pounds a year.'

The Reverend didn't know how to respond to such bluntness and turned away so that Bess was confronted by his perfect, black-clad shoulders. Mrs Penhaligon drew the interview to a hasty close.

Emerging at last from the nest of blankets and the self-indulgence of homesickness, Bess knelt on the hard floorboards and straightened her back. 'You have brought me very far from home, dear Lord. It seems certain that I am needed here but it's worse than I expected. Nevertheless I shall try to do your will.' Very grudging, she told herself sternly, you can do better. 'I shall do your will with a courageous and joyful heart. After all, if I am dismayed by my reception here, think of how it must be for the girls.'

But climbing between distinctly musty sheets she added mutinously: Does it have to be quite so cold everywhere I go? I could be so much more cheerful if I had warm feet.

At six-thirty the next morning Bess stood beside Miss Simms in the schoolroom where the stove had been lit perhaps five minutes earlier. Once this must have been the chief reception room of the eighteenth-century house but its gracious proportions were spoilt by a crowd of low benches and layers of distemper. A high ceiling and a row of long, unshuttered windows overlooking a garden still sunk in darkness did little to distract from the wicked chill in the atmosphere.

Miss Simms looked as if she had tumbled out of bed only moments earlier. Her cap was crooked, her face disfigured by sleep and her gown bunchy. A rank odour was exuded by every crease in her petticoats, every fold of her flesh.

From overhead came a shaking of floorboards and the tread of many feet. The pupils marched in and rows of girls stood before Bess, at first glance identical in their grey frocks and aprons, their hair neatly combed into long plaits. They were packed so close that the backs of their knees were pressed to the long wooden benches.

Bess ran her eye from face to face and was not encouraged. The children were thin and pale, their complexions blemished. Unwashed hair lay lank on scalps and clothing was skimpy. Bess, who had encountered similar signs of physical deprivation in other establishments, could tell that they were underfed.

Miss Simms began an interminable reading from the Bible, her emphasis falling unerringly on all the wrong words. Having already spent half an hour in prayer that morning, Bess excused herself from listening to Exodus and watched her pupils instead. Some returned her stare with insolent curiosity, others never raised their eyes. All were unnaturally still. Miss Simms, who next began on a misguided attempt at a homily, did not deserve such a passive response.

But despite the girls' outward resignation, Bess sensed that her own arrival had caused quite a flutter. How could it not, in a world as enclosed as this?

Her gaze fell on the senior pupil who had come into the room last. The girl's eyes were averted and her hands folded like everybody else's but she managed to be quite separate from the rest. It was as if she drew all the meagre light of the room to herself. Upright and graceful, she had a long neck and light, thick hair. Her features were pale, the curve of her cheek serene. Bess could tell at once that the girl was very conscious of her own difference.

At the end of prayers, Miss Simms made a grudging introduction. 'Girls, this is the new assistant mistress, Miss Hardemon. I know you will make her welcome.'

In silence the girls filed towards the dining room, pausing to shake the hand of first Miss Simms, then her assistant. One cold hand after another was placed into Bess's, with varying degrees of reluctance. Few were willing to meet her gaze at this close range. The last girl paused a moment and with deliberate significance extended her slim, smooth fingers. She gazed directly at Bess who had rarely seen such misery in a young person's eyes.

After breakfast Bess was to teach the older girls arithmetic. Seated at her desk on the dais, she folded her hands and looked calmly at the forty-five assembled faces. Not by a flicker of an eyelid did she betray her loneliness.

'Girls, I want to find out what you know.'

In five minutes she had plumbed the depth of their ignorance. The girls lacked even basic number skills and their powers of concentration were extremely limited. Little Miss Porter with her fluttering eyelids had obviously been a hopeless teacher.

'Then we will begin at the beginning. The addition of pounds, shillings and pence. Let us hope, girls, that you will all have a little money some day and will use it carefully.'

A girl in the back row sniggered. Bess, who had already marked her as a troublemaker, looked into her brash, brown eyes. 'Your name? Well, Mary Worth, you find arithmetic amusing?'

'No, I don't. I find nothing amusing about sums. Why should I bother? My father deals with the accounts in our house. Or his steward.'

Bess was surprised to learn that any pupil at Priors Heath came from a background wealthy enough to employ a steward. Perhaps Mary's behaviour was so dreadful she'd been sent to school as a punishment. 'But I assume you have come to school to learn. One day you will be a wife and mother, responsible for a household. You will need to measure, to weigh and to estimate. All this is arithmetic.'

Mary responded pertly: 'I intend to marry well so I shall employ a housekeeper, not be one.'

The girls shifted nervously. One or two suppressed giggles but most were frightened. From the junior schoolroom above there was an unnatural hush. Miss Simms, it seemed, had ways of imposing discipline on little girls.

Bess smiled and a few of her more sensitive observers shifted uncomfortably, for this was not a genial smile. Miss Hardemon's eyebrows rose, her forehead ruffled and sharp creases appeared at the corner of her lips. Nevertheless on this occasion she allowed herself to show a hint of sorrow as well as derision. 'Well, Miss Worth, if your aim is to live a life of complete idleness I hope you won't be disappointed. But I also hope you intend to make a good wife who will help her husband by understanding his concerns, even if she doesn't participate in them.'

'My mother says it's not genteel even to think about money,' put in someone else boldly.

'Your mother must always be your first guide,' replied Bess, 'but I'm sure she knows that a little sympathetic understanding can be of greater value than a wealth of ignorance.'

She knew that she had caught their interest. Her brief acquaintance with Miss Simms and her glimpse of Miss Porter had convinced her that these girls would hardly be used to reason. Their critical powers when it came to the cut of a dress or the size of a portion of bread and butter might be finely honed, but they would not have the words to argue with a teacher who taught with wit and imagination. She felt a pulse of elation. She would have influence, even here. She would fling open the doors of these girls' minds and show them what they might know and understand.

After lunch the girls had to walk in the garden, the one place where they could exercise, though they were forbidden to run. Everywhere else in the precincts of Priors Heath was overcrowded. The schoolroom was hardly large enough to hold them and the dining room across the hall was so cramped that the girls ate elbow to elbow. Pupils were not allowed to sully the gracious proportions of the entrance hall except to cross it in strict silence at meal-times and the main white marble staircase with its low, broad steps and wrought-iron balustrade was absolutely forbidden. Most of the girls' movements about the house were within its nether regions, along narrow passages and twisting back staircases.

But in the garden, which covered nearly an acre, there was plenty of light and space. On the other side of the far wall was the beat and clang of a brewery and sometimes the cloying smell of malt hung in the air but otherwise the garden was completely cloistered. A hundred years ago someone had dug an enticing pattern of paths between borders of trees and shrubs. Where there had once perhaps been flowerbeds were now lawns, naturally out of bounds to the girls, but overall there was still an air of retreat and variety. Not even the Board of Priors Heath could banish winter sunshine, or the brilliance of a pale, clear sky. Unfortunately the girls were too cold and subdued to do more than huddle together in whispering groups.

Bess took a book from her pocket and tried to read as she strode briskly from one path to the next. The book was her shield. By sheer force of will she had drawn her reluctant pupils through one lesson after another all morning, fixing them with her large, fierce eyes if their attention wandered, questioning and encouraging in an attempt to discover their strengths. Now her brain was clamouring for real stimulation. Her father had given her a copy of Coleridge's *Biographia Literaria* and for a few moments her mind sank gratefully among its measured phrases.

In 1794, when I had barely passed the verge of manhood, I published a small volume of juvenile poems. They were received with a degree of favour which, young as I was, I well knew was bestowed on them

not so much for any positive merit as because they were considered
buds of hope and promises of better works to come . . .

Buds of hope . . . thought Bess, and for a moment looked up in confusion at the grey garden with its high, brick walls and the dark clusters of girls.

'Miss Hardemon.' The senior girl she had noticed earlier had come up.

Bess usually paid little attention to her own appearance but this girl's cool perfection made her aware that her nose was reddened with cold and her bonnet shabby and unbecoming. Furthermore, she was at least a head shorter than her pupil.

'My name is Christina Riddell.' The girl was very shy, her voice so low as to be almost indistinct. Or perhaps her hesitancy was due to lack of practice; free expression of any kind was not encouraged by Miss Simms. 'I liked what you said. Something about sympathetic understanding. I feel . . . shut in. Do you understand?'

'I see.' For a moment Bess struggled with the longing to be left alone, just for a few more minutes, but then she reached out her hand and tucked it through Christina's arm. 'We'll walk on, shall we, it's very cold.'

The sunlight cast precise foreshortened shadows. At the end of every path was an angled turn, for on all sides the garden was enclosed. Above, bare trees extended thin fingers. On and on they marched in diagonals and parallel lines so that soon Bess knew the complete topography of the garden. Meanwhile, she questioned Christina about each aspect of her life in the school.

'How long have you been at Priors Heath?'

'Three years.'

'Why were you sent here?'

'I have several younger sisters. An uncle pays my fees. My family hopes that when I leave I'll be sufficiently accomplished to marry well, or at least teach.'

31

Bess, dwarfed by the willowy Christina, reflected ruefully that there was little chance that this particular girl would have to resort to teaching.

'What kind of teacher was Miss Porter?'

'We thought she was mad. She couldn't remember our names or the day of the week.'

'Where was she sent last night?'

'We weren't told. I suppose the workhouse in Faringford.'

'Tell me about your life at Priors Heath.'

Bess would allow Christina no direct criticism of the school or of Miss Simms, but the picture she painted was not promising. Furthermore, when Bess tried to broaden the conversation by speaking of wider, topical issues, Christina showed total ignorance and a disheartening lack of interest. At the end of ten minutes Bess was more dismayed than ever by the magnitude of the task ahead.

Christina, however, seemed much happier. Her lips had softened and her cheeks were rosy with pleasure because she'd been allowed to speak freely. Behind them trailed a gaggle of little girls, some as young as five, and on all sides they were watched with jealous or curious eyes.

Bess was wary of provoking the kind of petty rivalry that flared suddenly among girls. She moved quickly away and joined Mary Worth's group who rewarded her courtesy with contempt.

Even after supper that night Bess was not free. There were classes from six until eight and then she had to supervise the freezing dormitories until every pupil lay primly in a narrow bed.

As she had expected the Board was obviously much more rigorous about the cleanliness of the girls' souls than of their bodies. There was one grimy sliver of soap for each dormitory and a mildewed towel. The privies outside were filthy. Bess had seen and smelt rooms full of dirty girls before and was used to the mentality of authorities who saw nothing wrong with sore, greasy skin and unwashed clothes. Their reasoning was that the needs of the flesh should be ignored as far as possible. Female bodies were weak and disgusting and should be covered up. Immodesty was a cardinal sin. Bess thought of Mrs Penhaligon with her smooth fingernails and elaborate gown and wondered how she could hold up her head during her visits to Priors Heath.

She went from bed to bed, calling each girl by name and wishing her a good night's sleep. They were amazed that she bothered and some pressed their faces into the pillow to stifle laughter. Poor things, she thought, what a loveless world this is for them.

When she at last returned to her own room the surly maid, Annie Laidlaw, was waiting with a message from Miss Simms.

This time the Headmistress, wearing a scruffy dressing gown, was busy cutting her ridged fingernails.

'Miss Hardemon, one or two matters.' She flicked the clippings into the fire where they spat and hissed. Her voice was slow and ponderous. Why should she hurry when nobody in the building had the power to interrupt her? 'First, over-familiarity. You seem to think it necessary to curry popularity with the pupils. It is, I believe, a fault of many inexperienced teachers. But be warned. They will exploit you mercilessly, Miss Hardemon. Worse, you will undermine the absolute authority upon which Reverend Carnegie, and I, his officer, insist.'

She didn't dare look at Bess to see her reaction but continued: 'Second. Discipline. I am aware that you were spoken to with some insolence. We use the birch here, Miss Hardemon, in such instances. The school has a code of behaviour which I expect you to enforce.'

So, thought Bess, there is a spy among the senior girls. She concentrated on Miss Simms's puffy left cheek gleaming yellow in the firelight. The headmistress now took a slice of bread and speared it with a toasting fork. 'Finally, the content of your lessons. Reverend Carnegie has devised a programme of study which you should not vary without his express permission. There are copy books and there are Mangnall's excellent "Questions". I presume, Miss Hardemon, you are acquainted with Mangnall? Any other knowledge is superfluous to the girls, and misleading. These are the daughters of clergy, Miss Hardemon. Their delicate minds mustn't be exposed to any radical influence.' She eyed Bess with intense dislike. There was no doubt that she had recognized in the new mistress someone who would probably make a thorough nuisance of herself.

Bess merely nodded. 'Will that be all?'

'I trust you have learnt much from your first day here, and that you will do better tomorrow.'

Reverend Carnegie made frequent visits to Priors Heath, some regular, others unannounced. On Wednesday afternoons he taught scripture to the junior children and heard their lessons. Meanwhile Miss Simms gave a sewing lesson in the big schoolroom and Miss Hardemon was supposed to engage in French conversation with the small number of girls whose parents had paid a few shillings extra for the privilege. After the first of these sessions Bess asked permission to take her little group of students into the entrance hall to be free of interruption. She was refused.

Wednesday afternoons were extraordinarily oppressive to Bess, not only because Carnegie was in school, but because she sensed that Miss Simms was actually putting on a performance for her and that the girls were, as usual, the victims. By the third week Bess's nerves were jangling at the very thought of what lay ahead.

Plain sewing was a euphemism for the girls making their own dresses and aprons. The fabrics were of uniform grey and of such poor quality that they creased quickly and in the hands of inexperienced needlewomen were soon reduced to a pulpy consistency, like blotting paper. The pupils were grouped around six lamps while Miss Simms crammed herself behind the desk on the dais and worked on a piece of elaborate embroidery, calling the girls up one by one to have their stitching inspected.

'*Alors, Mademoiselle Riddell, où habitez-vous?*' asked Bess.

'*À Abbey Wood près de Coventry.*'

'Susan Potter, bring your work to me,' commanded Miss Simms. Out marched Susan Potter, a favourite of Miss Simms as she had neat, straight hair and deft little fingers.

'*Avez-vous des frères ou des soeurs?*'

'Very good, Susan. Excellent. Now I'll show you satin stitch and you can work on the tablecloth for the boardroom. Sit by me.' Smug Susan sat shoulder to shoulder with Miss Simms who loved to press close to her favourites. The tension in the room momentarily relaxed.

'*Oui, j'ai cinq soeurs plus jeunes que moi . . .*'

But Susan knew just when to lift her blue eyes and draw Miss Simms's attention to clumsy Caroline Wentworth who had dropped the scissors with a clatter.

'Caroline Wentworth. Stand up. Bring me your work.' All the girls jolted upright, fingers flew and the usual atmosphere of suspicion and fear returned to the room. Poor, myopic Caroline took her grubby little apron to the front, her blue eyes almost black with terror.

'*Quels sont vos passe-temps favoris?*'

'Hedge-stakes,' spat Miss Simms, spreading the apron before her and examining the waistband. 'Nobody could wear that, slovenly girl. Pass me the scissors.' Snip, snip went the rusty blades. 'And now unpick the rest and bring it to me. You waste far too much cotton. Every inch of it must be reused. Don't break the thread.'

'All of it, Miss Simms?'

'Are you questioning me? Look at the state of this apron.' By now, both pupil and teacher were half weeping as they studied the useless rag of a garment. Hours and hours of

Caroline's time were spent unpicking and resewing so that her apron was peppered with tiny holes where previous rows of stitches had been. 'The waste, the waste,' screeched Miss Simms. 'Not even you will be able to wear this. Think of all the money that's been thrown away on this garment. Out of my sight, over to the corner.' And there Caroline had to stand for half an hour with her head turned to the wall, without leaning or slouching.

Occasionally Miss Simms looked slyly across at Bess to make sure she was impressed. This is power, said her small, cruel eyes. See how these girls cringe. Look at the control I have over them.

Much later, having been fortified by tea with Miss Simms in the boardroom, Reverend Carnegie let it be known that he would inspect the work of Miss Hardemon's senior girls.

At his entry into the schoolroom, every girl leapt up. Bess saw his rigid presence in the doorway and was suddenly pierced by a cold sword of anger. Most of the glaring faults of Priors Heath were due to this man who called himself a philanthropist, and who expected such deference and inspired such fear that the mere sight of him made over forty young girls silent and still. A fortnight ago, Bess might have smiled when he came in. Now her eyes were cold.

'Please, Miss Hardemon, do continue.'

'Very well. We have begun a study of English poetry. I'll read on, girls.'

This was a calculated risk. Literature was a subject advertised on the curriculum but Bess suspected that it had never been taught at Priors Heath with any competence. Nor would Keats be Carnegie's idea of a suitable poet for his girls. She continued in a clear, ringing voice: '*Thou wast not born for death, immortal bird . . .*

What do you notice, girls, about the beginning of this penultimate verse?'

But there was no hope of a response. Carnegie strolled

among the girls, hands behind his back, pausing to peer more closely at their slates.

'Can you feel the awe?' Bess demanded. 'Do you see how perfectly the poet has juxtaposed the words "death" and "immortal"? This is a religious poem, girls, in every sense of the word. The nightingale transcends the mortal.'

As the girls had no copies of the poem she had to declaim line after line. All the while Carnegie circulated the room.

'*No hungry generations tread thee down.*

'Now, listen to the words "hungry" and "tread". Perhaps Keats was thinking of our own time, girls, the greedy industrial age. Hungry. I'm sure we can all identify with that word.' Here Bess again looked at Reverend Carnegie who happened to be quite near the dais, staring fixedly at her face with his ice-blue gaze. He suddenly extended a large hand and pulled her precious copy of Keats from the desk. Always afterwards she would think of its pages being turned by his scrubbed fingers.

'Later there is an allusion to Ruth, of the Old Testament. Perhaps Reverend Carnegie could explain it for us.' But Carnegie simply bowed his head and lifted his shoulders as if to say, that is scarcely my role. I would not stoop.

'Keats writes:

> '*Through the sad heart of Ruth, when, sick for home,*
> *She stood in tears amid the alien corn.*'

A few lamps flickered, the rest wouldn't be lit until supper. Outside the schoolroom now the garden was in darkness. Carnegie was a column of disapproval at Bess's side. *Sick for home*, thought Bess and looked at the girls who, cowed by his presence, had scarcely listened to one word she said, except perhaps for Christina Riddell, who sat with her head flung back and her dreamy eyes on Bess's face.

'The name, Ruth, means "the beloved",' Bess said, moving further from Carnegie whose rather laboured breathing oppressed her. 'Well, we all know what it means to be homesick, don't we, girls?'

Carnegie was heading for the door. He never spoke directly to Bess but conveyed his disapproval via Miss Simms. This afternoon, however, Bess followed him from the schoolroom. Closing the door behind her, she called his name, causing him to pause as his foot struck the lowest step of the marble staircase. He had a small office on the first floor.

Though his features were as rigid as ever, a blink of his dark-lashed eyes suggested that he was surprised. 'Miss Hardemon?'

'Have you any comment to make on what you have observed today?'

He remained still for a moment, measuring his reply. 'I consider it necessary to address any remarks I might have to Miss Simms, your superior.'

'Well, that may be but you must understand that I find it irksome to have no right of reply. Furthermore, I have several urgent observations to make to the Board. I have already spoken to Miss Simms about all these matters and she says she can do nothing without directives from you.'

He was preternaturally still for a while but then sucked in his breath and replied: 'The next meeting of the Board is in April.'

'I had not realized it met so seldom,' replied Bess steadily, though her heart sank. She had been relying on the support of Board members such as Mrs Penhaligon who might at least be sympathetic to some practical innovations.

Carnegie took several steps upwards. Bess dogged him. 'April is too far away. These are matters of great urgency.' He stopped but did not turn, forcing her to make her next remark to his back.

'Reverend Carnegie, I hope you will understand that any criticism I have to make is with the greatest respect and spoken entirely from my concern for the girls' welfare. This, I am sure, is also at the heart of all you do for the school. My first worry at present is for their petticoats.' The Reverend's shoulders were pulled back in astonishment. 'They are washed only every two months, I understand. The girls are so crowded that such a system can only result in disease. Miss Simms tells me that three left only last month with some kind of wasting illness.'

'The laundry is a matter for Miss Simms,' he murmured.

'She will do nothing unless you order it.' But he had climbed the stairs at such a pace that she could not reach him.

That night she was informed by a furious Miss Simms that she had no right to interfere with the running of the school. 'To suggest a weekly washing of petticoats is ridiculous, a burden on cloth and labour. Have you any idea how much this school relies on Reverend Carnegie's generosity? Perhaps you weren't aware that he founded the school in memory of his dead sister and has been unstinting in its service ever since. He has donated many hundreds of pounds of his own money. And you want to waste it on soap.'

One Saturday a month Bess was allowed a half-day's holiday. On the first of these precious afternoons she wrapped herself against a wet February wind and set off for the town centre.

Leaving Priors Heath by the servants' door beside the kitchens was like stepping from a murky, stifling cave into clear air. The weight of responsibility and the oppressive lack of privacy rolled from her shoulders. She felt absurdly glad just to be walking swiftly along the muddy road, alone.

Faringford was a small, compact town, although its relative closeness to London and the projected construction of a railway station had already caused some new large houses to be built beyond Priors Heath. The brewery was at the lower end of the High Street which was surrounded by rows of small terraced houses. Further west were a couple of much wider, leafier roads and beyond them the parkland of the Edgbaston Estate. Bess thought the town very dull and hated its dark brickwork. She was used to steep hills and stone cottages. Faringford High Street was busy and shabby and she knew no one.

It didn't take her long to locate the workhouse infirmary, quite newly built near the cottage hospital. Even as she pulled the bell she regretted the highly developed sense of duty which forced her to spend a precious free hour in yet another mean institution instead of out in the lanes.

The wardress had a thin but not unpleasant face and inquisitive eyes.

'My goodness, so you've come to see Miss Porter. She gets more visitors than all the rest of them put together. Poor thing.'

Bess, the daughter of a country rector, had plenty of experience visiting workhouses. She was pleased to note that the infirmary in Faringford was quite modern and smelt a little more savoury than the dormitory at Priors Heath. But still Bess felt glad to be only twenty-one and a member of a close-knit family. Presumably her three brothers would ensure she would not end her days in such a place.

There was little decoration in the ward except a series of improving texts carved into the stonework and on the central rafter the words: 'GOD IS TRUTH. GOD IS GOOD.'

Miss Porter sat beside her bed with her knees pressed together under a rug and her eyes very round and vague. She was taller than Bess had realized, gaunt, with white hair pulled back into a carefully pinned bun. She sat perfectly still, as if waiting. She had been a teacher at Priors Heath since it was founded fifteen years previously and now that she had finally been released seemed petrified, as if poised between that world and the next.

Bess touched her hands. 'I've come from Priors Heath to see how you are. My name is Bess Hardemon. I'm the new teacher.' A tiny measure of privacy was provided by a shoulder-high partition separating each bed but Bess was conscious of the presence of twenty aged, sick women, listening if they could.

But the wardress would permit no private conversation. 'Oh, she's very well, aren't you, Miss Porter? A lovely little lady. And she has so many visitors. Dear Reverend Carnegie comes at least once a week. But then he would.'

But then he should, corrected Bess silently. Look at the state of the woman. How on earth did she carry on teaching for so long?

Miss Porter said nothing though her head trembled on her neck as if it were attached by a tiny, worn spring. Her lips were pressed shut and the blue of her eyes was hazy.

'You know she taught at the school until a month ago,' Bess told the wardress.

'Oh, they were wonderful to keep her on,' said the wardress. 'Real charity. Mind you, I will say this for her, she is very clean.'

'Was she as bad as this when she arrived?'

'Oh no. But, you see, I think it was the shock. She couldn't adapt. Could you, dear?'

Bess expected retribution for her visit to Miss Porter, but not a word was said. It seemed incredible that only a few weeks ago her room at Priors Heath had been occupied by that pitiable figure. Miss Porter's ability to manage a class which included the likes of Mary Worth was explained in a few words by Christina Riddell, however. She had been excessively free with the strap. Hence the girls' deadly subservience.

After her visit to the workhouse infirmary, Bess was more determined than ever that Priors Heath should be swiftly reformed. It became a ritual for her to goad Carnegie. A tense, subdued exchange took place between them again and again near the staircase on Wednesday afternoons and always ended in her defeat.

Bess insisted that the primers, from which the girls learned answers by heart, were old-fashioned and tedious. The Reverend replied that the girls' tender minds must not be stretched by any method of instruction which demanded reason or imagination.

Bess said there should be rewards for good marks, rather than punishment for bad. Carnegie said that it was quite wrong, even sacrilegious, to encourage a desire for praise in young female minds.

Bess stated that the girls should have proper exercise, winter and summer, to allow their young bodies to develop. Carnegie, overcome by her brazen use of the word 'body', protested that such an innovation would lead to a vulgar display of physical movement and might do untold damage to frail muscles. He wished to instil restraint.

'But they are the mothers of the future,' Bess exclaimed. 'They must be strong and well to bear healthy children.'

From his high neck-cloth to his forehead a puce flush suffused Carnegie's pale skin.

At the end of each of these bouts Bess was left quivering with rage and frustration. But Carnegie, rather than avoiding her, seemed to be in the school more and more often. It occurred to Bess that she must be the first person ever to argue with him. His authority, based on his status as a clergyman and his considerable wealth, went unchallenged by members of the the Board who were relieved to have their duty to the poor clergy daughters so ably managed. He treated small, tenacious Miss Hardemon rather as an animal-tamer might deal with a new, fierce species. He watched her all the time, baited her, and even, at the end of a conversation, seemed to be lit by a tiny hot flame of excitement.

The moment Bess had an inkling that he might be enjoying their arguments, she stopped them. Next time he visited the schoolroom she didn't follow him out. She was aware that he hesitated for several minutes in the hall before beginning a slow ascent to the first floor. From then on there was a silent enmity between them. She had taken something from him and felt he would never forgive her for it.

His punishment was to envelop himself in a skin of steel when in her presence. Even his voice was coated in shiny metal. But worst of all, he treated her pupils with the same punctilious precision. Not by a flicker did he reveal whether or not they pleased him. You are my duty, his curt indifference seemed to say, a burden I must bear for the sake of my dead sister.

3

September 1970

By the beginning of the girls' fourth year at Priors Heath Mrs Taylor had left the house in Hampstead. 'She's found a lover,' announced Imogen. For the life of her Sarah couldn't imagine Mrs Taylor shedding her customary outfit of tight skirt and jacket which surely must happen if she had taken a lover. The illicit sexiness of the phrase suggested lace negligées and rumpled sheets, hardly images associated with acerbic Mrs Taylor.

Imogen seemed not to mind much, indeed announced that life would be much more peaceful without her mother. 'At least now Lawrence might come home,' she said. Sarah did not confide the news to her own mother, aware that it would lead to endless whispered speculation and words of condemnation. Also it would touch on the question of sex which was best avoided in the Beckett household as it caused everyone acute embarrassment. Sarah did look speculatively at her own mother, however, and try to imagine her creeping forth in the night to conduct an extra-marital relationship. But the backdrop to her mother's life, the aisles of Bishop's supermarket, Dewhurst the butcher, or St Thomas's church on Sunday, simply would not permit such a possibility. Sarah rested easy in her absolute security.

In the Taylor house a clinical air of rigid order now descended, imposed by a housekeeper. Mr Taylor hardly emerged from his study at all, though Mahler still ebbed and flowed. But in fact Sarah rarely visited any more because often

Imogen stayed with her mother at weekends. Few details of these visits to Mrs Taylor and her lover were volunteered. At school functions Mrs Taylor put in the odd appearance but bore no signs of the scarlet woman. Her hair was short and permed, her figure razor thin in a smart black suit and her feet shod in knife-sharp stilettos. She would give Sarah a slight, tense, smile as if she felt she ought to remember her.

By the following summer Imogen had grown dangerous. It never occurred to Sarah to bring her home any more for she seemed to be wholly preoccupied by boys in black leather. Her fingers were stained by chain-smoking and she sometimes spent days and nights at live music concerts. In any case, a final escapade with Imogen brought Sarah to the brink of disaster.

They had been closeted together in the cloakrooms eating Sarah's sandwiches. Sarah had cherished this rare moment of intimacy for Imogen was in a quiet and dreamy mood. Lawrence had written her a long letter. He had rented a flat, a penthouse – whatever that was. It sounded very decadent. The flat was in New York and there was plenty of room in it to accommodate Imogen. 'Maybe you could come out with me for a holiday. We'd have such brilliant fun,' suggested Imogen. Sarah knew at once that such a wild plan would never come to fruition but the sheer romance of Imogen's dreams was intoxicating.

'Ah, Sarah and Imogen.' It was Mrs Washbourne, officious head of PE, who sometimes patrolled at lunch-time. 'You should be outside. No sandwiches in the cloakrooms. But as you're here I wonder if you'd take this folder up to Art Room 3. It's "A" level work. Someone must have left it behind. Hurry up now.'

The corridors in the New Building were largely deserted at lunch-time. Through the art-room windows poured dazzling sunlight. In the centre of the room a large cloth concealed some bulging arrangement set out ready for the afternoon's lesson, a sixth-form still-life class.

Imogen sprang forward and whisked off the cloth. It was a bowl of fruit, heaped with precision, globed and curved, waxy skins glowing in the sunshine. There was a moment's hesitation. The stillness and colour in the room were perfect and untarnished. Already Sarah sensed Imogen's intention.

Imogen grabbed an apple and took a great bite. A banana lurched forward and tumbled on to the floor. She stuffed grapes into her mouth and a pear.

'Help me,' she spat between mouthfuls, laughing so much that she nearly choked.

Sarah stood by in horror. 'What are you doing? Come away.' She plucked at Imogen's arm, gripped by the horrible knowledge that life was plunging out of control. But Imogen pulled away and bit into more and more fruit. Sarah felt herself like a figure in a nightmare who cries out and is not heard by the evil forces that threaten to consume.

When they left at last Imogen replaced the cloth on a pile of half-eaten oranges and apples, banana skins, a peach stone and a mess of pips. Sarah was weeping and sat frozen in her seat all afternoon awaiting the retribution which was not long in coming.

Imogen was excluded for a day, her punishment reduced because she admitted her sin so frankly. Sarah had an interview with Miss Stone who specialized in history but was also a senior teacher.

'Imogen tells me you tried to stop her from wrecking that still life. Did you try hard enough, Sarah?' She fixed her sparrow-like eyes on Sarah.

'I suppose not.'

'I think Imogen needs all our support. Imagine how chaotic and lonely her homelife must be. You know her father suffers from depression. And of course Imogen is always anxious about her brother, who is rarely home and I believe may have had a drug problem. I'm telling you this because I believe you know her family.'

'Not the brother. I've never met the brother.'

'You could be such a good influence on Imogen, Sarah. You're the only one of her friends who might have a positive effect on her. She would listen to you.'

Sarah was astonished that any teacher had noticed her friendship with Imogen, particularly Miss Stone whose dealings with the girls were focused and curt.

'I don't think anyone could have an effect on Imogen,' Sarah said, trying to draw Miss Stone into an adult conspiracy of exasperation with Imogen.

'Then you'll go on reacting, will you, Sarah? You'll take the easy route, and keep your head down?'

'No, no, it's not like that at all.' How could she explain to steely Miss Stone the war that raged eternally within her?

Shine, shine, shine, Sarah, was the unspoken demand made by Mrs Beckett. Be the best at everything. 'A-' or 'Good' is not good enough. I'll be so disappointed if you don't excel. But at the same time be modest, tread quietly, know your place, above all *don't show off*. Because if you do, you risk ridicule when it all goes wrong, as it almost certainly will when they find out you're not really as clever as the rest.

The battle to save Imogen was caught up in the conflicting requirements to succeed but not to stand out. Of course, reasoned Sarah, I am bright, strong and good, and love Imogen so I will give her all my time and exercise my will over her. But then, who am I to try and change anyone? Imogen can't really care what I think. I am colourless, tame and ineffectual beside her.

'So, Sarah, I believe you must ask yourself, what can you offer Imogen?' The interview was at a close. A pile of exercise-books were pulled forward, and a red pen. Sarah went miserably away from Miss Stone's room, aware that she had made a bad and selfish impression.

*　　*　　*

A year later they were sitting 'O' levels. External exams were taken very seriously at Priors Heath. Candidates hovering in the lobby of the Wyatt Hall glimpsed an ocean of desks and chairs among which bobbed sombre teachers setting out papers. Exhibited nearby were signs bearing the words: 'SILENCE. EXAM IN PROGRESS.' The fifth-formers engaged in tense, muttered conversations.

'I did no revision at all last night. I was too scared. I can't remember a thing.'

'God, Sarah, why are you worried? You're bound to get straight As.'

Imogen yawned. 'I'm so tired. I didn't get in until two. My brother came home for the night so we hit the town.'

'Your brother? Lawrence? What's he doing at home? You never told me he was coming.'

'Oh, he didn't give any notice. He's between contracts.'

'But that's amazing. Aren't you delighted?' cried Sarah who desperately wanted the long-waited Lawrence, the wild-haired boy in the photograph, to live up to Imogen's expectations.

'Yeah. It's great to see him. Of course he's really tired, deep down. He sleeps a lot.' Sarah saw Imogen's disappointment and grieved for her. So Lawrence was no real comfort. But as usual Imogen had attracted an audience and must play to it. 'Oh God, Miss Washbourne's invigilating. When she sits behind that desk in her gym skirt you can see her knickers.'

'Imogen Taylor. No talking outside the hall. We've told you that.' The girls were lined up in rows and ushered into the hall where Imogen did an admirable impersonation of Miss Washbourne's rolling, hockey-player's stride for Sarah's benefit.

Afterwards the girls' voices screeched along the corridors: 'God, it was dreadful, my mind went a complete blank.'

'Sarah Beckett, you filled four extra sheets, I saw you.'

Imogen said, 'I finished three-quarters of an hour early. Boring. Do you want to come home and meet Lawrence?' she asked Sarah.

'Oh no, no, I've got to revise for Maths tomorrow. Perhaps next weekend, when we've finished.'

'He might be gone by then,' said Imogen, her manner cold. She gave a dismissive wave and strode off.

The truth was that Sarah was terrified by the prospect of meeting Lawrence Taylor. What would she possibly have to say to a rock guitarist?

In the first year of the sixth form the cork was pushed down tighter. The facts that Sarah must learn for the history exam that summer stretched from one end of the house to the other when listed on perforated computer paper brought home as scrap from Mr Beckett's work. Mrs Beckett told her daughter: 'I'm sure you're overdoing it. We'll be proud of you whatever marks you get.' But Sarah knew this was untrue. Mrs Beckett was accustomed to her daughter producing excellent marks and there could be no question of presenting only mediocre grades now. Sarah was terrified that if this careful veneer of intelligence created by years of conscientious study were to slip, the true Sarah would be revealed for all to see, a Sarah who was feeble, a struggling misfit at Priors Heath.

They took internal exams in the summer term and Sarah's marks were exemplary. But on her report her careless form teacher had scrawled: *Sarah continues to work hard. However, she must not take her studies too seriously. If she loses her natural pleasure in learning she will not live up to her former promise.*

Not live up . . . former promise. The phrases grafted themselves into Sarah's heart and haunted her summer. Imogen had suggested they might go youth hostelling to the Lakes but now Sarah insisted that she couldn't afford time out of studying.

In the autumn term of the upper sixth Imogen wasn't around much and attended a minimum of lessons. Sarah studied English, German and History, whilst Imogen, who had just scraped the required grades at O level, had chosen Pure and Applied Maths and Physics, so they scarcely had cause to meet at all. Imogen had the air of totally despising the establishment of Priors Heath which she said was a den of privilege, full of frigid virgins. It was rumoured that she now smoked reefers and certainly she smelt of some musky, oriental substance. Her hair and skin were dulled by an unhealthy, high-alcohol diet and too many late nights. After school she was met by a succession of besotted youths.

When she was with Imogen Sarah was conscious of a relaxation of pressure, a breath of air from a world not obsessed by public examinations. Imogen was cool and wayward, her preoccupations far removed from Priors Heath. Sometimes at lunch-time Imogen would link her thin arm through Sarah's and urge her out of the library and into the salty autumnal air. They walked in the enclosed rose garden behind the Old House where Sarah could shut school from her mind and imagine she was a former incumbent of Priors Heath, in the years before it became a school. The women of the house must have strolled along these same paths in elaborate bonnets, with nothing to do but kill time. Imogen occasionally allowed herself to be carried along by such speculations but mostly she just listened. 'You're quite mad,' she said. 'Can't you ever just switch off completely?'

'I can never switch off. Can you? I can never think of nothing. Sometimes the inside of my head feels stuffed with thoughts all crowded and jumbled together. I wonder I ever manage to write anything that makes sense in my essays.'

'The inside of your head. God, what a frightening prospect,' said Imogen.

In the centre of the garden was a sundial, its pointer long since broken. Warm September sun bathed the lawns and shrubs in thick, golden light. A bench nearby was occupied by Miss Stone whose short legs barely reached to the path beneath and whose face was turned to the sunshine with unexpectedly sensuous enjoyment.

She called: 'Sarah, a word.'

Imogen grimaced and moved on, her long feet soundless on the paving stones. Sarah stood apprehensively above her teacher who closed her eyes against the glare of sunlight.

'Your plans?'

'What do you mean?' Miss Stone never answered a question if its reply was obvious. 'Oh, well, university, I suppose.' Goodness, did Miss Stone not think Sarah Beckett was good enough for a degree?

The eyes jolted open and fastened their disapproving glare on Sarah. 'You should know. By now you should be certain. Oxford. History.'

'Oh, I don't think so. I'm not bright enough. I'd never thought of Oxbridge.'

'You have a gift. Don't waste it.'

'I don't believe I have. I only ever got Bs in my essays last year.'

Sarah could feel herself sinking deeper and deeper into disfavour. Miss Stone clasped her arms tightly under her heavy bosom. 'What you have is imagination. You move about in history with perfect ease. You are curious to know cause and effect. I envy you.'

'But you . . .'

'I want everything packaged. I want the past to be simple, though I know for sure that there is nothing straightforward about the past. I see the past in two dimensions and like it to look tidy. You could be a great historian because you are not satisfied with any one solution.'

'I thought I irritated you by asking too many questions.'

'You do.' It was possible that Miss Stone was smiling. 'I am irritated by anything I cannot grasp or any question I can't answer.'

The bell rang and the interview was over. Sarah was reeling.

At the end of October it was arranged for members of the upper sixth to enter the first heat of a national debating competition. The subject was vivisection and elections for the team took place in the common room on the Friday before the half-term holiday. The girls unanimously nominated Imogen Taylor who was a brilliant and ruthless debater. Sarah Beckett received one more vote than Laura Harding and was to second the motion.

Laura was bitterly disappointed, especially as vivisection was her passion. A whispering campaign was set up against Sarah. 'She voted for herself because she couldn't bear anyone else to be in a team with Imogen. She knew I'd win otherwise. I'm an expert on animal welfare. All she wants is to be able to write "debating" on her application form for Oxford.'

Sarah, with two essays to complete for history and another for English, wished she had never allowed her name to be put forward. The Oxford Entrance was in a fortnight's time. Later that day she took Laura aside and told her she'd be glad to relinquish her place in the debating team.

Laura's gaze was contemptuous. 'Why?'

'Partly because I haven't time.'

'Oh no, of course, you're much too busy. So in demand. Such an intellectual.'

Sarah shrugged and moved away. The common room had fallen silent. Imogen was not present.

'I wouldn't dream of taking your place, Sarah Beckett. Everyone would be so disappointed that Miss Perfection had dropped out.'

'Let me know if you'll do it.' Sarah had reached the door.

Laura followed. 'I was just amazed you'd be prepared to second Imogen in anything. It would be the first time you've ever supported her.'

'I'm sorry?'

'She's propped you up all these years. You take and take and take. You're like a sponge. Have you got any personality of your own? Who are you, I wonder? You're a parasite.'

'Laura, please.'

'I feel sorry for Imogen. I like her. God, what a drag you are. Not an idea in your head. Imogen will have to win the debate on her own with a little puppet sitting next to her.'

Sarah was a rabbit caught in the headlights. Someone pulled at Laura's arm. 'Drop it, Laura. Don't you think you'll regret this later?'

The next morning was Saturday, the first day of half-term. After a sleepless night Sarah got up early and tried to work. Her mother fussed about with cups of tea and extra toast but Sarah huddled in her room learning nothing, trapped within her misery like a rat in a cage. At mid-morning, her eyes bright and dry, she ran downstairs and told her mother she was going out.

'Of course, Sarah, the fresh air will do you good. Shall I come? We could have a coffee somewhere.' Mrs Beckett stood at the sink eager with concern. Sarah longed to be five again, to bury her head in the cool folds of her mother's apron and be made safe in that dark, comfortable place, but there was no escape. What Laura had said would be dismissed as cattiness by Mrs Beckett, who would then worry that her daughter had indeed upset someone badly. If Sarah mentioned that she was struggling with the volume of work Mrs Beckett would suggest a more lenient timetable of study but then live in fear of her daughter failing.

'No. No. I'm fine, really. I thought I might take the bus over to see Imogen.' And indeed, once voiced, this idea seemed to offer a solution which made Sarah's heart sing with hope. Imogen would dismiss Laura as a stupid, spoilt cow and the mountain of studying would be relegated to its proper place: 'For God's sake, Sarah, if you did no work between now and June you'd still sail through. Stop whining and imagine how you'd feel if you were me. I haven't opened a maths text book since last Tuesday.'

The journey passed swiftly. It was a sparkling day, so warm that winter seemed far away. Sarah fretted a little at the time spent between connections but managed to crush the voice in her head that whispered: You ought to be working. Think of all this wasted time.

The breeze had strengthened by the time Sarah reached Imogen's road and as she stood at the front door her hair flew out and the hem of her coat flapped. At first there was no answer and for the first time she was faced with the possibility that Imogen might not be there. She rang again.

There was the sound of feet on the stairs and the door was flung wide by a tall young man whose dark hair fell to his shoulders and framed a pale, angular face.

'Oh. I came to see Imogen.'

He stared at her for some moments. 'You're Sarah Beckett.'

'I am. Yes.'

'I'm Lawrence. Imogen's brother. She's not here.'

'I see.' She staggered a little, weak with disappointment and the thought of the long homeward journey, the bedroom where her books awaited her and no relief all week, not even the routine of school to distract her.

'I hope you'll come in,' said Lawrence Taylor. 'Haven't you noticed that I knew you straight away? Imogen always used to write about you. She sent me photos of you and her.'

Sarah followed him numbly inside the familiar hall with its chessboard tiles.

'You looked very frail and sad on the doorstep just then. Here, let me take your coat.'

She perched on a stool in the kitchen with her hair tousled on her shoulders and sipped coffee with Imogen's brother who must now be twenty-seven, every inch a rock musician in worn jeans and a short, ribbed sweater. His hair was tangled and wiry, very unlike Imogen's pale locks, but his strong nose and high cheek bones betrayed their relationship. The Taylor skin was so thin that their fine bones shone like polished ivory through it. Lawrence's mouth was fuller and softer than Imogen's, his blue eyes kinder.

Sarah's polite voice said: 'It's very nice to meet you after all this time. I had begun to think you didn't actually exist.'

'Oh well, you know. I've had a wild time. I try to call by occasionally though I don't exactly love this house.' His hand made a dismissive gesture and she noted that his fingers were strong and long, like Imogen's.

'Imogen tells me you're a musician.'

'Imogen tells you that, does she?' He was mocking, she noted wearily. His years in America had softened his vowels but he could mimic Sarah exactly. Nudging her coffee mug aside she gave a deep sigh and stood up. The complexities of conversation with Lawrence Taylor required more energy than she possessed.

'Where are you going?' he asked.

'Home. Will you tell Imogen I called in?'

'She's away, you know. I flew in last night and found that my mother had taken her up to York for a few days. Rather disappointing for me, too. I only really come home for Image – and my dad. I'm off again at the end of the week.'

Image. This nickname, unexpected and intimate, somehow made Imogen less powerful.

'Oh, all right then. It doesn't matter. I'll go.'

'Hey, hey, don't look so disappointed. I'll substitute. What did you want?'

A hopeless little laugh bubbled in her throat as she picked up her coat.

'Sarah Beckett. Don't rush off. Listen, you should eat. You're like my father. He forgets to eat. I have to cook him omelettes.'

'He seems to manage all right all the time you're away,' she remarked, surprisingly waspish.

'Oh, I know. I know I'm a terrible son. I expect you realize that. But even when I was very young he was completely out of reach. I didn't think he needed me.' The moment when she might have left had gone and Lawrence had taken a mixing bowl from a cupboard and was cracking eggs into it. Because she really didn't want to face the windy pavements again just yet, Sarah perched once more on her stool.

'And are you a successful musician, Lawrence?'

'I could be. I'm lazy. I lack ambition and you have to be hungry for success.'

'Some rock stars seem to make a great deal of money.' Sarah could hear her father speaking from the depths of his Sunday paper.

He laughed. 'Some do, Sarah Beckett.' His movements were very deft and he had a fierce concentration which prevented him from talking much as he grated cheese and chopped mushrooms. Sarah began to wonder where they would eat and how the meal would be managed. She was so tired that the prospect of sharing a lunch with Mr Taylor was dreadful. Perhaps after all she should go.

But Lawrence had set a tray for one, poured a glass of wine and carried it across the hall.

'Isn't he lonely in there?' Sarah asked when he returned.

'I think he is lonely. And very angry about my mother still. But he's working well these days, I understand. He's writing a lot, and has a new contract with a company in Sweden so he's doing OK.' Sarah was rather taken aback, having imagined somehow that Mr Taylor was a fixture in the study, with no life beyond the house.

Lawrence and Sarah ate in the large, under-used drawing room where light streamed through high, wide windows. He poured her wine, despite her protests, and she sank deeper and deeper into her chair, soothed by the sunshine. She was conscious that there was scarcely a moment when he was not watching her. When she held her glass up to the light the wine was a beautiful ruby pool. Her senses were dissolving a little.

He crouched at her feet and took her plate and glass. 'Image says you work harder than anyone she's ever known. Your eyes are so tired.' Reaching out his hand he ran the tip of his thumb under her eye in a slow smooth gesture that took her breath away. 'I'll play you a bit of music if you like and then I'll take you home.'

They climbed the stairs together. Sarah recoiled from the intimacy of Lawrence's bedroom which had come miraculously alive, strewn with clothes and with a guitar lying on the rumpled bed.

Lawrence laughed at her. 'It's OK. Here, sit. Listen.' With practised ease he withdrew into his professional self as he crouched on the bed and made minute adjustments to the tuning of his guitar. Sarah found his face and movements entirely fascinating, like Imogen's. He was a maverick, slow and sleepy one moment, quick and alert the next.

He was disappearing, she realized, into a world from which she was excluded. She relaxed in the knowledge that just for a moment she need neither say nor think anything. When he began to play she knew that he had understated his achievement for his fingers on the strings had an unfaltering precision and the music, a pulsing beat with a high eerie melody, was piercingly fluid.

He stopped abruptly and gave her his slow, sweet smile. 'Like it?'

'Oh, it was lovely, lovely.'

'I wish everyone was as appreciative as you.' His gaze moved lazily from her eyes to her lips. Then he got up abruptly, returned the guitar to its stand and stood over her. In one of his odd, sudden gestures he placed the back of his index finger under her throat on the warm skin at the base of her neck and drew it upwards to her chin. Then, with a shake of his head, he gave her his hand and pulled her to her feet. 'Come on. I'm meeting someone at three. I've just time to take you home.'

All the way down the stairs she felt a terrible sense of urgency. He was moving out of her life. She might never see him again. He was leaving at the end of the week, or so he'd said.

She did not at first register that the lift he offered was on a motor-bike. At once she was torn between the longing to have a ride and the prospect of being killed and her mother finding out what she had done. But Lawrence didn't pause to argue. He discussed her address, gave her a helmet, instructed her to hold tight, and off they went.

It was very cold. Her coat blew open and was in any case scarcely wind-proof. Within minutes she had overcome her fear of clutching his waist and was clinging tightly, her face held close to his back for protection. After a while she gave in to the joy of being carried, the complete abandonment of responsibility. She had enough sense, however, to insist on being dropped a few roads away from her house.

He took her helmet and strapped it to the seat. 'Bye bye then, Sarah Beckett. I have loved meeting you.'

'Yes.' She lingered on the pavement, wishing she could say more. He smiled at her, head to one side, as if waiting. 'Do you think Imogen might be back in the next couple of days?' she asked desperately.

'No idea. I doubt it somehow. But I'll be around. Is that any good?'

'Well, yes.'

'We could go to the pictures or something. What do you think? I'm at rather a loose end too, with Image and my mother away.'

'Yes. I think . . . that would be nice.' To sit beside Lawrence Taylor for two hours or more would be impossibly wonderful.

'Right then, we'll do that.' He reached out and pinched her chin gently. 'Keep smiling, Sarah.' With a squeeze of the accelerator he roared away, hand raised in farewell.

The next day, Sunday, Sarah refused church, claiming she had to work. In fact she was afraid to leave the house for fear of missing a call from Lawrence. As far as she knew he had neither her address nor her phone number but Imogen would have them in her bedroom, or they were in the phone book. She raged from room to room during her parents' absence, waiting and waiting, occasionally sitting at her desk to study but the words danced and memories of the previous day flickered in her head.

A couple of years before, Sarah had dated one previous boyfriend, David Parr, whom she had met at Claire Tomkins's sixteenth birthday party. David was a clean youth whose shirt collar smelt of soap powder and who pressed her close to his hot, frail chest when the lights went out at the end of the evening and Claire's dad put 'Bridge Over Troubled Water' on the record player. They had gone out together a couple of times and Sarah was relieved that at last she could talk about a boyfriend. David had been preparing for 'A' levels and intended to study engineering, but he was too slight and diffident to hold her. At the end of their second date he had put out a tentative hand to stroke her hair and darted his head forward for a kiss but she had shrunk from the touch of his dry, timid lips.

But Lawrence. The memory of him ate at her. He was not a boy but a man; his self-sufficiency was wonderful to her; it had rested her so that with him she had felt like a little bird rocking on a calm ocean.

But he didn't phone.

The next day followed the same pattern. Claire Tomkins rang and actually suggested a trip to the cinema in the evening, but Sarah wouldn't leave the phone. The thought that Lawrence might not even think of calling her had crossed her mind and she despaired. Once or twice she went to the phone with the intention of dialling Imogen's number, but what would she say if Lawrence did answer, or worse, Mr Taylor? Perhaps the suggestion that they meet up again had merely been a joke on Lawrence's part, or a courtesy.

At ten-thirty that night, when she and her parents were in bed, the phone rang at last. She shot downstairs, her nightie catching at her knees, and grabbed the receiver. Mr Beckett appeared at the top of the stairs.

'Sarah Beckett. Is that you?'

'Yes. Yes. Hello.' She gave her father a little wave to indicate all was well and he disappeared but she knew her parents' bedroom door was ajar.

'What are you doing tomorrow?'

'Working. I've got to work.'

'Pity. I'm going to Brighton to see a friend. Wouldn't you like to come?'

Brighton. All day. 'No, no. I couldn't possibly. I've got so much to do.'

'Well, I'll call in anyway, shall I, see if you've changed your mind?'

She agreed to meet him outside the station at ten.

This time he brought her a proper wind-proof jacket upon which the sun fell warmly as they skimmed along the A23. She fell against Lawrence's back, half asleep after so many wakeful nights. The Oxford Entrance and the history essays trailed away in streamers behind her so that her mind held only the shreds of their memory. She never wanted the journey to end because then the difficulty of meeting Lawrence's friend, male or female, would have to be faced. And the last time she had visited the Pavilion at Brighton had been years ago with her parents on a day return by train. To pass it again, in these circumstances, seemed a double betrayal as of course she had not told them where she was going, or with whom.

The friend lived in a dirty little terraced house well back from the sea. Sarah sat passively on a plastic couch and sipped coffee from a stained white mug while Lawrence and Geoff discussed the sale of a guitar. Geoff had limp, trailing hair, grubby nails and a hesitant manner. His eyes were sunken, dreary pools.

When they left at last Lawrence put his arm round Sarah. 'Geoff is the best guitarist I know. The most talented. Easily. I will never do what he can do. But he's blown it. He's a fucking idiot.' He released her and they rode off through the town to the sea.

Sarah had never felt such a sense of holiday. Holy day. The light was mellow on the long expanse of promenade. This was seaside at the close of season, with pensioners strolling by in heavy coats and comfortable shoes, and the occasional mother with her buggy out for perhaps a last morning by the sea before the winter came. Children careered on roller skates but they were locals, blind to their surroundings. Sarah was dazzled by the sea which was still a treat for her, visited annually but a virtual unknown.

She moved closer to Lawrence who was light-hearted and companionable. He bought her coffee and a hot dog, infecting her with his pleasure in the day. They walked to the end of the pier and she hung over the rail to gaze down at the lapping water and knew herself to be exactly on the cusp of her life, with a man beside her she hardly knew. Despite her confused fear of the unknown, she turned recklessly to Lawrence, smiled up into his face, caught the brilliance of his blue eyes and brushed against him, as if by accident.

They went on the beach and sat on the pebbles. He wanted to know about her family and school and she made him laugh with her anecdotes of Imogen but wished after a while that her friend had not been mentioned for Lawrence grew sombre when he talked of his home life.

'My mother is a grasper,' he said. 'When I stopped worshipping her I started hating her. She is too impatient to be a decent parent. My dad's not much better. They're both preoccupied and loathe each other, which doesn't help. There must once have been some passionate attraction but it died years ago. And yet they want us to be perfect and brilliant. You could never please them, you could never win their atten-

61

tion, you could never earn anything except disapproval, however hard you tried, so I gave up. I left. But I guess I dumped Image.' He reached out his hand and pushed aside the curtain of Sarah's hair. 'Only you were loyal to Image.'

Oh no, no, don't say that, she thought, I've neglected Imogen. I had no idea she had invested me with so much influence and anyway she drifted away from me ages ago. Why has she gone on talking about me all these years?

'And this time,' he added, 'I doubt I shall see her at all. We've tried to contact them but I gather they're travelling round. Anyway, I don't think my mother would come rushing home to see me.'

His hand shifted under Sarah's hair to the back of her neck and his thumb stroked the hollow under her ear. Every nerve in her body attended to the point where his thumb moved. He kissed the side of her forehead and talked softly into her hair. 'You smell of the sea, Sarah Beckett.' His arm came round her shoulder and he drew her down on the warm stones.

I'm lying on Brighton Beach being kissed by Lawrence Taylor, she thought, and burrowed closer and closer, lips, arms, breasts wanting him to shut out the jagged intensity of her life which seemed to hurt her so much. The simplicity of being kissed by Lawrence made her senses reel.

'Really, Sarah, we should not do this,' he whispered, his breath warm and moist under her ear. 'You do remember that I am going away on Thursday? I won't be back. You do know that?'

But you might be, you might be, she thought, now this has happened. She loved his hand that moved gently under her shirt at the neck, and his sure, hungry lips. The body which had been so unmoved by poor David Parr was wide open to Lawrence.

When they got up he held her tight and they crunched over the stones back to the bike. On the journey home her arms crept tighter and tighter round his waist.

All that night the house washed about her so that she lay in her familiar bedroom holding to the mattress lest she float away. I have fallen in love with Lawrence Taylor, she thought, and reworked every moment of the day. Across the room, faint in the glow of a street-light outside, were her open books, waiting for her. But who cared about a few essays? What did school matter compared to a love which lifted her from the slow, grubbing world of 'A' levels and hurled her into a new, glimmering dimension?

On Wednesday he didn't ring all morning. It was his last day. Time was slipping past. Surely he would phone? She had a little more confidence now and at last dialled Imogen's number. After a very long time Mr Taylor answered and she slammed down the receiver.

Two hours later she caught the bus to Hampstead. It was worth a try. Perhaps Lawrence would be back from wherever he had been. She knew that Mr Taylor rarely heard the front-door bell because of the Mahler so she would be safe from him. Somehow her legs carried her to the Taylors' front door. Lawrence answered at once and stood on the threshold staring at her. It was not possible, it couldn't be, that he looked impatient.

'Were you going to call me?' she asked.

'Oh sure. I've been packing.' The heart-stopping smile was there again. 'You can come and watch if you want.'

The house was intensely quiet as she tiptoed behind him up the stairs. 'Dad's out,' Lawrence said.

Once they were inside his room she leant on the closed door. 'Have you got to go tomorrow?'

He was busy with his music, his hair falling over his cheek as he sorted and packed. 'Of course. My contract begins on Saturday. I told you.'

'I know. I'm sorry. I didn't realize.' Dwarfed by his adult, business-like world, she sat hopelessly on the edge of the bed.

'Mind that guitar.'

'Sorry, oh sorry. Look, I'll go.'

'No. It's OK. Really. Just let me finish this.'

'No. No. I must go.' His coldness was so unbearable that she was almost crying. To escape the shame of it she made for the door and headed for the stairs. He came after her, gripping her upper arm.

'You're all in a state. We can't have this. Calm down. It's OK.' He held her against his chest and she sobbed into his shoulder.

'I'm sorry. I'm so sorry.'

'Don't be. You're such a silly girl.' He kissed her tears and then her wet mouth. Oh, his lips tasted so beautiful.

They backed along to his room where he kicked shut the door and pushed her on to the bed. 'Listen, Sarah. I think I know what you're feeling but I want you to understand I really am going tomorrow. I have commitments in the States. I won't be back for months and in any case I refuse to be tied by anything here. Do you understand?'

'Yes. Yes.'

'All right then. You just stay there and think about it while I do this.'

He worked on and on, stowing away clothes and papers until the room was neatly packaged into two bags. She watched every movement, committing it to memory. Occasionally he glanced up and smiled at her.

Finally he took up the guitar. She tried not to be disappointed. It was Lawrence she wanted, not his music, but he sang her a love-song of a kind which ended on a melancholy, trailing note: '*And how I wish I were in love.*'

Aren't you in love, Lawrence? I am. I am.

He threw the guitar aside, twisted the key in the lock and fell at last on to the bed beside her. His kisses were slow and deep, his face lost in that same daze, absorbed and sensual, as when he played for her. The afternoon was a tunnel along which he drew her deeper and deeper.

His tongue sank into her mouth, then away as his lips trailed across her cheek to her ear. 'Are you sure you want this, my lovely Sarah? Are you sure? I will be very safe and very gentle.' She gripped his thick hair in her hands and pulled his face to her breast. His touch was so slow and deft that her bared flesh shuddered. She bit on the palm of his hand and felt his coarse hair brush the untouched skin of her thighs. Spreading herself like a trailing, elemental thing, she sailed away with him into a plunging red sea.

The next morning Sarah woke to the pink light of her bedroom at home and knew that Lawrence would be gone. She had not fallen asleep until three and now it was very late. The memory of him sustained her for a little while but then the harshness of the morning crowded in on her, the mountain of work that hadn't been started, the blankness of weeks ahead without Lawrence who had given no date for his return.

Next day a letter arrived, sent first class. Lawrence's writing was as definite as Imogen's, though perhaps less flowing. For some minutes Sarah lay on her bed with the envelope unopened beside her, its contents safely unread.

> Dear Sarah Beckett,
>
> You were worth a trip to England all by yourself. I don't need an aeroplane to fly me to the States today, I could fly without one. But Sarah, we men are very different to you. The way we behave doesn't always reflect the way we feel. You are seventeen and very sweet but that's all you are to me. You do know that, don't you? I say it clearly again because I don't want you to waste any of your precious thoughts or hopes on me. I probably made a big mistake yesterday, but I won't regret it if you won't. But that's all, Sarah. Please, please understand that.
>
> Lawrence

By the Tuesday following half-term Sarah had not slept more than two or three hours a night for nearly two weeks.

Travelling to school was like forcing her body through a world where the hold of gravity was scarcely adequate. She felt all bone, no flesh, exposed to thin icy air that wouldn't allow her to breathe properly. The loss of Lawrence had left her spinning in frantic isolation. She could confide in no one, not her parents, not Claire Tomkins, who would be practical and prosaic, certainly not Imogen, who in any case was still absent.

Miss Stone was in a rage. 'Where are your essays, Sarah?'

'They're not done, Miss Stone.'

'What's happening to you? I've never known you late with work.' She brought her broad, coarse face close to Sarah's. 'What is it, Sarah? Come and see me after school. I'll be in my office.'

But Sarah didn't go. Instead she went to the end of Imogen's road and waited and waited in case the phantom of Lawrence roared past on his bike though she knew for sure he had gone. His intentions had been clear from the first and crushed in her pocket she carried his terrible letter. But how could he be in the States when his reality to her was stronger than this blustery evening or the blankness of nearby houses? If she could only see him one more time some of the pain caused by his words might be undone.

At seven she wandered home to find her mother in a state.

'Where have you been, Sarah?'

'I was working late.'

'You should have rung. You've been so quiet and strained recently. I never know what you've been up to. I worry so much.'

'You need not. Nothing's going to happen to me between school and home, is it?'

'You look so tired. You must ease off, Sarah. Tomorrow I want you home straight after school. I'll be waiting for you.'

Oh Mother. Your world is a darting, two-dimensional place to me. I can't reach you in it. You lead a shallow, pointless life in your small rooms. What do you know? The effort of saying a single word to her mother, all those light years away, was too much for Sarah, who had to squeeze out sentences from a dry, tight throat. She couldn't eat her supper but sat where she had always sat, meal after meal for seventeen years, facing her mother, on the left of her father, smiling out at them from a numb face.

All evening she hunched over her desk, supposedly studying *King Lear*. Her eyes followed speeches, annotations and references but only the odd phrase entered her consciousness. Cordelia. The name was a fruit that dripped its juice through her brain. Sad, doomed Cordelia: *Her voice was ever soft,/Gentle and low, an excellent thing in woman.* Lucky Cordelia, dead in her father's arms, grieved over, laid quietly to rest under sorrowful eyes. Wrong-headed Cordelia, inflexible Cordelia.

Later Sarah lay in the bath and watched her body float limp in the hot water. Only when completely submerged did the pain ease a little and even then Sarah could not sink her head under for more than a few moments without rising for breath and being faced once more with the narrow little bathroom and the steamy mirror on the shaving cabinet. Here was her enemy again, the real world, her home, her school, all the ordinary places where there was no Lawrence. And words and words that must be learnt and reworked by a brain that fought ever more feebly to make sense of them. In the night the easy, magical time with Lawrence faded hour by hour to be replaced by the cruel rejection of his letter. And then other rejections grew, other surprises. The image of Laura Harding with her bright, hard eyes was vivid in Sarah's mind. Everything Laura had said was true. Sarah barely coped at Priors Heath where each minute of her school-days now seemed to her to have been a struggle. She didn't have the casual intelligence of Laura Harding nor the stolid dedication of Claire Tomkins. Sarah's learning was emotional and obsessive. She had forced herself over every hurdle by sheer will-power. The background from which she came was paper thin for she had been bred on a diet of mashed potato and Sunday walks in suburban woods, not nourished by the rich brew of Imogen's cultural inheritance or the broad brush-strokes of information wielded by Laura's journalist father. Lawrence for a few days had offered her an escape from this deceit but now she was once again trapped at Priors Heath in a landslide of work.

By morning her whole being was fixed in a bright beam of certainty. She wrote and posted a letter withdrawing her application to Oxford.

At school her eyes were fierce and wide open. People looked at her a little warily though they smiled often. The row with Laura Harding had already become a legend. A few people had approached Sarah and told her they hoped she wouldn't give up her place in the debating team. Sarah smiled and shrugged. Imogen was still away.

At last school was over. Sarah was driven by the knowledge that there comes a moment when a decision is inexorable, as when Lawrence Taylor had opened the front door instead of Imogen and Sarah had stayed to watch him cook lunch. Before the start of the meal she might have escaped easily but then her will had become fixed and she had known she would not turn back.

She waited on and on in the library, tucked away in a corner with a book called *The Wheel of Fire* by G. W. Knight open in front of her. Normally she loved this mellow room in the Old House with its high oak shelving and ancient rugs but today it seemed merely another prison. At last the librarian locked up and sent her away. 'You look pale, Sarah. Don't overdo it. You'll be fine in the Oxford exam.' But Sarah had done no studying in the past hour, only gazed fixedly at a page number: 92.

The rose garden had not emerged from a fine mist all day and was now sunk in translucent darkness. A few classroom windows were still lit in the New Building and above, in the Old House, the Headmistress's light was on.

Sarah had decided on the place she would choose, a little

tucked-away nook under the brewery wall where she some-times went with Imogen, though there seemed less shelter than she had remembered because at this time of year the nearby bushes were wind-blown and spare. Clumsily she removed her coat and folded it over her schoolbag then sat down cross-legged on the grass. The blood ran warm in her veins but she was shaking with cold. Beneath her the earth was damp and yielding. She could have lain down and slept for a year.

She had selected an unused razor blade from her father's pack of five. It was still wrapped in its little paper envelope so she unfolded it and ran her finger carelessly along it, surprised by the instant, painless cut that appeared. The thought of her father's large fingers fitting this blade innocently into his razor almost prevented her but she closed her mind to him. His huge, unquestioning love was part of the burden she could no longer carry.

The complexity of her world fell away as she looked at the glinting, rectangular blade and saw it slice through her white skin like butter. At first there was no pain, then a sharp, hot sting. The other wrist was much more difficult for she was trembling violently and the blade seemed blunter. The cut was jagged and despite the hurt, blood refused to flow at first. Then it trickled on to her cold hand and she felt as if she were a warm bath slowly emptying.

Overhead the rose bush was absolutely still. She rested her fingers on the grass, closed her eyes and felt like singing in the peaceful moments of certainty. And then, almost at once, came a sense of horror at what she had done. How unutterably cruel. How unbearable for her parents. How could she have squandered her living self so wickedly? But the deed was done, she was committed, sliding down a slope which offered no handholds. Down, down, slithering and jolting, the world a black map below. Down, down until the grass reared up to meet her.

'Sarah. Sarah.'

She stared stupidly up at Imogen.

'Your mother rang my house. She didn't know where you were this late. I had the car so I offered to . . . My God. My God, what have you done?' Imogen reached down with merciless fingers and grabbed Sarah's hands. She clasped the red cuts and raised Sarah's arms high above her head so that soon her own hands and coat sleeves were wet with blood.

'You fucking idiot. You bastard. Why have you done this? How could you?' Imogen's eyes as she stared into Sarah's face were outraged and terrified. 'Get up. Get up. My God.' She was fumbling for something to stanch the flow but then gave up and instead took Sarah's elbow and began to pull her along.

The walk was interminable, along the edge of the quad and down the alleyway beside Ryder Street to the front of the Old House where Imogen had left her car. Sarah's knees wouldn't straighten and she couldn't feel her feet. All the time Imogen muttered abuse and instructions. 'Keep your hands up. Don't let drips fall on the path. God help me.'

In the car the shouting and scolding went on and on. 'Keep your arms up. Prop them on your elbows. Have you any idea of what a bad job you've made of it? You'd have been there all night and still not died.' She had found a scarf and was binding Sarah's left arm above the cut. 'I wish I knew what to do,' she muttered, and then shouted at Sarah: 'I bet you know what to do, you're such a fucking know-all. But you're past it, aren't you? Sarah.' She gave Sarah another shake. 'Don't go to sleep.' Freezing air blew from open windows as they drove away from the school. Imogen cursed and cursed, her driving erratic as she occasionally jerked Sarah's hands higher or nudged her awake.

They came to a strange street of high houses. Imogen tumbled out of the car and leant on a doorbell. A prolonged argument in low voices took place with someone inside while Sarah sank into her seat, dozing and weeping. She hadn't yet shed the feeling that her life had been abandoned, so meekly allowed herself to be hauled over the pavement by Imogen, across a polished floor and into some kind of white office where a young man was waiting. He was very angry. At last she could lie down on a cool, hard bed. The man scarcely spoke and Sarah, who longed to be comforted and forgiven, turned her head to the wall.

Imogen's voice cracked through the silence.

'She'll be all right?'

'She will. The cuts aren't that deep. Messy though.'

'Oh, cheer up, Steven, you told me you owed me one. This is it.'

'I could be struck off,' he muttered.

'Don't talk rubbish.'

He took a needle to Sarah's torn wrists and repaired them for her. On the way out she managed to thank him but he shook his head.

Next Imogen drove to her own house. 'No, no,' cried Sarah, 'I don't want to go in there.' How could she stand the sight of those stairs or Lawrence's closed door? But Imogen would have none of it. She pulled Sarah out of the car and frog-marched her up the steps. Inside, the staircase threatened to rise up and hit Sarah as she climbed.

When they were inside Imogen's room and the door was closed, Imogen turned on her. 'Are you listening carefully, Sarah? The reason I didn't take you to casualty was because I don't suppose you really want everyone to know you've done this. We can't risk your parents finding out. It would destroy your mother. I phoned her and said you were staying the night with me. Sarah, if you ever tell your parents what you've done today I swear I'll kill you.'

So saying, Imogen rushed away to make tea. Afterwards Sarah was allowed to huddle deep under Imogen's duvet, a hot-water bottle burning across her thighs. Imogen sat beside her and stroked her hair.

'I hate you for this, Sarah. I hate you.' She was shaking a little and flicked a tear angrily aside with her hand. 'Why? Why?'

The hand went on and on stroking. Sarah was sinking into sleep. She was too tired. 'Work. It's too much work.'

'Don't be so bloody ridiculous. If you can't handle a few "A" levels what about the rest of the human race?'

'I'm useless. I can't do it.'

'I don't believe that's all it was. You're not so stupid that you would take your life for the sake of a couple of exams.'

'That was it. I swear.' How could she tell Imogen, who worshipped her brother, that she had made love to Lawrence? Unpredictable Imogen might respond with distaste, or anger, or possessive jealousy. Worst of all would be disbelief and endless questions. 'Last week was terrible,' Sarah added drearily, 'I couldn't work at all. And then there was a row with Laura. Did you hear about that? She said I was a parasite on you. Other terrible things. And you were away.'

'So I should bloody well think. What good were you stewing over your books? Why can't you forget about school, ever, and have a bit of fun? It was great in Yorkshire, even if it was with my mother. Though I missed Lawrence. He was here, Dad says. I never even saw him.'

The hand continued stroking Sarah's hair. Imogen was calmer and more thoughtful now and her voice had softened. An odd word would reach Sarah like the volume being suddenly turned up on a radio: 'drive . . . my mother . . . Laura Harding'. Imogen gently lifted the cut wrists to check that the bleeding had stopped and even as she released them sleep came to Sarah in a warm, black flood.

The next day Imogen lent Sarah a long-sleeved jumper that covered her hands. She drove her to school and forced her through the familiar routine though Sarah was weak and tearful. At the end of every lesson, Imogen was there to encourage Sarah and protect her from fellow students and teachers who might question why she was so wan and pale. The debating project was summarily dismissed and Laura Harding taken to one side and verbally castigated.

Priors Heath that day became an extension of Imogen's domain: her candle-lit room; her bed with its billowing duvet; her long, strong hands; and above all the constant flame of her loyalty which danced and blazed.

4

April 1849

In April the icy dankness that penetrated every ill-fitting pane of glass at Priors Heath was at last banished by a delicate spring breeze that ruffled the girls' skirts when they walked in the garden and brought a slight bloom to their thin cheeks. Merciful heat could be found in long patches of sunlight falling on to the low forms in the schoolroom and by nightfall the dormitory in the attic had absorbed warmth from roof-tiles which had soaked in sunshine all day.

The rise in temperature, coupled with the dazzling blue skies and the brilliance of new leaf and bloom in the gardens, was troubling to the authorities. The girls had been quiet in the winter months, dulled to lassitude by cold, hunger and the monotony of grey weather. Now, in the spring, their voices were more high-pitched. They grew inches at a time and couldn't sit still. Their cumbersome skirts didn't hide the twitchings of their confined limbs and their feet clattered on the steep wooden stairs. On the Sunday walk to church they dawdled, lifting their faces to the light and peering excitedly round their bonnets to examine the new life in the hedgerows or to touch blossoms and soft buds.

Reverend Carnegie's visits to the school became still more frequent. He prepared little homilies on the excesses of nature and told his charges that they should be grateful such flashy colour was restricted to the exterior world from which he protected them. Miss Simms, delighted by the increased attention of her idol, now sported a skittish, fringed shawl and a new cap.

Bess had developed considerable funds of self-control but the almost constant presence of Carnegie was more than flesh and blood could stand and her inability to make changes made her reckless. She was near the end of her endurance. Her energy and resourcefulness were being dissipated on impossibly ambitious schemes to improve the school and there was no outlet for her ideas. Reading over the letters she sent to her family she was aware of a tone of frantic, biting criticism for Priors Heath and overcharged emotionalism, quite unlike her normal balanced phrases.

Her latest bid now the weather was so fine was that the pupils should be taken for long walks. As usual the very idea had been crushingly refused. Exposure to the sun was ruinous to the complexions of young girls, she was told by Miss Simms, and worse, their natures would become savage and saucy if exposed to too much fresh air.

One Tuesday lunch-time Miss Simms retreated to her bed-room with a prostrating headache, caused, thought Bess, by her refusal to open any windows in the school. All morning Bess had sat in the schoolroom tormented by the blowing movement of the trees in the garden. Every window held a shimmering image of pink blossom, brilliant sunshine and toss-ing shadows. She was struck by a yearning for her Derbyshire home where, in the rectory garden, the grass would be thick and verdant and her mother's flowerbeds newly raked and planted. Beyond the garden wall, the woods would be sappy with spring and the hills softly green. And here was Bess among the bare, distempered walls and hard benches of Priors Heath. She couldn't breathe. A brief walk in the garden at lunch-time where she was more than ever exposed to the demands of her charges only increased her sense of enclosure.

And now, on this exceptional afternoon, she found the entire school in her charge. All were gathered in the schoolroom.

'Today, it seems to me, is the beginning of spring, so we must celebrate. You may take into the garden your sewing or drawing, anything which will keep you gainfully employed. If you wish you may collect your cloaks. Because it is spring you may run about for a few minutes.'

There was a mutter of surprise. Inevitably Mary Worth demanded: 'Is it all right if I stay inside? It's too bright for my eyes out there.'

Bess took no notice but began to work on the latch of the large French window giving access to the garden. The wood had swollen and the hinges rusted with disuse but at last she was able to fling it open and allow the girls into the sunshine.

For a moment even Bess felt a little daunted. The unexpected deliverance from afternoon lessons had the same effect on the girls as the release of birds confined in a small cage. For a while the girls hovered near the schoolroom. Then they began to spin into the light, glancing back occasionally for reassurance before skipping out of reach so heedlessly that Bess experienced a wave of irrational panic in case they should indeed fly away. Their voices rose in excited twitters and Bess was thankful that Miss Simms's bedroom was out of earshot in the front of the house.

After a quarter of an hour most had calmed down. Some wandered about, others sat on their winter cloaks. A few of the youngest lay curled up in the sunshine fast asleep, their squares of cross-stitch abandoned. Bess found herself a spot under a tree near the middle of the garden and was soon surrounded by a gaggle of children. Christina Riddell sat close by, absorbed in her drawing but pausing occasionally to raise her eyes to Bess's face.

Bess rested her head against the broad, reassuring trunk of the tree and for a moment was at peace, entirely herself. Above, a canopy of pink blossom swayed and rippled. She was absorbed by the extravagant beauty of nature. Occasionally a child came up with her drawing for Bess to admire or correct. After half an hour a small sheet of paper was pushed gently into her hand.

'Christina. Is this your work?'

Christina's face was tense. 'What do you think?'

'I think it's exceptional.'

Most of the girls had no idea how to draw. They had never been properly taught and had been encouraged to make only feeble little sketches of each other, or still-lifes. But Christina was obviously very gifted. She had drawn a blossom tree and the brewery wall. The contrast between the movement in the branches and the solid brick of the wall was extraordinary.

'I used to think I had some talent,' Bess said, 'but I have never been able to draw like this. Who taught you?'

'Oh, I draw all the time. Mostly when I shouldn't.' They smiled at each other, a conspiracy of light-heartedness.

'I have some water-colours. Why don't you borrow them? I'm sure you could make better use of them than I.'

'No, Miss Hardemon, I . . .'

A hush fell on the garden, as if someone were snuffing out each child one by one.

Reverend Carnegie had arrived. He towered at the school-room door like a black-clothed avenging angel, his smooth gold hair agleam, his curved mouth set in stone. Annie Laidlaw trembled in his shadow but jumped to attention when his flat, voice ordered her to fetch Miss Simms from her sick-bed.

One by one the girls rose to their feet.

You have nothing to fear, Bess told herself firmly. It's absurd to expect retribution for something as trivial as this. As she walked the length of the straight path between herself and Carnegie she could feel sunlight hot on her hair. Her bonnet dangled from her right hand.

'Reverend, we have brought our work into the garden, as you see. It seemed a pity to waste so glorious a day. Don't you think?'

It was as if his gaze penetrated every fibre of her gown, every stray, floating hair, every pore of her flesh.

'The girls will take their places in the schoolroom immediately.'

She remained by his side and spoke softly as the girls hurried past. 'I hope you won't punish them, Reverend. This was my idea. You seem angry.'

He took the work of the older girls. The last pupil was Christina Riddell who barely paused as she handed him a blank page. Her hostility was tangible but she gave Bess a look of anguished love. Carnegie did not favour her with even a glance.

Miss Simms had tottered into the room, hair in a mess, eyes dull with sleep and pain. She stood swaying by the desk.

Carnegie turned on the pupils. 'I will not have girls at this school behaving like common labourers' daughters. Sitting on grass. Bare-headed. Drawing from nature. These pictures are cheap. The flowers on those trees will fade in days. They have no substance, and you have allowed yourselves to be seduced by their shallow charm. Caroline Wentworth.' Poor Caroline was often a victim of the Reverend's ill-humour for her cheeks were irrepressibly red, her hands clumsy and her hair wild. She had stuck a little spray of blossom behind her ear. He wrenched it out and tossed it to the floor. 'The birch.'

Bess was now full of dread. This was entirely her fault. She had tried and failed time after time to curb an inflated sense of her own power. She should have read his character more accurately. He couldn't bear to be disobeyed.

Now she could do nothing. If she tried to reason with him further his rage would be even greater. She fixed her eyes on his face and understood from the way he so fiercely avoided any communication with her that it was she who was being punished, she whom he sought to hurt.

Caroline was already crying when she brought the birch to him. Her extended arm jolted as it lashed her hand. After the beating she was shaking from head to foot, tears spraying from her nose and eyelids.

He began a slow circuit of the room. One of the smallest girls, Helen Moore, was sent to the front for crumpling her embroidery. Her huge eyes made a mute appeal to Miss Hardemon but Bess pressed her lips together. I can't save you, she told the child silently, and this must be a bitter lesson to you. The worst forms of injustice and persecution isolate one human being from another.

Many of the girls were by now weeping quietly. Carnegie had found a stray wisp of grass on another's sleeve.

Christina Riddell was sent forward for handing in a blank sheet of paper.

They stood in a row with their palms extended. He took the first child's fingers in his own to hold her hand rigid. The birch was brought down savagely. When he came to Christina she held out her beautiful hand and her eyes were burning with righteousness. At the first lash she turned to Bess and bit her lip. The atmosphere in the room was charged with lurid excitement.

There would be no jam for a week. There would be no daily exercise. Instead the girls would sit in silence in the schoolroom.

Bess neither moved nor spoke. But she did not look away. Many girls stared at her in confusion and anger. Christina Riddell fixed on her loving, rebellious eyes.

When Carnegie finally strode to the door Bess went after him. He looked down at her, his eyes glazed as if intoxicated, his breathing quick and heavy through thickened lips. 'I have nothing whatever to say to you, Miss Hardemon. It is for the Board.'

'But I must speak . . .'

He called sharply for his stick and hat. They stood side by side and she was aware of the tension in his body. Annie came with his things, but for a moment he remained completely still, his upper arm level with Bess's head, his elbow actually touching her shoulder.

When the door had slammed behind him Bess returned to the schoolroom. Miss Simms swayed, her brow knotted with the pain in her head. She gave Bess a slow, triumphant smile.

That night at bedtime the girls wouldn't speak to Bess, whom they blamed for the misery of the afternoon. When she was at last alone in her room she buried her face in her hands.

Why, why, why Lord? Did I do so wrong? Forgive me. Those poor girls. Why make them suffer for my mistakes? Why?

She intended to resign at once. Nothing but harm could come of her staying in the school. She would go home and attempt to recover her shaken confidence and sense of vocation.

When there was a knock on the door she couldn't bear to answer.

'It's Christina Riddell.'

Bess sat up. 'Come in, Christina.' Dear God, she thought, am I never to be left alone?

'I'm sorry to interrupt but I wanted you to have this. If you don't mind. I saved it for you. Take it, please.' She held out the square of paper with the sketch of the blossom tree, crumpled where she'd hidden it in the pocket of her apron.

'Miss Hardemon, about this afternoon.'

Bess held up her hand. 'Christina. There's something you must understand. And tell all the others the same. I am entirely to blame for what happened.'

'He is —'

'Reverend Carnegie did his job. He is in a position of authority, Christina, and I should have respected his rules. I have caused untold unhappiness.'

'He caused it. It was him.'

'Authority must be respected. I chose to come to this school and I am the most junior teacher. If we all behaved as I did today, society could never work. No institution could function.'

'But you only wanted to make things better for us.'

Bess shook her head and turned away.

'Miss Hardemon.' The girl was graceful in her skimpy night-gown, a blonde plait falling over her shoulder, eyes huge and lustrous in the candlelight. 'If you have to leave, should you leave . . . may I write to you?'

'My dear girl, of course. If they let you. My home is the rectory at Mereby Bridge, in Derbyshire.' Christina nodded but still seemed unable to go. Bess went to her trunk, took out a flat, black box, and pressed it into the girl's hand. 'Here are my paints. See. There's a flap to use as a palette for mixing colours. Take it and keep it safe. Today has been very terrible, Christina, but it's not the end of the world for any of us. You'll see.'

But the next day at breakfast the subdued clatter of spoons in bowls was disturbed by the sounds of hacking and sawing. When she reached the schoolroom Bess saw that in the garden two men were attacking the blossom trees with sharp tools. First, branch after laden branch fell, then the trunks were sawn off a few inches from the ground. All morning the sawing went on and on until every tree had been felled.

Miss Simms gave no explanation.

Bess spoke in a dull voice and her movements were heavy as she found a copy of Mangnall's 'Questions'. She was in no mood to teach anything else. Although she kept her head turned away from the window flashes of movement, pink, green and brown, caught her eye.

Dear God, she thought, where have you gone?

At ten o'clock at night three days later Bess was left by the horse trough in Mereby Bridge, three-quarters of a mile from the rectory. There was no one from the family to meet her as she'd not written to them about her abrupt departure from Priors Heath. Instead she'd commandeered a lift from Buxton with an affable but dumb labourer from Hill Farm who didn't have the wit to take her home, despite the pouring rain. Neither cart nor horse were his own and he dared not go beyond his usual route.

The weight of her bags dragged at her shoulders, her muddy skirts flapped and she was further hampered by a wet cloak. Yet Bess made good progress for she knew every pothole and twist of the lane. The familiar scent of dark woodland and the sound of the river in the valley to her left were soothing and at last her pleasure in being home dulled her anguish at what had happened. By the time she turned in at the broken gates of the rectory she was almost ready to face the family.

Mrs Hardemon, who had been on her way to bed when the knock came, opened the door. 'Bess? Good heavens above! Whatever are you doing here? Cathy, Cathy, come quick.' She bustled her soaking daughter into the study where the Rector had been reading at his desk. The housekeeper, Cathy, rushed in. 'Take off your cloak, Bess, it's dripping all over the rug.' Meanwhile the boys, Martin and John, had tumbled downstairs, roused from sleep, noisy with excitement.

Bess stood in a puddle of rainwater and wailed with melodramatic self-mockery: 'They threw me out, Father. I was dismissed.'

She was wrapped in a warm shawl and tucked into the chair nearest the fire. John hopped about and shouted: 'Hallelujah, it's not us in trouble for once.'

The Rector stood bolt upright by the mantel and his slow voice cut through the commotion: 'How dare they?'

'Oh, they had every right.' Bess was now halfway between laughter and tears. Mrs Hardemon plucked off her daughter's ruined bonnet and took a towel to her hair. Cathy brought a pot of tea.

'Boys.' The Rector turned on his young sons. 'Go up. You'll hear more about it in the morning.' Cathy took them out and whispers could be heard in the hallway before they were finally persuaded up to bed.

Bess let her wet head fall against the faded chair-back and the warmth of the fire at last began to penetrate her stockings. Mrs Hardemon, never at home in her husband's study, hovered nearby. The Rector sat opposite, sipping his tea. Bess, watching his ruddy face and the deceptive mildness of his eye, felt a pang of sorrow that she had returned to him in disgrace.

'I failed, Father.'

'Failed is a strong word, Elizabeth.'

'They haven't even paid me to the end of the week. I was too proud to protest.'

'No pay,' cried Mrs Hardemon.

'I thought I would drown in their ignorance. It was a prison. Those little girls were only there to be out of the way and have their childhoods used up until they were old enough to marry. And the worst thing of all was that most of them never protested, however bad the food, or the cold, or the humiliation. But of course you can guess why they never so much as murmured. They were terrified. And my small rebellion has had terrible consequences.'

Still the Rector was silent, dipping forward occasionally to sip at his tea so that the firelight glowed on his high forehead.

'Oh, do tell us quick, Bess, what you did,' said her mother. 'I can't bear it.'

But the crime of taking the girls out into the garden now seemed so absurdly insignificant that Bess was laughing as she explained. Mrs Hardemon cried: 'What a terrible place. You're much better off at home. I'd never have let you go if I'd known. I must tell Gerald what I think of him for recommending you.'

'Oh, Mother, those lovely, lovely trees. You would have wept.' A muffled thud from upstairs indicated that the boys were giving trouble. Mrs Hardemon dropped a hurried kiss on her daughter's head and turned to go. But Bess suddenly took her mother's rough hand and pressed it to her lips.

'Well, Cathy will take supper up to your room. Don't stay too long talking to your father,' said Mrs Hardemon, withdrawing her hand but pleased by the caress.

After Mrs Hardemon had left, the quiet of the study seeped into Bess's weary bones. In this house no one depended on her, no child's nightmare would break her sleep, there were few restraints and no rules.

But suddenly she turned on her father. 'What have you done? You have filled me up with knowledge for which there is no demand. You have given me an understanding of my world which has made me see what is possible for a woman, but there is no school in the country right for me. I have nowhere to go with all this learning, this independence of mind. Do you know, once or twice at Priors Heath I even thought those girls were better off before my arrival, expecting, demanding, hoping nothing.'

Hardemon put his teacup to one side and his sensitive hand to his forehead. 'One institution hardly represents the entire nation. You are allowing yourself to feel a great deal of despondency over a very small setback.'

'No, it was more than a small setback. Because of me three girls were beaten. The whole school was punished.'

He was silent for a moment. 'You were not responsible for the cruelty of the authorities, Elizabeth.'

'But I should have known what would happen. The humiliation.' She moved her head from side to side with the remembered pain of her dismissal: the descent of the staircase at Priors Heath; the girls in the schoolroom listening for the rustle of her skirts as she passed; Reverend Carnegie in the heat of the boardroom, flanked by his committee of whiskery men with sorrowful faces turned to her in outrage. Her letter of resignation had lain unopened on the vast, bare table. Mrs Penhaligon had sat apart, stately in tartan satin, expression unreadable, eyes discreetly lowered.

'Did you value the opinion of the people who dismissed you?'

'No. I did not. Carnegie was particularly hateful.'

'Well then.'

She couldn't help laughing. 'Why is it that when I sit in this room with you everything is so clear but as soon as I set out on my own I trip up?'

'My dear Bess,' he said, rising to snuff the candles on his desk, 'be like other girls if you like. Stay in the safety of this house until some fortunate man finds you and transfers you to his own household. That would be a calm, safe life for you. But I thought you had chosen otherwise and it's not like you to go back on a decision.'

The next day, Sunday, the family attended church. News had of course already reached the entire village of Mereby Bridge that Bess Hardemon had come back after barely three months away and her progress up the aisle to the rectory pew was watched with great interest. Mrs Hardemon gripped her arm as if afraid her daughter might collapse under so much scrutiny but Bess lifted her chin and smiled cheerfully.

Most eyes were sympathetic. Miss Eliot, in her spring shawl, beamed in anticipation of having unpaid help again in the little village schoolroom. And the curate, Jonathan Cage, came up to the pew and took her hand. Bess tilted her head and smiled up into his diffident, longing eyes.

'Well, Jonathan, you see I'm back.'

'I see, Bess. I'm very glad.' His clasp was warm and strong.

'Perhaps you'll come up and have tea at the rectory.'

'I should like that.' He gazed at her wistfully a moment longer but her eyes answered firmly: No, Jonathan, nothing has changed where you and I are concerned.

But after he'd moved away she sighed. Perhaps we would have been very happy as man and wife, she thought. We might have been so peaceful. For a moment she was distracted by the thought of herself and Jonathan in the church cottage, a clutch of infants clasping the skirts of motherly Mrs Bess Cage. But this vision, though amusing, was stifling. Would he ever stop worshipping me, she wondered, or would I be pursued for ever by those doggie brown eyes?

As if in direct response to this question she had to sit through a reading from Proverbs, articulated in the slow, careful voice of Jonathan Cage himself.

> *'Who can find a virtuous woman? for her price is far above rubies. The heart of her husband doth safely trust in her, so that he shall have no need of spoil.*
> *She will do him good and not evil all the days of her life.'*

But despite its subject matter, these words reminded her not of Jonathan but of Priors Heath. At this time on a Sunday morning the girls would be kneeling in the pews of St Matthew's, stomachs cramped with hunger, while Carnegie preached one of his interminable sermons. How he would love this particular text on the duties of women. And who now would he employ to take the place of Bess?

She thought of the garden at Priors Heath dotted with tree stumps, still white and resinous. Am I wicked, she thought? Here am I, among so many who love me; and I have left my pupils more unloved and deprived than ever. Surely I could have tried to save them?

At lunch there was a good deal of noise as the boys stated their opinion of a school that could turn away their sister whilst expressing some sympathy for her late employees. 'They could never have expected anyone to be quite as awkward as you, Bess.'

Mrs Hardemon was more than usually flustered. She treated her daughter as a returned prodigal and critical house-guest and was agitated when Bess carried in a pile of plates or offered to help serve. And after an hour of worried reflection in church she couldn't quite resist the occasional reproachful comment. 'If only you had kept your opinions to yourself, Bess. Do you think if your father wrote to the Board they might reconsider?

Dismissal. Dear, dear. John, do sit up. And hold your glass properly. The carrots aren't quite cooked. I told you to leave them another few minutes, Cathy.'

'Mother,' cried Bess, 'your roast beef is ambrosia to me. Night after night I lay awake at Priors Heath imagining a feast like this.' She began a much embellished account of meal-times at Priors Heath which had the family laughing and exclaiming in outrage.

Afterwards the women shared the clearing of the meal. Cathy's slow, gentle conversation did much to heal Bess's bruised heart. She gazed fondly at the warm kitchen where all was wholesome and orderly, pans gleaming, surfaces scrubbed. I am a little boat come back to harbour, she thought, moored up in a safe place to become whole again.

And then she was free. She took her charcoal and sketch-book and left the house. She rather regretted the loss of her water-colours, but thought they would have a good home with Christina Riddell. It was quite wrong to lament an impulsive and generous gesture.

Spring had deepened later in Derbyshire than at Priors Heath. The season's clock was set back a little this far north. The air was crystal clear and a soft breeze blew from the hills.

A rough path ran from opposite the rectory gates through woods to the river. In summer cattle were brought to graze in a clearing by the water but this early in the season the grass was untrampled. Bess ran headlong to the water's edge and rested on her favourite mossy boulder.

On and on hurried the river, flashing over stones, regardless of Bess who loved it so. The heathery smell of the air was so sweet to her that she shed a few tears of relief. Stooping, she gathered a few stones from among the grass and tree roots on the bank.

Splash went the first rough flint. Goodbye, Carnegie.

Splash. And Miss Simms.

In went a handful of little pebbles. And the Board.

The old energy came flooding through her veins. In a dark pool near the bank the water was still and deep, but further out it flowed quickly over a jumble of rocks. I could have been more patient. Had I been someone different I might have managed a few changes by a discreet word with Mrs Penhaligon perhaps, or by flattering Miss Simms. But it's too late for regrets. I am what I am. Perhaps it was for the best.

With a rush of joy she felt the light return to her soul. She spread her palms so that the sunshine fell directly on them. She heard birdsong and the rushing water. The breeze played on her face.

When she walked on it was with a slow, purposeful stride though her mind was busy. She would resume her studies. Even the ignorant pupils at Priors Heath had uncovered areas of weakness in her skills as a teacher. She would return to her unpaid work at the village school, answering truthfully questions about Priors Heath. And all the while she would be seeking another position. She could not be a burden on her father's overstretched purse again. Something would come up.

The Vicarage,
Abbey Wood,
Hertfordshire.

April 30th, 1849

Dear Miss Hardemon,

I couldn't stay at Priors Heath without you. I heard the door close behind you and I despaired. I couldn't live in that hated place knowing you had gone and I became so ill that at last they sent for my father and I was brought home.

Perhaps you think me very weak. Before you came I accepted everything that happened to me. My fees were being paid by my uncle's generosity and I thought it my duty to make the best of things. But you taught me that I must ask questions and use the few gifts I have. How could I do either there?

I'm very afraid that you won't get this letter, or you won't reply. Perhaps already you're teaching some lucky girls somewhere else.

Your ever affectionate,
Christina Riddell

5

---— ——

'Typical. Typical. It hasn't rained for months but now look at it. Where shall we put them all?'

'The weather man said it would be dry by this evening.'

'I'll have mud all down the hall whatever happens. And Aunty Win can't sit in a damp garden.'

'My friends won't mind. They won't worry about the weather. We'll put them outside.'

'Sarah, if it's raining they can hardly stand about on the grass.'

'Oh, Mum, it doesn't matter if there's a squeeze. People will have a great evening. Look at this spread.'

The party food, planned months ago, was laid out under tea-towels on the overloaded dining table. Mrs Beckett had pushed the boat out and bought salmon and a real ham which had caused her hours of anguish over the boiling and dressing. Chives had been snipped over the lettuce, little sausage rolls bought from the freezer centre, French bread sliced and buttered though perhaps too early for it was already rather dry.

'You've gone to so much trouble,' said Sarah.

'Oh, it's no trouble. It's the least I can do.' But Mrs Beckett's pointed face was crumpled with worry and she looked exhausted. 'Come and have another look at the puddings. I'm sure there'll never be enough for thirty. Shall I send Dad out for another tub of ice-cream? He won't mind.'

'Mother, there's heaps.' The doorbell rang and there was David in the porch bearing flowers for Mrs Beckett and a long, loving kiss for Sarah. It was such a relief to see him, scarcely recognizable in a suit and tie, his unruly hair brushed very flat.

David had the knack of imposing near calm on Mrs Beckett. He admired her handiwork, insisted on making her a pot of tea and pronounced firmly that the sky was definitely clearing. In a few minutes he had persuaded her that she could take time off to get changed. Mr Beckett crept down in a new cream shirt and his best suit but was immediately ushered away to put on a different tie. Sarah and David were left alone in the living room where they admired the engagement cake, iced and inscribed by Mrs Beckett.

He kissed her, his eyes full of excitement and triumph. 'How's my lovely girl?'

'Fine. Worn out, but fine.' Instead of meeting his eyes she kissed his cheek. 'And now come and have a look at how we've arranged the garden. Mum thinks it's going to rain.'

'Sod the garden. Your parents won't mind if we close the door and make love under the table, will they?' He covered her face with hot kisses, his eyes glazed with love and desire until she pulled away, laughing. But she had felt the customary tremor of irritation that he wanted so much of her these days. Reaching for her hand he kissed her knuckles and then deliberately pushed back her sleeve and ran his tongue along the raised white scar. 'Are you sure you're all right?'

And this was irritating too, his proprietorial attitude to her well-being because he knew the origins of the scars and tried to protect her from herself. Yet she had run to him, not he to her. It was she who had been persistent in their relationship at first.

On a freezing February day in the spring term of her 'A' level year, less than five months after her attempted suicide, Sarah had travelled to Durham for her interview at the university

91

to study history. After Oxford it had been her first choice, though she was rather dismayed when she discovered how far Durham was from home.

However, she loved the train journey which seemed to stretch on and on for hours. The motion of the carriage soothed her body and her mind dozed. She thought of all the quotes she knew about journeys and of Imogen reading Robert Frost: *Promises to keep . . . before I sleep . . . promises to keep . . . promises to keep.*

The moment of arrival tumbled her into a cold, windy station. Grit blew in her face and buses bound for unknown destinations wheeled away from the forecourt. Sarah clutched a typed page of directions sent by the university and stumbled about looking for the right stop. The light was fading rapidly and the bus journey along an empty road filled her with dismay for she seemed to be driving away from, rather than towards a new or promising world. She pulled her gloves firmly over her wrists and wished she was at home.

In the college she recognized the safety of a familiar institution. There were lots of other young women, officious notices on boards and long passages down which seeped dull cooking smells. At supper-time Sarah managed a conversation with a deadly girl called Sue who had straight greasy hair and severe dietary problems. Afterwards they sat in the common room and watched a slide show about student life. Sarah felt defeated by the sight of so many energetic young people engaged in rowing, singing or voluntary work with the elderly. As soon as she could escape she went to her allocated student bedroom and lay on the hard bed staring at the walls where grey paint was pitted by drawing pins and blobbed with Blu-Tack. She made a small gesture of preparation by rereading the first chapter of C. V. Wedgwood's book on the Thirty Years' War.

The next morning, after their interviews in the college, Sarah and Sue, who still hadn't washed her hair, were ferried to the city. Sarah had several hours before her appointment with the history faculty, so she said a firm goodbye to Sue and set off to climb the steep cobbled streets alone, trailing her overnight bag. The thought of working in a city where one could at any moment call in to an echoing cathedral filled her with awe. Sarah too might one day leap heedlessly down that flight of stone steps with hair flying and a rucksack of books bouncing on her shoulder, so used to the sight of the ancient city that she wouldn't even bother to glance around her.

A tour had been arranged of the library and union building. Sarah saw herself stooped over a pile of books or perhaps leaning nonchalantly on a student bar. From almost every window she glimpsed the river where moorhens bobbed their busy heads. Here was a sheltered world where the beauty of nature, ancient architecture and the vibrancy of student life went hand in hand. Surely here she would be all right, immune to the old demons of Lawrence Taylor and the fear of failure. She floated through the interview on a wave of euphoric confidence, still under the spell of the city. To be in a place where there was so much history, rather than a glum suburb in Middlesex, seemed wonderful.

Travelling home through the night she was breathless with hope, enchanted by the way her reflection hung in the dark window, a young elusive face with beautiful eyes.

Three weeks after receiving the offer from Durham, Sarah met David Parr again.

For her eighteenth birthday Claire Tomkins held a party in a church hall. Stephen, her older brother, supplied a willing gang of males home for the Easter holiday and half the upper sixth at Priors Heath were invited with boyfriends if they possessed one. Sarah generally refused all social outings but her mother was sufficiently friendly with Mrs Tomkins to be aware of the party and insisted that Sarah should go and have a bit of fun for a change. A new long skirt was bought in blue and grey checks with a flounce at the hem which Sarah modelled before her admiring parents in a moment of rare joy. At her dressing-table mirror she applied more make-up than ever before, like a mask. She brushed her hair until it fell in a thick dark veil through which her huge, black-rimmed eyes peered. With this flimsy screen between herself and the world, she set forth.

Despite some sixty guests the hall was too big and the lights too bright. Claire formed a reception line with her parents, as though at a wedding. The boys hung around the buffet scooping up handfuls of crisps and looking anywhere but at the unattached girls. Many of Sarah's school-mates had come with boyfriends whom they paraded triumphantly, suddenly not at all interested in the girls they met daily in the classroom. After a couple of moments Sarah felt intensely irritated. Who is going to enjoy this, she wondered?

Music was played quite loudly and one or two people jigged about. Sarah wished violently for Imogen who would have seen through the vanity, insecurity and disloyalty that set friend against friend. The evening would have been lit by her laughter. But there was no chance of Imogen being invited to Claire Tomkins's party.

And then, just as she was about to escape to the nearest phone-box and summon her father, Sarah became aware that she was being watched. A thin boy in glasses with a fuzz of dark hair and wearing a plain white shirt was standing in the midst of a small group. It was David Parr whom she had been out with two years ago, and then dropped. This time her heart lurched when she saw him because he reminded her of Lawrence Taylor, with his dark hair and intense, rather scholarly face.

Claire Tomkins came up, grabbed Sarah and insisted that she meet her brother. As she was dragged past David their eyes met. In a moment of secret understanding she saw that he had noted her reluctance and was amused by Claire.

Stephen Tomkins was engaged in a mannish conversation about the Hertfordshire cricket team. He and his cronies gave Sarah accommodating smiles, their eyes straying to her breasts and thighs in mild, automatic interest though their attention didn't waver much. They opened their bunched group to include her but were too gauche to change the conversation. She began to ease away.

David was at her shoulder. 'Supper's ready,' he said. 'Shall I get you a plate?' By this simple question the evening was saved. They sat on the floor against a radiator with their plates on their knees and gradually Sarah's sheer relief at being with someone changed to a renewed interest in David Parr. He was a student, an engineer, who had been at school with Stephen Tomkins and vaguely kept in touch but not much. The subtext of this admission was that David didn't quite get on with the blond, heavy-shouldered Stephen. Sarah liked the way David talked very quickly, as if he was full of observations and ideas that must be expressed in a hurry. He wanted to know every detail of what she was studying and concentrated his appreciative gaze entirely on her, so that for a while she forgot the envious eyes of her class-mates across the hall and her earlier desire to escape.

They tried dancing but he was a terrible mover. They didn't touch but joggled about awkwardly, their eyes darting across each other's shoulders if they threatened to become too intimate. Before the slow dances David announced that he had to leave and Sarah was deeply disappointed. He gave her a quick kiss on the cheek and wrote her phone number on the back of his hand. Sarah remembered Lawrence, who had been so substantial and so certain. As soon as David had gone she went to the telephone and then waited outside for her father. There had been enough exposure for one night, she thought.

David didn't get in touch for many weeks, not that Sarah minded much. Her only regret was that she hadn't taken his number so that she might have had the pleasure of not ringing him in return. She had ceded him too much power.

But one night, just after 'A' levels, he phoned, giving no explanation, and asked her to go to a Dylan concert with him. In her new, heady freedom from studying Sarah couldn't quite bring herself to turn him down. He had nothing but his grant to live on so the tickets must have cost him his beer money for a term. They met in the great crowd outside the Wembley Arena and she felt extraordinarily glad to see him again. Both were in high spirits, David because he'd just taken his second year exams and done brilliantly. They were swooped along by Dylan's music. Halfway through he took her hand and at the end he began to kiss her. People in their row pushed past and they were left in the emptying auditorium locked together. His kisses were quite different to Lawrence's. David's were dry, reserved kisses, but she still enjoyed them. Nevertheless she was quite relieved when he deposited her outside her house, having travelled with her all the way in the train even though it would take him hours to get back to his flat.

By the end of a fortnight they were scarcely apart. David looked after her as if she were a precious, breakable thing and wanted to share every detail of her life. She told him about the scars on her wrists and he kissed them tenderly, promising to keep her secret safe from the Becketts. They had never seemed to question her mumbled excuse that the wound on her left arm had been caused by a careless jab with the vegetable knife at Imogen's.

David was a great favourite with them, indeed the way in which he accommodated himself so snugly into family meals threatened to undermine the relationship for Sarah couldn't help comparing him unfavourably to the restless Lawrence who would have been very bored.

But then David set off for Camp America, leaving Sarah alone once more, although it felt rather glamorous to announce to herself that she now had two lovers in America. She spent some weeks waitressing at a local café and then went to a horrible hotel in Tenby with her parents, her last holiday with them. When David came back she fell on his neck with joy. He seemed immensely dear.

She went up to Durham but the gloss had gone from the city and Sarah told herself that it was because she was so far from David. It rained constantly and the wind funnelled through the narrow streets. She seemed to spend hours travelling to and fro in the company of girls she scarcely knew and found little comfort after all in the cathedral, which was too grand. Desperately homesick, she sat over dry textbooks in the library and her love of history fell to pieces. Every night she wrote to David who responded with occasional, cryptic letters.

At last, desperate, she got into the train one weekend and journeyed to London, tense with anxiety and anticipation, to arrive unannounced at his flat. He opened the door and stared at her for a moment without speaking. They fell on his bed and made love at last. The duvet kept sliding from her thin shoulders as they removed each other's clothes awkwardly, incurring several bruises. She was in mortal fear of the unlocked door flying open and one of his flatmates bursting in but she loved his intense, hard body and the smell of him. Nothing can touch me now, she thought, curling deeper and deeper into his side, nothing can take away from the certainty of being this in love.

By Christmas she had transferred to London University and was sharing his room. Two years later they were engaged, mostly because she could no longer stand the weight of her parents' disapproval of their living arrangements. David had been recruited by a company which would eventually require him to work abroad and the obvious and easiest option for Sarah was to apply for a teacher training course. As Mrs Beckett said, with a teaching qualification behind you, you could go anywhere.

*   *   *

Sarah danced up to her room to dress. A patchwork skirt bought from an Indian shop in town hung from the wardrobe door. On the third finger of her left hand the new ring shone, its chip of a diamond catching the light if caught at a precise angle. 'Mrs Parr,' she told herself, 'you will be Mrs Parr,' and gazed deep into the dark eyes in the dressing-table mirror. The excited gleam in them died away.

'I love him. I do love him,' she whispered, her breath misting the spotted glass. For a moment doubt came in a physical pain under her ribs. She applied beige lipstick and smiled at herself again. Sarah Beckett. B.A. Engaged to be married. Twenty-one. Her skirt swung as she moved through her bedroom, dabbing Coty's musk oil on to her wrists and pulling on a clatter of beaded bangles. She gave a last, approving twirl and galloped downstairs.

The great-aunts arrived first and installed themselves in easy chairs, their best frocks pulled tight over their knees, their ankles thick in low-heeled best shoes. Aunty Win wore muddy green and wouldn't take off her hat which had a little stalk in the middle, like on the top of a plum. They accepted sherry from David with daring abandon and gave Sarah gifts of tea-towels and face-cloths which had been carefully wrapped in tissue paper and stowed away in their large, flat handbags. Sarah thought delightedly of a home full of new things which were just hers, not rented, not borrowed and not old.

Mr Beckett circulated with a bottle of sherry, allowing tiny refills.

'Top them up, top them up,' urged Mrs Beckett, hovering in her husband's wake. The bell kept ringing now and Sarah flew between the kitchen and the door welcoming her friends. Claire Tomkins and her new boyfriend Tony arrived, Claire full of self-congratulation that the pair she had introduced at her sixteenth birthday party had come to this. 'I think I'll start a dating agency,' she laughed and thrust a heavy parcel into Sarah's hands. Claire had been working in a bank since she left school and was always better off than the girls who had gone on to further study.

'Oh my goodness, what a lovely casserole,' exclaimed Mrs Beckett, who loved Claire. 'How generous. It must have cost a fortune. Denby Ware!'

Claire settled herself beside Aunt Victoria who held the casserole in her lap and lifted off the lid. 'It can go straight from the oven on to the table,' enunciated Claire into Aunt Victoria's best ear. 'So it's very handy.'

'Of course the lid would get very hot,' said Aunt Victoria, trying it out again.

Sarah was grateful to David for the way he accepted all the mild eccentricities of her family. He never judged her parents but included them in his love for herself. His own family lived on the outskirts of Manchester and were quite wealthy. They had already held an edgy drinks party for the newly engaged couple.

'Everything seems to be going down all right,' whispered Mrs Beckett to Sarah. The guests swarmed up to the food and consumed it with satisfactory enthusiasm. As David had promised, a warm, low sun shone in Mr Beckett's summer garden where the younger guests, student friends of Sarah and David, sat cross-legged on groundsheets and forked up mountains of supper.

Mr Beckett had been told to make a speech. This was a great ordeal for him and it showed in the way his hand and voice trembled. He had not been known to speak in public since his wedding day. When he glanced up he looked at Sarah and after a while she began to weep, smiling and shaking her head to toss away the tears.

'It's a great day for my little girl,' he said. 'To be twenty-one, a graduate in history, and engaged all at once. David Parr is a very lucky man. And I think these two will have a wonderful future. David, I gather, is already turning down offers of work from other companies and Sarah has chosen to go into teaching. I hope she will give as much pleasure to her pupils as she has to us. She has given us so much joy over the years, our sunshiny girl.'

Had David's hand not clasped her firmly about the waist Sarah might have crouched down to hide her face and howled. Daddy. She burned with shame that his trust in her should be so misplaced. Her wrists ached. But people were amused by her tears, which were considered completely appropriate after a speech like this. They laughed softly and touched her shoulder while David kissed her damp cheek. There was a toast and then the party lost its focus as people drifted apart.

One more ring came on the doorbell. Sarah, high with sparkling wine and compliments, sprang to answer. Through the bevelled glass of the front door she saw a thin, tall figure whom she recognized at once. Her pulse began to race and she was full of dread.

'Imogen. Imogen, I thought you were away.'

'So I was. I'm back. Can I come in?'

Imogen was very tanned and thin in cheese-cloth shirt and jeans, her hair caught tightly back from her face in a chunk of leather with a spike thrust through it. She brought with her the tang of far places and a grace which made the house seem for the first time desperately overcrowded. Springing up to Mr Beckett she enclosed him in her taut, sudden embrace. 'I'm so glad to see you,' she said. Claire Tomkins was favoured with a brief wave but Mrs Beckett was kissed fiercely on the cheek. Imogen was at home here, drawing attention to herself without lifting a finger and apparently unaware that the atmosphere had been newly charged by her presence. Her voice was low and musical and her gaze missed nothing. From her manner she might have been gone a few months rather than nearly two years. Sarah was assaulted by the same old mix of love and despair. Wafting through the house behind Imogen came a cloud of memories, tangled and disturbing. When Imogen's clear eye fell on Sarah what must she see but guilt and shame, darkness and pain?

Imogen came upon David in the garden and her expression hardened. He shook her hand and uttered a few words of pleasure for they had met briefly twice before. Sarah watched their encounter and noted they were the same height. Imogen's light hair was dyed orange by the evening sun and David looked very young in his creased shirt with the ends of his tie boyishly wide and flapping.

The aunts were leaving. Sarah summoned David and there were minutes of kisses and promises to call soon. No, the date of the wedding isn't quite fixed, the engaged couple repeated, but you'll be sure of an invitation. Outside the sky was darkening with more than the end of the day. The aunts removed telescopic umbrellas from their handbags, ready for a downpour even though they had a lift home.

Then the evening was almost over and David scurried about in the wake of Mrs Beckett offering coffee and collecting empty glasses. Imogen stood at the end of the garden, where she used to help Mr Beckett with his bonfire. 'You should go and talk to her, Sarah,' Mrs Beckett urged. 'You haven't seen her for years.'

A thunderous grey cloud had nearly covered the sunset though red light streamed from beneath it. Sarah's thin blouse could not protect her from the little breeze which frilled the leaves on the apple trees and she clutched her upper arms for warmth.

'Imogen.'

Imogen's eyes were dreamy and affectionate as she drifted among the fruit bushes in Mr Beckett's garden.

'I really had no idea you'd be home. I sent the invitation completely on spec.,' Sarah said.

'Would you have posted it if you'd known I might turn up?'

'Of course. What do you mean?'

'God, Sarah, you know what I think of David.'

'I thought you liked him.'

'Oh, I *like* him.' The word 'like' was spat out.

David and Imogen had met once after 'A' levels. The only other time was when Sarah had left Durham to join him at London University. Imogen, about to begin another trek across a new continent, this time Australia, had called at Heskwith Close to see the Becketts and had met him there with Sarah. Her visit had been only a few minutes in length and to the Becketts she had been her usual affectionate self but as she was leaving she had asked Sarah: 'So what was so wrong with Durham?'

'Too far away.'

'From what?'

'From David.'

'Oh, for God's sake,' Imogen had said. 'What is it with you? Why are you wasting yourself on him?'

This time Sarah was more courageous in the face of Imogen's hostility. What right had Imogen to turn up after so long and pass judgement? 'Imogen, what's your problem with David?'

'God, you're so cosy, Sarah. Is that what you want, to be cosy? An engagement party. How grown up. Well done.'

'What is this? What's wrong? You know I love David.'

'What do you know about love? Sarah, you're twenty-one and what have you done? You're already in his pocket. What about a life?'

'I've got a life. It's just that I've decided to share it with him.'

'You're afraid,' Imogen exclaimed triumphantly. 'You've gone for the safest option.'

Sarah was shaking violently in the chill of the evening. The little garden seemed too small and cramped to contain Imogen's rage. 'But he's a good man,' she cried, 'he loves me,' and she looked to the currant bushes and the lupins for encouragement. This dangerous conversation should not be happening. There was betrayal in the air.

'He'll smother you. He's dull and he doesn't challenge you. Is that what you want? To be buried all your life?'

'No, no, you're not right. I love him. I want to be with him. Besides, we're only engaged.'

'Give me strength. You're binding yourselves hand and foot. Well, I thought you had more guts. I've known you selfish and frightened but never a coward before.'

'Imogen. It isn't cowardly. It's right. You haven't been in love so . . .' But the words twisted on her tongue and she was assaulted by wave after wave of searing pain, such as she had experienced immediately after her affair with Lawrence. She gazed at Imogen with horror. 'We've not spoken for so long,' she said. 'I don't think you understand.'

Imogen shrugged. 'I just think you're running away.'

'And what are your own immediate plans,' Sarah asked in a small voice, to break the silence.

'Still not sure. Still testing.'

'Imogen, isn't it just that we're opposites? I go for a fairly conventional route, it's true. But you duck out of things too. What are you avoiding by all this travel?'

'Travel is not avoidance.' Imogen was stone cold. She turned a chill, unfathomable gaze on Sarah. 'Remember I've had examples before me all my life of real avoidance. Look at my father, and my mother, who ducked out of all her responsibilities for us. Look at Lawrence.'

Sarah flinched. Lawrence was there among the raspberry canes, his dark hair cloudy about his face, a guitar hooked under one arm and a haunting smile playing on his lips. But Imogen didn't notice. She was looking away from Sarah.

'Sarah.' Mrs Beckett stood on the lawn. 'Come on, Sarah, people are leaving.' David was in the kitchen window, watching them. The grey, massed clouds surely couldn't hold their rain much longer. Sarah nodded at her mother and turned to Imogen. 'Coming?'

'I'll stay here a little longer, thanks.' She would not smile at Sarah.

'All right then. See you in a minute.' Sarah hated to leave Imogen in this unyielding, isolated mood.

When she at last returned from the front door Sarah saw that great spots of rain were now falling. Imogen had left the garden and was in the kitchen helping Mr Beckett with the washing-up. Sarah was again called away and next time she looked for her friend, Imogen had gone.

6

September 1854

Bess spent the summer of 1854 with her brother Gerald and his wife Laetitia in their house near Baker Street, in London. Although she had been invited to view her stay as a holiday, in fact she was there to help Laetitia through the exhausting weeks following the birth of her fourth child.

Gerald, who was so like his father that Bess was forced to apologize to Laetitia for the dreamy indolence of the Hardemon male, made himself scarce during his wife's confinement. Unlike her offspring, Letty was undemanding, gentle and touchingly grateful to Bess. Her children, of whom the eldest was not yet six, ruled the nursery so despotically that their harassed nurse crumpled under the strain of controlling their high spirits. It therefore fell to Aunt Bess to play games with them in hot London parks in the hope of exhausting them sufficiently to ensure silence for the greater part of the night.

Overall the visit was a success. By the end of August the baby and his mother were thriving and the children had accepted the restraints imposed on them by Bess. She, meanwhile, had made time to plan the next step in her own career.

She broke her journey home to call on Christina Riddell who had been a regular correspondent in the five years since they met at Priors Heath. Christina's last letter had announced her engagement and imminent marriage to one Charles Lytton.

The best wedding present I could receive, wrote Christina, *would be a visit from you.*

The Riddell family lived in a stone vicarage on the outskirts of the small market town of Abbey Wood. Bess, who had been met at the station by one of Christina's young brothers, climbed down from the trap with relief, for conversation during the drive had been stilted. Having disclosed that he was the third of nine surviving siblings of whom Christina was the oldest, and that he intended to be a soldier, Richard Riddell had become monosyllabic.

It was immediately clear to Bess why Christina had been sent to Priors Heath. The school's main attraction to impoverished clergy parents had been the modesty of its fees. Judging by the state of their home the Riddells must be very poor indeed. Weeds grew among the gravel in the drive, paint peeled from the window-frames and tiles had slipped from the roof. Bess, who knew only too well the privations suffered in underheated church houses, was glad that the season was still warm.

The door was opened by the lady of the house. Mrs Riddell, a toothy woman in an ugly green dress, had prepared a wide, deferential smile which faded rapidly at the sight of Bess. 'I thought it might be Mr Lytton. I expect you're Miss Hardemon.' She turned away but called over her shoulder. 'She's in the drawing room.'

Bess was left to deal with her own bag which she placed beneath the hall mirror, aware that she was watched by a number of young faces pressed between the rails of the upper banister. She crossed quickly to the door indicated by Mrs Riddell.

Christina didn't look up at the sound of the latch and it occurred to Bess that she too might have been anticipating the arrival of her lover, so carefully was she arranged at the window. Miss Riddell had lost none of her opalescent beauty. Her head, poised on its long, creamy stem, was lit by sunlight diffused by the swagged muslins shrouding the glass. She was sketching a delicate posy of garden flowers. Her long fingers held the pencil softly as if it were pliant and the smooth oval of her face was tilted to allow the light to fall cleanly on her page.

Apart from Christina's luminous figure the room was quite dark. Bess longed to leap over to the window, sweep aside layers of fabric and let in clear daylight. 'Christina,' she called a little sharply.

The spell was broken as the sketch was flung aside. Christina sprang to her feet, smiled with unaffected pleasure and manoeuvred her way through the crowded room to take Bess's hands. 'Miss Hardemon. You've really come.'

Bess knew that her own looks had changed very little since Priors Heath. In fact she wore the same blue gown as then. The alteration in Christina, however, was startling. When Bess had last seen her she had been a pale unhappy child whose face could yet be wonderfully transformed by a kind word. The woman who had taken Bess's hands in her delicate white fingers was completely assured. She had a full, graceful figure and whatever meagre funds were available at the vicarage had obviously been lavished on her gown. Feeling insignificant and Quakerish in the shadow of this tall beauty, Bess reflected that Christina was probably her family's only saleable commodity. Whatever would she find to say to so elegant a young lady?

But Christina took charge. She drew up a chair for Bess and offered tea.

Bess was acutely uncomfortable in this feminine, pointless room but seized on the one thing she could genuinely admire. 'I see you still draw. You've lost none of your talent. Is that your painting of fruit by the door?'

'Oh yes, I paint all the time. Your box of water-colours was my salvation, Miss Hardemon. I've taught myself as best I can and begged help from friends though I never get the result I really want. Please don't look too closely. My mother won't let me draw outside so I have to limit myself to still-life or copies.'

'I don't understand. Why can't you draw from the life?'

Christina laughed, an unpleasantly manufactured sound. 'You must know better than anyone after what happened at Priors Heath. It's not genteel to be exposed to nature.'

'Well, as you know I'm an amateur. But I certainly admire that painting. I can feel the weight of the peaches, and their texture. You've taught yourself well.'

At that moment tea appeared, brought by three of the younger Riddell sisters and their mother, in whose presence Christina's shoulders drooped and she looked bored and sullen. Meanwhile the flurry of so many voluminous skirts in so cluttered a space was unnerving. Bess, whose own neat gown was tucked about her ankles, felt as if she had been deposited among the swirls and baubles on an elaborately iced wedding cake. She couldn't fail to notice, however, that with the exception of Christina's, the girls' dresses were of the cheapest possible material and, judging by the little unravelled lengths of frill and ribbon which trailed from cuffs and hems, had been made by hurried, untrained fingers.

Bess thought Mrs Riddell insufferable. Her head was filled exclusively with the arrangements for her daughter's wedding which was obviously a matter of great satisfaction to her. It transpired that Mr Charles Lytton, a widower, was the wealthy owner of a glove factory. For five minutes Mrs Riddell detailed every dish of the wedding breakfast and every item in Christina's trousseau, and its cost.

Finally, however, she focused her attention on Bess. 'Christina never stops talking about you, Miss Hardemon. We've grown quite sick of your name, haven't we, girls? No, don't blush, we know you're a paragon. But I believe you left Priors Heath very suddenly.'

'I was dismissed,' responded Bess sweetly and turned her cup to avoid the long, discoloured crack running from rim to base.

Mrs Riddell's sensibilities were offended by such plain speaking. She glanced pointedly at the younger girls. 'And since then, Miss Hardemon?'

'I've been teaching in Yorkshire. And I've just interviewed successfully for a position at Queen's College, London where I shall start work at Christmas. The school's curriculum is very advanced and I shall be able to attend lectures there in the evening which are held for women, so I was particularly glad to be appointed. You may have heard of Queen's College?'

Mrs Riddell had not. 'As you see, Miss Hardemon is a teacher, girls,' she whispered artfully, 'so you'll have to mind your Ps and Qs.' This provoked a few giggles and pitying glances at the plain sleeves and skirt of Bess's gown. 'Just don't ask them any of your difficult questions, Miss Hardemon,' added the mother. 'They don't know anything. I can't seem to cram any facts into their heads.'

'What do you read, Emily?' Bess asked the youngest girl gently.

'Not much.'

'Oh, we don't have time for reading here,' intervened Mrs Riddell. 'I keep the girls very well occupied.'

Dinner was served in a room as over-furnished as the parlour. The family crowded round a long, stained cloth and were waited on by a clumsy girl whose resentful manner suggested that she was considerably underpaid.

Reverend Riddell arrived at the table only after the soup had actually been ladled. Bess, who had encountered very few men who were not clergymen, soon had his measure. She knew him to be an academic for her father had shown her essays by him. Riddell was a clever theologian, acerbic in his criticism of the Oxford Movement, but in the flesh he was lazy and cynical and disregarded completely the many defects in the behaviour of his children. Instead he ploughed his way through a substantial dinner with an application which explained the straining buttons of his waistcoat.

Only when he had tossed aside the cheese knife did he pay any attention to his guest. 'I understand you're a rector's daughter.' He had the clipped tones of a well-bred man and Bess wondered whether he had married beneath him.

'I am, sir. My father knows your work.'

'Is that so? And where does your father stand on the Oxford issue?'

'My father is an evangelical. He has few sympathies with the High Church.'

'Now, now. We never talk religion at table,' put in Mrs Riddell.

'What's his name?' asked the Reverend of Bess.

'The same as mine. Hardemon.'

'Never heard of him. You're a teacher of girls, so I'm told.'

'I am, sir.'

'Uphill struggle, I should think.'

'I don't find it so, though I always face the same problems: unenlightened management of the curriculum and lack of funds.'

'I've never seen the point of educating girls. Our Chrissey came back from school full of mad ideas. She was much easier to please when she was ignorant.'

Bess was by now heartily sick of her brief stay in this inhospitable house. 'Sir, as I told you, I am a teacher and it's my duty to encourage girls to use their many talents. How can we make a useful contribution to the world or to God if we are ignorant and dissatisfied?'

'Well said, Miss Hardemon,' cried Reverend Riddell. 'But does your education buy those girls rich husbands? I think not.'

'I would have thought most men would be glad of an intelligent and rational wife.'

'Rational. Hah! Women are relative beings, Miss Hardemon, who should look pretty and keep quiet. That's the best we can expect from most of them.'

He was not used to being challenged, it seemed, for he soon

rose from the table and stumbled across the hall to the sanctuary of his study.

The following morning at breakfast Bess announced that she must go home that evening but Christina pleaded with her to stay one more day. 'Mr Lytton is sending his carriage at ten-thirty. I wanted you to meet him and see my new home.' She was so eager and youthful in her pink muslin that Bess could not resist.

In the carriage where the comfort of the seats and the smoothness of the ride bore witness to the wealth of its owner, Christina became a little more lively. 'I would give everything I have to be you, Miss Hardemon. You're setting out on yet another adventure. From January you'll live in London, an independent woman.'

'But you're about to be married,' cried Bess in astonishment. 'Surely you anticipate that with excitement?'

'Oh yes, I do. In many ways. Charles is taking me to Europe on honeymoon. I shall see all the greatest art galleries. And he is already looking about for a drawing master for me. Perhaps when I'm married I might even be able to study a little anatomy, and then I could try portraits. I know I should be grateful and excited but part of me still feels dull and hopeless. You see, even married to Charles I shan't be free.'

'Free from what?'

'No. Free to direct my own life. Surely you understand?'

'But you have chosen freely to marry, I presume.'

'Because I had no other choice. Don't you see?'

Bess, having reached the limit of her understanding, couldn't reply but gave silent thanks that she had always been clear about her own destiny. Her vocation hadn't wavered since girlhood, even when under assault by the curate John Cage's shy adoration. The essential thing is to be whole-hearted, she thought sternly. Christina really is an irritating companion, so gifted but so dissatisfied. She proceeded to question Christina briskly about Mr Lytton and discovered that he had two children by his first wife, a boy of twelve who was away at school and a daughter of eight.

Charles Lytton was waiting for the carriage and greeted Bess with courtesy. He was unexpectedly old, probably over forty, but good-looking in a conventional, restrained way.

Clasping Bess's hand in both his he looked warmly into her eyes. 'Christina talks of you as having had a great influence upon her. You encouraged her to paint, I understand, and comforted her in that dreadful school. I hope to know you better.' He led her inside the house, casting loving glances back at Christina. Well, good heavens, thought Bess, he seems a fine man. Surely Christina is extremely fortunate and ought to count her blessings.

Abbey House was very old, parts of it dating back to the fifteenth century, and Bess was impressed by its tranquillity. Servants moved quietly over thick carpets and polished floors, doors were closed with a delicate click of the latch and there were no draughts. Though the rooms were low ceilinged and the windows small and mullioned, there was an air of space created by a careful placing of substantial but unostentatious furnishings.

The daughter, Rebecca, was a jumpy child with pale, plain features and mousy hair but she had astonishingly eloquent brown eyes. She came running forward to be embraced by Christina, whose kiss, it seemed to Bess, was given more with an eye to pleasing her future husband than with real affection.

'We have something to show you, Miss Riddell,' whispered Rebecca, her extraordinary eyes aglow with excitement.

She led the way up a shallow oak staircase above which hung a portrait of a lady. 'That's the first Mrs Lytton,' murmured Christina. Bess paused to study the face of a calm, smiling woman whose limp hair and thin features were very like those of Rebecca.

The surprise was a sitting room for Christina, so newly

decorated that there was still a strong smell of fresh paint. 'I helped choose the materials and arrange the flowers. And look, we've put your paintings there to make you feel at home. What do you think?' cried Rebecca, gazing with pride at her handiwork, a child's dream of frothy lace and nosegays. Opposite the window hung a series of water-colours, three of flower arrangements, one of a wild sky above a field.

'Charles doesn't mind what I paint,' Christina said smiling up at him, 'so I've had a go at colour wash. It was lovely to make the colours of sky. At the end of the garden here is a stile where I sat to paint this.' She ran her beautiful index finger along the line between field and sky in her painting. They all watched her for a moment; the smooth coil of her glossy hair, her slender, pearly neck. Then she took Rebecca by the hand. 'I am a very lucky woman.'

She gestured Bess towards the window from which there was a fine view of a large garden with a sweeping lawn. 'Over there among the trees is the old abbey gatehouse. The wall is just visible. Can you see? I hope there are no ghosts.' Turning to Charles she gave him another tender, teasing smile.

'No ghosts here, my love.'

But as they were on their way downstairs Christina whispered to Bess: 'I had hoped I might decorate that sitting room myself. I wanted to have one room truly to call my own.'

Bess's heart ached as she watched Rebecca's prancing little form. 'The child has high hopes of you, it seems.'

'Oh yes, more than I deserve, I'm sure.' She paused. They stood on the half-landing near the portrait of the former Mrs Lytton. 'Did you notice that he's hidden all my pictures away? I gave them to him and he's put them in my room.'

'Surely it was to make you feel at home.'

Christina sighed and closed her eyes for a moment, as if overwhelmed by exhaustion. 'Miss Hardemon, do you think I might find peace here? Surely I shall.'

Bess looked up fearfully into the girl's pleading eyes. All this longing for peace and freedom seemed to her a very poor foundation for marriage.

Charles Lytton was an easy and intelligent conversationalist. Although a little inclined to listen with over-pointed courtesy to the comments made by the females at his table, he at least appeared to take an interest in Bess's work. He explained with enthusiasm the enlightened way in which he ran his factory and how his profits had not been affected by his reforms.

'I'm interested in your ideas on education, Miss Hardemon, because my workers are so ignorant. You see, they can't think. They just await instruction. I try to make life easy for them, but they don't know what to do with their time or money. I don't want them to be so dull. I'd prefer them to have initiative and ideas.'

'Then you're ahead of your time, Mr Lytton, I wish others thought as you do.'

He looked pleased. 'I am indeed ahead of my time. I've thought of providing reading lessons for some of my hands. What do you think?'

Bess was aware of Christina toying with her food. Were I in her shoes, she thought, I'd leap at this opportunity to work alongside my husband. 'Perhaps you could help, Christina, by devising a course of study.'

Christina was startled from a daydream. 'Oh, in the factory. Perhaps. But of course I shall already be teaching Rebecca.'

After lunch they walked in the garden and Charles explained the layout of the former abbey. The gatehouse, the only part still almost intact, was built of dark, golden stone and above its arch was an oriel window. Henry VIII had first demolished the abbey and then presented the land to one of his favoured lords, typically generous with spoils that were not his to distribute.

'You'd think such a violent history would have marked the place,' commented Christina, 'yet it's so peaceful. I always love it out here.'

She moved away with Charles while Bess and Rebecca explored the boundaries of the garden. Their skirts brushed against bracken and brambles in the wilderness which had been allowed to grow against the wall. 'I like to play here,' said Rebecca. 'I like to imagine I'm a monk living in a cold cell. Sometimes at meals I don't speak to see if I could keep a vow of silence.'

Bess decided that these were the games of a lonely child. 'Do you go to school, Rebecca?'

'No, I have a governess and once my father is married he says Miss Riddell will help teach me.'

They turned back but Rebecca stayed behind a moment to pick up a white feather caught on a strip of bark. Rich September sunlight fell among the trees and on to the honeyed stone of the gatehouse. Bess was drawn to its dark archway. For a moment she wondered what it might be like to live here as mistress of the house. Then there would always be time to walk slowly among trees.

At the entrance of the arch she halted. Christina and Charles Lytton were standing there in deep shadow, her pink dress pale beside his taller, darker form. They were kissing and Christina's head was pressed back by the weight of Charles's lips on hers. His arms were folded tightly across her back and his jaw moved as the kiss was prolonged.

There was such a startling contrast between this passionate embrace and the courtesy Charles had shown Bess all afternoon that she caught her breath. She had witnessed village couples kissing in the lanes, the polite embrace of her parents and the teasing caresses of Gerald and Laetitia. But the sight of Charles's hands on Christina's back and his complete absorption in the kiss were a severe blow to Bess's composure. An hour before she had shared a meal with these two, as their equal. Now she was excluded.

She pressed her hand to her stomach to soothe a grinding, low pain aroused by unexpected envy and sexual longing. But though outraged both by such a public display and by her own response to it, she couldn't move away. She saw how Lytton's knee was pressed into Christina's skirts and how his hand moved under her arm and on to her breast, the palm softly circling the pink muslin. His closed, vulnerable eyelids flickered and his forehead was creased and slightly moist as his lips opened a little more, twisting and working hungrily on Christina's soft mouth.

The kiss ended at last and Charles folded Christina closer still so that her head rested on his shoulder and he stroked her small waist.

Christina opened her eyes and looked straight at Bess. Her expression was astonishing, cool and alert as if she had taken no part in the kiss at all. She seemed more interested in Bess and gradually a look of curiosity and sympathy lightened her gaze.

Bess, who knew what her own eyes must have betrayed, darted away to call Rebecca. As she hurried through the trees she felt only shame. The chill voice of her conscience told her she should never have lingered to watch.

When they all re-entered the house Bess realized that she had now conceived a distaste for these quiet, luxurious rooms. Everything was too carefully placed, too far removed from the essence of things. Charles Lytton was a man who arranged his business, his house, and now even the courtship of a second wife with complete assurance. But under the surface, she sensed, ran a deep vein of passions he would never understand or control.

What of Rebecca's grief for her dead mother, of Christina's love of her art, of his own physical desire for her? These were things that could never be regulated by the chime of an exquisite clock or the gentle ringing of the dinner gong.

As she and Christina drove home through a dusty twilight Bess thought ahead with relief to her purposeful drive north the next day and the relentless demands that would surely be made on her during another term's teaching. Intimate relations with others clouded and complicated matters. Certainly Bess had been foolish, possibly sinful to yearn for such passion even for a moment. Best to walk cleanly in the cold light of solitude, she thought.

7

July 1995

Sarah Parr approached Priors Heath on foot, passing through the iron gates, across the oil-stained forecourt and up the three worn stone steps to the shallow porch where she rested her hand on the tarnished door-knob. It was a sacred moment, weighted by months of anticipation and by a desire to find more than might reasonably be expected.

The door swung inwards and her gaze flicked across the busy scene: dusty sunlight falling from high windows, long floral dresses and sherry glowing in small glasses.

'Sarah, my God, it's Sarah Beckett, isn't it? I scarcely recognized you. Here, have a label. Use your maiden name. Fiona, it's Sarah Beckett.'

Sarah moved from one group to the next, embracing and exclaiming. Curious eyes fell on her face, tanned shoulders brushed hers, she caught brilliant smiles and snatches of other people's conversations.

'You know Nicola's here. She studied music at Cardiff...'

'No, I ended up doing PR, but now I run my own consultancy...'

'Three kids, all under five? How do you stand it?'

'Sarah, you're so brown. Where've you been?'

It took nearly half an hour to ease across the hall to the staircase. Bess Hardemon still presided from her portrait in the middle of the back wall, her uncompromising gaze falling on the excited clusters of women as if she sat in judgement on their bright clothes and restless eyes. 'Who's this? Are you wearing a badge? Sarah Beckett. I can't say I recall . . .'

Sarah, recognizing that voice at once, was sixteen again, heart in boots, caught out in some trifling inaccuracy. 'Miss Stone. I remember you well. You taught me history at "A" level.'

Madeleine Stone ought surely now to be in her dotage but in fact seemed little changed except that her plump shoulders were stooped and her clothes even more extraordinary. For today's celebration she wore a striped canvas dress tied at the waist with a knotted rope dangling above grimy, sandalled feet. As if to focus Sarah more intently through a narrowed slit in her memory, she half-closed her eyes. 'I have it. Weren't you great friends with Imogen Taylor?'

'In a way. Yes, I suppose. We're not in touch any more.'

'Pity. Now, there's an extraordinary thing. Of all people. You know I'm a deputy here now. I have to work with her.' Miss Stone's mouth cracked open to reveal strong yellow teeth. She laughed, but bitterly. Her age must have been grossly overestimated at school, Sarah thought guiltily, if she still taught at Priors Heath.

'Will Imogen be here today, do you know?' With a sickening sense of anticlimax Sarah had realized at once that Imogen was not present. Yet she had not given up hope and her eyes betrayed her by darting across the room to each new arrival. Was that blonde head Imogen's? Was that her red dress?

'No. She won't come. Busman's holiday for her, as it is for me, though I always like to see how girls have turned out.'

'Of course.' For Sarah, who had persuaded herself that Imogen would be bound to attend, the gloss of the occasion blurred and dimmed. Tightly rolled in her hand was a copy of the school's latest prospectus and there inside the front cover was a photograph of Imogen labelled 'Head-teacher, Priors Heath, 1994 – present day'. Even in this official pose Imogen contrived to look unprepared. One strand of fine, straight hair fell over her angular forehead. She had attempted a benign smile but the peculiar glint of her long eyes gave instead a glimmer of malevolence. 'She's done well, hasn't she?' Sarah added to Miss Stone.

'She has planned her career very skilfully, yes.'

'Oh, surely she must also be an excellent teacher.'

'Perhaps. It's managers they go for these days.' Miss Stone spoke as if from a great distance. Really, it's beyond me how anyone could have appointed Imogen Taylor, was her obvious opinion. 'And you,' she demanded, 'what do you do?'

'Oh, you know, a bit of teaching, marriage, kids, the usual.'

'Not usual. I have neither marriage nor children. How do you mean "a bit of teaching"?'

'My husband's a civil engineer. We've lived abroad for years. It's not always been possible for me to do paid work so I've done some voluntary teaching.'

'Abroad?'

'Yes, Hong Kong, mostly.' And for a second she stood again at the window of her apartment there, looking out one last time to the beach where windsurfers floated by on the blue sea.

'Lucky girl.'

'Lucky. Yes. It's a beautiful place. We were there six years and I grew to love it. But now my husband has a new contract in Malaysia which is something of an unknown to us.'

Claire White, née Tomkins, organizer and perpetrator of this, the twenty-one-year reunion of the leavers of '74, was ringing a handbell to indicate that lunch was served. 'We're in the upper dining room. Straight across the quad to the New Building in case anyone doesn't remember.'

The women began to edge towards the narrow passage at the back of the entrance hall. Miss Stone was greeted by Laura Harding and Sarah sank back against the panelling, her mouth fixed in a bland smile. For a moment Laura's ruthless gaze met hers and they disliked each other with as much vehemence as in their youth.

Other women flowed by. 'Sarah Beckett. How brilliant. You look exactly the same as ever. Except for the hair. You really suit a bob but how could you bear to have it cut?'

'Sarah. You dreadful woman, how do you stay so thin? Do you keep in touch with Imogen Taylor? Nobody seems to have heard from her.'

Sarah smiled into eager faces as memories came thronging across the polished floor and for a moment she breathed tremulously beneath their soft fingers.

Sunlight pierced the stained glass on the half-landing above. The three bright-eyed maidens in their vibrant gowns ran forward as they had always done, hair floating, throats pure, clasping in their white hands the scroll bearing the school motto: FIAT LUX. How has this happened? Sarah wondered. Thirty-nine years old, twenty years of my future already gone. The more recent past, the heat and light of a far country, a million strange faces, the beige apartment she had called home all became a picture-postcard memory, six years as empty as a pillar-box slot. By contrast the Priors Heath years were rock solid.

Tap, tap, tap came the high heels of Claire Tomkins who had left a folder on a bench nearby. 'I don't think we ever quite identified with that trio when we were here,' she remarked with a nod at the maids in the window. 'I never appreciated its quality before. Pre-Raphaelite, designed by Christina Lytton. Remember the spiel on Founder's Day?'

Sarah smiled and found herself perilously close to tears. 'I hope you feel pleased with today, Claire. What an achievement, getting us lot together.'

'Persistence and lists. My watchwords. Let's go and eat.'

After lunch the women had a shock. Three years after they left, Priors Heath had amalgamated with the adjacent Ryder Street Secondary Modern and thereby gained comprehensive status, doubled in size and admitted boys. Now the leavers of 1974 found themselves confronted by blocks of glass and concrete classrooms where they had run barefoot on grass tennis courts. They walked mutinously along straight paths outside the bleak structure they had always known as Ryder Street Secondary Mod., but which now housed the Humanities and Languages departments of Priors Heath. Former hockey pitches had been adapted for football and some of the grounds had been subsumed by a swimming pool and a technology block. The women, most of whom had not been back for twenty years, regarded these changes with astonishment.

For Sarah the impact of the transformation acquired tragic proportions. What she remembered most about her school was the quality it had of being eternal. Even in the so-called 'New Building', built in the late 1920s to accommodate the rapid expansion of Priors Heath School for Girls, there had been a sense of immutability. The girls' feet had trodden sturdy, tiled floors, their hands gripped smooth oak banisters. The Wyatt Hall had a parquet floor and a stage of polished beech boards. There had been plenty of space. Now it seemed as though too many feet had pounded these same interiors and some of the chill anonymity of the Ryder Street Block had blown through. The dusty cubbyholes which Sarah and her friends had annexed for their intimate lunch-time chats were crammed with metal lockers.

Sarah had one further pilgrimage to make, to the rose garden. The image of herself there had haunted her down the years. Perhaps by facing it, the horror and guilt of what she had done in that place would fade away. It might be like lifting the bandages on a terrible wound to find that the cut had not been too deep and jagged after all.

The garden, at least, was little changed. Traffic surged on the other side of the high wall but here, if one disregarded the new green litter bins, all was much as before. The same paths criss-crossed between the rose-beds, the same broken sundial stood at the centre. There was still an illusion of not being in a school bound by a hundred constraints, but at liberty in a green space where the mind and body could roam freely.

Sarah found a secluded bench and closed her eyes. People had begun to go home or were still careering up and down corridors exchanging addresses and 'do you remembers?' so the garden was empty. She was conscious of birdsong, women's voices and the scent of dry soil. Two worlds swirled about her consciousness; the troubled present and the past, where were sown the seeds of the future. Deliberately she had brought herself back to the setting where some of the most vivid moments of her life had been enacted. Here she was the same performer on a familiar stage. She remembered so well standing by the sundial while Miss Stone made her surprising pro-nouncement regarding her ability.

And then there was the other moment. Over there, where a yellow climbing rose swayed away from its trellis, had huddled seventeen-year-old Sarah, long hair draped about her shoulders like a shroud and above her, Imogen. The look in Imogen's eye was as piercingly vivid now as then.

Nevertheless, Sarah found that there was a kind of peace to be found by confronting the memory and knowing how far she had come from the girl capable of such a thing.

Her nail scraping gently at the rough stone bench where lichen grew, she lapsed into a kind of half-slumber. A bee banged against her arm and hummed away. Traffic purred, a thrush sang loud and pure and a high female voice called through an open window.

Six weeks later Sarah began packing for Malaysia where David was soon to begin a two-year engineering contract to build a couple of road bridges. The children were absent on a long weekend in Frinton with Sarah's parents. David had meetings in town. The house enclosed Sarah in its greedy arms as she worked on and on, sorting, tidying and folding.

Cedarview had been built wide and narrow to draw maximum advantage from a south-facing garden. Although

Sarah despised the aspirations of its architect to include three bathrooms, three receptions and a pretentious kitchen, she and David had bought the house eagerly enough. The garden with its copse and little bubbling stream had seduced Sarah. Furthermore, Hadeleigh Wood, still termed a village though squarely in the Hertfordshire commuter belt, seemed far removed from the cramped sameness of her suburban childhood. Besides, the house was an investment, visited by the family only once every few years, a gracious accumulator of wealth that could be discarded at whim. It had been rapidly furnished and carpeted eight years previously, without love.

Sarah's movements slowed. Then she found that she had been sitting for some time on the bed with a silk scarf twined in her fingers. The bedroom was full of hot, damp air. Outside an August storm had brewed and the sky lay heavy on the trees in the copse.

On the bed nearby lay an old photograph, unearthed from last summer's white shoulder bag. It was a snapshot of the children when toddlers, posing beside some pool in Korea. Sarah stared at their young figures: Jamie stolid and blond, Lorna dark and merry. She scarcely recognized in them her teenage son and daughter. After a while she picked the photo up and took it downstairs.

There was scarcely a breath of air in the garden. On the little bridge Sarah kicked off her sandals and stepped down to paddle among reeds and pebbles. The water was cool on her skin. She sat on the bank, scuffling her toes in the cold water as the storm broke and rain fell in huge drops.

She had an acute, watchful sense of herself as a still figure in a drenched garden. Occasionally she felt a flicker of interest in what might happen when David came home.

An hour later she heard his car but didn't move. The front door closed and faintly came the sound of his voice calling her name. Then after a few moments there was a tap on the kitchen window. 'Sarah! Sarah!'

One part of her yearned towards him. She knew how gladly he would respond to her smile and embrace. It might be a relief after all to pick up her old role and wear it like a well-worn, heavy pullover. But lassitude was stronger, the sense of being drawn onward over the edge. She sat quite still, shivering a little, waiting. Soon his footsteps spurted on the wet grass, his warm hand descended on her shoulder and his kiss touched her streaming hair.

'Sarah!' He ran his finger along her spine where the fabric of her blouse clung. 'My darling. You're so cold. What on earth are you up to?'

She wouldn't speak.

'Did you get sick of packing? Let me give you a hand if you're swamped.'

Still she didn't reply. He held out his hand. 'Come on. I'll make you tea. You're a nutcase, sitting out here in the rain. Or did you want to make the most of your last English downpour?'

Her voice was so faint that he had to stoop to hear her response. 'I'm not going.'

'You're not going where?'

'I'm not going to Malaysia with you.'

'I'm sorry, Sarah, I don't follow.'

'I don't want to live abroad any more. I've decided.'

She allowed herself a glance at him and thought he looked a little ridiculous in his business shirt and trousers, rain dripping from the spokes of a large umbrella, his face contorted with puzzlement. She was sorry to have been the cause of the distress in those alert brown eyes.

He was normally a patient man but they were expected for dinner with friends at eight. The soothing tones he might have employed to coax a reluctant cat into its basket concealed an edge of irritation. 'You know you always dread it when we go away. You'll be fine when we get there.'

'No, I won't. I don't want to leave the children.'

'They've left us, practically. They didn't even want to come

125

on holiday with us this year. Good God, they wouldn't know what to do with us if we were always about.'

'I never wanted them to go away to school.'

'It really is a bit late to say that now. They've been happy enough. And we'd be very foolish to unsettle them when they're sitting exams.' He paused, presumably to stifle the note of exasperation in his voice. 'Look, I'll finish the packing. You have a bath and I'll bring you a glass of wine. How about that? You've probably got very low on your own in the house with everything to do. It was a nuisance I had the meeting this afternoon, though incidentally it went rather well.'

She didn't move. He stood over her but short of dragging her up, what could he do? 'Anyway, I'll pack. You come on in when you're ready.'

Her shoulders sank in despair as he walked away. Had he sufficient tenderness for her he might have sat beside her and buried his warm face in her neck. He could surely have conquered her anguished self-doubt by the strength of his will. In imagination she followed his bewildered re-entrance to the house. When he came to the bedroom he would complete the packing with his usual methodical movements, giving the task his full concentration so that his thoughts need not dwell on her.

After half an hour he returned with a drink and a blanket, although the sun had re-emerged and now shone warmly on Sarah's back. Her bluish toes still dabbled in the water.

This time she turned to him and accepted the glass, as if they had actually agreed to meet together companionably by the stream. Her voice was clear and strong. 'I feel so — disappointed. I must act now. Before it's too late. I have done nothing, nothing with my life.'

Again, this was familiar territory. 'Sarah, we have two great children. I hope a successful marriage. Think of all the wonderful stuff you've done for the ex-pats. What about those Korean children you once taught?'

'It was just passing the time. Making meaning. I wasn't shaping my own life.'

'I'm afraid that's one of the penalties of being married to a civil engineer.'

Her voice was cutting. 'I don't want to be defined by you. I'm as talented as you. You have recognition. I have none.'

'Sarah, I think you're exaggerating. There are thousands of women who would kill to be in your shoes with your life-style.'

At last she did begin to cry. 'I can't bear the waste. I had such high hopes. I wanted to be someone.'

'We all want to be someone. But when all's said and done we can only do our bit, as well as we can.'

'But I've been doing your bit.' She turned her sad gaze upon him and pitied him for the fear in his eyes.

'I'm sorry. I thought you were happy. You've never really complained before. I always thought, when you got like this, it was a passing thing, your nature, as you used to say. I've feared for you, you know, tried to keep you safe. I thought everything was fine.'

'I've never had the sense to work it out. I never looked beyond the obvious reasons for being unhappy sometimes, like homesickness, or separation from the children. I was never miserable like this when I was a small child, lethargic and dull. I've cut myself off from my sense of well-being. Oh, I know I'm difficult, I know that, and I know this is partly my own fault. I never worked it all out, you see, instead I rushed headlong for you. You think I'm fragile because I cut my wrists.' They had not alluded to that episode for years and David looked away. 'I suppose I have quietly agreed to being cosseted. Poor Sarah, a little emotionally unstable. But I'm not, David. And if I am, you've never given me the chance to toughen up. You have been so careful, *too* careful, and I let you. It suited us both. But what I can't understand now, what I really can't understand, is how a man who married someone because she was bright and full of ambition and all the things you used to tell me you so admired, how he could bear to see all that die away, until she was just a kind of consort and housekeeper.'

'That's not how I see you. Not at all.' But he denied it a little too sharply.

'So what do you love about me now? If you love me.'

'Of course I love you. My God, how can you ask? I love you because I know you so well. Because you're so lovely with people.' He sounded angry. 'Look, there's no time to talk this evening, and anyway, I think we're both committed to this particular posting, don't you? You should have come out with all this months ago. Let's discuss it next week, when we're settled. Maybe I can go for a job in the UK in a year or so.'

She was scarcely listening. 'You haven't asked me whether I love you.'

He had risen to his feet but bent to kiss her ear. 'Do you?'

'How could I, any more? How could I when I see that you are content for me to be reduced to so little?'

The news that she would not be accompanying their father to Malaysia was broken to the children by Sarah whilst she and Lorna were sorting clothes in Lorna's bedroom. Jamie was prised away from his computer to listen. Sarah wanted her casual tone to imply that this was hardly a matter of great moment to the children, especially as they were both leaving Cedarview anyway to go back to school.

Jamie merely gave a slight shrug at the news, his face between its dead-straight curtains of hair completely expressionless. 'Is that it? Can I go back to work now?' But Lorna exploded with rage.

'So. You're getting a divorce. Thanks for letting us know.'

'No, Lorna. That's not the case at all. I want to try and develop a career of my own at last. And I couldn't face a long spell in Malaysia, more time away from you.' At this point of high emotion, Jamie slunk away. Sarah watched him helplessly. But had she really hoped that on hearing the news that she'd be staying in the country he would hug her for the first time in five years, or at least smile? What must I do to win you back, Jamie? she thought.

Lorna shouted: 'I don't need you. Don't worry about me. I'm fine.'

'Yes, I know you're fine.'

Sarah was dwarfed by her daughter who was large-chested and heavy-jawed. Lorna's nature had always seemed wide open, painted as if by the illustrator of a crude children's story book in bright, unsubtle colours. She could be cruel, impulsive or affectionate in rapid succession. Her certainties were daunting. Sarah, remembering herself at fourteen, had an image of cringing insecurity, a crippling need to please. 'Well then?'

'I'm not worried about you in the least. I just want to see more of you.'

'But why? You've never bothered before. Poor Dad, all alone in a new country. Jamie and I have each got a school-load of friends. We're not isolated.'

'I'm glad to hear it.'

'What does Dad say about it?'

'He's sorry I shan't be with him but he understands it's about time I did something for myself, if I want to.'

'What about Granny and Grandad? I suppose you told them about this before me.'

'They're taking it in their stride. After all, it's not such a big deal. Dad will be home for Christmas so we'll only be apart for four months. There's no need for anyone to get upset.' Her mother had responded to Sarah's news absolutely as her daughter had anticipated. Mrs Beckett was constantly guarded against disappointment. She avoided severe shocks and unpleasant surprises by always expecting the worst and if things went well never allowing herself to become too excited or committed. And she had made it a rule not to pry beneath the surface of her daughter's emotional life. 'I hope David will manage all right for meals,' had been her only remark.

Lorna's large bedroom was decked with sunflower prints, Oasis posters and a collection of assorted ornaments. Some of these were usually allowed to remain at Cedarview, others Lorna took to school with her. Now she began to bang open cupboard doors at random and hurl back all the little souvenirs of home she had piled into her box. 'Well, I shan't need these after all. Who wants to be reminded of this place? What's the point when you're going to be here all the time?'

Sarah understood her daughter's dismay. When Lorna thought of Cedarview it would not be of an empty house waiting for the family to return, or in the hands of strangers who let it for the winter, but of the place where her mother lived in solitary splendour.

Suddenly Sarah felt overwhelmed by an exhausted recognition of what she had let herself in for. Living abroad all these years she had escaped the clutter of the past and the stifling trivia of family life. A stab of longing for the clarity of walking on to a plane assaulted her. She could have flown cleanly across the sky to a new world, there to step brightly along in her bubble of foreignness.

Lorna yanked open a drawer and heaped underwear from it into a case.

'Don't you ever wish we all lived permanently together?' Sarah asked, her voice made quavery by insecurity. 'Haven't you ever wanted to go to day school?'

'God no. Boring or what? And look at where I've travelled because of Dad's work. You always used to tell me how lucky I was considering you hadn't even left the country by the time you were eighteen.'

'I don't think you're being honest. You've often said how cut off you've felt at school.'

'You mean you don't like what I'm saying now. Why would I lie to you? Anyway, you seem to have made up your mind so that's that.' She flicked down the lid of the suitcase and made for the door.

'Lorna, whatever happens, however resentful you feel, don't shut me out.'

'Why? What right have you to have access to my mind?'

'I mean I want to know what you think of me, even if you're critical. I don't want to be protected.'

'All right, I'll tell you again. What I think is that you should be on the plane with Dad tomorrow. I think you're excessively selfish.'

'But surely at least you understand my longing to have a career. How would you feel if when you finish school someone says: Well there's no point in all the work you've done because you're never going to need any qualifications?' It was as if she and Lorna had exchanged roles and that she, Sarah, was the wheedling child, unattractively wielding a well-worn armoury of ploys to win parental approval.

'I'd love it. Imagine, someone to look after my every need. Never having to work. Bliss.'

'You love sport. Sport is what you do well. I want something like that, of my own.'

'You couldn't run to save your life. What could you do?'

'Teach. I thought I might go back to that. I am qualified.'

'Teach. God. You'd give up a year in the East to teach! Who'd have you, anyway?'

'I'm not sure. I suppose someone might be desperate enough.'

Lorna's hostile, wide-open hazel eyes met her mother's. Sarah reached out and slid her fingers through Lorna's hair. 'I used to have hair as long as this when I was your age. Mum always complained about it. We didn't wash our hair as often then so mine wasn't silky like this but lank and greasy, I expect.'

'Yuk.' But for a moment their understanding collided in a shared image of Mrs Beckett with her unsuccessful perm and worried mouth. Then Lorna began hurling sports equipment into a bag once more as if to say: You see, my life is full of activity and purpose. Don't spoil it by tiptoeing about on the periphery, shattering my peace of mind.

Sarah longed to reassure her daughter that there was no question of a permanent separation between herself and David but her tongue would not make such a promise.

The next day a car came for David. While Lorna clung to him and sobbed, Jamie hovered in the hall and Sarah tried to look casually cheerful. David was too hurt to do more than kiss her cheek for the sake of the watching children. His body was rigid. But then he gripped the side of her neck and spoke into her hair. 'Sarah, if you need me, let me know. Please. Please.'

She turned her head to the familiar warmth of his face. 'I'll be all right. And you. I hope you will.'

She watched his head as the car drove off and felt nothing but pity.

That afternoon she gave the children a vague excuse and drove away from the house. There was no escaping her next move, though she despised herself for all she had omitted to tell David about her intentions.

The town of Faringford, once so familiar, appeared to be faded and dusted over on this late August afternoon. The shops were shabbier and unfamiliar: charity shops, antiques and delicatessens predominated, rather than utilitarian little ironmongers or butchers. There was a new pelican crossing opposite the main entrance to Priors Heath. She pulled into the forecourt where three other cars were parked. At least the school would not be entirely deserted.

Sarah's visit to the school was a gamble based on the assumption that the head-teacher of a large comprehensive might need to work in her office before term started. In the quad she saw that windows were open in a room on the second floor of the New Building. She pushed boldly against the door to the Old House and found it miraculously unlocked, though the air in the passageway within was stale and the building was frighteningly quiet.

Upstairs in the administration corridor a fly ticked against a light fitting. The door of the office was wide open and a woman typing at a computer raised cold eyes to Sarah. 'Yes?'

'I wondered — is Imogen Taylor here?'

'She is. Yes.'

'Do you think I might speak with her?'

'Can you tell me what it's about? I try to let her work undisturbed.'

'Actually I'm an ex school-friend. I mean I was at school with Imogen.'

'Oh.' There was a gleam of a smile. 'I should think that would be all right. That's her door opposite.'

The head-teacher's door, painted white as of old, was very slightly ajar so it was possible that Sarah's conversation had been overheard. Indeed when she knocked softly and pushed back the door it seemed as if Imogen had been listening, for her head was raised in expectation. She wore a black T-shirt and her straight, shoulder-length hair was pushed behind her ears. Her face was as raw and impatient as ever.

'Sarah Parr. I mean Beckett. I'm Sarah Beckett.' Sarah, when imagining this moment, had thought that Imogen might leap forward and embrace her in her long arms. Or perhaps, remembering their last encounter years ago at Sarah's engagement party, Imogen might shun her, anything but joyful about this visitation from the past. What Sarah had never anticipated was that Imogen would rise coolly, reach across the desk and shake her hand.

'Sarah. I'm really pleased that you called in.' She regarded Sarah with slightly raised eyebrows, her gaze politely enquiring.

'I missed you at the reunion,' murmured Sarah. 'I missed you.' Imogen's absence had been one of the most disturbing

133

aspects of a day that had torn the flimsy veneer of satisfaction from her life.

'You wouldn't catch me going to that,' Imogen retorted.

Sarah seized on this opening with relief. 'We were all terribly impressed that you'd become a head-teacher. The last time I saw you I don't think you had even begun higher education.'

Imogen's face was a mask showing not a glimmer either of pleasure or dismay. She offered nothing, neither a gesture of hospitality nor a conciliatory smile.

It now occurred to Sarah that of all the women she had met at the reunion, Imogen was most altered. Physically, of course, there was much of the old Imogen, though time had made her wrists and collarbone even more knobbly and her skin was quite lined. Her voice had deepened and her accent become clipped, less middle-class Hampstead. But the expression in her eyes and her total self-containment suggested someone entirely poised, at ease within her role, quite unlike the prickly, impulsive creature of their school-days. It seemed not at all extraordinary now that Imogen should be a head-teacher for she was every inch a woman of authority.

What had happened to the Imogen whose saggy schoolbag had been randomly stuffed with plimsolls, sandwiches and books? The mere appearance of Imogen in the doorway of a classroom, skirt hitched on hip, had meant disruption. Imogen had always been more interesting than the lessons she attended.

'Claire sent me a copy of the news-sheet,' Imogen said. 'I saw that you had two children.'

'Yes, I do. Sixteen and fourteen. Jamie and Lorna. And you?'

'I never married. No kids. Well, twelve hundred here.'

They both laughed uncomfortably at this winsome remark, so woefully out of character.

'And how's David?' Imogen asked.

'He's well, thank you. He's recently been made a director. At the moment he's in Malaysia. I'm not joining him out there until later.'

If Imogen remembered that she had once been highly critical of David she gave no sign, merely smiled faintly and nodded.

'But tell me about you, Imogen. How on earth did you get to be Head-teacher? I can't help being surprised.'

At last Imogen softened into real laughter. 'Your amazement is most insulting. I did it by the conventional route. Degree in maths. Teaching up through the ranks. A bit of research. A Masters in Education. Deputy. Head. Simple.'

'But Imogen, why Priors Heath? You used to hate it here!'

'Did I? I don't think so.' This knack Imogen had of closing down a conversation by a crinkling of the brow and a twist of the head was presumably well practised. It must deter all but the most officious parents from outstaying their welcome.

'And how is your family?' Sarah asked in desperation. Oh, we are playing this game so well, she thought. Twenty years' maturity have given us the ability to dissimulate perfectly.

'Dad's still alive. Much as ever. Often depressed. I live with him.'

'Ah.'

'My mother is long dead. Cancer.'

Mrs Taylor in her smart red suit and knife-sharp stilettos shot through Sarah's memory. 'I'm so sorry.'

'And my brother Lawrence is in the States. Second marriage. Two kids, like you. Quite a conventional career in the end with a recording company. Mixing sound or something.'

Sarah had prepared herself for news of Lawrence but still flinched at mention of his name. He was always among the shadows of her mind, appearing occasionally in a dream or a flicker of recollection to startle a response from her body and heart. Now his sister had dragged the three-dimensional, living Lawrence into sharp relief. Two marriages. That didn't suggest contentment.

'My own parents moved down to the sea,' she said smoothly. 'They were most impressed when they heard about you. My dad said he always knew that girl would go far. Meaning you.'

Imogen was smiling again and Sarah, for the first time, was

reminded of how it felt to be loved by Imogen and to see the rare tenderness in her eyes. 'Your father was the kindest man I ever knew,' Imogen said.

'Apart from just wanting to catch up with you again,' Sarah went on hurriedly, 'I had something else to ask. Actually I wanted your advice.'

Imogen gave a tiny sigh as if suddenly tired by this conversation. Was I such a burden in the past, Sarah thought in panic, that I make her so weary? Was that all I was to her?

'It's about teaching. I haven't taught for fifteen years. I was wondering if I might return to the profession.'

Imogen shrugged, that familiar crushing gesture.

'It's your professional opinion I want. How easy would it be to get back into teaching after a long gap? When I'd qualified I taught for two years then nothing really except a bit of voluntary work abroad, teaching English.'

Imogen narrowed her eyes. 'Are you asking whether there are any vacancies at Priors Heath? I thought you said you were going out to Malaysia.' Her ability to assimilate information must be one of her most formidable weapons as a head-teacher. Sarah was floored by the need to explain half-formulated plans.

'Oh I may, yes. But not yet. Not until I've re-established some kind of career for myself.'

'And what does David think of that?' Was there an edge of the old contempt for Sarah's marriage?

'He always supports me.' She thought of the hard grip of David's hand on her neck before leaving, the forlornness of the children at Cedarview. Surely Imogen couldn't see the web of dissatisfaction and failure that enmeshed Sarah?

'Your subject is history, yes? There are loads of good history teachers about. You will have a problem because you obviously lack experience. And you'll be more expensive to employ than a newly qualified teacher.'

'Right.'

'You might get a bit of supply. But not here. We have a

good pool of supply teachers already, I'm afraid. I've an excellent deputy in Miss Stone who's got it all sewn up.'

The Imogen of their school-days had never made excuses. Her honesty had been ruthless but now such obvious evasion was just as cruel. Sarah stood and spoke quite harshly. 'It's OK, Imogen, I don't want to intrude on your work here. I can tell you don't want me underfoot. I understand that.'

Imogen, she thought, I took you right down to the bottom with me. Is there nothing worth retrieving?

The secretary tapped lightly at the door. 'I'm sorry, Imogen. I've got the *Observer* on the line. They want a statement about the GCSE results.'

'Thank you. I'll ring back in five minutes.'

For the first time the yawning gap of time and experience unfurled itself before Sarah who had nothing in common with this busy woman. She held out her hand but suddenly Imogen whisked round the desk and hugged her.

Their eyes met. It was like the opening of the shutter in a camera. In Imogen's blue gaze Sarah read an awareness of all they had once meant to each other. But already Imogen had withdrawn and her hand was on the phone.

Sarah reeled away to the door. 'Well thanks. Thanks. I'm sorry to intrude.'

Along the corridor she ran and took the marble steps two at a time, oblivious to the girls in the stained-glass window. The afternoon had turned blustery and cool. When she reached the snug interior of her car she sat for several minutes, laughing a little and shaking her head, breathless but aflame.

A couple of days later she drove the children west to their respective schools near Winchester and Marlborough. Their relief that they were being returned to a more predictable environment was all too evident.

It was not Jamie's habit to speak or smile but on their arrival before the Georgian frontage of Alston Park he did apply slight pressure to his mother's arm before lifting his cases from the boot. 'Good luck. No need for you to get out of the car.'

'And good luck to you, Jamie.' She watched her lanky son amble away, his shoulders stooped by the weight of heavy luggage. Tailing him was a much smaller Jamie on his first day at the school, a sturdy eight-year-old in grown-up blazer and trousers that only served to emphasize his childish cheeks and bright, brave eyes. He had tried not to cry and Sarah had thought, Is this the environment I want for my boy, one in which an eight-year-old may not weep for his mother? The pain of separation had knifed her through and through.

What had possessed her, she now wondered, to send him here? The seduction of peer pressure, presumably. She and David had spent hours in the company of their friends, agonizing over the question of education, deciding to go for what they understood best, public school in England.

Sarah had traded Jamie and Lorna for the sake of a privileged life in a foreign country; for days of tennis, swimming and shopping and for dinner parties in the company of friends who would later mean so little that communication between them was reduced to circular letters at Christmas. Her only bond with her son for months at a time had been his dutiful air mail letters, written in a round large hand: *We're having great fun in art. I got B+ for my science practical. We were doing pressure. I still miss you sometimes in the night but I'm really fine. Lots of love, Jamie.*

And then that young boy who had been given to making endearing confidences and displaying sudden bursts of enthusiasm had disappeared completely to be replaced by a taciturn stranger who never wrote and who lived in a closed-up world where his most intimate relationships were with his computer and his head-phones. As Sarah watched Jamie go through the side entrance of his school she acknowledged that she might never now reclaim him. Walking away had become second nature to Jamie. But she also felt a wave of resentment for David that he had so deftly escaped these feelings of guilt. If I hadn't chosen to be here I wouldn't have to face up to all this, she thought foolishly.

Lorna slotted a different tape into the cassette recorder and took a large bite of apple, unmoved apparently by her brother's departure. She was still moody and disapproving of her mother and had intimated once or twice that she couldn't wait to get back to school.

A couple of hours later she bounced out of Sarah's car and was gone with a flash of acid-green leggings. She had barged her way through boarding school like an eager spaniel pup, seizing the many opportunities extended to her, excelling in sport and falling out spectacularly with her friends, but inviting these same unmentionables for lengthy spells of the holidays. As Sarah and David had often said, boarding school was the perfect environment for a sporty, gregarious girl. Lorna was thriving.

Sarah turned the car and prepared to drive away but at that moment she caught a glimpse of the green leggings again as Lorna came running back, her sturdy thighs scissoring vigorously along the drive. She flung open her mother's door and embraced her so tightly that afterwards Sarah's ear burned and she felt a rare wave of pure, joyous love for her child.

Cedarview lay smug behind its laurel hedge. A fine drizzle fell and with it the first dead leaves in the copse. Autumn was tousling the garden and the windows of the low house were blank in the evening gloom. The car spat gravel against the door-step but when the engine died, so did all sound. Sarah stepped into the moist twilight, stiff from the journey. The impact of her foot on the drive seemed of terrible significance and she faced the oak front door reluctantly, aware that her isolation now was nothing to what would she find inside.

She ran through the house closing curtains, flicking light switches and bolting outside doors. She turned on the heating, the cooker and the kettle. The preparation of scrambled eggs on toast created a brief spate of bustling purpose. Her existence was reduced to this; a woman in a kitchen breaking two eggs. That was all.

After supper she dared herself. On stealthy, bare feet she visited every room, flinging wide the door and walking to its centre, twirling round in its silence. Only the children's rooms gave her pain by the small remembrances of them that were left, indentations in the pillow and an old trainer thrust under a wardrobe. But it was her own guilty relief in their absence that hurt her most. Alienation was what she and David had bought.

In the drawing room she searched David's CD collection with deliberation until she came to Mahler's ninth symphony.

The music, like a cold finger, worked along her nerves. She couldn't stay in the room with it but flung wide the French windows and stepped out into the garden.

The thrust of the music was so powerful that it wrenched her memory back to her first visit to Imogen's house when Mr Taylor's crackly recording had filled the hall with melancholy and Sarah had understood with a thrill that here was a culture far removed from her own. In that same hall she had later met Lawrence, who had given her a casual few hours but with whom she had fallen so violently in love that she had never fully recovered. And in the wet, autumnal air she remembered the rose garden at Priors Heath, where she had tried to rid herself of Lawrence once and for all. How deeply she must have experienced life then, to have known such profound despair. The best she could manage now was a feeble abandonment of responsibility, but even that was clouded by damp, clinging fronds of unease.

At great cost, she had created for herself a blank sheet again.

An offer of a few days' supply teaching came from St John the Evangelist, a notorious comprehensive near where the Becketts used to live in Hillingdon. As she drove through the playground youths shuffled reluctantly aside, giving her the impersonal stare which her own daughter had recently perfected. The reception area smelt of chips and a flustered secretary sent

Sarah across a scarred linoleum floor towards the staffroom where she stood in the doorway like a reluctant sheep at the gate of a market pen. Teachers shouldered past with bulging bags and steaming coffee mugs until at last Sarah plucked up the courage to accost a balding man in a track suit. 'I'm a supply teacher. I'm looking for Mr Balfour.'

Balfour, bulky and shiny-faced, was a man who, for the sake of self-aggrandizement, made a simple task impenetrably complicated. He was in charge of cover and sat at a desk running his fingers through stringy hair as he crossed and recrossed names on a timetable. He thrust a list into Sarah's hand and she began a trail of the staffroom seeking out the various heads of departments who would give her lesson plans.

Her first double lesson was covering year ten chemistry. 'Oh, you're OK, it's a video on catalysts, all set up,' said the head of science. 'I'll take you up there now if you like.'

'I'm afraid I know nothing about catalysts,' she said.

'They won't expect you to. They're used to supply teachers.'

She was taken into an empty lab, instructed how to work the video recorder, issued with a list of questions and a tape and left alone. The school clamoured and roared in the background, a great whale carrying a thousand Jonahs.

Having dealt out the questions and tidied the rows of stools Sarah had a few minutes to take stock. She was intensely excited, though many of the old fears of the classroom had returned. For a year immediately before and after Jamie's birth this had been her familiar world. Then as now there had always been a dread of being entirely overwhelmed. But this time, she told herself, she was much older. Before she had been of practically the same generation as her pupils. Now, surely, she had perspective. She was here to do a job, only that, and the pupils could take it or leave it.

A bell rang offensively in the corridor outside. Sarah stood in the doorway to welcome her class.

There was so much she had forgotten. The thirty fifteen-year-olds who crowded into the room and crammed themselves behind the long, scratched benches were enormous as they hunched awkwardly on their high perches. The noise they made seemed uncrushable. Bags were dropped at their feet as if they had no intention of withdrawing anything from them and if they deigned a glance at Sarah or met her eye, their faces drained instantly of all animation.

Sarah stood at the desk, deliberately still, waiting, but they took no notice. Unswerving will-power was her first strategy for gaining silence and it wasn't going to work. When she shouted at last her voice was a flimsy straw which reached row three and died among the gelled hair of the two girls who were studying the instructions on a bottle of nail varnish. She went to the door, opened it and slammed it with a bang that caused a boy in the front row to say: 'Shit, you gave me a fright.'

In the moment of silence which followed Sarah rapped out instructions and switched on the video. The flickering of the screen quietened them a little.

The first shot was of a boy in a burger bar cramming a bun into his mouth. The title read: 'FOOD FOUR. GRAIN.'

It was the wrong video. 'Oy, Miss, we saw this in Biology last week.'

Sarah cursed herself for not testing the tape before the class arrived while an undersized boy in the front row offered to fetch the head of science. Once the television was switched off the attention of the class sucked away and the pupils sank back into their own worlds. Sarah perched by the window with nothing whatever to say. Outside there was a netball court and beyond, a row of maisonettes. A woman stood in her garden hanging baby clothes on the line. Sarah weighed her own situation against the woman's and felt a strange pleasure at being immured in the classroom safe from the cauldron of emotion and tedium that was domestic life.

The head of science appeared at last, very irritable. His great height and overbearing manner imposed some calm on the group. 'Must have been put in the wrong box,' he shouted.

All his words were too loud. 'I can't find the right one. Sorry.' He began to toss text books along the benches. 'Page 131. There're some revision questions. Mrs . . . Um will take your answers in at the end of the lesson.' He scrawled the work on the board having plucked a pen from his pocket. Sarah had not been issued with a white board marker.

Paper was handed out, spare ball-points found and he departed again, leaving the door pointedly ajar. Sarah went to close it. Fifteen minutes of the hour-and-ten-minute double period had gone and still the class made no move to work. Sarah suddenly had a picture of herself in her navy blue trousers and red pullover, hair tucked behind her ears, insignificant as a leaf in the wind.

A register of names lay on the desk beside her. She plucked one at random and yelled it across the din. 'Carole Fenning.'

A head shot up. 'What?'

'You're not working.'

'Neither is anyone else.'

'You haven't even opened the book. Open the book.' She called another name and the class grew marginally more attentive. Seizing her chance, Sarah repeated the instructions, standing over them until they had all at least scribbled their names and the date. Then she had a handle on them.

Silence fell, blessedly, and then was immediately broken by a request for Tipp-Ex. Noise swelled behind the question and had to be picked apart, pupil by pupil, until there was quiet again. It took every ounce of will to keep them to the task, which Sarah knew to be dull and probably beyond the capacity of some. But she was merciless, accepting neither questions nor complaints. Their resentment fizzed.

She thought of herself as a pupil at Priors Heath. What had held her so fixedly to the path of righteousness then? The answer was simply that she had been ruled by the desire to please. She had not sought self-fulfilment particularly. No, she had wanted to make her mother happy, and people like Miss Stone, and ultimately Bess Hardemon in her portrait under

143

the stairs, who had set her school rolling across the years with such high hopes for her girls.

The group had grown restless and a few had finished. There was shuffling, whispering and the discreet tearing of a biscuit wrapper. Each member of the class in front of her now stood out for Sarah in brilliant relief.

'When I was at school I had a friend called Imogen,' She announced suddenly. 'Our physics teacher was so awful that she didn't notice that Imogen once spent nearly two-thirds of a lesson sitting behind a bench on the floor, playing Patience.'

The class sat in stony silence, not in the least interested in Sarah who had proved to be fierce and strange. 'You've worked well,' added Sarah. 'There are five minutes left. If you've finished you can hand your books and papers to the end of the bench.' She had made a hideous mistake by releasing them too early. There was an explosion of noise and movement and still three hundred seconds to be endured.

But Sarah no longer minded. She had brought Imogen into the room and the pair of them sat side by side perched on the teacher's desk. Imogen didn't care that the class had scraped back their stools from the benches, stuffed papers into their bags and shuffled towards the door where they jostled and swore. Sardonic and dispassionate, she murmured: You did pretty well, by and large.

Three days later a white envelope arrived at Cedarview, hand-written in black, confident lettering.

> Sarah,
> You asked me if there were any vacancies at P.H. A history teacher will go on maternity leave on October 30th. If you're available, let me know and I'll arrange for you to be interviewed.
> Imogen

The 30th of October. So Imogen had known of this when Sarah visited her before the start of term, but had said nothing.

8

November 1855

By 1854 Queen's College had become a flourishing but exclusive day school for the daughters of wealthy parents and had even been granted a royal charter. Originally, however, the college had been founded with a view to providing a higher academic education for teachers and governesses and to answer this continuing need lectures for women were still held in the evenings.

Bess taught at the school in the day and afterwards, on several nights a week, attended lectures herself on subjects as diverse as Astronomy, Hebrew and Algebra. At first she had been very happy on these evenings, partly because for once she was on the receiving end of instruction, and partly because for the first time in her life she did not feel an oddity. The environment was dignified and scholarly and the women, even though most made their living by teaching, were actually treated with respect.

During these sessions Bess was in the company of people as dedicated to the cause of learning as she was herself. There was a minority of wealthy, fashionable ladies on the roll, but most were poorer women intent on improving themselves in the hope of being appointed to more lucrative teaching positions. These students, desperate for knowledge, made laborious notes in their careful longhand, afraid of missing a single word. Like Bess, they wore sober, dark clothes. Under plain bonnet brims their eyes were shadowed with exhaustion and their hair was drawn back harshly from anxious foreheads.

All the tutors were men, mostly clergymen whose delivery tended to be a little jaded because they were repeating lectures given perhaps only a few days previously at King's College for men. The women were pathetically grateful for even poor lectures and knew well that their teachers were paid a contemptibly small fee for the dubious privilege of attending at Queen's.

Before very long, however, the novelty began to wear off for Bess. Her father's teaching in his study at the rectory in Mereby Bridge had been so broad and thorough that it was rare for anyone at Queen's to add much to what she already knew. However, she was intrigued by how her own interest in a subject could be stifled or enhanced by the personality of an individual lecturer.

There was one man in particular who fascinated Bess, not only by the diversity of his interests, which ranged from Literature to Economics and Geography, but by the vivacity of his face. Reverend George Peachey was a small man with a beaked nose and long black side-whiskers. His expression was warm and alert and his teeth white and even. He dressed with immaculate care and his dog collar flashed brilliantly between his whiskers.

Bess was amused by Peachey's obvious relish for the company of so many women. He had a gift for finding an exactly appropriate word or phrase and producing it with a teasing caress in his voice. She watched him steadily, trying to capture the essence of his charm. If only other teachers could copy his style, she thought, pupils would lap up learning as eagerly as a cat licks cream. She held a pencil at the ready to note any special trick, or indeed any moment when her attention wandered.

After three or four sessions it occurred to her that he had singled her out. If he cracked a joke he looked at her quickly to see if she smiled. When she made one of her rare notes she would look up to see his brown eyes watching her, puzzled.

Once she had become conscious of his interest she grew flustered and for a whole lecture couldn't look at him. She had no wish to appear eccentric or affected. After that he paid no special attention to her.

One fault she found in Peachey was that he always overran at the end of the session. After a day's teaching and then hours as a student herself, Bess was exhausted by nine-thirty p.m. But Peachey was never in a hurry. He took questions, thereby giving women anxious to ingratiate themselves the needless opportunity to make irrelevant or obvious points. Peachey responded to them all with unfailing courtesy but Bess was less tolerant and would snap shut her notebook, stow her pencil away in her reticule and tap her foot. What she despised most of all was his desire to be liked. They won't learn if you pander to their weaknesses, she thought, and they'll get an inflated sense of their own importance.

When the women were dismissed at last they surged from the hall and along the galleried corridor to the staircase. An odour of heavy dinners and domestic activity still hung on the landings, despite the more utilitarian use that was now made of the grand old house which had been bought by Queen's. On the ground floor an arched passageway led to a porch where a cluster of chaperones waited, having emerged from their little parlour in a flurry of wide skirts. They smelt of tea and had probably spent the last hour in the demolition of many a previously respectable character. The wealthier girls were scooped up by these older women and escorted to waiting carriages. Others walked off in pairs, or were met by a brother or a father standing humbly in the dank night air on the street outside. Gerald, who despite Bess's protestations always came to collect her, waited with unshakable patience by the railings, arms folded, bewhiskered face placid, sunk in an indolent torpor.

One night Reverend Peachey had apparently been hot on Bess's heels as she left the lecture hall for no sooner had

147

she taken her brother's arm than Peachey leapt forward and exclaimed: 'Good Lord, Gerald Hardemon! Whatever brings you here?'

'George Peachey.' Gerald wrung his hand. 'I'm meeting my sister. Bess. George Peachey.'

'Miss Hardemon.' Peachey bowed over her small, gloved hand, smiling down into her eyes, though he was by no means a tall man.

'Peachey and I were at Oxford together,' Gerald told his sister, gazing at George with a degree of hero-worship. 'I had no idea he was giving lectures at Queen's.'

'It's my great privilege.'

'Thin end of the wedge, George. If you start allowing women to attend lectures, what will become of us all?' Bess, displeased by this heavy wit, dropped her brother's arm.

The two men now began a conversation about a mutual university acquaintance. Peachey smiled encouragingly at Bess from time to time but she withdrew herself a little, eyes down-cast. During the evening lectures at Queen's she felt glad to be part of a valuable and unique institution but this exclusive conversation between the two men dampened her pleasure. Also she was aware that Peachey only partially attended to Gerald and was trying to draw her back into the conversation. She suddenly glanced sharply up at him. Don't you judge me or Gerald, her eyes told him. I don't consider myself in any way superior to my brother, as you so obviously do.

At a suitable pause in the discussion, George Peachey spoke softly to her: 'Miss Hardemon. I'm still so unused to teaching women that I would truly welcome your opinion of tonight's lecture.'

Her heart beat faster. It was rare for her to feel any power over a man but she knew Peachey would listen carefully to what she said and that she was about to surprise him. 'It's your delivery that interests me, not the content. You said nothing tonight I didn't already know.'

Peachey was dumbfounded. Gerald threw back his head and roared with laughter. 'Be careful, George. Bess isn't as harmless as she looks.'

The Reverend recovered enough to enquire: 'And what do you find interesting in my delivery?'

Before she replied, Bess pushed her head back a little to give herself a longer perspective. 'Reverend Peachey, forgive me for sounding rude. You see, the glaciation of the British Isles is of far less concern to me than how best a set of complex ideas may be put across.'

'And your judgement?'

The men looked down at her expectantly. Abruptly Bess's mood changed. I do believe Peachey is flirting with me, she thought in dismay. He plays with me as if I were a puppy or small child. He is no more interested in the opinion of a woman than are most men. 'My judgement,' she responded, 'is of value to me, but not, I suspect, to you.'

Gerald tutted with annoyance at this brusque reply. Peachey however seemed untroubled and offered her his arm, which she had no option but to take. They walked on towards Cavendish Square. 'Miss Hardemon, you thought I was humouring you. Your astuteness, for indeed, I was toying with you and perhaps seeking flattery, has doubled my interest. I really do wish to hear your opinion now. I think it will be invaluable.'

She cocked her head to one side and a glimmer of amusement flickered in her eyes. Her fingers barely touched his arm. 'Reverend Peachey, as you probably realize I'm a teacher and I find myself a member of a profession in which few have studied how to perform well. As I think it's possible to learn almost effortlessly if the teaching is pleasurable I'm trying to find ways of making even the dullest subject memorable. You're an admirable speaker. I'm fascinated by what you say though I'm afraid that much of your success is based on force of personality and one can only be born with that. However, your other great strength is the fascination you seem to feel for your subjects. I have seen you lecture now on a number of topics and your enthusiasm is always infectious. You are very clear and methodical. You begin with a résumé of what you intend to teach and end by a summary of what has been achieved during the lecture. You add variety with humour and anecdote. All these examples of good practice can, I believe, be learnt by other teachers in some measure.'

Peachey looked very pleased.

'But,' she continued, and they both laughed because he knew at once that she was about to criticize him. She found herself delighting in his quick-wittedness. 'I must add that your delivery is too quick and you give so much information in so little time that at least half of what you say is lost. Furthermore, you can't resist the odd flourish, a discreet brandishing of your superior knowledge by apparently casual use of technical or Latin terms, or obscure sources. What I admire most in a teacher is simplicity.'

He laughed again. 'Miss Hardemon, I've been completely found out.'

She withdrew her arm. 'I'm glad you're amused. My guess is that you will reflect at length upon the praise I have given your lecture, and disregard, or soon forget, the criticism.'

'Now there you're mistaken. I shall never forget what you have said. Miss Hardemon, I find you hit the nail with alarming accuracy. I don't know whether to feel sympathy or envy for your pupils.'

A fortnight after her conversation with Peachey, Bess returned to her brother's house in Baker Street late in the afternoon to find the maid hovering anxiously by the area steps, on the look-out.

'Miss Hardemon, there's a visitor for you in the drawing room.'

Bess barely paused on her way through the front door. 'I

do have the odd acquaintance in town who might call, Maggie. There's no need to be so surprised.'

'Mrs Hardemon said I was to let you know. She said you might want to be prepared.'

At that moment the inner door was flung open and Laetitia's anxious, long-nosed face made its appearance. Bess was drawn hurriedly across the hall and into the little dining room. From upstairs came a prolonged, childish screech of rage which caused Letty to flinch and draw her hand across her forehead. 'I've been with her in the parlour for an hour, Bess, and Ellen's having such trouble with the children this afternoon. Thank goodness you're home. You won't believe who's here. Mrs Penhaligon. From Priors Heath. Remember her? She says you'll know her at once.'

Bess placed a careful hand on the polished table. 'I remember, yes. What does she want?'

'She won't say. Bess, don't you think you should put on a better frock? You do look a bit dragged down.'

'Certainly not. If she wants to see me, she must take me as I am. How rude to call without prior warning.' Bess had removed her bonnet and cloak, revealing her hair only a little roughened by a day at Queen's, and a well-darned grey wool dress. She couldn't resist a quick glance in the hall mirror however, and a comical grimace at Letty. 'Don't you dare leave me alone with her for one minute,' she hissed, and flung open the door.

Mrs Penhaligon had taken the most comfortable armchair in Laetitia's ambitious parlour, though of course her rigid deportment wouldn't allow her to relax among its cushions. She was in black and her vast silk skirts, elaborately quilted, suggested that Mr Penhaligon's fortunes were still on the up. Mrs Penhaligon was the younger daughter of a baron but had married only a solicitor, though an exceptionally wealthy and successful one. A discreet diamond brooch glinted on her bosom. She had not removed her bonnet, a formidable structure with a white inner frill which framed her sharp features and translucent complexion. The sight of her reminded Bess vividly of the dreadful morning when she'd been dismissed from Priors Heath.

Her mind was working furiously. Surely the Board hadn't discovered, after six years, more fault to find with Miss Hardemon.

Mrs Penhaligon rose and advanced towards Bess, hand out-stretched, an unnaturally accommodating smile on her thin lips. 'Miss Hardemon.'

'Mrs Penhaligon.'

'My dear Miss Hardemon. How well you look.'

Twin impulses were at work in Bess. Her upbringing ordered her to forgive but her pride told her that Mrs Penhaligon should be punished. After all, she had been a member of the Board that had tolerated not only Bess's summary dismissal but all the other cruelties of Priors Heath. She was too com-placent, too unruffled to be forgiven. Therefore Bess stood quite still gazing at Mrs Penhaligon with cold indifference. At last Laetitia came to the rescue by sitting down by the window, thereby allowing Mrs Penhaligon to resume her own chair. With some reluctance Bess took a hard seat near the door.

'My dear Miss Hardemon, I come on a mission. I am in Town partly on private business, partly to settle school affairs. We discovered you were here quite by chance. Reverend Carnegie, as I'm sure you're aware, is a fellow of King's College and you share a common acquaintance there, I believe, in a Reverend Peachey. And of course your dear brother Gerald is also acquainted with Reverend Carnegie. It was decided that I should approach you at once, in person, though it had been our intention to write. You may perhaps have heard that Priors Heath has suffered a series of misfortunes culminating in an outbreak of scarlet fever last winter. Our numbers have fallen so far that we are threatened with closure.'

What possible reason could Mrs Penhaligon have for bringing

this news? Bess wondered. The very mention of Carnegie's name brought a flush of remembered humiliation to her cheeks.

Mrs Penhaligon had paused, as if waiting for a word of sympathy from Bess or Laetitia. Neither spoke.

Mrs Penhaligon had the knack of making such a silence appear discourteous. She shifted her weight as if to say: The people one has to deal with. 'You may wonder how the Board is dealing with this crisis. Reverend Carnegie' — and here she fixed Bess with a glare so forbidding that it was as if she was expecting Bess to leap to her feet and denounce Carnegie — 'has felt it right to step down from his position as Chairman. In any case, he is very busy with his work among the missions.' A pause, to signal Mrs Penhaligon's enduring admiration for the Reverend. 'I am taking his place, at least for a while, until someone more suitable is found. I need hardly say that it is highly unusual for a lady to take such a prominent role and indeed most undesirable, except in the very short term.'

Even Mrs Penhaligon couldn't fail to find the unresponsiveness of her listeners disheartening. The parlour with its frivolous trimmings had acquired the aspect of a courtroom.

'The Board has taken a brave step,' she continued, recovering her stride. 'We have decided that the school has to survive, for the sake of so many needy but respectable girls who must be educated. As you know many of our pupils go on to be teachers and governesses themselves. We must arm them with a proper education. The aims of the school have always been noble. Perhaps our fault has been a failure to move with the times. Modern girls are so demanding, not nearly so acquiescent as they once were.' Bess had trouble stifling a bubble of laughter for Mrs Penhaligon had given her a look of deep reproach as if to suggest she were personally responsible for a general decline in self-discipline among young females.

'There has been a public appeal and the school is to be refurbished. Fees will of course have to be increased but we intend to help the poorest applicants. We have also decided to take students from other than clergy families, so long as the father is engaged in a respectable profession. We will thus be enabled to open the school to a considerable number of local day girls. I need hardly tell you that this last innovation has been met with dismay in some quarters. There must be a danger that day girls will bring with them influences that are less than pure. However, economic constraints have forced our hand. We intend to revise the curriculum, sleeping and living arrangements and the school's routine. In short, Miss Hardemon, there are to be great changes. There must be if the school is to survive.

'Miss Simms feels unable to continue at the helm of so altered an institution so we are looking for a new headmistress. The Board and I discussed the matter at length and we decided to approach you.'

There was a quick intake of breath from Laetitia. Bess waited for a moment to find a suitable response and then said calmly: 'Your choice, under the circumstances, is a surprising one.'

'We know you. In the short time you were at the school you impressed us by your energy and ability. You obviously had a strong influence on your pupils. We have thought over some of the criticisms you saw fit to make of the school and in retrospect we feel that our conviction that you spoke entirely out of turn perhaps blinded us to the wisdom of some of your observations. You may not have been aware of it at the time, Miss Hardemon, but nothing you did at the school escaped our notice. My conversation with your sister-in-law this afternoon has confirmed my opinion that in approaching you we are doing what is best for the school. She tells me you have worked ceaselessly to improve your qualifications to teach. And I know you have gained experience in the most forward-thinking school in the country. I believe you have been working at Queen's College?'

Bess gave the slightest inclination of her head. Mrs Penhaligon was bound to be impressed by the reputation of Queen's among the upper classes. She said quietly: 'I wonder if the Board had forgotten the way I was dismissed.'

Mrs Penhaligon didn't flinch. 'I think it's to our credit that we are prepared to forget past differences.'

Bess rose to her feet, her skirts flicking dangerously close to the grate. 'Mrs Penhaligon, I won't pretend that I'm not surprised by your offer, or indeed a little flattered. But of course I must refuse. I was young and relatively inexperienced when I arrived at Priors Heath but I was subjected almost to slave labour. The pupils were crushed and deprived. I'm a religious woman but even my relations with God were compromised by the atmosphere of spiritual sterility within the school. Any suggestion I made, any changes I tried, were immediately repressed. I was dismissed without a character. Had the Board considered how that might affect an eager young woman of twenty-one years old? And you ask me to return?' By the end of this violent speech Bess was panting a little, and taken aback by her own vehemence.

'You must understand, Miss Hardemon, that Reverend Carnegie always acts from the best of motives. All his decisions were based on the desire to protect his young charges from harm. He thought he was doing right and, as he held the purse-strings and was very persuasive in his arguments, he was given almost complete autonomy. But the Board has considered deeply and has come to see that there were errors. Young minds must be allowed to develop in some freedom, young bodies must have physical exercise. Miss Hardemon, the Board regrets . . .'

There was the apology, tossed like a fragile, white flower between them. The tension within Bess began to seep away.

Suddenly, without taking her pale eyes from Bess's face, Mrs Penhaligon added softly: 'The garden, Miss Hardemon, is very much as you last saw it, waiting to be replanted. We thought the new Headmistress might like to oversee that too.' In Bess's mind the branches of blossom fell to the grass, piles of blowing pink cut down. She stood again in the bare old house with its closed windows and dark passages, and gazed out at the stumps of trees, the creamy newness of sawn wood.

Mrs Penhaligon rose to her feet, her rigid upper torso rising from the billow of black skirts like a goddess swooping from the ocean. 'Miss Hardemon, I shall not repeat my offer but nor will I withdraw it. I will only add that I'm sure careful reflection will convince you that our choice would not have fallen on you if we hadn't wished to make considerable changes. We know your character, Miss Hardemon. Were you to apply and be appointed, the Board is well aware that we would not in future enjoy the freedom we have previously experienced in managing the school.' It was possible that there was a gleam of humour in her eyes. She had drawn on her gloves and moved to the door, her swinging petticoats causing one of Letty's little tables to wobble.

Bess murmured: 'And Reverend Carnegie . . . ?'

'Miss Hardemon, the school is a project very dear to the Reverend's heart. As you are possibly aware his own sister died at fifteen, of consumption. In her memory he helped to found the school, investing a considerable portion of his family's fortune into its establishment. Reverend Carnegie desires only what is best for Priors Heath. He won't object to your appointment. In any case, he will no longer be living in Faringford as he's decided to work abroad for a while.'

Laetitia had remembered to ring for the maid, whose arrival was a little too prompt. Mrs Penhaligon sailed from the room with a gracious nod towards her hostess, who barely waited for the door to close before taking Bess in her arms and joining with her in a little jig of hilarity and excitement.

9

The history department was situated on the top floor of the Ryder Street Block and Sarah was escorted there on her first morning by a woman called Alison Atwood, second in the department.

Sarah was assaulted by a host of impressions: damp coats; a hundred unfamiliar, youthful faces; artificial light and scuffed paintwork. Youthful male voices called, there was a burst of laughter and she was before a door numbered 37.

Inside there was a rise in temperature, a teacher's desk facing sixteen grey tables and a display: 'CASTLES. *Please do not touch.*'

'All right,' said Alison, 'I'll leave you to it, if that's OK. See you at break.'

Sarah's new form of thirty-two fourteen-year-old children, quite well washed after a half-term break, regarded her curiously. She smiled at them with a brisk assurance gleaned from her few weeks at St John the Evangelist, which had proved to be a rigorous retraining ground. 'Good morning. My name is Ms Beckett. I'm here to replace Mrs Cornell while she has her baby. The register . . .' Her tongue stumbled on the unfamiliar list of Asian, Afro-Caribbean, Irish, Greek and English names. As she spoke them a whisper from the past drifted into her consciousness: *Sophia Bell, Sarah Beckett, Helen Carlton, Susan Edmonds, Jill Edwards, Margaret Goldstone, Helen Good, Laura Harding* . . . White, female, British names followed by obedient responses.

'And next the notices. My goodness, what a mixture. Karate Club, meet today in the gym, twelve-thirty . . .' A boy was discussing a football fixture with his neighbour, barely troubling to lower his voice. 'Excuse me,' Sarah said coldly. 'Why are you speaking? What's your name?'

The offender took his time registering that she had noticed him and then turned upon her a handsome face crowned by a precision haircut, long at the front, shorn at the back. Contemptuous hazel eyes stared into hers. 'Matthew. What's yours again?'

Sarah had been warned about Matthew Illingworth and told to avoid confrontation where possible so she ignored his insolence and continued with her pile of announcements. 'Geography Society. Craft Workshop . . .'

The moment she finished speaking the class withdrew the brief gift of its attention and Sarah moved across to the window. Outside autumn blew in chill gusts across the playing fields. She thought of her son and daughter in their gracious schools, Lorna exactly the same age as these strange children, and David under a hot, foreign sky. Her heart ached with the knowledge that she preferred those three to be absent from her life. It was a grim irony that she had chosen to work among a thousand youths when she had made such careful arrangements to dispose of her own two.

A bell rang and the class funnelled out. In the momentary respite Sarah's hands grew clammy with nerves. The sensation of having come full circle back to Priors Heath dragged her down and down.

A host of eleven-year-olds crowded through the door, eager to discover this new factor in their lives. Like jumping beans, the children were disorganized, anxious and shrill. 'Are you our new teacher? What are we doing today?' She watched with growing affection their frantic scrabbling for the right books and pens. Some threw hurried glances towards her and Sarah knew that they were poised on the brink of cynical adolescence and she wanted to catch them there in the brightness of their enthusiasm.

She sprang forward with a confident smile. The topic for the half term was Norman Britain and Sarah had prepared a lurid narration of life in a castle. Up perilous winding stairs the class followed her, along windy battlements and in and out of privies and bedchambers. They tumbled into the dungeon and lay on the freezing floor gazing up at a glint of daylight. Roasted meat from the cavernous kitchen was brought past the high barred window to tantalize the starving prisoners. In the great hall the Lord and his Lady nestled in furs and received the service of others as their birthright.

At the end of the lesson the children emerged blinking into the twentieth century.

Sarah thought: I love this.

Late in the afternoon she met her 'A' level candidates. Graham Hibbert, head of history, had warned that six of the seven students in this group were not in the least academic. Certainly their lack of punctuality and the reluctance with which they sank on to their small chairs did not bode well.

'Well,' said Sarah, 'I don't like this.'

They looked mildly surprised but did not otherwise respond.

'More than five minutes have been wasted because you're late and even now you're not ready. And why are you sitting in rows with your backs to each other? It's ridiculous at your age. Move the desks into a circle so we can communicate properly.' She was too tired to moderate her officious tone which had roused both interest and anger. A hideous scraping of desks followed.

One girl was certainly not lack-lustre. Her name was Sonia Castelino and she had a vivid face and dark shining eyes. Graham Hibbert had singled her out as an exceptional student, a starred A candidate at GCSE. She took copious notes, asked questions and gave lucid answers. Teaching Sonia was like conducting a talented instrumentalist. Her intellect was fluid, generous and searching.

The other students had put up with Sonia's genius throughout their school-days and were resigned to ploughing a lowly furrow in her bright shadow. Sarah tried to catch them into the net and make them listen and argue. But suddenly there was a rude interruption as the classroom door was flung open and Matthew Illingworth projected himself into the room as if fired from a gun.

He regarded the startled faces of the group with considerable satisfaction. 'Fenster sent me.'

Sarah took him outside. 'How dare you barge in without knocking? Who's Fenster?'

'Art teacher. He said he didn't want me in the art room and I was to find my form teacher or head of year.'

'Don't you mean *Mr* Fenster then? Why did he exclude you?'

'I don't know. He just said he didn't want me.'

'All right, I'll discuss it with him later. For now you can sit at the back of the lesson.' But the class didn't recover from the intrusion and for the next half-hour Sarah had to drag the discussion through its dying phases and dictate some notes.

After the bell she dismissed the older students and prepared to discipline Matthew who lounged against a desk, arms folded.

'You can't keep me after school. It's not allowed. I might miss the bus.' He was a manipulator, a well-seasoned player in this little game.

Because she didn't know the procedures Sarah was on shaky ground. 'Very well. I'll make enquiries and see you in the morning.'

'Just as you like.' He tossed his bag over his shoulder and sauntered out, giving her a familiar wave. 'See you, miss. Have a nice evening.'

Sarah put her hot hand to her forehead and breathed deeply. The Ryder Street Block had emptied of pupils with extraordinary speed and its cheap walls seemed to exhale.

Suddenly, instead of being ricocheted by the bell from one demanding class to the next, there was time.

'Ms Becket?'

'Sonia. I thought you'd gone.'

'I wondered, I don't want to interfere, but would you like me to take you along to the art rooms? I've got to go and collect some work. I could introduce you to Mr Fenster, you know, Matthew's art teacher.'

Sarah had intended to discuss Matthew with Graham Hibbert or her head of year, but Sonia looked so eager to please and yet so afraid of overstepping the mark that it would be a shame to reject her offer. There could surely be no harm in speaking to Mr Fenster.

The art room was awash with colour, as it had always been. Yellow light bulbs in translucent glass shades had been replaced by white strip-lights and instead of quavery easels there were long tables but the pervasive smells of glue and poster paint were as pungent as ever and the walls were decorated as before with exotic fabrics and rows of students' work.

Fourteen-year-old Imogen, fingers running with juice, mouth crammed, raised wicked eyes to Sarah.

'Mr Fenster.' A man in a creased linen jacket turned abruptly.

'Ah. Sonia.'

'This is Ms Beckett. She wanted to see you.'

Fenster was extremely young, presumably a new addition to the teaching profession. Tall and slender with fragile hands and coltish eyes, he sported a yellow tie patterned with zebras.

Sonia made careful introductions. 'Mr Fenster is supervising my special project for art "A" level. I'm researching the Victorian artist, Christina Lytton. Have you heard of her?'

'Yes, I believe I have.'

'Oh. Hardly anyone else has. Which is surprising, considering her quality. And she had links with this school.'

'Of course. Didn't she paint the portrait of Bess Hardemon in the entrance hall?'

'And she designed the stained-glass window, yes.' Sonia seemed a little piqued that Sarah knew about Christina Lytton. Fenster's gaze followed her as she went to a drawer and removed a portfolio of work. Her figure was supple and full beneath an over-sized jumper and when she swung round a flood of dark hair shifted on her shoulders. She smiled at Sarah. 'All right, Ms Beckett? See you tomorrow.'

'Poor girl. Not much of a home life,' Fenster murmured when Sonia had gone.

'Mr Fenster, I wanted to have a word because you excluded a boy from your lesson. Matthew Illingworth. I'm the temporary appointment in the history department. He's in my form so he came to me.'

'Of course, of course. I'm sorry about Matthew. He and I don't quite click, I'm afraid. He went too far this afternoon and swore at me.'

'I see. He didn't tell me that.'

'No. He wouldn't.'

'Will you mention it to the head of year, or shall I?'

The back of Fenster's head was endearingly angled like that of Sarah's son, Jamie. 'I'd rather you didn't. I've already had to refer a number of disciplinary problems this term. Newly qualified, you see, bound to make a few mistakes.'

'Yes, but no one should swear . . .'

'I allow them too much of a free rein, I suppose. And then it all gets out of hand so I shout and there's an argument.'

When Sarah agreed to deal with Matthew herself a great weight seemed to lift from Fenster's brow and he became bantering and flirtatious. Holding the door wide open for her he bowed her out, a charming young man used to winning friends easily.

Afterwards she walked slowly along the empty corridors and into the quad, pausing near the arched entrance to the rose garden. The leaves on the rose-bushes were shrunken and a chilly October wind scratched an empty yoghurt pot along a path. Perhaps familiarity would dull the pain of passing this place several times a day. Her stride had been purposeful and confident, but now she faltered. Impostor, she thought.

At the weekend Sarah arranged to collect Jamie from school and take him to spectate at his sister's hockey match. Removing him from his habitual environment was like levering a limpet from a rock and she could extract barely a syllable from him. During the bustle of family holidays Jamie's taciturnity went unnoticed but being alone with him was a disheartening experience. He responded to Sarah's questions with the odd grunt and then gazed fixedly out of the window. When they arrived at the match he wouldn't leave the car but sat in the front seat reading a maths textbook.

Sarah wondered if she was being reproached by her son for deserting David. How much easier it had been thousands of miles from Jamie, she thought wearily. This proximity forced her to scrutinize the many shortcomings in their relationship. But her encounters with pupils Jamie's age at Prior's Heath made her gentle with him. She saw that he shared their anguished unease with the state of their long, knobbly bodies and their terror of being singled out. She was patient with him and after a while didn't probe too much.

Lorna was pitifully pleased to have her achievements witnessed by her mother. She charged vigorously about the hockey pitch though her game lacked focus because she kept turning to wave as if to reassure herself that Sarah was actually there.

At lunch she gabbled on and on, tirelessly narrating the minutiae of her school life while Jamie worked his way through a meal a quarter the size of his sister's and then peered about him as if he had arrived in the restaurant unexpectedly and had no idea what he was doing there.

Lorna informed Sarah pointedly that her father had already written to her twice. 'He seems to be managing all right,' she admitted, 'but he's definitely missing you. He never used to write at all.'

'Whenever I speak to him on the phone he sounds fine,' Sarah told her firmly and Lorna absorbed this remark in silence, her honest eyes fixed on her mother's face. Sarah smiled back unflinchingly but her heart sank. That brittle cheeriness of David's hadn't deceived her. She knew that he'd buried his anxiety about her deep inside and was presenting a bland and capable face to the world. Fine. Fine. If he burrowed away far enough she would never find him again.

Afterwards, when they had said goodbye to Lorna and driven back to Hampshire, Sarah parked in a lay-by a mile from Alston Park. 'One word, Jamie. Tell me. Are you happy at school? Because if not you could leave at once.'

He made not a murmur of response.

'Are you miserable? What?'

But she didn't want him to make any such admission. How awkward it would be if he did decide to ditch Alston Park. She would have to bear him in her daily life like a growth on her side, heavy and unwieldy, a constant worry. What kind of mother are you, she asked herself wildly, that you should think like this? Guilt sharpened her voice. 'Well?'

He gave a shrug.

'Jamie.'

'Yeah. I'm OK.'

Realizing that the word 'happy' was not one that would readily enter her son's vocabulary, she let him go.

For the first time Cedarview seemed to welcome Sarah, promising her an easy few hours in its still company. She lay in bed that night and listened to the rise and fall of branches as the wind soughed through the copse. The stream made the merest trickle of sound.

The week had resolved itself into a pattern that could easily become a routine. In her darkest moments Sarah had anticipated great dramas that had not after all occurred. The modern Priors Heath had received her without question, grateful that here was a woman who could fill the gap in the history department. She had scarcely seen Imogen at all, except in passing when they nodded and smiled distractedly at each other. And she had engaged in several quite amicable telephone conversations with David who was, he said, already deeply immersed in the new project. For several hours a day, then, she was safe from the clamouring internal voices which insisted that her husband and children should not be discarded quite so smoothly.

Sarah spread wide in the double bed, her hands trailing the edge of the mattress on either side. The great house carried her quietly through the night.

Staff meetings at Priors Heath were held twice a term after school in the Boulder Library, the room Sarah feared more than any other. Her memory of it was sensitized by the hours she had spent there as a sixth-former. But of course the library had changed. Gone were the brown paper covers, the musty volumes of obscure essays nobody read, their Dewey number fastened to the spine with ageing Sellotape. Instead rows of glossy reference books and paperbacks gleamed above printed laminate labels. The shelving had been extended and computers installed.

Sarah's first staff meeting took place three weeks after she'd joined the history department. In a touching display of friendship Alison Atwood had saved her a place in the back row. Imogen sat a couple of metres from Sarah, flanked by her deputies, facing the staff. Was she deliberately avoiding eye contact, or was she simply oblivious to the fact that Sarah had come in? But how could she be when Sarah felt a physical jab of tension if Imogen was near? Indeed the possibility that she might at any moment encounter Imogen at Priors Heath added a piquancy to each day. But usually Sarah caught only glimpses of her loping across the quad, pale hair flying, or deep in conversation with a pupil, head ducked to minimize her great height.

Sarah's form had weekly assemblies in the Wyatt Hall with the Head. These were virtuoso performances by Imogen, amusing, topical and provocative. Her youthful audience was entranced by her extravagant gestures. Matthew Illingworth could perform a brilliant impression of Miss Taylor in full flood, arms flailing or a strand of hair thrust back with an impatient hand. But even he never forgot what she said and the same message was implicit behind every assembly. The pupils of Priors Heath were exhorted to make the most of each opportunity. They must discover their strengths and not waste time making excuses for poor performance. And they must be watchful and alert to the needs of others. A school should be a community intent on achievement by all, or it could not flourish.

'Was Imogen this driven when she was a pupil?' Alison had once asked Sarah.

'No. Far from it. She opted out of almost everything.'

These days Imogen's passion was electrifying.

It was evident this afternoon, however, that Imogen was ill at ease. She leant back in her chair and doodled whilst her most inept deputy Mike Morris fumbled to arrange his notes. Madeleine Stone sat slightly apart, her eyes fixed on the agenda. Imogen must feel quite isolated, Sarah thought. There was an evident lack of camaraderie among the senior management team.

'Tell me what you really think of Imogen,' Sarah murmured to Alison Atwood.

'What do you want to know?'

'Is she liked?'

'You've been here nearly a month now. What are your own perceptions?'

'People seem very loyal to her. But then they know our

166

relationship, so they would of course be careful in front of me.'

Alison considered Imogen for some moments with pale, calculating eyes. 'Imogen Taylor. No. She's not liked, but that's not her aim. She doesn't care a bean for popularity. She's obsessive about the kids and people respect that. Before she came eighteen months ago the school was plodding along, just about OK. We did our best. Then she arrived and set the place alight. There's not a single aspect of school life she hasn't overturned. She's critical, angry and hates incompetence. Several of the staff have been hounded into offering their resignation and we've all had to work much harder so of course we complain. She sometimes asks too much. It's the same with the kids. She drives them. She encroaches on their spare time and makes them get involved with sports and activities – all run by us of course. But though some kids hate it, most thrive. Imogen's like a shot in the arm.'

So, thought Sarah, all Imogen's energy is now concentrated on her career. It was characteristic of her that wherever the ruthless spotlight of her attention fell the subject of her regard would either curl up and crisp, like a spring bloom in the midday sun, or emerge more resilient, charged by her vitality.

Even Sarah, a newcomer, had detected that all was not well between staff and management. Resentment was bubbling to the surface.

'We note, Imogen, that the carol service at the end of term has been shortened by a quarter of an hour this year. Why is that?' The questioner was Malcolm Long, head of PE, bull-headed and surly. There was an expectant silence. Antagonism crackled.

'To minimize disruption. Previously the service has extended across break and beyond.'

'But surely the festival of Christmas might be allowed to interrupt the timetable a little.'

'A little, yes.' Imogen acknowledged her own refusal to compromise with a smile while Mike Morris studiously made a note in the minutes. Malcolm spread wide his hands as if to say: You see? What can you do?

The eighth item on the agenda was labelled 'Sports Hall'. Alison nudged Sarah and scribbled: *Watch out!!! Mike Morris tipped us off about this.* When Imogen began to speak it was immediately obvious that this was the real focus of the meeting. Pens were still, backs straightened, expressions frozen.

'We need a new sports hall. I don't have to tell you that the halls and gyms are desperately overbooked, particularly in winter. Our problem up to now has been funds. But the governors have agreed a site behind the Ryder Street Block and now someone has come up with an idea for raising the cash.' ('Imogen herself, I bet,' muttered Alison.) 'We could sell the site known as the rose garden, which is prime for development. As you know, Tesco is sniffing round the old brewery and hopes to build a supermarket there. They've actively expressed interest in the garden which would give them more car parking space.'

Sarah's mind was fogged with disbelief. How could Imogen do this? How could she even consider it? The rose garden was sacred. Not just for every pupil who'd ever been in the school but for Sarah especially, and for Imogen who had saved her.

Surely Imogen would look at her now. A flicker of apology, perhaps? Imogen, do you remember nothing? she wondered.

Glenys Morgan, head of Year 9, garbed in purposeful grey slacks and a lemon acrylic jumper, shot up her hand. She had been in the school for nearly two decades and her dislike of Imogen was palpable. 'You cannot possibly sell the garden site. It's an area of great historic interest like this library and the rest of the Old House. You'll never get planning permission.'

'The local council and the governors are divided, of course. They acknowledge the importance of Priors Heath in the history of girls' education but they also understand the shortage of funds. We can't even afford to maintain the garden properly.'

Sarah thought Imogen was like a great round stone, gathering momentum as she rolled onwards.

'This is only a suggestion,' Imogen added, tapping her papers together. 'There will be plenty of opportunity for discussion. But whenever I'm doubtful about something I think of Bess Hardemon and what she would have done. She would always have put the welfare of her pupils first.'

What right has she to play that card? wondered Sarah. When did Imogen Taylor ever have a morsel of respect for Bess Hardemon? Who had worn the school emblem, a white rose issued to the girls on Founder's Day, stuck behind her ear or in her sock? Who had taken the opportunity, every Founder's Day, of an unofficial half-holiday after lunch? How typically arrogant of Imogen to have been given the temporary stewardship of a school that had existed for generations, and yet to feel able to demolish part of its history which ought to be a bequest to the future.

Safe in her enclave of fellow teachers Sarah watched Imogen with some hostility but as the meeting drew to a close it occurred to her that Imogen was once more where she had always been at Priors Heath, on the outside. It was as if by perching on the edge, an onlooker, she was allowing herself the option of taking flight unhampered by emotional ties.

On her way out Sarah moved deliberately close to Imogen, wishing to show by some smile or gesture that however much she was personally wounded by her plans, she retained a degree of affectionate sympathy.

Imogen did indeed catch Sarah's eye and even came up. 'Sarah, I need a word with you about a pupil. I believe you're free period six tomorrow so I'll see you then.' And she was gone, on to the next matter.

Sarah had a double free lesson on a Wednesday afternoon and during period five the next day she sat alone in her classroom, knees pressed to a radiator. Before her were the thirty exercise books in which her Year 7 group had written their 'Castle Diary' (or 'Dairy', most wrote) as lords, ladies, prisoners, archers or kitchen maids, according to taste.

'Ms Beckett. May I come in? Do you mind?' Sonia Castelino stood tentatively at the door in a huge, shapeless jumper that contrived to make her look vulnerable and soft-fleshed.

'Of course I don't mind.'

'I have a big favour to ask you. It's about my art project.' She wove her way among the desks on which chairs had been slammed upside-down by the last class. 'Have you a moment?'

Already Sarah had grown used to conflict between a desire to get on top of all the marking, preparation and administration and the need to spend as much time as possible with the pupils themselves. Now she felt irritation at being interrupted coupled with pleasure that Sonia had bothered to come and find her.

'What it is, you see, I want to paint you.'

'What?'

'In "A" level art we have to do a number of special projects, and build up portfolios and sketch-books for each one. At the moment, as I told you, I'm working on Christina Lytton. Specifically my task is to find out why she is so little known. Is it that she's been consistently underrated because she was a woman, or simply that she's mediocre?' Sonia was producing sheafs of papers from her folders; pages of handwritten notes, coloured prints, sketches and photocopies.

'Mr Fenster and I have been working through the school archives together. He's amazed the school doesn't make more of its links with Lytton.'

Sarah watched as the girl's quick, flawless fingers leafed through the papers. She is deliciously young and dewy, she thought, like a velvety rose. I was never so ripe and self-assured at eighteen. I was prickly and afraid. If I have a wish for Lorna it is that she will be like Sonia appears to be now, personable and clear-headed. But the memory of Lorna brought misery.

Lorna, in Sarah's head, was sepia-toned and two-dimensional compared to this vivid girl. What was Lorna doing at this moment? Did she ever think of Sarah?

'You see, what I have to do is plot her development as a painter in relation to her contemporaries. So I'm going to focus on one particular picture and find out everything I can about it. And then I have to try and paint something similar myself, so I can show her technique. Mr Fenster says the best way of discovering how a painting was done is to try and do one like it. We don't know much about Lytton's formal training as an artist, you see, so by deconstructing a painting I'll be able to tell how much she might have relied on instinct, how much on technique.'

'I see.'

'I could have chosen one of her most famous, like "The Gatehouse", but there's such an obvious link between me and Christina Lytton it seems silly not to use it. We're both pupils of Priors Heath so I'm going to explore the portrait of Bess Hardemon, which also of course happens to be uniquely access-ible to me. Mr Fenster says Lytton couldn't have had much time to sketch Miss Hardemon, I mean you can't imagine a headmistress agreeing to sit for long, so she must have done a lot from memory. I've got to try the same with a teacher of my own. We'll even be able to date the portrait perhaps for the first time. We've trawled through all the archives but there's no reference to it. Christina's name is on an old 1845 register and there's stuff about the stained glass, but that's all there is.'

'Well, I'm very flattered you thought of me.'

'Oh don't be. You're sort of the same age as Bess Hardemon in the picture, well, you know, between young and middle-aged, so that helps.'

'Thank you very much.'

'That's not the only reason, don't worry. You have a really good face.'

'Sonia, what if you find that Lytton was very mediocre after all? Isn't there a risk that you'll spend months on someone who's not very good when you might have been studying any of a thousand great painters?'

'Oh, I have to look at her contemporaries too, to understand what influenced her. The portfolio will be very detailed. But I already know she's a brilliant painter. I love her work. And besides, I identify with her so much not just because of this school but because of what she did. She was so brave, such a free spirit. That's why Mr Fenster thinks she's a good subject for me. He reckons I'll understand her. Look, here's her portrait by H. Nelson O'Neil. It's supposed to be a good likeness. We think it was done just after her marriage.' Lytton's face in the portrait conformed to the Victorian ideal of smooth features, large, almond eyes and a full, submissive mouth.

It was typical of Sonia that once she had achieved her purpose she would sweep away. 'Anyway, that's all. Thank you. I'll let you go now as I think you've got a meeting.' And with brisk, deft movements the papers were gathered up. Sonia was an extraordinary mixture of assurance and diffidence so that one moment she'd be on the brink of tears because of a less than brilliant grade, the next she'd be lofty and almost arrogant in her obsessive pursuit of excellence.

I wonder which is the true girl, Sarah thought, as they set off together along the corridor.

It was only after they had parted in the New Building that she paused to wonder how on earth Sonia had known that she had a meeting with Imogen.

'Miss Taylor is with the chair of governors but I'm sure she'll be free soon.'

Power. The threads of Sarah's time were entwined in Imogen's fingers. Imogen was in a meeting so Sarah must wait. She withdrew a folder of marking from her bag while phones rang, a photocopier whirred and clunked and Imogen's door remained firmly closed. How had the scheme of things gone so adrift, thought Sarah, that it was Imogen who now occupied the hallowed office on the administration corridor, whilst Sarah, a mere temporary teacher with no real influence on the life of the school, hurtled from one classroom to the next buffeted by an endless stream of noisy pupils?

She became increasingly agitated. Imogen's request that they meet had extended shadowy tentacles over the last twenty-four hours. What was the matter? Sarah was consumed by the familiar dread of being found wanting.

When at last she was allowed into Imogen's office there was no awkwardness after all. Rising smoothly Imogen gestured Sarah to one of a pair of low seats while she rested against the front of her desk, elbows bent, back hunched. There was no smile in deference to their shared history. Imogen's narrow fingers drew a blue folder across the desk.

'One of your tutor group swore at Robin Fenster, I understand.'

'What? Oh, I see. Yes, three weeks ago. On my first day.'

'The incident has only just been brought to my notice. I gather that Robin sent him out. He should have gone to his head of year but instead he came to you.' Imogen cocked her head to one side and waited, an eyebrow lifted, rather as Sarah might look at Matthew Illingworth.

'Yes.'

'And you never reported the incident.'

'I gave Matthew a series of detentions.'

'In this school swearing at a teacher triggers an immediate suspension which lasts until I've held an interview with the parents and a letter of apology has been sent by the pupil.' Imogen was every inch the headmistress, unassailably right. Her voice was clipped and smooth. 'There have been a number of complaints from parents concerning art lessons with Robin Fenster which I obviously can't share with you but one was specifically about this incident. The father was outraged by the fact that a boy had shouted an obscenity in his son's lesson.'

'Only "fucking". Surely . . .'

'And that apparently no disciplinary action had been taken. So I've had to interview Robin Fenster, and the head of year, and the boy.'

Sarah was thirteen again, rowing with Imogen. She was tempted to sneer: bully for you.

'Have you got a copy of the staff handbook?'

'Of course.'

'What I wanted to say was, please read it and try to follow it, especially the code of conduct for pupils.'

'I've kept a careful watch on Matthew since then,' Sarah protested. 'He spent three lunch-breaks with me. I think I made the point.'

'You may well have done. But he needed to know that such behaviour was absolutely unacceptable to everyone in the school. You took too much upon yourself.'

For a moment they stared at each other, stony-faced. It occurred to Sarah that they were role-playing, as once they had crouched over the tape recorder in her bedroom at home. As soon as the machine was switched on they had become quite separate, intent on performance.

'Imogen, I don't understand. Why are you talking to me like this, as if you don't know me at all?'

It was almost as if she were a lover bewildered by her part-ner's sudden withdrawal of affection. Her question, once asked, seemed a huge risk, flung across the chasm created by the years they had never communicated with each other. For the first time it struck Sarah how very deliberate those years of silence had been on both sides. Whenever she'd been tempted to write to Imogen she had hesitated long enough for the urge to disappear. It had been like lifting the lid on a cauldron bubbling with dangerous memories and dropping it firmly shut again.

Imogen was apparently impervious to all this. 'My greatest concern of all is for Matthew. I want each child in this school to feel cherished and by that I mean made completely secure, as well as encouraged. It doesn't help Matthew if he's allowed to win a confrontation with a teacher. No incident of bad behaviour should get past us. And the other problem is Robin Fenster who is having extraordinary difficulties because he doesn't know where to draw the line. Teaching, as you know, is a matter of fine tuning. You seem to have no discipline problems and have proved to be both popular and competent with young people. It must be hard for you see how far Robin puts himself in danger.'

The compliment was unsettling. Sarah's mood shifted again. 'All right. I apologize if I acted out of turn. And actually, now I'm here, I wondered if I might have a word with you about the rose garden.' Imogen would not meet her eye. There was a pulse of understanding, a resonance. Surely Imogen had felt it too.

'I know. You protest. I thought you would.'

You. You. *I thought you would.* In a fleeting moment of joy Sarah understood that Imogen had thought of her enough to anticipate her response.

'I do oppose its sale.'

'Of course.'

'Imogen, surely there are other ways of earning money for the school? We have to preserve the garden or Priors Heath will lose a great deal of what makes it special. And is a sports hall really that important?'

'It is to our kids. I want them to have the same opportunities as the selective school down the road where the Head only has to click his fingers at the parents' association for half a million to be raised. Most of our parents don't have that kind of money. I won't refuse pupils admission to Priors Heath because they haven't got the right brains or background so I have to find other ways of funding the school.'

'Are you sure you don't have a vendetta against anything middle class, including the tradition of this school? I always had the impression that you rather despised Priors Heath because everyone in it had money.'

175

'I have a vendetta against snobbery, sure. I would rather people didn't have privileges simply because they can afford them.' Imogen indicated that the interview was over by returning to her chair behind the desk. Her fine straight hair fell over her ear and across her cheek. By a mere tilt of the head she had always been able to flick this fine curtain between herself and Sarah. She looked up one last time, as if slightly surprised that Sarah should still be in the room and gave a quick, preoccupied smile to suggest that already her thoughts were far away.

Sarah ran down the wide staircase and jumped the last three steps, desperate now to be away from Imogen. In her portrait the stern-eyed Miss Hardemon was ready with a further scolding: 'You were trying to provoke a scene. Naughty girl. Consider yourself well and truly chastised.'

Sarah went up to the picture and stared at Bess Hardemon, face to face.

Sonia suggests there are some parallels between us but I hardly think so, she thought. Heaven help me, I wish I had your certainty.

10

Autumn 1858

The girls at Miss Hardemon's school in Faringford, now known as Priors Heath School for Girls, came to Bess as empty vessels, or rather vessels into which a few dried beans of information had been dropped indiscriminately. As Bess remarked to George Peachey, their ignorance was beyond belief.

At first the curriculum she planned for them was wildly over-ambitious. They knew next to nothing and she wanted them to understand everything. On the same morning the girls might be propelled from Herschel's outlines of astronomy to an elementary drawing lesson and then on to analysis of English grammar or a potted history of the church in medieval England. The atmosphere was frenetic and tense, the hours punctuated by a handbell and by the sight of flocks of girls scurrying in silence up and down the main white staircase or along the narrow passages at the back of the house.

Within a year building had begun on a new boarding house. Bess, for whom the presence of boarders on the top floor of the old house was a terrible reminder of her first period at the school, was adamant that they must be moved out as soon as possible. She hated her lessons to be disturbed by the clash of pans from the kitchens and by the knowledge that some of her girls were separated by only a thin ceiling from where they slept. To her mind domestic arrangements must be kept quite separate from the academic. She argued that the girls were coming from homes where their education was not taken at all seriously, but crammed into odd gaps between calls, caring for young sisters or other domestic chores. At Priors Heath their academic education was all that mattered. There must be no distractions.

But above all she needed the rooms formerly taken up by laundries, sculleries and dormitories to accommodate her swelling numbers.

Finances were always stretched to the limit. The Board did its best but Bess was never satisfied. First the classrooms must be refurbished with secondhand desks Peachey had begged from a London boys' school, and oil heaters must be bought to warm the freezing rooms. The school must be painted from top to bottom and books, the most precious commodity of all, must be acquired. Mrs Penhaligon had found a local lady, Miss Boulder, who would come in two afternoons a week to manage the accounts. Within a month she was working full-time in a tiny office next to Bess. Every drop of ink was measured out by Miss Boulder, every last farthing counted, but still the school was constantly in the red.

By the second year things had calmed down. The upper and professional classes of Faringford had decided that Priors Heath was a good thing for their daughters. To educate a girl there cost less than the price of a governess and better still she returned in the evening brimful of knowledge to pass on to her young siblings. Once Mrs Penhaligon had persuaded her friend Lady Edgbaston not only to send her daughter Constance to the school but also to sit as one of the two lady governors on the Board, all the best families were lining their daughters up for admission. There were still bursaries for the daughters of poor clergymen but these soon became a minority. Wealthy parents were shocked that their girls had to sit an entry test for Priors Heath and were only mollified by Mrs Penhaligon's argument that such a precaution would ensure that none of the illiterate lower classes would gain a place.

Concerned for the poor physical condition of her charges,

not just the undernourished clergy daughters but the lazy girls of richer families, Bess had instituted a regime of daily exercise. The garden became pivotal to the life of the school. Much of it was replanted with rose-bushes and shrubs but some beds were left to the boarders who each had her own patch of soil to maintain in the spring evenings. After lunch the entire school was expelled into the fresh air and made to walk or play in the garden or to use the swing bought by Bess against the better judgement of Mrs Penhaligon. On wet days the cellars were used for skipping or hoops. No one in the school, pupil or teacher, had a moment to call her own from eight-thirty in the morning until four in the afternoon.

Bess's greatest problem was the recruitment of staff. After the first term when it became apparent that the school would definitely thrive, there was a constant flow of applicants but none of them had any formal training and few were educated beyond village or dame school standard. There was such a dearth of suitable textbooks that almost all the teaching had to be done by lectures so it was essential that teachers knew what they were talking about. Bess insisted on offering a gener-ous salary and unthinkably lenient conditions of service includ-ing a few hours' free time each day for resident teachers but there were pathetically few women with anything like sufficient skills.

Fortunately the school was close enough to London for part-time male teachers to be lured out by the vague idea that they were part of something important, and by Bess's unquenchable enthusiasm. Provided these men were clergymen nobody raised any objection. Even lazy Gerald Hardemon found himself teaching a regular two days a week of classics and Italian at Priors Heath. He was rather charmed by the rows of young ladies in pinafores who drank in his rambling but humorous discourses on Homer or Dante.

A more dedicated lecturer was George Peachey, who had proved to be a powerful and committed ally. He could charm any parent into donating funds and had a vast network of acquaintances among the more radical clergy and intellectuals in London. He made his living as a teacher at King's but he was also a writer and essayist, his extraordinary mind leapfrogging from one topic to the next with boundless energy, always interested, always excited. His greatest passion was for the railway and by train he travelled all over the country giving lectures and gleaning material for his articles on the morality of the new industrial age. But he was also firmly committed to the cause of educational reform. He had once hinted to Bess of a brutal and joyless boyhood at a famous boarding school.

One further stalwart was Caroline Wentworth who had been a young pupil when Bess had first taught at Priors Heath and who had since taught English conversation in a school in Paris. Her French was faultless, which was just as well for Bess insisted on the entire school conversing in that language on Tuesdays. Miss Wentworth was devoted to Bess and was one of the few female teachers who came anywhere near satisfying her exacting demands.

Meanwhile Bess could sense that her own character was maturing and expanding. It was as if for years she had been confined to a small room where her voice was muffled, her mind bound and her limbs constrained. For a year or two after her earlier dismissal from Priors Heath she had fumbled for purpose. Now her way was clear. Every day presented her with new obstacles but nothing pulled her down for long. Mrs Penhaligon had been true to the undertakings she had given in Laetitia's drawing room. Priors Heath was Bess's domain and she reigned in it supreme. Furthermore, her faith in the guiding hand of Jesus Christ was once more rock solid, and together she knew they were a force to be reckoned with.

In fact, in the autumn of 1858, two and a half years after her arrival in the school, things were going so well for Bess that she was contemplating a holiday. There was a reliable flow of funds from fees and endowments, and best of all a waiting list of pupils. Two hundred and five girls were now on the register. She wrote to her father in the rectory at Mereby Bridge that she was thinking of taking a two-week break at Christmas.

On Friday afternoons Bess taught history to the senior girls. The knowledge that she could teach in whatever style she chose was still intoxicating and she loved to combine lecturing with moralizing.

'Queen Elizabeth the First. Now, she is an historical character both to admire and criticize. Emily Cathcart, sit up. Slouching is the sign of a weak mind and a sickly body. Elizabeth succeeded her sister, Mary Tudor. Rachel Vaughan, the date of Mary's death, if you please? Very good.

'Of all those we have studied in history thus far, girls, I think the figure of Elizabeth is of the greatest relevance to you. Her upbringing was not ideal in any respect except that she received a classical training as fine as any boy's, which was just as well. This education enabled her mind to be so clear and rational that she could outwit many who wished her dead. For instance, had Queen Elizabeth not been an educated woman the Catholics might have succeeded in their plot to put Mary, Queen of Scots on the throne. And then we would all have ended up Roman Catholic. Imagine.'

This is poor teaching, Bess reflected, a rambling and speculative introduction to Elizabeth. But it was late on a dull, Friday afternoon and the girls needed a little anecdote to keep their attention.

'Here I have a print of Queen Elizabeth.' She held up a heavy book containing a tiny woodcut borrowed from her father. 'What do we learn from this picture?' Her eyes darted about the classroom. 'Constance Edgbaston?'

Constance peered at the print, her mouth heavy with reluctance. 'She's wearing a very large collar and has a tiny waist.'

'Yes, Constance. It was Queen Elizabeth's misfortune to rule her country dressed in such a tight bodice that she must have had difficulty breathing, let alone thinking. As I have frequently told you, the wearing of stays is detrimental to both mental and physical well-being.' She paused for the inevitable exchange of glances between the girls, who thought her obsessively critical of the modern fashion for minute waists and crinolines. Well, let them laugh, she decided, it's a small price to pay for ensuring they have healthy bodies. They'll thank me one day.

Emily Cathcart, hardly the brightest child, was now gazing out at the frost-bitten garden. 'Emily, if you can't resist the temptation to stare out of the window you'll have to sit next to the wall. Perhaps you would comment on the significance of the Queen's collar, known as a ruff.' But Bess's own gaze had now been caught by a figure near the sundial. Tall and thin, he stood quite motionless in the freezing air. Some of the other girls had also noticed him and were peering out.

'Girls. Inattention is the greatest discourtesy you can offer an adult. Face this way.'

The clang of the handbell came, shattering in its proximity. Bess made a mental note to speak to the housemaid responsible. In silence the girls packed their books away, in silence they stood until Miss Hardemon had wished them good afternoon and in silence they marched out.

The figure in the garden was Reverend Thomas Carnegie, who had been away in Africa since Bess's return to Priors Heath, but was now home due to ill health. A visit to the school had long been expected for he was still a trustee and a generous benefactor. In fact, as Bess was rather galled to admit, Priors Heath could hardly have survived even under her careful stewardship without his money.

The knowledge that he was now actually on the premises was deeply disturbing. By the time she had tidied her desk and straightened the chairs in the schoolroom the last girl was gone from the entrance hall. There was no movement on the stairs or the landing above, yet she felt Carnegie's dark presence.

On this same polished floor he had once trodden on silent feet to trap the young, upstart Miss Hardemon in the garden and thereby secured her downfall.

All sound was ebbing from the school. The day girls had put on their outdoor shoes and left for home while the boarders crossed the paved yard to the new boarding house. And as the absence of these modern girls filtered into the hall, Bess thought that a spectre of the old Priors Heath seemed to hover like grey cobwebs in the cornices above her and in the schoolroom at her back; a forlorn atmosphere of confined female flesh and too much failure and bad temper. For almost the first time since her appointment as Headmistress she felt weary to the bone.

The energetic maid, Mary, the ringer of the handbell, emerged from beneath the stairs. 'There's a Reverend Carnegie to see you. Miss Boulder said to put him in your office and bring tea.'

Bess felt the sweat prickle at the back of her neck where her hair lay in its heavy coil. I care nothing for his opinion, she thought. He can't harm me now. She wished he hadn't been shown into her office but since the old boardroom had been converted into a classroom there was nowhere else to entertain him. She took several deep breaths, straightened her back and went upstairs.

The door-handle, hip high to most people, was by Bess's waist and she felt more than usually conscious of her small frame which put her at chest level to Carnegie. He was at the window, his black figure dominating her little, unornamented room. She saw all her familiar possessions: the Bible beside the bentwood chair brought from her bedroom in the rectory; her diary; the inkstand presented by her father on her first day as Headmistress; and her instinct was to gather them up and protect them from Carnegie's censorious gaze.

From below came the sound of young voices as two more boarders spilled across the paved square. Bess suddenly felt a pang of longing for her own curtailed girlhood, a run in the woods on a winter afternoon, the rectory drawing room, her mother's old tea service and the luxury of a long read before supper.

Frost seemed to have clung to Carnegie. His nose was reddened by cold though the rest of his chiselled features were tanned by years in Africa. He had thrown his heavy black cloak across a chair and an acrid smell of freezing dusk lay in the room. Bess crooked her neck to look directly up into his face and noted that his mouth, if possible, had become more rigid. His hair had a slight glint of silver and his eyes were as blue and unsmiling as ever. He held himself as ramrod straight as she.

Bess had been subjected to several eulogies on the subject of the Reverend Carnegie by Mrs Penhaligon and knew that here was a man who spent his life labouring tirelessly for the good of the poor and destitute at home and abroad. Since his return to London only three months ago he had set up a mission and a soup kitchen. It was said that he had already turned down several offers of promotion in the Church so that he could continue to work for the poor. But what do the destitute think of the cold hand of charity that he extends to them, Bess wondered, and why can't he manage one cheerful smile?

'Reverend Carnegie.'

'Miss Hardemon.' He had not taken his eyes from her face since she first came into the room. His expression was unreadable and in turn she looked at him with the chilly gaze usually reserved for the most lazy and careless of her pupils. The pall of anger and bitterness in which they had parted nine years ago hung between them.

She sat on her upright chair and poured tea. 'Do please be seated.'

He remained standing. Her movements became brisker. She lifted the sugar tongs and raised her eyebrows questioningly.

Then, when he still made no move she got up and placed a cup in his hand. 'Reverend, have you taken the opportunity to tour the school?'

'I have visited the new boarding house.'

'Paid in part by your very generous gift when the school was reopened,' Bess murmured in a remote little voice.

His eyes were now anywhere but on her face. 'It has all been a great surprise.'

'I hope a pleasant surprise.'

He didn't drink his tea but stood with the little cup and saucer in his big hand as if fixed to the spot, his eyes still on her.

'You may wish to look at the accounts,' she said.

'I am told all is in order.'

'As you know, we have been through difficult times. Even now we exist from term to term. We have nothing saved, nothing to protect us in an emergency. It's no way to run a school.'

No word of reassurance was forthcoming and it occurred to Bess for the first time that the Reverend's sculptured features might actually be so rigid because behind them was a very limited intelligence. Perhaps he was inflexible because he was too stupid to behave otherwise. The thought comforted her.

'And you, Reverend, have been in Africa.'

'Yes.'

'Did you find your work there rewarding?'

'Oh, very.'

The entire continent of Africa, which in Bess's mind was full of colour and heat, exotic and unreachable, was quenched by the Reverend's flat voice and made as dull as the description in the textbook.

'Perhaps one day you'd speak to the girls about your work. I like them to hear from people who have travelled.'

But no sooner had Bess issued this invitation than she

became so irritated that she had to get up and move about the room. She didn't want this man corrupting her girls and poisoning their enthusiasms with his crushing brand of Christianity. Her agitation brought her closer to Carnegie and she was immediately aware that his frame was almost vibrating with tension. Did he find the changes at Priors Heath so intolerable? Or was it that he couldn't bear the thought of Bess being in charge?

She managed another question. 'Have you anything you wish to ask before I show you what we've done to modernize the school?'

He seemed to speak from a great distance. 'Yes. Yes. There is one matter. I believe Mrs Penhaligon —'

'Ah, yes.' Reverend Carnegie, you disgust me, thought Bess. How dare you so much as set foot in my school after the damage you did to generations of girls? And now you want to interfere again. 'Mrs Penhaligon mentioned that you were worried about the girls being taught by gentlemen in subjects other than mathematics and theology. Is that so? Reverend, I must tell you that the standard of education for girls up until now has been so poor that there are few women qualified to teach. I have to use whoever is willing and able to help, at least until some of my own students are old enough to become teachers themselves.'

'The character of these particular men —'

'They are all three clergymen. One is my own brother.' Of the two other male teachers one was the aged Reverend Michael Foreman, dry as a bone, who occasionally lectured the girls in church history. There could be little doubt, therefore, that the object of Carnegie's disapproval must be Peachey, presumably because of his many secular areas of study.

Carnegie gave a deep sigh.

'Have you any other questions? Very well.' Resentment coiled like a snake inside her. She rose briskly, removed the untouched cup and saucer from his hand and whisked from the room. Just wait until I tell George Peachey, she thought. He'll be delighted to hear that Carnegie has been casting aspersions on his character. She smiled to herself, already relishing the anticipated conversation with Peachey and the laughter they would share.

His ponderous tread followed her along the passage as she flung open the nearest door. 'Here we have the school office. Perhaps you have heard that our secretary, Miss Boulder, gives her services for practically nothing. No, Helen, please don't get up.'

Helen Boulder occupied a cubbyhole, at one time perhaps a dressing or laundry room, now the administrative centre of the school. Bess glanced at the Reverend and gave him a reluctant nod of approval for not flinching at the sight of Helen's scarred face.

Carnegie had extended his hand to Miss Boulder, another mark in his favour. Bess hurried him away. 'The stationery room. The sanatorium, very small, as you will see. I don't allow sickness. Here is classroom five.' She took him into one airy room after another. Miss Simmons wouldn't have recognized her bedroom which now had bare white walls, a map at one end, a dais and blackboard at another.

'This is the room I hope to make into a laboratory. We are living in the latter half of a century of invention and discovery. My girls must understand what's happening in their world.' Here Bess turned and glowered at the Reverend, in case he thought of protesting about the prospect of girls studying the sciences. He nodded.

The old dormitories had been converted into a sewing room and yet another classroom. 'Heat!' announced Bess triumphantly, pointing to the oil stoves.

Down two flights of narrow stairs she flew and out on to the ground floor. The kitchen had been made into a music room and the cellars into cloakrooms and a playroom. In the old schoolroom she showed him how the long, merciless benches had been banished to be replaced by double desks and chairs. The boardroom was now a middle school classroom. Does he remember, Bess thought, my last morning, and how he dismissed me? Here they were, side by side, in the entrance hall where they used to stand while she pleaded for small changes. She realized that she hadn't forgiven him at all.

'Finally, the library, which used to be the dining room.'

'Ah yes. I have had several conversations about the library.'

Her lips tightened. Stocking the library had been a contentious matter, with money so short she had to rely on contributions from parents. Mrs Penhaligon had recommended a lady who might be prepared to catalogue the books; Mrs Briskin, whose husband, a bank manager, was very well respected in the town and a member of the Board. Although this lady was willing and efficient, her approach to reading was maddening and puritanical. She banned modern novelists and worried about the girls being given access to philosophy and theology. 'They will start wondering. Girls' minds are not equipped to wonder.'

Carnegie, who looked warily at the titles on the shelves as if afraid one of them might leap up and assault his virtue, suddenly extended a surprisingly strong and roughened hand to withdraw a copy of *The Merchant of Venice*. 'Shakespeare makes very robust reading for young ladies. Is this an edited edition?'

'Don't you find Shakespeare's language beautiful, Reverend?'

'Beautiful?'

'Doesn't it stir you?'

'Stir?' A flush was rising to his cheeks. He moved away from her. 'Yes, I believe I was on occasions moved. It's a very long time . . .'

'Reverend, I don't pretend to be an expert on literature but my father, a clergyman, ensured that I was given free access to all the writers he considered great, ancient and modern, British and European. I believe that through reading my powers of imagination, judgement and understanding have been immeasurably improved. Furthermore, I know that my girls are emotional creatures, destined to love and suffer. I want them to know that they are not alone in these experiences. Literature will teach them what it is to be human.'

He was actually backing towards the door.

'I shall speak to Mrs Penhaligon,' he said.

And I shall speak to Reverend Peachey, Bess thought, and ask him to do battle with Mrs Briskin. This nonsense over what books are suitable for the library must stop. Of course the girls must read Dickens, Coleridge and Blake.

But as she closed the library door Bess understood that she and Carnegie had slipped into their old antagonism. At first he had bitten back any criticism but now the kid gloves were off and he was revealed as her enemy once more.

Carnegie was now heading for the front door, so anxious to leave that he'd forgotten his hat and cloak. 'Overall you are pleased with the school, I hope?' Bess persisted but didn't wait for a reply because she had noticed Mary deep in conversation with George Peachey himself.

As usual the sight of Peachey made Bess feel less burdened. He was so humorous and loyal, so unfailingly interested in every aspect of her work.

'Ah, I believe you and Reverend Peachey are old acquaintances,' she exclaimed mischievously.

Peachey, smiling and courteous, put out his hand though Bess was struck by the unusually wary expression in his eye. 'Carnegie. You're back at last. Delighted to see you.' Carnegie responded with the faintest of nods and there followed an absurd moment when all three waited in silence for another to speak. Bess, glancing up at Carnegie, noted that his gaze was fixed to a spot an inch or so above Peachey's head.

'Well, I was on my way,' Peachey exclaimed cheerily. 'Can I offer you a ride, Carnegie?'

'Thank you, no.'

'Very well.' Peachey actually seemed to retreat, bowing and

smiling until he reached the door where Mary still waited, eyes big with curiosity.

Bess, disconcerted by Peachey's retreat, was now left to deal with Carnegie who apparently intended to stand in the hall indefinitely. 'Will you be dining with us tonight, Reverend?' she asked, her voice dulled by sudden weariness. The thought of a meal shared with Carnegie filled her with dread. The food would turn to gall in her mouth.

'Thank you, no, I have visits to make. A cousin in Faringford is expecting me.'

'Of course.' Bess gestured to Mary who set off in search of his hat and cloak. While they waited Carnegie read a list on the notice-board by the door while Bess stood by with her hands folded and her mouth fixed in a small smile. At last Mary reappeared with his things and he left, sliding out into the dark, a grim spectre from the past.

Bess stood alone on the stairs, head thrown back, her hand clasping firmly the polished rail. It was as if she had defended her domain against the barbarian. But though triumphant she was bruised and battle-stained. She climbed the stairs.

'Tea, Helen. I need tea.'

Helen Boulder brought fresh cups and rang the bell for hot water. Meanwhile Bess whisked about tidying papers and adjusting the furniture. 'You'd not met Carnegie before, I suppose. Dreadful man. What did you think of him, Helen?'

'He seemed very reserved.'

'Reserved!' She laughed. 'Do you know, that's the unkindest thing you've ever said about anyone.'

Helen smiled. 'A letter came for you this afternoon, marked confidential. I didn't open it.'

Abbey House
2nd November, 1858

Dear Miss Hardemon,
    It is many months . . . It is many months since I wrote. I've been very ill.

My spirits are so low. I can only think of how much I would love to receive a letter from you.

Christina Lytton

Dear Miss Hardemon,

My wife begged me to write to you. I enclose her little note, which I think will show you only too clearly how weak she is.

It now seems probable, after the miscarriage of yet another child, that Christina will have no living children. She has taken the news very badly and her recovery has been painfully slow.

You are my last resort. Christina still speaks of you with great affection and I think if she spent some time with you she might revive a little. Could you accommodate her for a few weeks? All other devices have failed. Her mother and sisters don't seem able to help her. I will of course send her maid and reimburse you fully for any expenses you might incur. She is so low and quiet, I believe you will find her little enough trouble. For friendship's sake I believe you will help us.

Charles Lytton

Despite her success with the school, Bess woke each morning to momentary desolation. An annexe had been built to the boarding house with its own little garden and front door and here Bess lived on her own. Her experience as a young teacher had convinced her that she must have some privacy from the girls but such seclusion meant that every morning she faced solitude.

The quiet of Priors Heath was not the bird-loud peace of a dawn at home in Derbyshire. Birds did sing but the nearby town also made its presence felt in the rumble of cartwheels, the clang and cry of the weekly cattle market and the tread of many feet on their way to work. From her window Bess could see away to the left beyond the garden the chimneys of the brewery and the rolling Hertfordshire hills. No river ran in a steep valley, no woods rustled at the end of the drive, there were no high peaks.

On the morning of the Autumn Bazaar in mid November she dressed quickly and walked down to her parlour with its plain white walls and blue curtains. Already she had shaken off her sadness and the demands of the morning ahead were lighting sparks in her consciousness. She spent half an hour before breakfast in prayer, a habit learnt from her father. By keeping it up she knew that she was united with him as he knelt in the chill of the rectory study, the air heavy with last night's candle smoke.

Slowly the day's business took hold of her. 'Dear Lord, I commit into your hands my flawed and impulsive nature. Guide me in the decisions I must make and in the dealings I must have with so many young minds. Give me wisdom and patience to deal with the parents at this afternoon's bazaar. I wonder, did Helen Boulder order the extra teacups from White's. We ran very short last year. I pray for the poor and destitute to whom half the proceeds will be sent. Is half enough? The other half is for the assembly hall and we're desperately in need of that, but what is our lack of space compared to the starvation of orphaned children? Guide my teaching and my pen when I write. And, dear Lord, what am I to do with poor Christina Riddell, Mrs Lytton, who will arrive this morning?'

She then said a brisk 'Our Father', rose to her feet, patted her hair and went along to the dining room in the boarding house for breakfast.

> 'The trivial round, the common task,
> Will furnish all we ought to ask;
> Room to deny ourselves; a road
> To bring us, daily, nearer God.
> Only, O Lord, in thy great love
> Fit us for perfect rest above
> And help us this, and every day,
> To live more nearly while we pray.'

Miss Clatterboult's plump hands landed with their usual gusto on the last chord and the school subsided on to the floor with a collective sigh, like a forest of trees suddenly felled. The teachers sat eagle-eyed on chairs at the end of rows. Older girls were crushed against the doors and some were even forced out into the entrance hall.

Bess glared briefly at Emily Trowbridge, who had been whispering. The girl froze like a startled rabbit and went crimson.

'Today's reading was the story of Martha and Mary and Our Lord's visit to them. Of course, what is memorable about this Gospel is the way the Lord criticized Martha for bustling about, whilst Mary, who had done nothing, was praised for her holiness. I've always had great sympathy for Martha who was after all doing the best she could, though I expect she was the type who couldn't sit still, ever.' (Another forbidding stare at Emily Trowbridge.) 'There is a time for action and a time for contemplation. You modern girls at Priors Heath are given the opportunity to be both Martha and Mary. You must study, learn and listen attentively like Mary and then be busy like Martha, as you will be this afternoon at the bazaar. Can I remind you that the white covers for the tables should be collected from Miss Boulder at midday and not before. Incidentally, two girls yesterday were found wearing their outdoor shoes during afternoon school. Order marks were given.' Having strayed too far from Martha and Mary Bess added hastily: 'How can we be Mary, quietly attentive to our teachers, when there is mud in the classroom? Let us pray . . .'

Miss Clatterboult gave a turgid rendition of 'The March of the Queen of Sheba' as the school filed out in silence. Bess watched the girls' orderly exodus with pride and decided that their bloom of good health must in part be due to her insistence on regular exercise and woollen combinations.

Later that morning as she passed the library, Bess noticed that a flustered Mrs Briskin was deep in conversation with George

Peachey, his neat, slim figure providing a pleasing contrast to her bulging plumpness.

Bess paused and listened shamelessly.

'Whenever I come into this library,' exclaimed Peachey, 'I think: Oh, the joy of seeing a lady surrounded by books. A lady brings an immediate air of calm. Our great libraries should all be run by women, I feel.'

A simpering laugh from Mrs Briskin.

'I expect you have great difficulty choosing books suitable for the girls. But then you're probably better qualified than anyone. Your husband, I believe, is a magistrate?' Bess couldn't see Peachey but she imagined that all the warmth of his brown, kindly eyes would be directed on Mrs Briskin's loose-skinned face.

'Yes.' The reply was breathy.

'Mrs Briskin, you make great demands of our girls' intellects. Gibbon, Milton, Dr Johnson, and of course the Classics. My goodness, Homer. And for lighter reading? Now, that's where the danger lies, of course. Books which seem suitable for children because of the simplicity of their theme and language can be twice as seductive and damaging if they lack moral fibre.'

'I encourage the girls to read what I gave my own children.'

'Of course. Excellent. And I expect I will find Dickens and Kingsley, who so skilfully combine moral teaching with wonderful stories.' Bess knew quite well that neither author was in the library. 'And thank the Lord for Byron and Keats. So lucid in their understanding of the human mind.'

But Mrs Briskin was not quite so enchanted by Peachey that she could allow this to pass. 'We have no Byron in the library.'

'You do surprise me. It troubles me so much when I hear people say that a writer's work must be corrupt because his personal conduct is less than satisfactory.'

'Well, I . . .'

'We are all vessels for God's work. He has allowed each one of us, however frail, one precious gift or talent. It's easy to see,

Mrs Briskin, where your gift lies. Thank heavens he saw fit to give Byron, so flawed, poor man, the ability to write sublime poetry.'

Bess was shocked by the deftness of Peachey's onslaught. If he could be so outrageously insincere with Mrs Briskin, could he be trusted to be honest with anyone else? He continued: 'Our pupils must learn to be discerning readers, else how will they later be able to give proper guidance to their own children? You, I suppose, must read very widely, for you are the censor of all the books that arrive in this school. Dare I offer my assistance? Will you work with me?'

'Why, of course.'

'It will mean several hours in my company, I regret. Can you bear that?'

Bess never knew how Mrs Briskin responded to this outrageously flirtatious question for there was a commotion in the hall. The front-door bell had been rung with such violence that Miss Wentworth appeared from the schoolroom to see what was going on and Mary came hurtling out with her apron flying over her shoulder.

The weather that day was grey and sleety and when Mary opened the door all three women took a step back from the icy blast. Outside was a lady swathed in shawls, the hoop of her skirt extending halfway across the wide threshold. Her face was hidden by a heavy veil but its pale oval glimmered through the opaque folds. A coachman appeared, shouldering a trunk.

The woman swayed and her maid sprang to her side.

But Christina Lytton had already lifted her arms imploringly to Bess who hurried forward. 'Christina, my dear girl.' She gripped Christina's arm and felt its extreme thinness through layers of fabric. Christina fell against her. 'For goodness' sake don't faint in the hall. Come up to my office and have tea.'

Christina flung back her veil, her face emerging ghostly as a water spirit. Her eyes were huge and ringed by brownish circles. For a moment it struck Bess that Charles Lytton had understated her physical weakness and that she was dying.

But then Christina gave a sweet, lovely smile, even more extraordinary in the fleshless face. 'I wouldn't dare faint,' she murmured, and everyone laughed with relief.

Bess clasped Christina firmly round the waist and they walked slowly across the hall while Caroline Wentworth went reluctantly back to her class, perhaps a little disappointed that she hadn't been recognized by Christina despite their shared school-days. On their laborious ascent of the white staircase Bess noticed that below them stood Peachey and Mrs Briskin at the library door. Peachey's eyes were bright with interest. Bess smiled briefly down at him, gladdened by his ready sympathy and oddly pleased that he should witness Christina's deep affection for herself.

Christina had thoughts only for Bess. Her thin fingers clutched at Bess's shoulder. 'I can't believe that I'm actually here with you,' she whispered. 'It seems impossible that we should be climbing these stairs together.' Up and up they went on the white marble that had always been forbidden Christina when a pupil here. Bess was conscious of her own little figure supporting Christina's tall, light frame and the beautiful face above her own plain head.

After a drink of tea, Christina seemed much better. She had taken off her bonnet to reveal gleaming hair drawn into effortless coils over her ears and she wore a tiered crinoline gown which hung a little loosely at the waist and breast. Grief had given depth to her beauty. Two delicate creases on either side of her mouth now enhanced the curves of her lips, and her jaw was firmer.

She gave a deep sigh, looked at Bess and smiled. 'I can't tell you how grateful I am to you. Now I'm away I realize that the Abbey House itself was making me miserable. It's as if a great weight has been lifted.'

'I'm very glad to be of service.'

'Please, don't say that. It sounds so cold.'

'Goodness, Christina, I'm your friend. I wanted to help you.'

'Oh, such a friend.' She raised her hand to her eyes and tears fell. 'I'm so weak, so weak. But three babies. I've lost three. Oh, Miss Hardemon, how could God be so cruel? Tell me.'

Bess was silent. This was a very different Christina to the reserved girl she had last seen a week before her wedding. She had not anticipated such an open display of emotion. 'It is very hard.'

'I fought to keep them. Do you know that when I was very first with child I was so sick at times I doubted if I even wanted a baby? It all seemed so much trouble and I hated the way my body changed. And then in the seventh month when I lost her, when I had nothing of my hopes, no warm, precious, living baby, I understood that there could be no deeper joy in life than to bear a child and I thought maybe I was being punished for my vanity, for not wanting her enough in the first place.'

Bess's eyes strayed to the window. She was a little embarrassed and very uncomfortable. Conception, childbirth, confinement. These were areas of womanhood that happened behind doors closed to Bess. She did not like to confront too closely an area of life that she had deliberately rejected.

'So the next time I lay quietly in my room and prayed and prayed for a healthy child. Another baby grew. I felt him move and turn. But then he went still. I knew the instant he was dead. And now it's happened again. Another girl. I saw her, Miss Hardemon. She was perfect.'

In the face of such grief Bess felt unusually helpless. 'Your husband has been very concerned for you. He obviously cares about you deeply. That must be a comfort.'

'Charles has tried so hard to help. But the terrible thing is, Miss Hardemon, that all we had in common was the desire for a child and now even that's gone.'

Bess found this revelation unendurable. She remembered vividly the kiss under the gatehouse and Christina's eyes meeting her own to reveal a shocking detachment. I am required to feel sorry for this girl, Bess thought, yet I find her a little chilling. She has awoken in Charles Lytton feelings she'll never return. Suddenly Bess was struck by the idea that Christina might have been cruelly punished for her selfish marriage to Charles. But belief in such a vindictive God was not usually part of Bess's creed so she pushed the thought angrily away and asked gently: 'Your stepchildren?'

'My stepdaughter grieves too, poor thing.'

'She'll miss you, I should think, while you're here.'

'Yes, though she has a governess.'

'Poor child.' The thought of the isolated, motherless Rebecca distressed Bess even more than Christina's sorrow.

'To you I must seem very feeble.'

'No. Oh no.'

'I thought if I talked to you it would help. You at least would understand how narrow my life must be now, watching these children who aren't my own grow into adulthood, all my time frittered away on making calls and performing unnecessary household duties. It's so strange to be at Priors Heath again. I remember how unhappy I was here, and how homesick. Then you came and you changed me by showing me just a glimpse of how rich life could be. But when I went back home I allowed myself to be drawn into a marriage where I was expected to be quiet, undemanding and charming. No trouble to anyone. Well, I suspect I have been a great deal of trouble to poor Charles.'

'What about your painting?' Bess asked, hoping to raise her spirits a little.

'Do you know, Miss Hardemon, since the death of my second baby I have scarcely touched a paintbrush. I've been too sad.' With bent head she added: 'But through all my darkest hours I have remembered you.'

Bess was so moved that she crossed to Christina and took her in her arms. 'Perhaps here at least you will be able to paint,' she said, and actually kissed the top of her smooth head. My goodness, she thought, as she hurried downstairs to take a mathematics lesson, I don't believe I've kissed anyone outside the family for years. Her lips felt weighted by the touch of Christina's warm hair.

The Autumn Bazaar had a dual function. Not only did it raise money but it gave fond mothers the opportunity to see Priors Heath as they would like it to be. Books, maps and slates were put away and the desks arranged in long counters around the rooms so that the girls' handiwork could be displayed on starched white cloths.

Parents sent their girls to Priors Heath because they sensed Miss Hardemon was offering something enviable, but they were dismayed by the speed with which their daughters shed their dull acceptance of routine home life. Within weeks the girls began to acquire an understanding of subjects such as astronomy and literature, thereby leaving their mothers, and often their fathers and brothers, far behind. So it was a relief to find that the old skills of sewing and embroidery hadn't been abandoned altogether and that Miss Hardemon was aware of the fact that most of her charges would soon be married. The parents were pleased to see their daughters with brushed hair and neat frocks, proudly displaying the fruits of their labours: tea-cosies, pen-wipers, lavender bags, pillow-cases, miniatures in twig frames, collages, woven purses, even home-made biscuits and cakes. Nor could any fault be found with the girls' deportment. They moved about with deft, assured movements in the service of their elders.

Bess, who had stationed herself in an unobtrusive corner of the schoolroom, watched the proceedings somewhat wryly. The success of her modern school depended on old snobberies. All the town was here, from the Honourable Mrs Godalming, whose daughter Clarice was prettily displaying an array of cross-stitch samplers, to Lady Edgbaston, the fourth daughter of an earl and mother of Constance. These ladies were dressed in their second-best afternoon gowns, their status as much marked by the circumference of their crinolines as by the particular social ranking of their associates. There were a few gentlemen, mostly members of the Board, though thankfully Carnegie was not present. Mrs Penhaligon was in her element sailing about in formidable chocolate brown satin as if personally responsible for all the good things the school had produced.

Bess and her teachers stood outside this strict pecking order, rather like clerics at a church sale. As Headmistress, Bess was generally at ease with parents and pupils but when her role was less defined, on an afternoon such as this, she was more defensive, even afraid. The mothers and daughters were engrossed in a ritual that had little to do with Bess Hardemon who was in some ways just another servant appointed to ensure that the outer gloss of life was polished and lovely. A few years ago Miss Simms had stood in the same apparently unassailable position of Headmistress. Some day a whim of fashion might oust Miss Hardemon just as ruthlessly.

Much to Bess's alarm, she now noticed that Mrs Penhaligon was near at hand and had been taken aside by her great friend, Mrs Godalming. Ominously, they had waived an offer of tea and cake. Bess tried to escape into the entrance hall but she had left it too late. The two women were now actually bearing down upon her.

Mrs Godalming had a deceptively genial face, generally wreathed in smiles. This afternoon as she approached Bess her lower lip was caught firmly between her teeth and her eyebrows were raised in gentle question. Bess clasped her hands together and tilted her head, disadvantaged as usual by her small stature.

The conversation began with the usual courtesies. Mrs Penhaligon commented on the marvellous work produced by the dear girls and showed Bess the handkerchief she had bought from one of the youngest children. 'It's a little grubby but ideal as a birthday present for a housemaid.'

Mrs Godalming, whose eyes were darting about the room in anticipation of Lady Edgbaston's arrival, cleared her throat.

Mrs Penhaligon fixed Bess with a bland, practised smile and exclaimed: 'My dear friend Margaret has a little quibble to raise with you, Miss Hardemon. I suggested it might be better to wait for a less busy moment, but she thinks it can be cleared up immediately.'

Mrs Godalming smiled sweetly and touched her delicate, gloved hand to Bess's arm. 'I've heard a ridiculous rumour. It's said that the Wyatt girls may be admitted to Priors Heath after Christmas.'

Bess glanced to Mrs Penhaligon for support but she had picked up a pair of knitted gloves and was turning them over in her hands, apparently deaf to the conversation.

'I'm afraid, until the admissions for next term are finalized, it is confidential . . .'

'Of course, as I have said to Mrs Penhaligon, the little bird who gave me this information must be mistaken. She tells me you are quite autocratic in some matters, Miss Hardemon, and I must apply to you for reassurance. It is surely impossible that you would admit the Wyatt girls. The daughters of a grocer . . .'

'As I said —'

'Shall we take a look at the crochet, Margaret,' suggested Mrs Penhaligon, glancing a little fearfully at Bess. The undesirability of admitting the daughters of tradesmen to the school had become an increasingly large bone of contention among members of the Board.

'I scarcely need remind you, my dear Miss Hardemon, that many of us completely reject the modern idea of disregarding family. I'm old-fashioned enough to think it vital for our girls to attend school uncontaminated by the coarseness they would inevitably learn by association with girls from trade.' Mrs

Godalming fixed Bess with an alarmingly beady brown eye. 'My views are shared with many, many other parents.'

'Mrs Godalming, now is hardly the place or the time for this discussion. You will understand that with so many guests in the building I am needed elsewhere. But I must repeat that my prime consideration in accepting a girl at Priors Heath is that both she and her parents should want a serious education. I'm not interested in education as a frippery thing, one more accomplishment to help a girl on the marriage market.' Bess caught Mrs Penhaligon's eye and knew that she had exactly stated Mrs Godalming's motives for the education of her daughters.

At last Mrs Penhaligon manoeuvred Mrs Godalming away: 'I believe I've just seen Lady Edgbaston on the stairs.'

Bess, with the occasional discouraging nod to advancing parents, retreated into the quiet garden.

It was intensely cold outside but the wind had died and the evening sky was awash with a winter sunset of pink and purple. Bess leaned on the cold bricks of the old house and breathed in the clear air until the beating of her heart was calmer and her hot head cool.

A soft male voice was speaking. Bess recognized immediately the sympathetic tones of George Peachey and was surprised that he should have stayed for the bazaar. Oh good, she thought, he'll certainly be on my side. She moved forward quickly.

He stood behind a long, low bench upon which sat Christina Lytton in a billow of crinolined skirt. On her lap, gleaming in the fading light, was a sheet of white paper. Peachey stooped to admire her work, his head almost brushing the edge of her bonnet. Well, what an improvement already, thought Bess, Christina's started drawing again though she should never be out in this cold.

Ordering Christina inside she took Peachey's arm. 'I need your advice yet again, George. Mrs Godalming is after me.'

Together they watched Christina drift slowly towards the boarding house, her skirt catching here and there on stray thorns so that she had to lift it gently away.

Peachey patted Bess's hand. 'Now then, Miss Hardemon, what have you done to upset our dear friend Mrs Godalming?'

He was one of the few men with whom Bess had ever been able to keep in step. Her head was comfortably at shoulder level. As they walked briskly along the silent paths they could speak easily in low voices of the difficulty over the Wyatt girls. Behind the lit windows of the schoolroom the bonneted heads of visiting mamas waved and bobbed.

'I thought of myself as a radical until I met you,' Peachey admitted. 'You're the only woman I know who'd fight this battle, let alone win it, as you doubtless will.'

'I'm not radical,' retorted Bess. 'I'm sensible. How ridiculous to exclude girls because their father sells cheese. Heaven knows, if Wyatt had made his money from gold or slaves I presume it would be a very different matter.' She loved to make Peachey laugh. It made her feel young, even a little daring.

'You know quite well that Mrs Godalming is teetering on the brink of a slippery slope herself. Her husband's family is probably one generation away from moneylending.'

'Then I certainly shan't give in to her hypocrisy.'

'No, you must certainly not, my dear Miss Hardemon. One of your greatest strengths is that there is not a fibre of self-deceit in your being.'

She smiled and ducked her head. Peachey's compliments were acceptable because they were made so lightly, as if they came from a brother. They had reached a corner and their step slowed as they turned back to the school.

'Thank you for taking an interest in poor Mrs Lytton,' Bess said next.

'Ah, the mysterious Mrs Lytton. I've had to listen to her singing your praises for a quarter of an hour. You must watch your step, Bess. If you have the same effect on all your pupils the school will be crammed with young ladies come swooning back to be rescued by you.'

She laughed aloud at him. 'Nonsense. You talk such nonsense.'

His affectionate brown eyes smiled down at her. He squeezed her hand and they parted. Bess returned to the schoolroom which seemed hot and crowded after the clear air of the garden but she was full of energy again. It was time to usher mothers and daughters towards the entrance hall so that the school could be restored to normality. Any further attempts by parents to engage her in discussion about the principles of the school or the progress of their daughters were swept firmly aside.

11

December 1995

On her birthday Imogen sent tins of biscuits to the staffroom as a token of celebration. Glenys Morgan picked up the scrawled note inviting her to tuck in and replaced it with fastidious fingers. She chose not to eat a crunch cream provided by Imogen Taylor. Mike Morris, who would consume anything he hadn't paid for, scooped up handfuls and quipped: 'She'd have smeared them with arsenic if she knew I'd be eating one.'

Graham Hibbert was more generous. 'Good for Imogen. You wouldn't have caught old McArthur handing out free biscuits.'

Sarah, who'd never forgotten the date of Imogen's birthday, had bought a card which she delivered during lunch-break in what she hoped would be seen as a conciliatory gesture.

Imogen's door was open and she greeted Sarah this time as if she were a close friend, admired the card and even invited her to a small party on Saturday. 'There'll be a few people from the staff. Please come.'

Wrong-footed by so unexpected a display of friendship, Sarah said: 'Did you know that the dreaded Laura Harding has got wind of your intentions for the rose garden?'

'Yes. I'm glad. I want the subject well aired. It removes the responsibility from me. All I've done is toss the ball into the air. I'd like a sports hall and this seems a good way of getting it, but I'm not going to shed tears if it doesn't happen.'

'There's an informal meeting tonight in Laura's flat. I think I shall go.'

'I think you must. Madeleine Stone will be there, so you'll have some powerful allies.'

'Oh, I don't think it's a matter of allies and enemies, is it?' Sarah asked softly.

For the first time she detected a hint of weariness in Imogen. 'No, just colleagues with differing viewpoints to my own. So what's new?'

When she returned to her form room Sarah found Matthew Illingworth and a couple of his cronies draped over her desk. The ordeal of spending her precious free time with Matthew was self-inflicted. Since her exchange with Imogen about his insulting behaviour to Robin Fenster Sarah had confronted him head on.

The head of year had provided her with a snapshot of Matthew's background. The father had left and the mother worked nights if she worked at all, leaving Matthew in charge of his eight-year-old sister. Matthew's life had been a constant crossing of boundaries, not enough care, not enough food, too much freedom paradoxically coupled with too much responsibility. What he needed was stability and reliable constraints.

So Sarah hounded him and picked him up on every misdemeanour. If he handed in shoddy work she stood over him until it was rewritten, and if he was late she detained him at break. Today he was in lunch-time detention for coming to school without pencil case or rough book. The other two were here to catch up on missing homework.

'You're late, miss,' said Paul Irving.

She stifled the urge to respond with a cutting reprimand, arranged the boys in desks far apart from each other and issued them with orders.

'Oh miss, I'll be lonely over here, can't I sit next to Paul?'

'Matthew, I'll sit beside you and keep you company, don't

worry,' she said soothingly. The other boys leered and sucked the ends of their biros.

'Miss, I need a ruler.'

Sarah moved quietly to her desk drawer, unlocked it, removed a selection of rulers, erasers, pencil sharpeners, pens and crayons and arranged them carefully on each boy's desk. She then approached her face very close to Paul's and murmured: 'Don't dare speak again for the next half-hour.'

Matthew, who had enjoyed this floor show hugely, was making thick, wet wodges of blue ink from little pellets of paper. Sarah sat close to him, took a clean sheet of paper and began to draw lines across it. 'You and I, Matthew, are going to design an action plan. I've had three more complaints about you since last week. You're wasting your life and mine, and now you have to buy back privileges for yourself with good behaviour. Here goes.'

He moaned and shuffled his way through the lunch-break but she had a peculiar sense, as always with him, that he was pleased. He was a boy who struggled all the time for attention. Well, he would have it, but for the right things only.

There was the occasional tiny indication that he was beginning to respond to these methods. Although he often gave a low hiss when Sarah came into the room, or made a sign as if warding off the devil, in the morning hers was the face he sought when he appeared in the classroom and now occasionally he caught her eye and there was a hint of sympathy, an acknowledgement that she was taking some trouble on his behalf.

She dismissed them five minutes before the bell to give herself breathing space before the afternoon's lessons. They barged out of the room like bullocks from a pen but Paul at least bothered to gather up the things she had lent him.

'Right, miss,' he said.

'Right, Paul.'

When he'd gone she felt all of a sudden ridiculously lonely, floundering in a tiny vacuum before the arrival of her form for registration. It was in these odd pockets of time that she felt most displaced. At Priors Heath her relationships were many and varied and in most her role was very clear. There were failures and set-backs along with moments of great clarity and joy. But always in the background, behind Sarah's inter- action with her pupils, were her own children. And her relationship with them was a grey fuzz, a reluctant and occasional reaching out, always marred by a fear of what she ought really to be doing and feeling for them.

Laura Harding lived with her husband Henry in an attic flat in Ealing. Laura welcomed Sarah, arms outstretched. The moment they had withdrawn from the embrace and looked into each other's smiling eyes, Sarah understood the source of her dislike for Laura. Here was the woman she could never be. Laura's glinting hair slipped from its clips and fell in delicate fronds about her face, her white thigh-length shirt was crisp and spotless and her feet trod lightly in canvas pumps. She was neat and contained, at ease with herself. Her heavy jewellery pattered softly as she led Sarah across stripped boards and dainty rugs along a white hall to the living room where people sat on cushions and low sofas, their hands cupping tall glasses of wine. This was a clear and restful setting, expensive but understated, in effortless good taste. There was no evidence of children. Bach played lightly from a concealed CD.

Sarah knew no one present except Madeleine Stone who was seated on a low Edwardian easy chair and looked strangely at home amidst all this elegance. Her bright eyes moved over the assembled company and she actually smiled at Sarah, who went and sat at her feet.

'Who are all these people?' she murmured to Madeleine Stone.

'Some old girls. A couple of parents. Mostly environmentalists and historians. Laura wants to nip this thing in the bud and has brought in all her most influential friends.'

Sarah thought of the rose garden with its sad, wintry paths and wondered how it could warrant such a high level of interest from strangers. She even felt a pang of absurd possessiveness. It's mine to defend, she thought petulantly, what does anyone else know of its real significance?

Laura, it seemed, worked as a researcher for an MP, a junior environment minister. Her husband Henry who stood by the door for a few minutes to utter charming self-effacing words, was a barrister who must regretfully go to another room and plough through papers in preparation for the morning. Bantering laughter greeted his self-portrayal as overworked, proving that most here were intimates of Henry and Laura. Sarah, watching them wistfully, wondered if she and David had once appeared so infectiously witty and at ease together. Did Laura and Henry ever have difficulty thinking of what to say to each other?

There were groans of reluctance when Laura said they must at last get down to business. Am I truly so petty that it's just envy I feel? Sarah wondered. Has it always been that she epitomizes the self-confidence, beauty and quick-wittedness that have eluded me?

Laura was now talking about Bess Hardemon and her role in women's education. 'We owe her so much. Her school was a model, much more radical than any similar school for boys and the girls were taught a curriculum of astonishing breadth. Bess Hardemon encouraged them to be ambitious, to see themselves as women who could have roles in society. She must have been hugely influential among the Suffragettes.'

Sarah was not sure this was all true. Her memory of Miss Hardemon, about whom she had once written an article for the school magazine, was that she had actually been quite a conservative little body, at least at the end of her life. She was a rigid disciplinarian and her work had not been unique. Though certainly a pioneer, she had been part of a groundswell of change. What about Miss Beale and Miss Buss, or the founder of Girton, Emily Davies? Did they count for nothing?

'You see, what girls didn't have,' said Laura, mouth working fast, voice rising in excitement, 'was space of their own. The original school would have been desperately overcrowded and at home the girls would have been very much at the beck and call of their mothers. The garden was seen by Bess Hardemon as a place for reflection and recreation.'

No, it's not just envy that makes me feel so antagonistic, thought Sarah, it's that Laura is entirely lacking in generosity. She will never allow for the differences of others. Her face shines with conviction, as it always has. She is not a victim of self-doubt, ever, and maybe one needs a little, though of course not in spadefuls, like me. Sarah smiled to herself, contrasting Laura's rapid, emphatic tones with her own tentative approach to arguments, and indeed life.

In Laura Harding's attic living room stars shimmered through the sloping windows and Madeleine Stone was out-lining the history of the garden from its eighteenth-century, more natural design with trees and lawns to its radical transfor-mation into a formal garden in the mid nineteenth century. 'The garden has evolved,' she said, 'its function is the same but its appearance has altered. I use the garden at Priors Heath in my history lessons to show the children how the past is there, all about us, layer upon layer, if we will only look.'

'Perhaps it will go on evolving then,' Sarah said. The atten-tion of the room swung instantly in her direction, for she had been silent thus far. 'Perhaps we ought not to resist the sports hall, which is for recreation of a modern kind. After all, Bess Hardemon had the roses planted. She didn't seem to mind reshaping the garden.'

'The rose garden won't be the site of the sports hall. It will be part of the supermarket car park,' Laura said fiercely.

And suddenly Sarah was entirely out of patience with these

people. 'You've not yet mentioned the desperate shortage of sports facilities,' she said. 'How will that be answered?'

Everyone began to speak of the paramount need to balance the demands of modern pupils with the tradition of the school which gave it identity and would long outlive current trends. It was decided that the way forward must be to resist the sale of the garden, but to suggest other fund-raising alternatives.

Sarah, as nervous about driving in London as her father, had travelled by train. With considerable relief she left Laura's flat and set off on her own. She loved to walk in London by herself, a tiny speck on the pavements of the capital. She took the Underground back to Euston and here, more than ever, she was confronted by her solitude. In Hong Kong the trains had been full of talk, gesticulation and laughter and Sarah was not yet used to the insularity of English people on trains. There was a kind of weightlessness about descending the escalator alone and sitting elbow to elbow with a stranger, her face reflected dimly in the dirty windows opposite. She felt her mortality completely, this self-contained, breathing body which carried her from one platform to the next, yet would leave no trace. Through all the years with David, sure of a place, a niche in his life and in their shared future, she had never felt so conscious of her self. Now every action she took was self-generated and self-directed. It was exhausting and frightening but also wonderful and illicit. I am on sabbatical, she thought firmly. Surely that's allowed.

She took a taxi home from the station. The lane leading to Cedarview was dark and winding; there were a few orange street-lamps but their glow was dispersed by a fine mist. Sarah directed the driver to slow down and told him he could turn round in the drive.

The headlamps swooped across the lane illuminating one gatepost and in the slow swerve of the lights she saw a man on the grass verge. He stepped back a little as the taxi passed but she glimpsed his face and his eyes which deliberately sought out hers. They were obscured by glasses, his skin was pale and he wore a leather jacket and jeans. One arm lifted as a shield against the glare of the beam and then he turned away.

The driver's voice was drowned by the pulse of blood in Sarah's head. She fell back in the seat and would not look round. The car had stopped but the engine was still running. She was required to find money. Her fingers worked the soft leather of her purse and she drew out a fistful of notes and coins.

'Please, please wait until I've opened my front door. Sorry, I'm a bit nervous.'

It had to be done, she must cross the space between car and house. Yet the interior of the taxi had become the last outpost of a present in which she had begun to manage her life very competently. Beyond was chaos.

She apologized again to the cab driver for delaying him, fixed her eyes on the lock of her front door and stumbled up the steps. She slammed the door and sank down, holding her hand to her mouth.

The man at the gate had been Lawrence Taylor.

She sat with her back to the door. No footsteps came on the gravel outside, there was no ring at the doorbell. She stayed absolutely still, as if by moving she might weaken the reality of what she had seen. At last she crawled to a window over-looking the drive. She had a clear view of the gate, and there was no one there.

Lawrence Taylor, shadow or substance, had completely unhinged her. She had rocketed back to her seventeen-eighteen-year-old self, his hands on her skin, his lips on her mouth, his voice. Shuddering, she waited on and on at the window. If he came she would let him in and sink at once in his arms. Had she not been secretly longing for him all these years? Or so she thought for the first hour.

But slowly Cedarview began to calm her. She must prise herself away from all this turmoil. If he came she might not let him in, she decided. They must surely both be utterly changed from what they were. Of course she felt nothing for him any more, only a nagging desire for the intensity of love she had once experienced for him, and none other. If he came, what complication, what additional pain for herself and David would surely follow. I don't want him really, she thought, and stepped back from the window. If he's in London, then I shall meet him calmly and treat him as another ghost, like the rose garden, that must finally be laid to rest.

'Plans for Christmas?' David asked, his voice small and mechanical. 'I have to book my flight.'

'Well,' Sarah replied a little coldly, entering grades into her mark book, 'I assumed you were coming over.' It was several days since she had glimpsed Lawrence Taylor and a conversation with David seemed impossibly mundane by contrast.

'If I'm wanted.'

She thought his humility despicable. 'Of course you're wanted. The children would love to see you.'

Pause.

'How are they? Lorna always seems so tearful on the phone,' he said.

'Whenever I see her she seems cheerful enough. Of course she's worried about us but I tell her there's no need. Jamie works all the time. I can't get him to come out with me.' Her anxiety for Jamie was constant. What a lot of worry they'd avoided all these years by tucking him out of sight.

'You haven't seen much more of him, then, as a result of being in England?'

'No. But at least I'm here.' The beginnings of an argument hung between them. She snapped on the lid of her pen and held the receiver tighter against her ear. To fill a painful silence she said: 'I'm still at odds with Imogen about the rose garden. I can't think why she employed me when I'm obviously such a thorn in her side.'

'I didn't think it would be long before you and Imogen were at odds.'

And in that moment, for one fleeting second, she loved him. David knew, as none other, the knots into which Sarah had been tangled when they started going out together again after her 'A' level exams. Imogen had then been demanding that Sarah take a year off so they could travel together to Australia and America. She had insisted that Sarah was much too sheltered and took life too seriously to be a student just yet. But Sarah's parents had seen the need to be qualified as some kind of race. Sarah must complete her education quickly to be in on the job market. David, calm and sure, already well established in his degree course, had put a decisive end to the struggle.

'But it's OK,' Sarah added. 'She's asked me to her birthday party, along with the rest of the staff.' A notice had been pinned on to the staffroom board inviting everyone to attend. 'Typical Imogen. I might have known she wouldn't favour me with an exclusive invitation. But at least she bothered to speak to me personally about it.' She marvelled at the cool normality of her own voice. How could she talk so calmly of Imogen's party?

Once more, as in every telephone conversation they'd had since the summer, she could hear the silent subtext. Sarah, he called. Sarah, tell me you still love me. Don't say goodbye without a word of affection. She felt it stronger than ever tonight, after their moment of understanding. One unguarded mark of tenderness would bring him hurtling thousands of miles to her side. She did not want the bond of his love.

'Are you all right, then, I mean the job and everything?' she asked without much interest.

'I am. Everyone's had enough, though. We're all ready for a break.'

'I bet.'

'But the work's gone well.' This word 'well' was typical of

David. A tepid word. He might have said up to a few months ago that all was 'well' in his life.

'Good.' She had caught sight of her face in the mirror. 'I must go and make myself glamorous for Imogen's party. Can't let the side down.'

'No.' He laughed a little sadly. 'Goodnight, my darling, take care.'

As she got ready to go out he was there still, in the room with her. He watched her take her short blue dress from the cupboard and told her it had been bought for summer in Hong Kong, not winter in London. Would she be warm enough? He kissed her neck as she brushed and brushed her hair and smiled with satisfaction when she chose the little black leather bag he had bought her two Christmases previously. But she left him behind in the house, shaking her shoulders to free herself from him, an independent woman out on her own.

The night was wet and blustery and Sarah, who was forced to park far from Imogen's house, arrived with her hair in a mess and her face buffeted. Yet her pace slowed as she neared the house and saw that it was little changed.

The glamour of this moment was not lost on Sarah. So much of significance had happened to her in this house. It was a place that contained boundless possibilities.

Would Lawrence Taylor be there? Would he?

There were so many people crowding the hall that it was almost impossible to squeeze through the front door. Sarah recognized very few from Priors Heath and wondered if such a general invitation had actually been designed to dissuade any but those closest to Imogen from attending. Or perhaps, as seemed more likely, people chose to snub their unpopular head-teacher.

For a moment, standing on the familiar black and white tiles, Sarah felt a sense of displacement. This was her territory. In this house she and Imogen had spent weekend afternoons talking, reading and plotting. They had grown up here, evolving their ideas as they turned over and over the iniquities of school and home and other people. And the house had been the source of so much emotion that it had moulded her responses to the adult world.

Lawrence?

But now the hall was so thronged that she could hardly elbow her way through to the stairs. Rock music throbbed. She stumbled upwards, looking firmly ahead lest her eyes betray her. Where was he, was he here? She had convinced herself that it had indeed been Lawrence Taylor watching for her outside the gates of Cedarview but now her confidence ebbed away. Why had he made no move to see her again, if he was indeed in the country and had taken so much trouble to discover her address?

The door of an upstairs room was flung wide and a heap of coats lay on the bed. Sarah dumped her own and paused to glance at herself in the long wardrobe mirror. Sarah Beckett, tense with anticipation, cheekbones sharp, eyes hard under heavy make-up, on the brink of a great change.

Downstairs in the living room, which these days was decorated in brilliant greens and reds, Sarah was reminded of her teens before she had acquired the safety of David's company. Then she had experienced the same agonized fear that she alone had no one special to be with but that out of sight, concealed in some corner of the room, was the one person in the world who might change her life.

But he wasn't there and she felt his absence at once. Perhaps he had already gone from the country on one of his long periods of self-exile to the other side of the world. Or perhaps the figure at the gates of Cedarview had been a mirage after all.

Imogen appeared, shimmering in a skin-tight dress that barely skimmed her thighs and the atmosphere of the room was electrified by her presence. In one hand she carried a half-empty bottle from which she topped up her glass. She stood talking in the doorway for a while, the long expanse of her legs gleaming as she gently vibrated her body to the music. The gift of her attention was within reach and many eyes slid sideways to her wondering whom she would approach. It was towards Sarah that she hurried at last, bestowing on her a lavish kiss.

'Sarah, how fabulous that you came. God, you look great.' She hooked her arm about Sarah's neck and kissed her repeatedly on the cheek. The heaviness of her embrace suggested that she was quite drunk. 'You wouldn't think she was the mother of two teenagers to look at her, would you?' she demanded of a young geography teacher.

Sarah was led through the room and presented to strangers as an old school-friend. Old, old, old and faded, was how Sarah felt beside Imogen, whose compelling charm was tonight undimmed. She remembered her own reflection in the wardrobe mirror upstairs. Is that how she looked now, hard and unapproachable? Imogen insisted that they must find a quiet corner to have a decent chat and at last settled on a prominent sofa.

'What did you say they were called, these children of yours?'

'Jamie and Lorna.'

'God, what responsible names.' They had acquired an audience of people Sarah didn't know. 'Her kids are at boarding school,' Imogen informed them. 'Now tell me what they're like. I'd adore to meet them. What do they do?'

'They're just teenagers, you know.'

'Tell me what it's like to be a mother. To feel that these people somehow grew out of you.'

'I never think like that. Almost as soon as they were born they became individuals.'

Another woman seized the opportunity to speak of her own son.

Sarah was silenced by memories of her children: a steady

hand holding her own to cross a road; herself curled in a chair with a child in her lap, his cheek cool and firm as an egg. She recalled nursery rhymes repeated over and over and the weight of a sleeping child in her arms, a heavy head lolled on her shoulder. She wanted to reach out her hand and take hold of the past. But no, she was in Imogen's confusing living room with its exotic furnishing.

'I think I may take them out of boarding school if I do decide to stay in this country.'

'Oh you must, must stay. We need you. The woman you're replacing probably isn't coming back by the way. She's decided to stay at home with the baby so her permanent job is up for grabs. I hope you'll apply. I've always needed this woman,' Imogen explained to her audience as she put both arms around Sarah's shoulders and kissed her cheek. She smelt of musk and alcohol and it felt for Sarah like a homecoming to be seated hip to hip with Imogen, tight in her embrace. 'And now she's come back I can't be without her again. She kept me on the straight and narrow all through our youth. Mind you, she was so clever she used to get me down.'

Sarah laughed and shook her head but for a moment Imogen seemed on the brink of tears. 'You make me feel so sad, so sad,' she moaned and again Sarah was kissed and fiercely hugged.

'Why, why, Imogen, why do I make you sad?' They still had an audience but people were looking away. The pair were not teasing any more.

'Because, my dearest old darling,' and now Imogen nestled her face so close to Sarah's that she could whisper directly into the warm hollow under her ear, 'because I could never be you.' Then she laughed and leapt away. 'Who'll dance? What a boring old crowd. Let's dance. Turn up the music.'

The music doubled in volume and Imogen was tugged away by its beat. She shimmied across the room, arms held high, glass in hand.

Sarah, abandoned, went to the kitchen and found some

mineral water. The food had already been demolished so she had no excuse to linger there but she paused to digest what Imogen had said in her tipsy state. It was a great revelation to realize that Imogen had ever reflected on the differences between their two worlds, let alone crave Sarah's unexciting little childhood. And it was oddly exhilarating to think that Imogen had seen Sarah in an entirely different light. Sarah Beckett, special? Enviable? Now there was something new.

After a while she wove her way back to the hall. It would be good to leave feeling so encouraged but at that moment she was accosted by a bearded young man who declared himself to be a neighbour of Imogen's. 'She invites everyone living nearby in case we complain about the noise.'.

'Is she in a special relationship with anyone?'

He shrugged. 'Oh, you know, they come and go.'

The music was louder still and most of the lights had been switched off. More people were dancing. Through the door to the living room Sarah saw that Imogen moved sinuously, still clutching her wine glass. The fabric of her dress flashed iridescence.

'That,' said Sarah's companion, 'is the brother Lawrence, by the way. A musician of some kind. He's been around for a couple of months now. Most unusual for him. He lives in the States.'

The room swung round and emptied of all but Lawrence who stood in sharp relief against a cavern of sound. His hair was shorter than before, a dark cloud brushed back from an angular forehead. He wore gold-rimmed glasses and was altogether more substantial than her memory, broad-chested in a grey sweater and jeans. To Sarah's eyes he was just as beautiful.

He turned and his gaze fixed on hers.

'He's a dark horse, is Lawrence Taylor,' added her companion. Sarah glanced up at him and nodded blindly.

Lawrence thrust his glass into someone else's hands and moved forward to clasp Imogen's waist.

They danced together for some minutes, his strong hands on Imogen's hip and shoulder while she slid to and fro in his arms. Her head was flung back and her eyes were shut as her brother smiled affectionately down at her. But Sarah, aware that he was not dancing for Imogen at all, could not take her eyes from his hands, and every nerve in her treacherous body was fretted by the sight of those long, talented fingers. She had been waiting, then, all these years, for his return.

But the arrogance! To come back like this, after treating her so cruelly. How dare he look for her again when he had caused her so much pain?

Making her apologies to the bearded man Sarah headed for the stairs. But on the first floor she wavered for all the doors were closed. Where were the coats? At last she took hold of the handle of the furthest door. But at that moment it was pulled open from the inside and Sarah found herself face to face with Imogen's father, emerging from what was in fact his bedroom. She recognized him at once by his air of remoteness, the impression he gave of hardly bothering to dabble with the frivolous present. He smelt, as always, of mothballs.

Sarah ducked her head and mumbled: 'I'm so sorry.'

'Sarah.'

'Why yes, Mr Taylor. I thought you would have forgotten me.'

'I see few enough faces now and I saw plenty of yours at one time. There is no reason to forget. Imogen told me you were back.'

'Yes, Imogen very kindly took me on at the school.'

'Imogen has never done a kind thing in her life. You know that.' He put his head to one side and regarded her curiously. 'You saved our girl, you know.' He still had a strong Eastern European accent, which gave a peculiar significance to his words.

'Oh, good Lord, I don't think so.'

'Yes. You provided her with some stability. You saved her but I think too that you disabled her. You were too good.' He paused and corrected himself. 'What I mean is, you knew too well how to do the right thing. My wife and I often used to say, in the days when we spoke to each other, how we wished Imogen were you.'

'But think how much Imogen has achieved.'

'Oh yes.' He smiled at her in a way that she did not remember, paternal and loving. 'Poor Imogen. She is the greatest regret of my life.'

'I don't understand.'

'Imogen. We gave her a beautiful name.' He began to shuffle away to a door at the far end of the passage.

Sarah called after him: 'Mr Taylor, I remember that you used to play Mahler. Do you still?' But he merely lifted his shoulders in a gesture of dismissal. From below, Imogen's party music thumped. The Rolling Stones.

She turned back to the stairs and found that Lawrence Taylor stood at the end of the passage, watching.

His long hands were loose at his side, his head was tilted back and he had aged more than she thought. This new image of him grafted on to her consciousness; a face now scarred by vertical creases between his eyes and beside his mouth, hair almost entirely grey. But his expression was exactly as she remembered, dazed, lips parted, eyes unfocused.

He spoke her name like an incantation. 'Sarah.'

But now that the moment was upon her she felt again a flash of anger. Does he not remember the letter he sent me, she wondered? *You are seventeen and very sweet but that's all you are to me. You do know that, don't you?* He must begin by apologizing.

Smiling at him as if they had never met before she moved to another door, this time the right one. She fumbled among the pile of coats but was too agitated to recognize her own.

He was behind her. 'I never forgot you.' His voice seeped to the marrow of her bones, but she was incandescent with rage.

She turned to face him and her voice emerged strangled with emotion. 'Your letter was the cruellest thing anyone has ever done to me. Did you know? It nearly killed me.'

All the intervening years were gobbled up and gone. This was the confrontation he had never allowed her. A force of feeling which had lain dormant plucked her from herself and spun her out of control. 'It was a wicked thing to do. I was seventeen. You used me. You used me.'

Hot, bitter tears fell. And yet, a tiny, familiar part of her lingered on the outside and looked on in horror. Sarah, this happened so long ago. You don't know this man. What will he think of you?

Lawrence said over and over again, 'I'm sorry. I'm sorry. I'm so sorry.'

'So why come back? Why dig it all up again? I was happy. Why have you begun to haunt me again? What do you want?'

'Image told me you were working at the school. I had to see you because, like I said, I've never forgotten you. I was in a relationship, Sarah. When you and I met I had a young kid. It seemed I was doing the right thing by pushing you away. I've been punished too. God. My God. You were like a flower. You were so beautiful. I have never forgotten you.' His eyes with their dark lashes, a little obscured by the glasses, were tender and sad. She could walk into those eyes and drown. The anger was fading, leaving her weak and pliant.

There was a sudden burst of laughter on the stairs, footsteps chasing, more laughter and a couple burst in. 'Oh sorry, just getting our coats.'

They glanced at each other, laughed again and dived into the pile on the bed. Sarah moved forward and began fumbling for her own coat.

'Which is yours?' asked the other woman. 'I'm all right. Mine's on top.'

'Grey. A grey jacket,' Sarah said. She was conscious that

Lawrence had moved and for a moment, having no sense of him, was terrified that he had actually gone. But he was there on the other side of the bed, lifting coats and pulling out her jacket which he handed to her with a deliberate, careful movement as if he were passing a full cup.

To give herself more time with him she put it on as slowly as possible, buttoned it up, wound her scarf round her neck and removed gloves from her pocket. The other couple had long gone. All the while Lawrence said nothing. What was he waiting for? She would never give him a sign. Never. Finally she walked to the door and put her hand to the switch.

'Are you coming down? Shall I leave this on?' Her voice was bright and brittle.

He said nothing but moved to her side and his thumb covered hers on the switch. They were suddenly in half-darkness. Light fell through the door from the landing and her hand was ice cold under his. She felt the cool, flat wall and his strong fingers lacing through her own.

More voices approached. Sarah moved away down the stairs, holding tight to the smooth banister to steady herself. On the ground floor she stumbled about for a while looking for Imogen and saw her at last, far away, in the midst of a group of strangers. Someone dragged at her arm, the bearded man. 'Hello. I thought you'd gone. I'm glad you haven't.' She shook her head and pulled away. Lawrence waited by the front door and followed her out into the blowing wet night.

She began to walk rapidly to her car.

'Can I have a lift?' he called.

'Where to? I thought this is where you lived.'

'I don't mind where I go.'

She was helpless. Lawrence had to open the driver's door for her and guide her into the seat. The familiarity of the little car revived her and they set off through the empty streets.

The watchful, horrified part of Sarah found a voice and began a long monologue. Speaking in a breathless, rather high

223

voice, she told Lawrence about David in Malaysia and her children Jamie and Lorna. 'As you know I'm temporarily back at Priors Heath. It was the right move. I find I'm quite a good teacher. I mean, I'm making some headway.' Her hands and feet drove the car smoothly but a cold little woman in her head asked: Where are you going with this man? What are you doing?

Lawrence said nothing, only looked at her from time to time. The ease with which he had found his place at her side suddenly enraged her again. He played her like a fish on the line, waiting for her to flounder headlong into her old passion for him.

She snapped suddenly: 'So you went back to your girlfriend. What then?'

'We married, but it didn't work out. So we divorced and eventually I got married again. I have two children now. But you know, it's all a game. I've spent my life looking for a girl with dark chocolate-brown hair that fell like glass to her shoulders, full of hang-ups but also such a passion as I have never known. I found her once, and I let her go.'

'Well she's gone for ever,' cried Sarah. 'Can't you see? That's not me. Look at me, a married woman, half my life gone by. See, even my hair's different now.' She couldn't help laughing at this last statement.

She drove on and on with Lawrence until their arrival in her own lane caught her by surprise. Cedarview lay in darkness but the security light flicked on as the car turned into the drive.

'You said you wanted a lift to anywhere but you're not coming in,' Sarah said. 'I won't let you. This is the house I share with my children and David. I won't let you inside. Think of all that would be destroyed if I did that. When I told David I wouldn't go with him abroad it was because I wanted to make a life where I would be at the centre, directing my own self. I'm not going to start up with you again. What would it be? Another torrid little affair among so many million others.'

Lawrence was smiling. 'Calm down. I'm not asking you to embark on an affair, torrid or otherwise. I wanted to see you again. To be with you, that's all.'

'Good, well you have. Good.' She was smiling too, at the drama.

'It's a grand house. Very grand.' The frontage of Cedarview was before them, bathed in electric light.

'It's horrible,' she said, laughing still more. 'I don't know what possessed us to buy it. David . . .'

'David?'

'Is quite conventional. But do you know I don't think even he likes it. We never talk about it much. We put up with it, and live in it occasionally, but we don't discuss it.' Her voice faded because this was betrayal. David was part of the house. His finger punched out its telephone number almost every night. He was aware that she had been to Imogen's party, and had travelled with her there as far as he could.

'What sort of place would you like to live in?' Lawrence asked.

'Oh, God knows. Some smart little flat, I suppose.' She explained about Laura Harding and their mutual dislike. Why don't I gossip like this with David, she wondered. Because he never seems sufficiently interested? Or is it that I can't be bothered to tell him things?

The heat was seeping from the car. Sarah shivered a little and Lawrence suddenly moved decisively. 'You're cold. I must let you go in.' He got out and closed the passenger door.

'How will you get home?' she asked, her voice blown by the wind, her hand shaking as she locked up.

'Oh, you know, I'll be all right. I'm pretty resourceful and I'm glad I came with you. It was worth it. We had more time.' He took the arms of her coat and pulled it tighter against her. 'You're cold. You must go in.' But his body had moved against

225

hers so she couldn't walk away. Behind his head the security light switched off and then she saw clouds scud across a full, white moon.

His kiss obliterated her. His mouth drew her into the warm darkness that was Lawrence Taylor and she put her gloved hands to his face to hold him fast. The cold wind followed his tongue along her eyelids until they were pools of ice. She shivered uncontrollably and he locked his body against hers. Still kissing her, his arms tight on her shoulder and waist, he led her forwards, into the garden where her feet sank into the wintry lawn. At the stream he paused again and wrapped her tighter in his arms, his face buried in her neck.

The reasonable little voice in Sarah's head had been blown away. Lawrence led her on and on, over the bridge and under the trees. The moon on its ocean of clouds was sliced by dense, bare branches. Damp leaves and twigs broke underfoot.

Sarah locked her hands on Lawrence's back. He seemed not to feel the cold but elbowed off his jacket and spread it out for her. She curled on to its warm lining and pulled him down to cover her completely. Her breasts ached when his hand passed over them and away. When he was inside her his heat was a steady pulse. Clinging thorns and bits of bark knotted in her hair as she flung back her arms and grasped a stalk of bracken, tearing the ferns from the stem as it pulled through her fingers. With her other hand she hit the rock-solid trunk of a tree. Eyes wide she watched Lawrence in a spatter of moonlight, his face blurred by the intensity of love-making.

When he fell back the white light dabbled her exposed skin. Beside her a stranger lay panting and laughing, his unfamiliar arm thrown behind his head.

Sarah's flesh lay abandoned on the upturned saucer of the earth and her fingernails were heavy with mud. She thrust her head round and buried her face in old, cold leaves.

12

December 1858

Ever since Bess's appointment as Headmistress of Priors Heath the Chairman of the Board had been Reverend Rush, incumbent of St Matthew's, the parish church of Faringford where Carnegie had once preached to shivering rows of clergy daughters when he was assistant priest there. Rush was the town's foremost cleric and Mrs Penhaligon had indicated to Bess how fortunate the Board was to have such an exalted and hard-pressed gentleman at its helm.

It had not taken long for Bess to realize that Mrs Penhaligon had been speaking more from duty than conviction. Rush was the most infuriating kind of clergyman, believing himself to be benign and democratic when in fact he was stupid and pompous. If someone was male and high-born, Rush submitted to his opinion without question. To the ladies he was unfailingly courteous but he ignored most of what they said.

Poor Mrs Penhaligon, who had been brought up to defer to all gentlemen and especially all clergymen, was torn between exasperation with his patronizing incompetence and a reverence for his standing in the town. By the end of a board meeting her lips were generally so compressed as to be almost invisible. After all, during the interregnum following Carnegie's resignation she had presumably run the meetings much more efficiently herself.

The only other woman on the board was Lady Edgbaston who attended very rarely and whose contributions consisted of lengthy anecdotes about her unfortunate daughter, Constance. Miss Boulder, who took the minutes, was unnoticed by everyone except Bess.

Among the gentlemen Bess had very few allies. Although nobody but herself was at all qualified to speak about educational matters they all considered themselves experts on the subject.

By the last meeting of the winter term, Carnegie had become a regular attender again. He said very little though his presence cast a cloud, not least because everyone remembered his responsibility for the school's earlier failure. Bess was particularly oppressed by him. He often stared at her for minutes on end, his blue eyes fastened on her face either, she thought, with a desire to intimidate or to control.

By the time everyone had gathered it was five o'clock. Outside a gale blew and when people arrived they shook freezing moisture from their cloaks and complained about the cold. Board meetings these days took place in the library. Mrs Briskin, whose husband was a member, used the occasion to hustle the girls out at lunch-time so that she could tidy the shelves and have the table polished.

Bess, as the Board's officer, sat at Rush's elbow and therefore had a detailed view of the bristly hairs sticking out of his ears and nostrils. Rush treated her as if she were a wayward younger son. She didn't conform to his idea of womanhood and he was constantly out-manoeuvred by her dextrous arguments. Even after two years he didn't expect her to have valid opinions so he was always wrong-footed by her.

That night she had a particularly difficult fight on her hands. The agenda was lengthy and controversial. After sailing through 'Apologies for Absence' and 'Matters Raised from Minutes of the last Meeting', the Reverend found himself up against an item entitled 'Educational Standards – Examinations'.

Rush had struggled his way through several examinations in his distant youth and therefore was happy to give his opinion, which was that they were a bad thing. 'Perhaps Miss Hardemon would like to address us now, though,' he suggested, folding his hands and favouring Bess with a paternal smile.

'In order to know how well the girls are being taught,' Bess said, 'they must be examined.'

Mrs Penhaligon nodded. 'We know how rigorous you are, Miss Hardemon. The poor girls in this school are always being subjected to little tests.'

'But these tests are set by myself and marked by the staff. We are not able to judge our teaching by any general standard.'

Dr Michael Ford rubbed his huge hands and said with heavy chivalry: 'My dear Miss Hardemon, I think we all trust your excellent judgement.' He looked round the table, confident of agreement.

'Thank you. But I'm afraid I am not satisfied with my current system and I don't share your confidence. I want our girls to take the Cambridge Local Examinations, like their brothers. I have approached the Cambridge board and met with total opposition. None the less I believe we should make strenuous efforts to have our girls entered. I've already obtained copies of past papers.'

There were expressions of outrage and amazement. Rush said nervously: 'Dear me, Miss Hardemon, we never know what new idea you'll come up with next. I always go home from these meetings positively shaking in my shoes, as if I have been party to revolutionary activity. We must look to our backs, gentlemen. Soon she will have the girls at universities. And then what?'

'I have no intention of pressing for university education as I'm not at all sympathetic to the idea of women taking any part in the political or economic life of the country. But I need to educate well-qualified teachers. And for the sake of the school, so that our work is properly valued, I must show that we are as successful as any male establishment. Dr Ford, I'm sure you will understand my reasons. The medical profession relies on a universal qualification, some measure of excellence, so that the public can trust its practitioners.'

'Oh, I wouldn't trust any doctor just because he has a few letters after his name,' replied the doctor, beaming at his friends around the table, safe in his reputation for being the most expensive and therefore the best doctor in Faringford.

Bess could feel a tightening in the muscles of her jaw. She said softly: 'Perhaps you will allow me to look further into this subject. At some later meeting we could give the matter more time.'

Lady Edgbaston, who had been sunk deep in reverie throughout this exchange, now raised her heavy head. 'I don't want my Constance sitting at a desk and writing for hours on end. Her constitution wouldn't stand it. The poor child is overwrought enough as it is when she returns from school, especially after a geometry lesson. I always insist that she lies down before dinner.'

'You have raised an excellent point, Lady Edgbaston. Excellent.' Dr Ford rearranged his expression to his gravest bedside manner. Now, his sombre gaze seemed to say, we are going to take this seriously. 'There has been some new research which suggests that the female brain is quite different in structure to the male. I will try to speak the layman's language here. It is thought that whilst the brain of a male constantly renews itself, a woman's intellect is exhaustible. If over-used early in life, the female mind will be worn out and she will go into early and rapid mental decline. And then, you see, there's the, um, "organization" of the female body. There are times, each month, when a girl is weak, even prostrated, incapable of intense study. The strain on her then of examinations would be too much.'

Lady Edgbaston was pale with fright.

'Nonsense,' Bess said with unforgivable emphasis. 'Oh, please excuse me, Doctor, but really I cannot believe any of this has been proved.'

Mrs Penhaligon intervened. 'I think that at Priors Heath, Miss Hardemon, the girls are given such variety and such stimulation that their education can only do them good. The muscles of their minds, as it were, are as much strengthened as are the sinews of their bodies through daily exercise. But of course Dr Ford is right, we must be sure they are not over-stretched. We are on such new territory here.'

'We live in a world of great change,' Bess exclaimed, 'and we mustn't be afraid of innovation. Would railways have been built or factories mechanized if people had stood about saying: "We haven't done this before, best not try"?'

'Most of us would rather there were no railways,' put in Lady Edgbaston.

'Indeed,' soothed Mrs Penhaligon, giving Bess another quelling look. She had proved over the years an excellent gauge of how far the Board might be pushed but on this occasion Bess couldn't help persisting.

'Some girls are so bright and keen. We will hold them back if we don't allow them the challenge of an examination. And what better way to reward their efforts than by public certification?'

'Bookmarks, bookmarks have always been reward enough,' murmured Rush, bowing his head, as if asking guidance of his divine master. There was a hush as the Board awaited the result of his meditation and Bess looked at his grey, woolly hair with loathing. Finally he said: 'I think you are right, Miss Hardemon, in wishing to develop the minds of our young girls. We all believe that, or we wouldn't be here. But the most persuasive argument I have ever heard for the education of girls is that as mothers they are custodians of the future. We must ensure that their intellect is heightened by excellent schooling but we must not then use it all up by needlessly examining what they have learned. Their powers must be reserved for the rearing of their sons. If a woman's intellect is all wasted away, she will produce children of weak minds.'

Bess had rarely been brought to such a peak of irritation. Her ears were ringing and her cheeks burning. But Mrs Penhaligon had risen to her feet. 'Tea. Time for tea.'

As tea was poured, Bess wondered what Carnegie thought of all this. He had the quality, she thought, of marble. It wasn't simply that he made no contribution but that nothing passed him by, nothing was reflected from him and possibly nothing was absorbed either. Why is he here, she wondered, if he's not prepared to take part? If he would only stand down there would be a vacancy for George Peachey. I really need an influential and reliable ally on this Board.

The next items on the agenda were dealt with swiftly and matters generally went Bess's way for it was felt that as she had lost on the major issue of examining pupils she should be appeased in more minor things. It was agreed at once to set up a fund for an assembly hall and a brisk discussion followed on Miss Hardemon's policy of giving the girls lessons in callisthenics four times a week. Several parents had been anxious that their daughters' bodies would become too muscular and unfeminine but the Doctor stated unequivocally that he believed physical exercise, provided it was not competitive, was of great benefit to a growing girl.

The last item was the contentious issue of whether or not the Wyatt girls should be admitted to the school.

Rush knew when he was out of his depth. He gulped the last of his tea and gazed about him, weighing up the odds. Bess guessed that he'd canvassed opinion beforehand, for he was a man who liked to be on the winning side.

'We must settle once and for all the admission policy of this school,' he said.

'There is no admission policy,' replied Bess.

'It has never been an issue,' added Dr Ford as if to close a needless argument. 'It has never occurred to the lower orders to spend their ill-gotten gains on the education of their daughters.' He followed this with a needlessly hearty laugh, aware that he had perhaps overstepped the mark. He was after all sitting next to a titled lady.

'Too many people have too much money these days,' sighed Lady Edgbaston. 'How can a grocer be wealthy enough to afford our fees?'

Mr Briskin, husband to the librarian, said: 'Perhaps our fees are too low. If they were higher, only the best type of girl would be attracted to the school.'

Lady Edgbaston looked alarmed. 'We mustn't set them any higher. I applaud Miss Hardemon's economies. High fees would preclude many girls of noble family from attending. These are hard times.' And she stroked the glossy fringes on the skirt of her gown.

'Miss Hardemon,' said Reverend Rush, annoyed because people were ignoring their Chairman, 'perhaps you would tell us why you are so determined to accept these Wyatt girls?'

'Perhaps you, Lady Edgbaston,' retorted Bess, 'could tell me on what grounds I might refuse them.'

'So many ills of society are caused by this absurd mixing of one rank with another. Nobody knows his place any more. If we begin to rub shoulders with the lower classes there will inevitably be a coarsening, a levelling out.'

'There may be a levelling *up*,' Bess replied quietly. 'Think how the Wyatts would benefit from daily contact with your Constance.' Out of the corner of her eye she saw Mrs Penhaligon duck her head to hide a smile.

Lady Edgbaston nodded solemnly. 'They meet in church. That is surely enough.'

'Have you considered, Miss Hardemon,' said Dr Ford, 'what may be the harmful consequences of educating these girls? You will raise their expectations and make them dissatisfied with their lot in life. They won't marry well and yet they'll have become used to a refinement that they'll never find among their usual circle.'

'I suppose they'll be governesses,' murmured Lady Edgbaston.

'But surely it's our duty to raise the expectations of every girl who passes through this school? Ignorance can never be a blessing.'

'You'll be saying next that you'd like to invite the daughters of labourers into the school.'

'If they could meet the minimum requirements we expect at entrance, I see no reason why labourers shouldn't attend, but unfortunately elementary education is so poor in this town we're in no danger of that.' Bess fixed Rush, the trustee of a local elementary school, with her unfaltering stare. 'I see it as my Christian duty to offer education to every girl who has the attributes to receive it. How can we ask our citizens to behave morally if they are too ignorant to make choices because they live their lives in the dark?'

Unable to defend himself from this unexpected attack on his own territory, Rush looked to a fellow clergyman for support and at last Carnegie spoke, his voice as flat and repressive as ever. 'In this, as in all else, I admire Miss Hardemon's conviction. I believe her to be wrong, however. My own sister –' the Board duly sank its collective head in memory of this sainted girl – 'was a child of great delicacy and refinement. Undoubtedly, her classmates would have gained much from the example of her behaviour but I don't think she would have benefited from their company. The female mind is, I believe, particularly vulnerable.'

Nobody was capable of riling Bess more than Carnegie. 'You haven't met the Wyatt girls. They have been brought up in a hard-working, Christian household and are spirited, intelligent and good-humoured, just the type I long to see at Priors Heath. They have exhausted the education their mother can provide and want to make something of themselves. Are they to be punished simply for being born above a grocer's shop?'

'We all have to bear the destiny of our birth, Miss Hardemon,' replied Lady Edgbaston, 'otherwise I might aspire to be

Queen of England. It is no use my yearning for what I cannot have.'

The frivolous nature of this remark and the warmth with which it was received were too much for Bess. It now seemed certain that the Wyatt girls would not be accepted into the school if the Board had its way. In the face of defeat she could feel the layers of tolerance and forbearance that she had acquired over the past years peeling away. 'I am bound to tell you that I intend to admit these girls and any others like them who apply, so long as they can withstand the intellectual, physical and moral rigours of the school.'

'My dear Miss Hardemon, you must be guided by the Board, may I remind you . . .'

'And may I remind you, Reverend Rush, that one of the conditions upon which I agreed to be Headmistress was that I would not be obstructed at every turn by this Board. I have already been forced to agree to a great deal that I believe to be wrong. We teach cooking and sewing, even though these are subjects best learnt at home and a waste of precious school time. I've abandoned my idea of encouraging the girls to play games because of your groundless objection to competitive sports. I've modified the biology syllabus to satisfy your sensibilities, even though I still feel that at the very least we should give girls an understanding of their own bodies. But I will not be ruled by such antiquated views as I have heard tonight. I am the daughter of a rector. I was educated first in a village school where I worked shoulder to shoulder with the children of farm labourers and gained a sense of my own privileged status and a heightened understanding of what must be done to alleviate the hardship of others. Education, I decided, was the key to the future for all children. I don't see the particular rank into which I was born as a cage from which I must peer at those more or less fortunate than myself. I see it as my duty to give everyone the opportunity, if she can, to raise herself. And if this means that a girl must move from the enlightened world of my school to the unenlightened world beyond, then so be it. I will equip her with understanding and sympathy enough to endure anything.'

An uncomfortable silence followed. She suddenly raised her eyes and saw that Carnegie's eyes were fixed on her face. He was burning. Why did he go on and on hating her?

Lady Edgbaston said at last: 'Well, I think I have made my position clear.'

Reverend Rush coughed. 'Obviously, no action can be taken tonight.'

'I have in any case written to Mr and Mrs Wyatt accepting the girls into the school next term. As there was no agreed admission policy beyond the entrance examination, I didn't see I had any choice in the matter,' Bess said. Despite the glowing fire and popping gaslight, the temperature of the room dropped several degrees.

'Any other business?' asked Rush.

Miss Boulder took up her ruler and carefully drew a line under the minutes.

The meeting disbanded quickly. Bess hoped for a word with Mrs Penhaligon but she was sharing a carriage with Lady Edgbaston and left immediately. As usual, Bess stood at the library door to show them out one by one. Impeccable manners were restored for this ceremony. The ladies stooped forward to brush her cheek with theirs, the gentlemen bowed over her hand.

Once she was alone Bess moved about rearranging the chairs, pushing books into line and rattling the fire with a poker. She was so upset that she had no sense of the mellow, bookish world she had created in the library, normally her pride and joy. Over and over again she repeated to herself: I have no one, no one to support me. I am quite alone.

She was almost ready to pack her bags there and then. She had defied the Board and surely risked dismissal. At one of the windows she unfolded a shutter to reveal rain-lashed glass and then drew it back into place with a bang, snapping down the latch.

She was not alone.

'Reverend Carnegie.' He stood with his back to the door at the far end of the room. She had no idea how long he had been there, too intensely black to be a shadow, watching her.

She felt trapped and tiny but she flung back her head and dared to meet his eyes, flashing sparks of rage at him that he should have dared to invade her privacy.

'Miss Hardemon.' She detested the way he spoke her name, emphasizing the final syllable with a dying inflexion.

'Did you leave something behind?' Each word was bitten off with chill vehemence.

'I wished to speak with you.'

Neither moved. The light was too dim to see the expression in his eyes. There was a lengthy silence.

I won't help him in this, Bess thought. I've done enough tonight. She heard her own quick breathing and Mary's footsteps in the hall.

Dear Lord, give me patience, Bess prayed, her feet and thighs aching with tension.

At last Carnegie spoke. 'You express your views with great vehemence and you have considerable integrity. I admire you for it, Miss Hardemon.'

The unexpected compliment when she had expected criticism almost undid Bess and she was ready to sink in a pool of tears. Her throat tightened. 'Even if you don't agree with those views.'

There was another silence. He was still watching her. 'I've learnt a great deal from you, Miss Hardemon, and my views on many matters are altered. You'd be surprised, I think.'

She almost laughed. I certainly would, she thought and wondered whether there was the slightest hint of softness in his eyes. He cleared his throat. 'Miss Hardemon, I wish to speak to you on a matter of some delicacy. I understand that you ... that you and Mrs Lytton intend to take tea with Peachey and his sister on Saturday. I must warn you. I must implore you not to go.'

She was so surprised she couldn't speak.

'I've known Peachey for many years. His Saturday afternoons are notorious. You will meet people in his home who will do nothing for the reputation of you or your school.'

Her exhaustion forgotten, Bess exclaimed: 'Reverend Peachey has been a dear friend to me and to this school. I scarcely know how we could have survived here without him, he has been so generous with his time and his learning. He suggested that I, and my former pupil, Christina Lytton, might benefit from a change of scene and he's right. I rarely leave the school but when I do go into Faringford I am invariably recognized and have to spend half the afternoon discussing some detail of a particular pupil's education. I long to get away, just for an afternoon. Surely you won't deprive me of one small treat.'

'You must trust me, madam. The good name of the school is in danger because Peachey works here, though I believe we are far enough from the city for people not to be aware of what he is.'

'What do you mean?'

'I can't say.'

'I don't understand you. Why do you dislike him so?' But Bess thought she already knew the answer to this. Carnegie was jealous of Peachey who had great charm and was universally liked. Of course Carnegie misunderstood George Peachey completely. They were opposites: Carnegie frigid, aloof, cerebral; Peachey warm, witty, even tender.

Carnegie muttered: 'The company he keeps . . .'

'Reverend, is there anything else you wish to say to me? If not I'll ring for Mary. It's late and I still have letters to write.'

She went to the fireplace and put her hand on the bell but suddenly he crossed to her, reached out his great hand and gripped her fingers. They both stared in astonishment at their joined hands.

'Don't, please don't, think badly of me for this,' he said.

Mary burst through the door. Carnegie dropped Bess's hand, gave an abrupt bow, and walked out.

Despite the discomfort of the carriage Bess spent the journey to Peachey's afternoon party in Hampstead reading with furious concentration a pamphlet by Herbert Spencer on the teaching of science. As a result she very soon felt sick and a small throbbing pain in her temple warned of a much worse headache later on.

There were so many things she ought to be doing back at school. The prospectus had to be revised, as did the class lists for next term. Seasonal messages of goodwill must be sent to benefactors of Priors Heath, and one to Miss Simms who now lived with a cousin in Taunton.

Furthermore, the hem of Bess's grey dress needed attention and she had lessons to prepare for Monday. And yet here she was dressed in her best russet merino gown, gallivanting in the company of Christina Lytton who sat opposite, her beautiful face lit by a low beam of orange sunshine. At least she was looking a little healthier, her mouth had lost its hopelessness and she was less fragile.

To Christina's right, unable to hide her pleasure, sat Helen Boulder, whom Bess had invited on this little spree by way of chaperone. No one could ever accuse Helen of impropriety and although Carnegie's warning had made Bess more determined than ever to go to Peachey's afternoon party, she wanted to be above criticism.

Helen Boulder loved Christina. Bess thought it was her beauty that attracted poor Helen, and her sad history. It was as if Helen could never get enough of drinking in Christina's physical perfection. Christina, who had tried to make herself useful in the school by taking slower girls for French conversation or elementary arithmetic, also helped Miss Boulder in the office by addressing envelopes or copying lists or letters in her precise, looping handwriting, so the pair had become quite intimate.

'Do you drive into London often?' Christina asked Miss Boulder.

'Good heavens. Never. No. Why should I come into London?'

'It isn't so very far.'

'Oh, no, no.' The very thought made the scarred side of Miss Boulder's face discolour even further to a deeper puce.

'I expect you're always too busy,' suggested Christina. 'I can't imagine Miss Hardemon giving anyone a spare minute. But you should get out, you know. You're fortunate to have London so close. Think of all the galleries you could visit.'

'I'm not like you. I have no real appreciation of art.'

'Oh, I'm just an amateur. I dabble, but I do love it, and I don't see enough good paintings.'

'I've seen you in the garden a good deal with your sketch-pad.'

Bess, who had been listening attentively, was conscious of a deepening of her own unease. Yes, she too had noticed Christina in the garden and had at first been delighted to see her so busy and absorbed. Charles Lytton had given his wife a handsome box of oil paints which she had brought with her to Priors Heath. Bess had encouraged Christina to sit in at the back of the girl's drawing lessons, to help them and to pick up a little free instruction. But even as Christina blossomed and grew stronger through all this attention and renewed interest, Bess felt herself becoming troubled and anxious.

Last Saturday morning she had watched Christina from her office window in her thick coat and blue bonnet, a rug tucked round her knees, intent on sketching the wintry, brilliantly lit garden. Occasionally her work had been interrupted, first by Mary bringing tea, then by one of the boarders coming to admire it and finally by Peachey who had an appointment with Bess to discuss next year's timetable. And Bess had felt dissatisfaction grow like poison. When had she time to paint? When had she time simply to sit and absorb her surroundings, and the attention of those who came to watch?

'At Priors Heath everyone has to keep busy,' Christina said to Miss Boulder. 'It would be impossible to be in the building more than five minutes and not feel that one must find an activity, and quickly. You have no idea how much I envy you all so much.'

'Oh, good Lord, even me?' Miss Boulder put her hand to her mouth, her face flushed under her little grey bonnet.

'I was so sick to death at home of doing nothing. At school every single one of you has a function. There's a feeling of dignity. Nobody is wasted, nobody ignored. Yesterday in the hall I watched two teachers discussing some pupil and I longed to be like them, engaged together in serious work. Or like you, when I go up to your room and there's a queue of girls wanting to see you about music lessons or lunches or holidays or whatever it is. You matter. The staff at Priors Heath are part of something that couldn't work so well without each of them. Do you see?'

'Yes. I see. But then you have your family.'

'Oh yes. But if I had my time again, I'd be like Caroline Wentworth. You know she and I were both pupils in the old Priors Heath. She chose an entirely different path to me, though we started with the same opportunities. She has a real vocation to teach. I've watched her.'

Bess couldn't help interrupting. 'She works extremely hard and has the prospect of low wages and spinsterhood ahead of her, like the rest of us. Aren't you forgetting that?'

'There are worse things than being unmarried,' said Christina, her face bleak and sad again.

When they arrived at Peachey's new brick house the driver was told to call back in two hours. Christina had offered to pay for the hire of the carriage and already Bess felt tainted by the unusual luxury of private travel and by this journey into a part of North London she didn't know at all.

Peachey came leaping down to the carriage so quickly he must have been watching out for them. He flung open the door and looked immediately to Bess, his eyes full of delight like a child who has at last received a long-awaited present. But for once she felt a little oppressed by his obvious partiality to herself. Carnegie had spoilt the afternoon for her and she was alert for the tiniest hint of indelicacy. She was determined to return to Priors Heath triumphantly assured that Peachey and his afternoon parties were without blame.

He handed out first the shy, amazed Miss Boulder, then Bess whose hand he held a little longer than necessary, and lastly Christina. They were ushered into a dark hall where Peachey waited attentively while Bess fumbled with the fastenings of her cloak. Then he led her through to the drawing room which was clustered with people. The room was not large, though a pair of double doors had been opened into a smaller reception room beyond, but it seemed huge because it was so full of strangers. Bess, in her unfamiliar best dress, quivered with alarm. Matters were made much worse by Peachey's excessive solicitude.

'I hope the journey hasn't worn you out. Are you cold? What can I get you?'

'I'm quite all right. Thank you.'

'I'm so glad I've got you here at last. I couldn't keep people away when they heard you were coming. They all wanted to meet you.'

There did seem to be a lot of very tall people all looking towards her, though not, she thought, necessarily with pleasure. A dark-haired man with a strong nose and fleshy lips came up and bowed low over her hand. 'Ah, Peachey, this must be your Headmistress.'

'Martin Stuart-Harris, Miss Hardemon. Martin's a contributor to the *Westminster Review*, like myself. We thought of writing an article on the state of girls' education with Priors Heath as an ideal.'

'In some ways, Miss Hardemon, you are so much more radical than your male counterparts. Did you know that? They are still clinging to the old classical education which is all very well but hardly takes account of our scientific century. We thought possibly a comparison of Priors Heath with say Rugby, or, if you prefer, a local boys' school of your choice. What do you say?'

Bess felt herself diminishing. The room was a brilliant kaleidoscope of colour swinging round and round. She was used to pale or subdued shades. All the schools in which she had taught, including Priors Heath, had been functional and stark and at home in the rectory at Mereby Bridge the furnishings were dull and shabby. Here, in Peachey's house, were jewel-bright colours. The women wore draped, loose clothes in emerald, gold or crimson, very different in design to either Christina's vast crinoline or the plain frocks worn by Bess and Helen Boulder. They dressed their hair in nets threaded with ribbons. And the room itself was highly coloured, the walls papered in a heavy floral print, the floor covered with rugs patterned in lozenges of blue, coral and cream.

Stuart-Harris's conversation seemed to reach Bess from a great distance and her lips didn't know how to formulate a reply. She could give an assembly to a couple of hundred girls, interview parents, lecture her staff or speak at a meeting with complete assurance but here, in Peachey's modern drawing room, she was knocked completely off balance. The gaze of twenty pairs of clever, judgemental or amused eyes fell on her, very different to the diffident glances she usually encountered at Priors Heath.

I know nothing, I've done nothing, I seem nothing, she thought in despair. Dear God help me. Get me away from here. My motives in coming were muddled and I'm paying dearly for it.

Christina's soft hand fell on her arm. 'Miss Boulder has found herself a seat by the fire. We'll join her in a minute, shall we? Reverend Peachey, we're all shaken up by the journey. Is there tea? Come and see this wonderful painting, Miss Hardemon. I saw something similar at an exhibition in Birmingham last year, but nothing so fine as this.'

In an alcove was a woodland scene with a woman dressed in some strange, Grecian garment wringing her hands. The picture was entitled: 'A Wood Near Athens: I'.

'You see the clarity of detail. Every leaf. Look at the droplets of water on this fern.'

'Poor use of perspective,' Bess said.

'Perhaps perspective didn't matter so much to this artist as the need to show the texture and colours of nature, don't you think? You can feel the exact weight of the berries and their moistness.' Christina looked anxiously at Bess who was pre-occupied by the seesawing pain in her temple.

Christina cut a swathe for them through the crowd, one smile from her smooth lips causing conversations to falter and little groups to fall apart. There was Helen Boulder, hands folded on her lap, a little table beside her. Her scarred cheek was turned away so that from a distance she looked a serene and happy woman, which of course she is, thought Bess, dropping with relief beside her friend.

Another woman appeared and introduced herself as Meg Peachey, George's sister. Here was another surprise, for though over thirty, Miss Peachey was dressed in a girlish frock and her hair was a frizz of untidy curls. Bess recognized the kind of woman who had been a clever, admired girl and who has spent all her disappointing adult life trying to be that girl again. She couldn't help feeling a little dissatisfied with Peachey who should have guided his sister's taste and so prevented this pitiable display.

Meg gushed over Bess and Christina, put her hand to her mouth at the sight of Miss Boulder's scarred face and then managed a string of insincere compliments to compensate for her lapse. 'Tell me everything about your school, Miss Hardemon, though actually I probably know more than you do because my brother so admires your work. He talks about you all the time. And what advice can you give my neighbour, who has two very wayward girls? There is Miss Buss's school, the North London Collegiate. Do you recommend that? I understand Miss Buss is very particular about behaviour. Is it right, do you think, for girls to be rigorously disciplined? I was allowed to run a little wild, I'm afraid, but at least I have always been free to think my own thoughts.'

'I've heard that Miss Buss runs an excellent establishment,' said Bess. She watched Miss Peachey twirl one of her unnatural curls about her finger and wanted to smack the hand down.

George Peachey was across the room, a slight, distinguished figure in clerical black. His eyes, as usual, sought Bess out, but they were a little troubled. Perhaps he was doubting the wisdom of inviting her here. Well, what did he expect, she thought? I have no time for people like this. The women were behaving particularly badly, tipping wine from their glasses into moist mouths, fingering their flowing hair and touching each other's hands and shoulders. They spoke freely and boldly to the men.

And yet the atmosphere was not particularly easy. At first Bess wondered why people who seemed to know each other quite well could yet be so at odds. In the end she realized that it was because they were vying with each other. The laughter was a little too loud. Eyes strayed around the room, as if worried that someone else was being more amusing, or they were missing out on a more interesting conversation.

Christina, in pearl-grey silk, sat between Bess and Miss Boulder. Bess thought they must have looked an odd trio, scarred Miss Boulder, plain Miss Hardemon, and between them the fair, mysterious Mrs Lytton. Meg Peachey had obviously heard all about Christina's tragedy for her eyes brimmed with sympathy as she offered to take her round the room to view Peachey's collection of modern art. 'I understand you're quite an artist, Mrs Lytton.'

'Oh, no, not at all,' cried Christina.

'George says you are. Come and tell me what you think. Miss Hardemon?' Bess rose dizzily to her feet. The pain above her right eye was a pendulum striking again and again. A sip of tea had increased her nausea. They stood in front of a picture of a woman with trailing hair and soulful eyes leaning over what seemed to Bess to be a large pot-hole. The picture was entitled: 'Ceres at the Gate of Hades'.

'Now this is our latest, what do you think?'

Christina lifted her slender hand and used it to cut out the sound and colour in the rest of the room. 'It is wonderful,' she said. 'The quality of the light. Such clarity. Yet the artist has deliberately knocked back the woman's character, don't you think? I wonder why?'

A man was standing near by, heavily bearded and with pale, thick eyelids and glistening lips. Bess had to step aside for him.

'Ask the artist yourself,' said Meg Peachey. 'Here he is.'

Bess stood on the edge of the little group, her feet hot on the thick rug, looking and looking at the painting in which she had no interest. But she was aware that a change had come over Christina who was suddenly entirely in her element. She knows what to do at this kind of gathering, thought Bess, and she has become an expert on modern art.

Christina knew how to smile directly into the young artist's eyes and how to draw poor Meg Peachey, who obviously admired the man excessively, back into the conversation. When someone else came up seeking an introduction Christina stepped aside, then put out her hand to him with an easy and graceful gesture. She spoke gratefully about her friendship with Bess and then returned the group's gaze to the picture with a word about the velvety texture of the goddess's robe. Soon they all moved on to a print near the door and Bess seized the chance to return to the sofa by the fire.

George Peachey was now seated next to Miss Boulder. He moved up to make space for Bess who sank down beside him. She had an absurd desire to rest her throbbing head against his shoulder. Instead, to show her displeasure with him for subjecting her to all this, she tucked her skirts under her hips to avoid any contact.

'I've been watching you. You're not happy,' he said in a low voice.

She wouldn't smile at him. 'I'm afraid I'm out of practice. I don't know how to spend time talking to people with whom I've nothing in common.'

'You think we're all very frivolous. But you might learn something by broadening your circle.'

'I have no circle. It's precisely to avoid becoming part of a narrow clique in my home village that I took up teaching, that and financial constraints. I hate talk for its own sake.'

He threw back his head and laughed. 'Miss Hardemon, I can always depend on you to speak your mind.'

'Why did you invite us here?'

'Because I think Mrs Lytton has real talent and should meet other artists. And because I wanted you to see what I am.'

She sat very still with down-turned eyes. At last she said: 'Reverend Peachey, I know you to be an excellent teacher. That's all I ask of you.'

'And do you think,' he murmured, bringing his face so close to her own that she actually felt the heat of his breath on her lips, 'that all I ask of you is that you be an excellent headmistress?'

The room swam in its blaze of heat and colour. Across the room Christina's glossy head was thrown back in laughter. Pain was a hot nail driven into Bess's skull and Peachey's clear brown eyes with their dark lashes smiled directly into her own. She knew that her face was slack and dull, her eyes exhausted.

And yet her body yearned towards him. She was remembering the kiss under the gatehouse again, Charles Lytton's lips on Christina's, and she wondered how it would feel to be kissed like that by George Peachey.

Bewildered by this image she straightened her back, lifted her chin and looked sternly away from him. His gaze lingered on her face and he seemed to be waiting for a response from her. After a moment he spoke again, but this time in an unusually flat, depressed voice. 'Mrs Lytton has proved a great success,' he said.

'Yes, she seems very happy today.' At that moment Christina glanced across the room. Her eyes caught Peachey's and a smile passed between them.

'There's another chap, Madox Brown, here. I'd like her to meet him.' Bess watched Peachey cross to Christina and place an easy hand on her shoulder. They have become friends, Bess thought through her headache. I hadn't quite realized that.

But of course she had seen them together quite often at Priors Heath. In a classroom at the end of a lecture they would be found standing at a window talking earnestly about philosophy, or art, or a novel Peachey had recommended. They walked together in the garden, her slender frame supported by his firm arm, or paused on the stairs to talk.

I'm glad I have given Christina new friends, thought Bess. A life should be full of people. But she wanted to get away from this room, which was too hot and too full of confusion for her. She didn't know herself as she sat in her steel blanket of migraine, frightened, angry and unsure. What had Peachey meant by that whispered question? She thought longingly of the empty cool rooms at Priors Heath, of her little office and the white staircase leading to it.

Peachey was soon back at her side. 'I wonder if you would see if our carriage is here yet,' she said at once.

'Yes, all right, I can tell you're longing to be away. But I do think it good for you to meet with other reformers and revolutionaries. You're too isolated at Priors Heath. All the world is changing. It must be reassuring to know that education is part of a great liberalization.'

'As I told you before, I'm not a liberal,' she retorted. 'Girls should be educated because they have intellects that mustn't be wasted. That's all. I have no thought of overturning the order of things.'

He bowed his head. There was none of the usual sparkle in his eye. 'Very well, Miss Hardemon, but try not to look quite so much the headmistress. I promise never to subject you to an afternoon like this again. I wouldn't dare.'

At last they were in the carriage, and the bumping and twisting along the narrow suburban lanes began. Bess's head jolted against the hard cushions and she fell back in a half-sleep, longing to be unconscious, away from the pain and the unfamiliar sense of failure. She thought about Peachey and the rather cursory way he had shaken her hand as they left. She had lost something by this afternoon, and not just her time or a little confidence. She had lost Peachey's whole-hearted approbation because she had failed him. He had wanted her to shine and instead she had drooped. But he had disappointed her, too, surrounding himself with those people with their indulged mouths and loud voices.

And do you think that all I ask of you is that you be an excellent headmistress? Had he been declaring himself to her in some way? Surely not. But what other explanation could there be? He would surely not jeopardize their friendship by flirting with her.

Oh, what does it matter, she thought wearily, as long as he continues to teach at Priors Heath. If I simply behave as I've always done, all this will blow over.

On the other side of the carriage Christina and Helen Boulder spoke in low voices. Christina was delighted with the afternoon. 'I am so grateful to have been able to meet such people. I talked to a woman who earns her living by writing. She made me feel dependent and feeble, ashamed.'

Helen said suddenly: 'What I loved was listening to so many people talking at once. It was wonderful by the fire, just to watch and be warm. I understood something about us all that's completely new to me. Perhaps we are born to be gathered together like that.'

Bess, who listened but did not open her eyes, was suddenly alert to the fact that Miss Boulder was speaking more intimately than ever before.

'When I was a child I would never have believed that I might some day sit among soft cushions in the company of so many people who were unafraid.'

Christina said: 'Were you often frightened, Miss Boulder, when you were a child?'

'Frightened. Oh yes. I had no idea that one human being could speak kindly to another. I didn't believe there could be a home that wasn't full of anger.'

'What about school? Someone must have given you a good education or you would never have learnt to write so beautifully.'

'My aunt came for me after my mother's death. She taught me at home.'

The story of Helen Boulder's childhood was legendary in Faringford. Her father had been a wealthy farmer, though so fond of the bottle that he had driven his wife to an early grave with his violent rages and killed himself soon after with liver poisoning. Helen, his only child, had probably been subjected to unimaginable bouts of cruelty in the two years between her mother's death and her father's. The farm had been remote and people had not intervened until he was dead and it was too late to save the child. All Helen had ever said about her scarred face was that she had once fallen into a fire and her father had dragged her out.

At least, when he died, Boulder had left his child in comfortable financial circumstances. The farm had been sold and since the age of eighteen Helen had been an independent woman, living in a small double-fronted house on the south side of town, near the school.

'I kept thinking to myself this afternoon,' added Helen, 'how amazed I would have been twenty years ago, if I could have seen myself now. I would never have believed it possible. As a child I was so ignorant I didn't even know what there was to hope for.'

At Priors Heath Mary was waiting with an urgent letter for Bess.

> *Faringford Place*
> *December 12th, 1858*

My dear Miss Hardemon,

I have canvassed the opinion of fifteen other mothers of my acquaintance. We are all agreed that if you persist in admitting the Wyatt girls, if you refuse to listen to the best advice of the Board, we will be forced to withdraw our daughters from the school. I think you will understand, Miss Hardemon, what this could mean. I beg you to reconsider, especially at a season of the year when conciliation must be in all our hearts.

> *With all best wishes*
> *Judith Edgbaston*

13

Christmas 1995

The sixth-formers at Priors Heath did their best to create a seductive atmosphere for the senior Christmas disco. In the Wyatt Hall the dark green curtains were drawn, a complex lighting rig had been set up by an entrepreneurial old boy and silver balloons inflated. These measures were only partially successful, however, for the hall's pervasive smell of floor polish and sweaty feet persisted and nothing could hide the badminton court markings or the piles of chairs.

Alcohol was absolutely forbidden. Miss Taylor ran the bar herself, dressed from head to toe in black lambswool, her pale hair scooped into a leather slide. She handed out Coke and crisps with the air of one bestowing illicit whisky and caviare. The students were a little wary of her but hung about to chat, their faces attentive and pleased.

Other teachers shouted comments to each other about pupils' choice of outfits or partners and averted their eyes from more ostentatious displays of petting while occasionally a couple of senior staff went off to patrol the cloakrooms and larger cupboards.

Sarah loved watching the students. They were so young. The girls' skin was plump and clear and the boys had sharp shoulder blades and bony wrists. They padded round the girls in their huge trainers, shifty and watchful. Sonia Castelino stood a little apart in a black dress which revealed her soft brown limbs and slender ankles. Her eyes were dark, glowing pools. Boys hung about making clumsy jokes and jockeying for her attention but she, delectably aloof, preferred to talk to members of staff or work with Imogen behind the bar.

Sarah suddenly felt deeply grounded in her own age and time. These teenagers gave her joy when she saw them at the brink of their adult lives, but she no longer yearned to be young again. She was changed. A week after making love to Lawrence, Sarah's body still ached, as if it carried his imprint.

He had telephoned her every night and asked to see her again but her answer was always the same. 'No. No. I am not punishing you. No. I just don't want to see you.' For hours after each call she had to skirt around the telephone in case she was tempted to ring him back. It got harder, not easier, to refuse him. But what she remembered most about the night of Imogen's party was the smell of the copse at Cedarview, the vegetable, earthy scent from the leaves in which she had buried her face. It had reminded her acutely of the evening at Priors Heath when she had made jagged cuts in each wrist. Half-naked in the moonlight, her body blown by the cold wind and scratched by thorns, she discovered that she had turned a full circle.

Lawrence had pulled her to her feet and, with her clothes clutched in her arms, her jacket flapping on her shoulders, she had trailed back to the house. He had followed until they came to the front door where she had moved quickly inside. Leaning on the closed door she could just hear his feet scrunch away on the gravel.

The house had been blessedly warm, the carpets soft on her icy toes. In the drawing room she turned on the gas fire and sat in front of it, the heat bathing her clammy skin. She had fallen at last into bed with torn leaves still clinging to her so that when she woke the next morning the sheets were gritty and smeared with earth.

Only then did the implications of what had happened dawn

on her. Appalled, she had pulled on her dressing gown and wellingtons and let herself out into the garden. Stumbling, as if in a nightmare, she had rushed back to the copse and found the place where bracken and thorns had been pressed down by the weight of their bodies. With frantic fingers she had tried to pull them upright, then as violently stamped them down again.

Look, Sarah. Look what you came to. Once again you did something irretrievable. In the rose garden at Priors Heath you cut your wrists because you had been discarded by a worthless man. Now, for the sake of that same man, you sacrifice husband, children and any sense of self-esteem. Why? Why? Because you refuse to take control. You set something in motion and then watch it roll away with you, howling because you don't like what's happening. Well, this time there's no Imogen to pick you up and make it better.

Sarah had stood a while longer in the punishing cold and then returned to the house, her feet dragging on the muddy grass, reluctant to enter Cedarview's respectable interior.

At the Priors Heath disco Sarah, supported by a square white pillar, felt safe in the beat of her solitude. On the night of Imogen's party she had watched herself disappear down the tunnel of desire for Lawrence like a little fish swimming less and less strongly away from the vortex of a whirlpool. But now she saw clearly what had happened; the old Sarah Beckett trick. Such had been the pattern of her life. She had the instinct for the grand gesture, but not the moral courage to take the consequences.

The disco was drawing to a close. As the last slow numbers played, the students who didn't have a partner moved self-consciously away. Sarah leaned against her pillar, hands behind her head, eyes closed, washed by the noisy, sentimental gloom of the hall. The advertisement for a permanent history position would be out in January. Lawrence Taylor was leaving for the

States in a fortnight. David would be home for Christmas and she must decide whether to return with him or not. She was at the centre of a tangled web for which she knew she had only herself to blame. There was a burst of laughter as Robin Fenster, who had spent most of the evening shoulder deep in a bevy of female students, performed a mad tango with a female PE teacher.

The lights were flicked on and the dancing couples split apart, blinking and coy. The disco was over. Through freezing wind and lashing rain Sarah fled to her car. Once inside she sat shivering and fumbled for the ignition. A female figure in an inadequate jacket, dark hair flapping in the wind, made her way to the blackness of the alley which led beside the Old House. Sonia Castelino. Silly girl, Sarah thought, what's she up to? Why make the foolhardy gesture of walking home alone when she might have asked anyone for a lift? This time she could not quite admire the girl's fierce independence.

By now other stragglers had reached their cars and were driving away and Sarah was caught behind a battered Metro which crawled along the narrow drive to the front of the building, its headlamps illuminating the rain. If she could only drive more quickly she might catch Sonia on the main road before she disappeared into the maze of side streets.

Sonia was waiting at the pedestrian lights, her hair already wetted into ringlets. The Metro had stopped and its passenger door was thrown open. When Sonia climbed into the front seat Sarah sighed with relief that after all she would not need to take Sonia home.

Jamie's headmaster rang to suggest that Sarah should call in for a little chat with him when she came to pick her son up for the holidays. Oh Jamie, she thought, what has happened? It was as if a net was tightening around her.

The Headmaster occupied a study of quite staggering elegance. Its large bay window overlooked a sweep of drive shaded by graceful lime trees and the desk was eighteenth century with a top of tooled leather. Flanking a mahogany coffee table were armchairs upholstered in blue velvet. An open fire burned in the wide grate.

David and I are funding this opulence, Sarah thought, for the first time affronted by it. Why does a headmaster need a priceless desk in his room?

Jamie was not working as hard as previously, revealed the Head, whose aesthetic features and refined, unassuming manner were probably better suited to parental sherry parties or masonic meetings than awkward discussions on under-achieving pupils. 'We have always had a good opinion of Jamie, and now, just when he should be studying so hard for his GCSEs, his concentration is drifting. I'm afraid it's also my painful duty to inform you he has been caught a couple of times a little worse for . . . over-indulgence. So common, more's the pity, in boys of this age.'

'I'm surprised he should have any access to alcohol,' Sarah said at once, her voice reedy in the plush room. How did the Headmaster manage to make her feel so guilty about her son when the school was paid thousands of pounds a year to take responsibility for him? It was the power he had over her child's destiny that intimidated her and the comparisons he could make between her imperfect boy and a hundred others.

She had put him on the defensive. 'This school is not a prison. We act *in loco parentis* but we cannot forbid the boys excursions to the village, or the houses of friends, not of course that any of our pupils' parents would condone . . . We trust their good sense . . .' He fixed her with a sad eye. 'We under-stand that you have not been abroad with your husband as in previous years.'

'No. I haven't. I wanted to be nearer my children.'

He placed the tips of his fingers together and bounced them apart. 'That is possibly not the interpretation your son is placing on events.'

'Has he said anything about it?' Sarah demanded. 'He's never mentioned it to me.'

'No, but James is not a great one for expressing . . . James has always been exceptionally withdrawn, wouldn't you say?'

Sarah rose to her feet, nodded and excused herself. Bastard, she thought. Bastard.

The Parr family was to follow its usual custom of spending Christmas with Sarah's parents who now lived in a bungalow near Frinton. It would be a well-ordered affair. No natural tree entered the glass porch to scatter its needles on the fawn carpets. A little artificial tree, bought in the January sales three years previously, and 'very life-like' as Mrs Beckett said with satisfaction, supported with some difficulty the ancient ornaments and tree lights extracted by Lorna from the shoe box into which they were annually stowed. This box, which had once accommodated a pair of Mr Beckett's tissue-wrapped Hush Puppy casuals, was so ancient that the price of the shoes was marked on the side in shillings and pence. Lorna loyally enthused over the aged treasures, retaining her sense of enchantment at their annual uncovering through all her cynical teenage years.

Meanwhile Jamie, on entering the bungalow, set up his computer in the smaller spare room and removed himself from sight.

Christmas Eve was spent in demure last-minute festive activity. Mrs Beckett was a great one for preparing things in advance, to the extent that her Christmas shopping was done by the end of November and the vegetables peeled and left soaking for the next day by ten a.m. Sarah, flicking through her mother's magazines, read an article entitled: 'Rushed off your feet? The guide to staying cool this Christmas' and yearned for a house party of twenty at Cedarview, anything but this numb apprehension. She was so tense that her limbs seemed to move stiffly, like those of a puppet. The contrast between the familiar minutiae of Christmas with her parents, the detail of tying a ribbon round the cake and polishing the wine glasses, with the turmoil she felt at the prospect of seeing David again threatened to break her in two.

All, all revolved on the question of how she would feel when she saw him. Surely when they met the vacuum would be filled and the conundrum resolved. Do I love him or not? Do I love him enough?

And then there was the burden of her parents' joy in yet another family Christmas. Watching her father carefully tap another pin into the wall to support a ribbon of Christmas cards, Sarah was lashed by guilt at the pain the destruction of her marriage would cause them.

At five o'clock she set off for Heathrow. Neither of her children would accompany her, presumably because they were afraid to witness their parents' reunion. She drove with obsessive precision, never overstepping the speed limit. Her dread of the coming meeting was not founded in a fear that she would love David less than in August but that she would feel precisely the same. She had anticipated that by now she would be sure either that their separation must be final, or that she couldn't live without him. Instead, all she knew was that she was worn out by the constant, exhaustive dissection of a seemingly insoluble problem. Did she wish to restart the engine of her marriage, which had been satisfactory, or did she want finally to end it?

She could not now remember the quality of love she had felt for David, only that two weeks ago when she had been touched again by Lawrence Taylor, David Parr in his neat, city suit, with his measured progress through life, had been reduced to a mere flicker in her memory. Yet she had understood precisely where further contact with Lawrence would lead. Oh, she was in love with Lawrence, certainly desired him, carried him inside her head every waking moment of the day and anticipated those abortive little phone calls with anguish. But she had seen enough of him on the night of Imogen's party to recognize one thing, that he was fundamentally unchanged. He had a wife and child, yet he was pursuing an old love affair. And he had not come from America to find Sarah, so much was clear. Happening to be in England he had discovered that she was working for Imogen. Sarah thus had been brought to the forefront of his consciousness and he had rediscovered an old passion, as she had done. But Lawrence Taylor had a poor record of commitment. As a youth he had run from his family: a lonely young sister, tortured father and ambitious but dying mother. He had since run from one wife and was busy deceiving another. Nor had he flourished in the music business. All this, in the moments when she was not clutching at the kitchen table in Cedarview to prevent herself from moving across to the telephone, Sarah understood very well. So why did she love him? Because he was Lawrence Taylor.

Not good enough.

When David's flight arrived she saw him in the distance wearing his dark overcoat and wheeling neat luggage. His hair was a shade greyer than she had expected and his figure very compact. He smiled and gave a cheery, casual wave.

Her first thought was one of pity for a man who had flown home in such uncertainty, and her next was despair because she felt no tremor of desire. When he gripped her shoulders and kissed her he smelt of travel and food.

As they walked together towards the exit she was stifling tears of sorrow.

After lunch on Christmas Day the Parr family walked to the sea, leaving the grandparents to watch the Queen's speech.

Mr Beckett was a great collector and usually Lorna liked to humour him by gathering stones and other bits of marine treasure to take back but this time she stayed close to her father. Jamie shuffled by the water's edge, stepping across the seaweedy breakwaters, eyes down. Sarah kept to the top of the beach where the stones were large and dry while David meandered between the various members of his family, head held high, apparently enjoying the bracing salt air.

Lorna skipped and loped along, occasionally taking her father's arm. She was playing the little girl this Christmas, perhaps to cover up with gaiety her terror at what was happening to her family, as if the pulling of crackers might keep them all from the abyss.

David had a blitheness about him that made him unreachable to Sarah. He seemed quite oblivious to her turmoil. She couldn't decide if he was being deliberately obtuse to put off the evil hour when they must face the future, or whether he genuinely thought they were all right. All day she had been waiting for something to happen that would make the way forward clear to her. But David was simply as he had always been, courteous and patient, affectionate with his children and teasing with his in-laws. He and Sarah played their roles easily, exchanging appropriate presents and quick kisses.

Lorna could not keep her parents apart for ever. A wind had polished the sky an arctic blue and it was very cold. At the bungalow a Christmas tea would be ready and afterwards party games. Suddenly the figure of Sarah's father appeared, muffled in scarf and cap, sent by his wife to offer them a lift because it had grown so icy since they went out. Jamie accepted with alacrity. He was underdressed as usual and his complexion was whitish blue except for the red tips of his ears and nose.

Lorna looked anxiously from her parents to her grandfather. 'Are you coming by car, Dad?'

'No, I'll stay with Mum if she doesn't mind. Sarah?' David pressed his daughter firmly into the back seat and took his wife's arm. The car drove away and they began to walk up to the deserted high street where the lights on a municipal Christmas tree flashed bravely.

Sarah was even reluctant to leave her arm in his, so terrified was she of committing herself to something she might regret.

'I missed you,' he said at last.

'Did you?'

'I missed you most after I'd spoken to you each night because I knew how confused you were and I couldn't be there to help you.'

'How could you help me, when you were part of the problem?'

'I don't know. Habit, I suppose. I was used to looking after you when things were bad and I missed being able to do that this time.'

'You make our marriage sound very one-sided, as if you were constantly having to pick me up.'

'No, not at all. But I always knew you had the harder deal, being with children in foreign countries. And you take everything so much to heart, and so suffer more. You know me, I never think about how I'm feeling until things go wrong and then I'm caught off guard.'

Sarah realized that this was not an impulsive admission but something David had carefully rehearsed. He was so reasonable. She really didn't want the breakdown of her marriage to be treated with reason.

'And the other thing is,' he continued, 'I know that when you're sad, you think only of the bad side of things. The world goes black for you. I've thought perhaps that's how you would start to regard our years together. But it wasn't all bad, not at all. We had a lot of happy times. I was hoping you hadn't forgotten about them.'

'Of course not. Though actually I've been too busy to think about anything much.'

He deliberately ignored the irritable edge to her voice. 'Tell me about teaching. Is it right for you?'

'How can I say? The job isn't permanent, though it could be, by the way. Imogen wants me to work at Priors Heath until the summer at least. Because I was only temporary it was as if I was playing this last term. I couldn't tell how I'd feel if I truly made a career of it.'

'No. Of course. You know, I've often thought I'd like to try my hand at teaching, or at any rate something other than engineering.'

'Whatever do you mean? You're so good at what you do.'

'I mean I suppose I envy you this opportunity. It's made me think that I might like to consider other options too.'

'I see. But surely not teaching.'

The conversation was not going at all as Sarah had expected. Where was the drama? Where were the words of despair and hatred? 'All this sounds very pragmatic and matter of fact,' she said. 'What about us? You and me. Don't you worry about our marriage?'

'I'm more worried about our children and what they think.' Sarah realized she had stirred him after all. Beneath the surface she detected a hard core of anger. 'But while we're cooped up in an overheated bungalow with your parents and Lorna and Jamie, who you tell me is so unhappy that he's taken to drink, I'm not going to provoke any discussion about our future. I'm going to look after our family by being as level and cheerful as I can.'

Ah, so he was determined to appear unshaken. He would occupy the moral high ground so the demolition of their security would be all her fault. But he must take responsibility too for coasting through the last fifteen years on the safe little raft of being David Parr, father of two, married to Sarah.

'I wanted to tell you, I can't hide it, that I saw Lawrence Taylor recently,' she said.

The quality of the space between them became electric with the implications of what she had said.

'Lawrence Taylor,' he said carefully. 'Imogen's brother? Didn't you have a fling with him once, in your "A" level year?'

'I did, yes.'

'Oh, and how is he now?'

I see what you are doing, she thought. You are trying to contain this so it fits into the category of Sarah meets an old friend. She averted her face and spoke clearly into the night air. 'He had the same effect on me as before.'

David trudged along beside her, hands thrust into his pockets. 'I do find it fiercely cold here after Malaysia,' he said.

'I want to tell you, so you know the score. David, I slept with him. I'm sorry. I had to. I couldn't help it. It won't happen again, I don't think. But I can't say it meant nothing to me. That wouldn't be true. I'm sorry.'

He said nothing, though perhaps slackened his pace. She twisted her head to see his expression and realized that there was a great deal about David that she scarcely knew and she had no idea how he would react to what she had done. What had actually happened was that he was no longer there. The man who had been on her side all these years had sunk away and she now walked next to a dead-faced stranger.

So, she thought in despair, perhaps I will discover at last whether or not I want to fight to keep him.

They were at the narrow side road with the Becketts' bungalow at the turning circle, its artificial Christmas tree winking in the window between parted curtains. When they unlocked the door a rush of centrally heated air greeted them. 'We must talk,' Sarah hissed. 'What shall we do?'

He looked at her quite calmly but from a great distance. 'Oh, as soon as I saw you last night I knew that plenty was decided already. You won't ever be coming back with me to Malaysia. I know that.' He tilted his head to unwind his scarf, kicked off his shoes, and padded away from her into the living room.

On the day after Boxing Day the family returned to Cedarview where at least there was space. David had meetings in town and Sarah breathed more freely when he had gone. She wanted rid of him for his coldness was repellent to her. She would much rather he had filled the hours with violent reproaches but he had scarcely changed in his outward manner. They had even slept together side by side, their bodies held carefully apart to prevent contact.

More of the Christmas season had to be endured because Sarah had invited Claire Tomkins and her family to lunch. The preparation of food and the polishing of furniture brought life to the house. David shuffled a newspaper in the drawing room; there was a clatter of cutlery as Lorna reluctantly set the table and vegetables simmered in pans on the under-used stove.

Claire brought chocolates, wine and her unquenchable air of brisk good sense. Tony gave David a detailed account of their journey across London while their children sat in a silent, awe-struck row and then spilled with Lorna down the long carpeted passages into other rooms. Of Jamie there was no sign.

Sarah felt that she was subsiding into a familiar role of amusing, capable host and that she and David were a team again in the service of guests who shared their world. The conversation flowed smoothly from schools to business to houses.

At lunch Claire and Tony's children consumed huge meals, smiled from time to time at Lorna, whom they obviously admired, and cast covert glances at the silent Jamie. Even Claire was forced to abandon her attempts to draw him out. Questions about his studies were met again and again by monosyllables. 'Fine. Sure. OK . . .'

Afterwards Lorna took the children into the garden whilst their elders sat in deep armchairs in the living room. Bright jackets could be seen bobbing among the wintry trees beyond the stream.

'Why is the house called Cedarview?' asked Claire. 'I don't see any cedars.'

'I think there was once a very beautiful cedar nearby,' said Sarah, 'but it blew down. That's all.'

'Shame. Still, it is a very lovely garden. I bet it's wonderful in summer.'

'Oh yes. Though it's so difficult to maintain flowerbeds when we're away. Spring is best, I expect, because of the bulbs, but again we've never seen them in bloom.'

'But there are plenty of perennials that give gorgeous colour. Imagine if you were to plant beds of delphiniums and lupins high on the banks of the stream. It's so wonderful to have a water feature, I think.'

Her husband shifted in his chair. Claire's voice died away and for a moment they all stared aghast at David. His head had sunk and he held his hand to his eyes. Between his fingers tears flowed so fast that they dropped from his wrists and darkened the leg of his trousers.

The children were called inside and ushered away. In the hall Claire embraced Sarah warmly and whispered into her hair: 'You want to watch him. That's the first sign of breakdown. But don't mind tears. Excellent outlet for emotion. I wish I could cry, never could. Oh dear, I'm so sorry. But we all play such a good game of being happy, don't we, it's a shock when it all cracks.'

Tony edged himself out on to the drive and their highly polished car swooped away, leaving Sarah alone on the steps.

Lorna was surprised by their sudden departure. 'They were all right, those kids. I think I might consider some kind of youth work for my voluntary service next year.' She glanced into the dining room, noted the quantity of unwashed lunch things and took herself hurriedly upstairs.

For a while Sarah worked alone in the kitchen but the clash of cutlery falling into the dishwasher compartments could not quieten the horrified pumping of the blood in her veins. Her movements were clumsy and she exhausted herself in senseless journeys from one room to the next. David was in terrible pain, but what could Sarah do when she felt nothing for him? How could she comfort him when she had so little to offer?

At last she burst into the living room which was now in almost complete darkness. David sat where they had left him in a chair by the window, completely still. Sarah went up and enclosed his wrist with her hand.

'David.' She edged closer.

Suddenly he put the palm of his hand to her cheek and roughly pushed her so that she fell to her hands and knees. 'Tell me about him, Lawrence Taylor.'

She shook with fear.

He covered his face. 'Was he at the back of all this from the outset? What is he?'

Sarah put her hands on the window-sill and drew herself up so that she could see a faint reflection of herself in the glass. Outside a liquid winter sunset blackened the trees in the copse. She thought of herself crossing the bridge with leaves in her hair and her body shaken wide open by Lawrence Taylor's love-making.

'I think he is selfish and feckless but I can't help being obsessed by him. I have never been able to put him out of my head. Perhaps because he treated me so badly he left me scarred. And he was part of that terrible time, you know, at Priors Heath when I cut my wrists. But David, he's not the danger. I don't think I'd give him another thought except that —'

'You feel nothing for me.'

'No, not it's not like that. Oh, David.'

'So what do you want to happen now?'

'We must both surely have a say. What do you want?'

'Sarah, I'm not going to begin to think of that until I know whether I have a choice. At the moment I want to kill you.' From another man this might have sounded wild. From gentle David Parr it was unspeakably violent.

'I still don't know for sure what I should do,' she whispered.

He slammed his hands down on the arms of his chair but at that moment there were footsteps in the hall and Lorna flung open the door.

'What's the matter, why are you sitting in the dark?'

David went over and hugged her tight. 'I was thinking about tea. Toast. Will you help me make it?' He went out leaving Sarah crouched in semi-darkness. It was as if Lorna had found him alone in an otherwise empty drawing room.

14

Christmas 1858

Three days before Christmas Bess travelled north by train, fretting at the need to stay the night with a dull cousin in Sheffield. The next day she made the last slow miles to Mereby Bridge by pony and trap.

Moment by moment, as she was drawn deeper into the landscape of her childhood, the tight knot that bound her to Priors Heath and Faringford loosened. Cloud shadows skimmed the steep hillsides and darkened the little valleys and gullies. The peaks were huge and smooth under a racing sky.

Human beings should not have to live crammed tight in a small town like Faringford, Bess thought. In the streets people were crushed shoulder to shoulder so that petty jealousies and intrigues festered. Almost every family and every building in Faringford was new. The ancient order of the countryside had been replaced by a society scrambling over itself in the acquisition of rank and wealth. Rich industrial families, precarious in their new-found status, constantly looked over their shoulders at those who coveted their position, or down the pile to where so many toiled in genteel poverty. There was a ridiculous obsession with respectability. By contrast, the old social structure of Mereby Bridge was simple, with the Longcross family at its head, the rector next and below him the doctor, then the farmer and the tradesmen. And here, thought Bess, turning up her face to the blue and white sky, we are all put firmly in place by the sheer grandeur of nature. What did it matter if Lady Edgbaston was afraid of her daughter mixing with the wrong type? The petty problems of a girls' school in the distant south were reduced to nothing by this eternal landscape. The hills would still cast a shadow on the valleys and the clouds pass overhead whatever actions were taken by the ladies of Faringford.

And at this distance from Priors Heath, the recent puzzling episode at Peachey's afternoon party seemed less significant, possibly even imagined. In the new term they would meet each other with their old, comfortable pleasure. Bess had merely been confused then by the onset of a headache that had taken three days to clear. Time, rest and walks in these hills would put all to rights, she thought. Soon the sad, nagging pain he had caused her would be completely forgotten.

They came within sight of Mereby Bridge pressed close to the hillside and below it the broad water meadows running down to the river. From far away Bess could see the stone walls of the rectory bathed in afternoon sunlight.

The house fitted about her like an old glove, its battered corners as familiar as her own face in the mirror. On Christmas Eve she woke to the quiet of the wintry countryside, the dying call of a December bird and the riddle of the poker in the kitchen hearth. Shaking with cold she dressed and joined her father for prayers in the study though she was shivering so much that her lips trembled.

> 'The Lord said unto my Lord, Sit thou at my right hand, until I make thine enemies thy footstool.
> The Lord shall send the rod of thy strength out of Zion: rule thou in the midst of thine enemies . . .'

After breakfast she helped with the bed-making in preparation for the boys' imminent arrival and then went down to the village where Miss Eliot, the retired schoolmistress, gave her tea in her stark little parlour. The Longcross family had given Miss Eliot lease of the cottage for a peppercorn rent, and she was supported by various gifts from local families and a tiny inheritance from her father, but by the end of half an hour yesterday's romantic idyll of country life had faded for Bess. There should be a pension for teachers, she thought indignantly, remembering the visit she'd made to poor Miss Porter, her predecessor at Priors Heath, in the Faringford workhouse. Miss Eliot had nothing to show for years of service to the boisterous children of Mereby Bridge except a few samplers and a proudly displayed bone china tea set. There was something terribly unused about Miss Eliot's body with its long, dry bones and flaky skin. It was as if now that she had no function she was dying from the inside out.

With some relief Bess next called on her father's curate, Jonathan Cage, who had once proposed marriage but was now the husband of Susan Kidd of Home Farm. Bess had bought a precious picture book for their two children. Susan, a mousey, thin-faced woman, was tediously proud of her unremarkable infants and told Bess every detail of their progress whilst making an unnecessary fuss with the best cups and a fluted milk jug. Bess took a gracious interest in the Cages' domestic arrangements whilst giving heartfelt thanks that she had declined the position of Mrs Cage for herself.

By the time she got back to the rectory all the family had assembled. John and Martin, down from Oxford, were lounging untidily in the kitchen and Gerald's children spilled into the hall, attracted like a magnet to Bess who frightened them but not quite enough to keep them at bay. Laetitia ran down the stairs and fell laughing into her sister-in-law's arms. Lunch was a noisy, messy affair.

During the afternoon it dawned on Bess that there had been considerable changes at the rectory since her last fleeting visit the previous summer. Her father was slower and refused to join her for an afternoon walk. When she tried to persuade him outside he looked wistfully at the fire and clenched his thin hands together. Nor would he participate in the domestic life of the house. He cast vague smiles of approval on his grandchildren but moved away if they became too demanding.

Meanwhile Mrs Hardemon, though still quick and energetic, had slipped further away from her husband. She worried about every aspect of her housekeeping but in particular the need to provide nourishment for so many mouths. To spend more than an hour in the kitchen with her was torture to Bess, for Mrs Hardemon did not spare her daughter either from her many worries or from a finicky inspection of every task Bess undertook.

'Your father's catching too many colds. He never picks up from one to the next. That's far too much salt, dear. Nobody will be able to eat the mince pies. He won't wear enough or keep the fires in at night, though heaven knows there's plenty of wood. How are we going to manage with so many for dinner tomorrow? Bess, you never used to be so heavy-handed with pastry. There certainly won't be enough spoons for dessert. I'll send Cathy out to borrow some. Have you seen how the wallpaper is hanging from the landing, by the way? Damp. And we only had it put up last summer.'

Bess reflected how sad it was that her mother, who in her younger days would probably have coped competently with the problems of running an institution the size of Priors Heath, was quite crushed by the day to day domesticity of the unwieldy rectory.

A few minutes later one of the children came in with a large rectangular parcel from Mrs Christina Lytton which Bess opened with some reluctance.

She and Christina had parted just over a week previously with a mixture of emotions on both sides. Christina had been tearfully grateful to Bess, sad to be leaving but eager at last to return to her husband and stepchildren. Bess, by contrast, had been ashamed of her own overwhelming feeling of relief. She had begun to find Christina, with her observant eyes, gentle manner and massive skirts, a disturbing presence. When they embraced on the steps of Priors Heath Bess's face had been level with Christina's shoulder and her nose had been pressed to the soft, perfumed wool of her cloak. Long after the carriage had gone Bess had smelt that flowery perfume and been rather sickened by it.

The painting was a portrait of Bess.

I hope you don't mind, *read Christina's accompanying letter.* I knew I would never persuade you to sit for me so I stole your face without you realizing during assembly or while I was observing a lesson. Besides, I think I know your features by heart. I wanted to give you something to say thank you. I almost feel as if you and your school have saved my life.

'The girl has talent,' said the Rector, rescuing the picture from the floury kitchen and propping it up on the hall stand. 'It's a very good likeness.'

'Oh, I hope I don't look like that.'

'You should see your face first thing in the morning. Enough to frighten the daylights out of your pupils, I should think,' said John. 'She's got the jaw exactly. Hatchet face.'

'That blue dress is so shabby now. I can't think why she's painted you in it,' said Mrs Hardemon. 'What about that nice reddish merino I bought you last winter?'

'Mother, I had no idea that she was painting me at all,' said Bess. Are my eyes really that large and questioning? she wondered, rather pleased by their size and clarity. Her hair in the portrait was smooth and glossy.

'It doesn't look like the work of a woman,' pronounced Gerald, who had an opinion on most things. 'Look at the flesh tones, the texture of the hair. Very modern. Excellent technique.'

'What will you do with it, Bess?' asked Martin. 'Hang it in one of the classrooms to scare the wits out of your poor gels?'

'I hardly think so.'

'I should like it in my study,' said the Rector. 'I think it's very fine.' He smiled at Bess, proud and loving, her dear father and mentor once more.

On Christmas morning the family walked to church. Bess and Cathy followed in the wake of Letty and her brood who were all so bundled against the Derbyshire cold that they skittered along the lane like over-stuffed puddings.

'So, Miss Hardemon, when can we expect you home for good?'

It was so unlike the nervous Cathy ever to begin a conversation that Bess was caught off guard. 'Oh I've no intention of coming back to Mereby Bridge permanently.'

'I see. It's just I had thought with the boys gone and your father's strength failing you must be planning to come back.'

Forgetting that her future at Priors Heath was currently in the balance Bess exclaimed: 'No. Certainly not. I'm sure everyone realizes that I'll be at Priors Heath indefinitely now. I have so much to do there, Cathy. Besides, you and mother always manage much better when I'm not around getting irritable with everyone.'

'Miss Hardemon, when you come home we're all pleased. You're so capable and understanding. You have a sense of proportion.'

'What nonsense. My pupils would laugh to hear you say that.'

But a cold hand clutched her breast. Duty. Where lay her duty?

Later she watched her father take with painstaking care the low altar steps he had climbed so briskly for the past thirty years. Beside her in the pew her mother searched fretfully for a handkerchief she had left behind at the rectory.

Dear God, is it my duty to come home and support my parents in their old age?

*　　*　　*

The next evening after tea, though his grandchildren dragged at his coat tails and begged him to join in a parlour game, the Rector withdrew to his study. As he passed Bess he said: 'I see you've lost your old habit of quiet study in the evening, Elizabeth.'

After a few minutes she followed him away from the boisterous turmoil of the drawing room, took up a copy of Carlyle's *Life of Sterling* and began to read. But the book, her father's choice for her, couldn't hold her attention. Her thoughts were far away with a plan to introduce philosophy into the curriculum at Priors Heath. She shifted her weight and her hand tapped the arm of her chair.

'You seem to have become very impatient with us all, Elizabeth,' Hardemon said at last.

'No, no. It's just I'm so used to being busy that I hardly know how to be still any more.'

'Then you have lost a precious gift.'

Bess obediently tried to read again. But this time she was distracted by shouts of laughter in the drawing room. 'Mother seems very tired sometimes,' she said.

'She wears himself out unnecessarily. We are better off financially now. She could employ other servants. We already have an extra girl on Mondays for the laundry, I believe. And Cathy is very capable.'

'Mother would be lost without domestic tasks to keep her busy, don't you think? What would she do?'

He sighed and Bess recognized his old impatience with his wife, a woman who essentially bored him.

Bess closed her book. 'Father. Do you think I should come home? Am I needed here?'

'Why do you ask?'

'This last term has been very difficult. Recently I have begun to question what I'm doing. Perhaps I'm too ambitious for the school. At every turn I'm faced with intense opposition. Perhaps I should come back here now and let someone else take over.'

'This muddled thinking is very unlike you, Elizabeth. It sounds to me as if you're suggesting that you're being given a sign from on high. Life as a schoolmistress has grown uncomfortable, so the Lord shows you your aged parents to remind you there is another possible life for you. I don't share your concept of Him, Elizabeth. Our Lord doesn't plot a woman's downfall because she has been ambitious. He isn't vindictive. Nor does He encourage her parents to grow old so that she might be reminded of her duty to them. I'm surprised at you.'

'You know very well what I mean, Father. It's not easy being a solitary woman so far from home. And by your own admission, I no longer have to teach to make my contribution to the family purse. I've always felt so certain I was doing right but now sometimes I'm lost. How can I be sure I am not becoming an eccentric, out of touch with the times? And really, aren't I needed here?'

'Your mother would be happier if you were home, although you'd drive each other mad. She thinks that people pity a rector's family whose only daughter is unmarried and earns her own living.'

'But in the south, in London, there are plenty of independent women, often by their own choice, who prefer to make a useful contribution other than through marriage.'

He said gently: 'You asked me what I thought of your coming home.'

'I need your judgement on what is best for us all.'

'I will never make that judgement for you, Elizabeth. And I suspect that it is a question you will have to ask yourself again and again during the coming years.'

'Is there no answer?'

'There are several answers. It depends whether you believe that you, Elizabeth Hardemon, are the best person to run your school. You must balance the demands of Priors Heath against the demands of your home and your nature. Remember, the humblest path is often the right path, but not always. Self-sacrifice can be very alluring, but martyrdom, Elizabeth, can be disgustingly self-indulgent.'

He had already hung Christina Lytton's portrait over the fireplace instead of the old print of Westminster Abbey that had always been there. A pale mark on either side of the new painting betrayed the change. Bess looked up into her own, uncompromising eyes.

'I understand that you're giving me my freedom,' she said softly.

'My dear Elizabeth, I don't believe your freedom is mine either to give or take.'

On the last day of her holiday Bess, perhaps inspired by Christina's painting, took her own sketch-pad from a dusty drawer and walked up-river on one of her favourite routes to the head of the valley. The path, pressed firm by the tread of a dozen generations, ran through a steep, wooded gorge where the river surged with foamy energy.

Gradually, as the trees became less dense, Bess lost the protection of the valley and emerged on to a wide plateau where the river ran wide and calm. Here a bitter wind blew but she dragged her cloak tightly across her chest and looked with pleasure on the faded heather and harsh grey outcrops of rock. For a moment the prospect of coming back for ever and taking this walk every week seemed very alluring. But then Bess remembered Christina Lytton, who had once told her of the anguish of waking each morning to the knowledge that the day ahead would be exactly as the one before; the same household tasks, the same faces, the same demands. The only changes for Bess if she came back to Mereby Bridge would be the decline of her own youth and of her parents' health.

She began to walk rapidly across open moorland to the

wooded plateau which marked the edge of the Longcross Estate, hoping that the trees might give her a bit of shelter. Among the scrubby woods on the boundaries of the park was a circular pool, said once to have been used as a bathing place by Robin Hood's man, Little John. Here, between the roots of a huge beech tree, Bess did find a dry spot out of the wind where she could sit and sketch. Occasionally the clouds cleared and wintry sunlight fell on her page and warmed her hand.

But there was no pleasure to be gained from drawing any more. She was impatient with her own lack of practice and knew now that her limited skill would never be enough to satisfy her. She wanted to capture the pool with its tiny jetty, the ducks and the brown, dead leaves at her feet all in a few minutes. It was hopeless. After a little while she pulled her gloves back on, tucked her hands into her sleeves and leaned her head back against the trunk.

Her solitude was no longer perfect. There was a crunching and tearing of the dry bracken to her left. A black, slim figure was crossing between sparse birch trees to reach her, his hand raised in greeting.

George Peachey. Bess, amazed, sat completely still. Surely not. But yes, it was certainly Peachey, his smile as bright and humorous as ever. He stood in front of her, took her gloved hand and kissed it, boyishly thrilled at having taken her by surprise.

'Gerald gave me very clear directions from the rectory. He said I'd find you up here. I could see you from the lane but didn't want to disturb your drawing. Let me see. Oh yes, very competent.'

She snatched the book away. 'Whatever are you doing in Derbyshire?'

'My latest interest is geology, specifically the effect of industrialization on the rural landscape. Where better to undertake such a study than in the north of England?'

Her nerves were tingling with joy at being in his company

again. He made her alert and quick-witted. And best of all, the awkwardness of their encounter at his house seemed to be completely forgotten. 'Reverend Peachey, you never cease to amaze me. How can you marry your extraordinary array of secular interests with your position as a clergyman?'

'Very simple,' he responded cheerfully, perching on the broad, dry root beside her. 'God's earth must be protected and so must His people. I believe the Church can't afford to ignore the great changes that are taking place in our country. The lives of its people are being transformed, its landscape is altering. We must respond to new needs and new anxieties. And besides, I wanted a journey. It's been very quiet without you and your girls to keep me busy so I thought I'd come up and have a look at you Hardemons in your natural habitat.'

'So you called at the rectory?'

'I did. And was greeted very warmly by dear Gerald who insisted I must stay until tomorrow. He would have come with me up here but he's a lazy scoundrel and the fireside was too attractive to him.'

Bess couldn't help smiling at Peachey with unguarded pleasure. It was so good to see him. She thought that here was a figure from Priors Heath who was unequivocally affirmative, who brought with him a sense of mission that convinced her she must carry on. He represented all that she loved best about her school: the excitement of introducing new teaching methods; the pleasure of talking and arguing with an equal; and the knowledge that she was admired and liked by someone whose affection she returned.

She shook her head. 'I can't believe you're really here.'

'Yes, yes, I am here, my dear Bess. As you see.'

It took her a moment to realize what was happening to her. The unhappiness and lack of direction she had felt since receiving Lady Edgbaston's letter had blown away. So too had gnawing worries about the rectory and her parents. She was no longer cold, or irritated that she couldn't draw well enough.

And all this because George Peachey had appeared out of the blue and was seated beside her, having taken and kept possession of her hand which was still tucked warmly under his arm.

But in the wake of such clarity appeared the clouds of new complication. The dancing pleasure of surprising her had gone from his eyes, and he now looked at her more solemnly than ever before. His face was so near her own that she could see how individual hairs in his dark beard sprang from his fine pale skin and how the creases at the corners of his eyes were etched by kindliness and laughter. She remembered seeing him in the garden with Christina Lytton; the sickening ride in the carriage home from his afternoon party convinced she had failed him, and she thought: It's all right, it's me after all that he likes best or he would never have come so far to see me.

He said: 'I don't believe you've ever been in one place long enough for me really to study your face.'

'It's a very ordinary face,' she said, from a dry throat. 'Though do you know, Christina Lytton has done a portrait of it?'

He looked away from Bess, across the pond. 'I saw her sketch-book once or twice and guessed what she was up to. I should like to see the finished product.' He was like quicksilver. A part of him that had a moment ago been entirely Bess's had slipped away.

'How did you spend Christmas?' she asked, to draw him back. Her hand was still held tightly. They had often walked arm in arm through the garden at Priors Heath and she had revelled in the intimacy and physical contact with him. But their situation now was more weighted. There was a tension between them that hummed with possibilities.

'At the risk of sounding immodest, madam, very profitably, and mostly on your behalf. I have been working away at Rush and he undertook to preach a Christmas Day sermon on the Christian virtues of generosity and charity. I think I managed to convince him that the Church should have no truck with snobbery.'

Bess looked directly into his puzzling brown eyes. How had he known of her difficulties with the Board?

'Oh yes, Miss Hardemon,' he told her softly, 'I am well aware of your current troubles. I make it my business. Mrs Briskin, remember, is a great friend of mine.'

'I see. I feel you should consult with me before you begin interfering on my behalf.'

'Oh, I was only sowing a few seeds. Forgive me, Bess. Perhaps you are not aware of how serious your situation is. You really are in great danger. The Board is very angry. I came to warn you. You risk losing everything. If you would allow me to advise you . . .'

'By all means.'

'You move too fast, Bess. Perhaps on this one issue of admitting the grocer's children you must relent, at least for a while. It would be quite wrong to sacrifice all you have achieved for a principle that can perhaps be tried with greater success in a year or two. Several other parents have withdrawn their support during the last week and there is a petition going round.'

'What do you think I should do?'

'Be patient. Compromise. My dear Bess, I believe you must compromise in the case of this one family.'

'And those poor girls?'

'Will suffer if they are the sole pupils of the school, don't you think?' She gazed down at her free hand and nodded, but for once she was not attending fully to what he said. All the time they were talking about Priors Heath she was conscious that something else was not being said. And the longer they spoke of other things, the more that other subject diminished, dancing away from her.

She was suddenly breathing very fast. Oh God, she thought, why didn't he sit down beside me and say simply, I love you, if that's why he came? I think I would have loved him in

280

return. Yes. I love him. For an instant he had seemed a breath away from taking her in his arms and she had even braced herself, preparing her body for the shock of his embrace.

But now the moment had passed.

Peachey shivered suddenly. 'Soon it will be dark. Perhaps we should move on.'

Why doesn't he tell me what he came to say? she wondered. I don't know how these things are done. I don't know what to do. He was again looking at her, but with a degree of calculation she had never seen before. Suddenly he shifted and put his arm around her shoulder. The touch of his fingers on her upper arm made her conscious of how cold she was. Her flesh felt unyielding.

'Bess, shall we go back?'

I can't help you, she cried silently. You must tell me why you're here. Please. He released her hand, reached up and ran his knuckles over her chin.

'Ever since I first saw you I wanted to touch your hair,' he said. He was undoing the ribbon of her bonnet, but there was a limpness about his fingers that was intensely disturbing. When he had loosened the strings and lifted off the bonnet, he stroked her hair from crown to nape where it was fastened in a net.

They looked at each other for a moment, then he gave a long sigh and awkwardly replaced the bonnet. She reached up to adjust it and tie the ribbons. All the time he watched her with hooded eyes.

'I don't understand,' she said. 'What are you doing?'

But he had sprung to his feet and reached out his hand to her. 'It's very cold. We should be walking back. Look, it's almost night.'

She was enraged by the thought that they might return to the rectory and part company with nothing more said, leaving her in this state of turmoil. What was the matter with him?

'No,' she said, shaking the leaves from her skirts and tucking her sketch-book under her arm. 'I won't be treated like this. Why did you come? Why did you touch me as you did?'

'I came because I want you to marry me,' he said, but he was looking away again at the silvery water.

Without thinking she replied: 'No, you don't want to marry me.'

'Don't I?' He laughed. 'No, well perhaps you're right. As you usually are.'

He walked so quickly through the trees that she had to run to keep up with him. She called, as if to one of her pupils at Priors Heath: 'Stop walking away. Tell me what this means.'

He laughed again and suddenly came back to her. 'I'll tell you, my little ice maiden. Dear God, I came here because I wanted you to save me. I thought you could.'

'From what? From what?'

He took hold of her upper arms so tightly that her flesh ached. 'Can't you see, with all your wisdom? Can't you? No, of course you can't. You know nothing about it. You're so innocent and untouched.'

Despite the pain in her arms she preferred the physical contact to none. Behind him the sky was a deep blue with the sun dipping away behind the valley side. She understood in a moment of utter desolation that her friendship with Peachey was at an end. 'Try me,' she begged. 'Tell me what you want.'

'No. I'll leave you in peace, my poor lady. I ought not have come. It was a whim. I thought, when I saw you, I might find a way of redeeming myself. But it's no use. You can't do it.' It was as if the corner of a heavy curtain was being lifted and behind it was a world she had never seen before. Her days were directed by order, by lists and learning, not by passion and confusion. She was cruelly aware of all the experience she lacked.

Peachey leaned forward and kissed her cheek. 'You are chilled to the bone. I should not have come. We'll go back to your home and I'll take tea, but I'll not stay.'

They walked side by side through the dusky woods. She was heavy with sadness. This was her dearest friend who had wounded her and was now moving far away.

'Is there nothing more we should say?' she asked.

'Nothing that you would want to hear. Nothing that would not destroy your peace of mind.'

'Don't say that. What has changed? I scarcely know how I would have managed these last years without you. Can't I now help you in return?'

'I'm not free, my dear Bess. If I were free there are all kinds of ways you might have helped me.'

'You are free. None more so. Look at the way you've suddenly travelled here. Of course you're free.'

But Peachey was silent. They had reached the lane and were walking swiftly along it. Ahead lay the rectory, with Bess's trunk packed ready for her return to Priors Heath and the long fight with the ladies of Faringford. Afterwards would come the struggle to build the assembly hall and the question of examinations.

At the gates of the rectory he halted. 'When I saw you by the pond, you were perfectly calm and strong and that's how I want to remember you. Forgive me, Bess.'

In the hall, a small nephew hurtled towards them and flung himself on Bess's neck. From the kitchen came the smell of burnt scones. Peachey gave Bess a long look from wistful, liquid eyes, and went to find Gerald and her father in the study.

The little boy clung like a monkey to Bess as she climbed the stairs. At the top she put him carefully down and told him to wait for her. She went to her room, closed the door and stood alone in the dark.

15

January 1996

Three weeks of the spring term had passed and Sarah was now a permanent member of the history department at Priors Heath. Every morning and for days and years to come she might step over the threshold and be enclosed by this institution. Nobody questioned her right to be there.

This morning there was consternation. A poster in lurid orange gave details of tomorrow evening's open meeting on the fate of the rose garden. Next to it, much more discreetly, were set out the proposed arrangements for Founder's Day in April. Normally on this hallowed occasion there were services of thanksgiving at St Matthew's Church in the morning with form entertainments, parties and fund-raising events in the afternoon. But now there was a new directive from Imogen. This year, due to curriculum pressures, there would be a curtailed service followed by normal lessons until the very end of the day when the fund-raising would take place.

'She's so high-handed,' exclaimed Alison Atwood. 'Did she consult anyone about this? I don't think so. She's the limit. Nothing is sacred to her.'

'I wouldn't mind if she was an effective head,' someone added, 'but she seems to destroy all that's good. The basic running of the school is in chaos. Look at the arrangements for cover. I lost more than half my free lessons last term.'

Sarah was dismayed by how little Imogen seemed to care about the opinions of the staff. It was as if she deliberately put herself out on a limb, just as she had when a pupil, pushing the patience of those around her to the limit. Yet most of her innovations were rooted in sound educational practice and based on her perception of what was best for her pupils. This matter of Founder's Day was typical. The fact that the day had always taken a particular form meant nothing to Imogen. She had guessed, presumably, that to consult on the matter would lead to endless argument so she went ahead and put up with the criticism as a necessary evil.

'I enjoyed Founder's Day when I was a pupil but I did think it a bit of a waste of time,' Sarah murmured to Alison.

'I'm amazed at you. I thought you were all for tradition. Look at the fuss you made over the rose garden.'

Sarah turned away, ridiculously shaken. At Priors Heath she had hoped for refuge. It was not as if she could continue to regard the school with the amused detachment of an outsider. The alternative of Malaysia, warm and exotic, no longer glimmered in the background. She felt oppressed by the demands the day would make on her and the way the bell would pull her from one lesson to the next.

Her own class quietened down immediately she entered the classroom.

'Miss. Miss.'

Mark Hopper was probably the least attractive boy in Sarah's form. He had been cursed with a huge pink face, pale hair and the conviction that he was the wittiest child in the school. Sarah had learnt that it was best to ignore his waving hand when possible. 'Miss.'

'Yes, Mark.'

'Have you heard about Matt?'

'No, what is there to hear?' There was a rather alarming quality to the silence in the room. A ghoulish excitement lay beneath the quiet.

'He had an accident, miss. Off his bike. He's in intensive care.'

'Oh really, when did this happen?'

'Last night, miss. He was racing down the hill, you know, down the Rushforth Estate. He went over a kerb and was unconscious for three hours.'

'And how is he now?'

'Don't know, miss. We thought you might know.'

'I'll do my best to find out.' Their trust in her was touching. Ms Beckett would sort it out, just as she acted as a referee when there was a falling out between a group of girls, or unravelled a misunderstanding with another teacher. She thought of Matthew Illingworth in a hospital bed. Perhaps he was relieved to be there, away from his chaotic family life. Should she visit him? She was suddenly exhausted by the responsibility of all these young lives. And what right had she, who had shelved the upbringing of her own children, to take on other people's offspring?

David had left three days after Boxing Day. Refusing Sarah's suggestion that she should give him a lift to the airport he had instead been collected by taxi. He looked neat and calm in his grey overcoat, its tailored shoulders perfectly fitting his slim figure. Sarah had stood with him by the gate at the end of the drive and kissed his cheek, sick with sorrow for this lonely stranger. Lorna cried on her father's neck and bolted back to the house. Jamie hovered at the front door, murmuring some impression of a farewell.

Sarah had felt a kind of violent tenderness towards the children, whom she must now protect from the crisis she had initiated. Her feet closed on the frosted lawn where each grass blade was sharp with white ice. Behind her she left a trail of crushed, wet stalks.

On the sofa in the drawing room lay a disconsolate figure, long hair draped around her face.

'Right, Lorna, what do you think, shall we go swimming this afternoon?'

'I'm not in the mood, thanks.'

'How about the cinema? Or a matinée? We could go into town.'

'No, thanks.'

'Is there anything else you need for school? Do you want to come shopping?'

'I'm not bothered.'

'Anything else you fancy doing?'

'I'm OK here.'

'But you can't just watch telly all day.'

Silence.

'What about homework?'

'Done it.'

'Can I see? I'd love to know how you're getting on. Especially your history.'

'Later.'

Sarah stood for a moment sick with frustration. She was locked in a battle with her daughter that Lorna would win time after time. Lorna saw herself as the victim of her mother's wilful behaviour, and was certainly not reliant on Sarah's approval for her peace of mind.

Jamie, when approached, had muttered that he had too much revision to do for his mocks. He didn't need any help, he said.

Still Sarah couldn't leave him alone. She stood at the door of his room which was as usual immaculately tidy.

'Jamie, are you all right now? I know you were miserable last term.'

He didn't reply.

'Jamie, I hope you understand that all is well in this family. We want to give you every support in your studies.'

Still no answer.

'I expect you've been a little worried about us, but we're OK, you know. Dad will be all right on his own for a few months more. Really.'

Jamie began to click the switches on the mouse of his computer.

'I want you to promise me that if you feel depressed, you'll ring me. Please don't drink too much. Jamie.'

I'm here. I'm available, thought Sarah in exasperation. We mustn't waste this rare time together.

At the end of the day of Matthew Illingworth's accident she finished her 'A' level lesson precisely on time. Tonight she had promised Sonia the second of two half-hour sittings. She didn't relish the prospect, however, for Sonia, who had a histrionic tendency, had been silent and soulful throughout the lesson, sighing occasionally and throwing Sarah wounded, desperate glances.

After the rest of the group had gone Sarah closed the door and went rather awkwardly back to her desk but Sonia had made no move to get out her art materials.

'I've finished my project on Christina Lytton,' she said. 'It's all over.'

'Oh, well, good.'

'Miss Taylor's made me stop working on it.' Sonia's lower lip trembled.

'I wonder why Miss Taylor felt the need to get involved,' Sarah prompted.

'She said art was occupying too much of my time, and I wasn't getting a balance between it and my other subjects.'

'I see. Well, was she right?'

'I don't know. You think my history's OK, don't you?'

'I'd say so, yes.'

'You only gave me a B+ for my last essay, though,' murmured Sonia. 'What was wrong with it?'

'Nothing in particular. I just didn't think your argument was as balanced as usual. And you can't expect an A every time, Sonia. History isn't like that. It's too subjective. But I still think you're a very strong candidate.'

'So did you tell Miss Taylor my work was slipping?'

'Certainly not.'

'I hadn't nearly finished my portfolio on Christina Lytton. There was this portrait to do, and I was going to go to a gallery in Birmingham where some of her best pictures are. And now I've got to stop it halfway through. I don't understand why.'

'Well, what does Mr Fenster say?'

There was a pause while Sonia scribbled lightly on the edge of her history notebook.

'Oh, I haven't talked to Mr Fenster. I haven't been able to find him.'

'Well, you must go through your portfolio with him. I'm sure there'll be enough work in it. He's given you a lot of help, hasn't he?'

'Oh yes, he's been wonderful. We've found out so much. He says Lytton makes a brilliant point of reference for the development of mid-Victorian art. You see you can really chart the influences on her work. The portrait she did of Miss Harde-mon was so full of character that she'd obviously been well taught, but rather conventionally, about flesh tones and tex-tures, you know. Later, she followed the Pre-Raphaelites and to them character was less important. She set the rest of her paintings outdoors and filled them with passion and light, and loads of botanical detail. But it wasn't just that she was influ-enced by a particular school of paintings.'

Sonia's smooth forehead, heavy brow and full lips reminded Sarah of the kind of Pre-Raphaelite models presumably once so admired by the likes of Christina Lytton. There was even that same self-conscious meekness. Look, I am beautiful, tragic and yearning, said her expression. It definitely seemed as if she were on the brink of some revelation.

'I think, Ms Beckett, what it was, she fell in love soon after doing this painting. I think I understand her completely. Art is terribly emotional. A painter can't keep her feelings about the world out of her paintings. I find, anyway.'

'You obviously speak from experience.'

There was a long, pregnant pause before Sonia gave a slight nod and gathered up her things. 'I'm sorry, I have to go now,' she said and rushed away, as if terrified of breaking down in front of Sarah.

In the children's ward of Faringford General a busy nurse with glossy black hair and kind eyes directed Sarah to the right door. Sarah, unused to the informality of an English hospital, crept along the highly polished linoleum with her mother's fear of authority, especially of the medical profession, tugging at her heels. Matthew's high bed was visible through the open door of his bare little room. It seemed extraordinarily intimate and inappropriate to see this boy lying naked to the waist with his narrow chest exposed and his head supported by a neck collar. The white bones of his ribs were visible and Sarah thought suddenly of a frail animal skeleton she had once seen high on a mountain-side.

'I came to see whether this was yet another excuse for not handing in your homework,' Sarah said, and he cracked a smile. 'I'm told you must have a thumping headache and ought not to talk. But I brought you these. The form drew them for you. Pretty rude, most of them.'

She pushed a pile of get-well cards under his hands. Even Matthew's sworn enemies had come in during the lunch-break to write to him, disarming Sarah by their urgent desire to do something immediate for their class-mate.

'And apparently Mr Morris mentioned you in assembly so you've really made it, Matthew.' She wished she could speak words that might really matter to him. I want you to know that I like your spirit, Matthew, was what she could not say.

An exhausted-looking woman wearing a nylon overall under a cream anorak came forward. Sarah shook Mrs Illingworth's hand and said she was there to represent Priors Heath.

'Bet you're all glad to see the back of him for a while,' said

Mrs Illingworth, who had a smoker's dry lips, and hands that trembled for want of a cigarette.

'You must have had quite a night,' Sarah murmured.

'Oh God, these kids. They're always up to something.' And she cast Matthew a nervous, affectionate glance which was instantly obscured by renewed anxiety. 'I told him he shouldn't be riding that old bike. I've had to take the day off work.'

Sarah, suddenly conscious of her own expensive shoes and manicured hands, felt like some ridiculous Lady Bountiful. Certainly she didn't deserve this woman's deference.

'Matthew,' she said, giving his arm a little nudge. 'I'll be off now. Hurry up and get well. I haven't anyone to bully when you're not at school.' The boy had closed his eyes when his mother walked in but now reopened them. His expression was one Sarah had come to expect from him, surly and defensive, but with a hint of lazy affection. In a few years he would cause women a lot of heartache, she thought.

Outside in the corridor the same nurse was pushing a trolley.

'Is he doing all right?' Sarah asked.

'Oh, he'll be fine. Nice of you to visit from the school, though, it'll make a big difference to him. I've noticed kids pick up so quickly when they're valued by people. You'd be amazed how often a boy of his age has no visitors from one end of the day to the next.'

By the time Sarah left the hospital it was six o'clock and the traffic was even heavier than usual. Already she had forgotten the days before Priors Heath when there'd been no drive home through the rush hour to Cedarview. Windscreen wipers were a rhythmic accompaniment to the news on Radio 4 or the folksy theme tune of *The Archers*. At Priors Heath she felt safe and involved but once away from the school she sailed danger-ously on the edge of order, her nights and weekends breath-taking absences of commitment that had to be filled.

Tonight at last it happened. Lawrence Taylor was perched on the top step at Cedarview, a shadowy figure hunched in his shiny leather jacket. She walked past him up the steps and into the house. He followed and closed the door behind him.

So here was Lawrence Taylor on the pale green carpet inside Cedarview. Energy surged in the hall radiator, responding to the waft of cold air from outside. On the landing above was darkness.

Sarah knew that were she to put her head on his shoulder, the pliant leather of his jacket would smell the same as new shoes which as a child she had sniffed to savour their untouched perfection. Under the jacket he wore a well-worn checked shirt, soft as lint. His skin against the collar would exhale a scent of soap and his own salt fragrance.

She sank on to the bottom stair and resolutely folded her arms, not saying a word.

'I'm off to the States on Saturday,' he said. 'My work here is done. I thought this time I ought to say goodbye, in case I got another telling off in twenty years' time.'

She had to laugh at him. His gaiety was so completely unexpected.

'You will note how obedient I have been. Christ, Sarah, the hardest thing I've ever done is keep away from you over the last weeks.'

Was she to thank him for this? she wondered. Something had held him at a distance but she suspected that it wasn't entirely respect for her wishes. If he loved her as once she had loved him, nothing would have kept him away. He didn't look her in the eye but leaned against the door with his head to one side, one knee bent, like a seventies rock star on a record sleeve. With a tremor Sarah acknowledged her own detachment from him.

'We're both too old to think that a relationship could change the world, Sarah, but I think we might have astonished each other. Have you ever wondered what we might have become, if we'd had the chance? I feel that I could have discovered in you something that's always there, but under the surface. What is it? A sort of instinct for impulsiveness and joy. I recognize your quickness. I feel it. I might have drawn all that from you.'

And in return what would I have found, Lawrence? A man who turns me inside out, whom I want to watch and watch because I'll never have enough of looking at his mouth and eyes. And what else? Music. Oh, you would sing and play for me and introduce me to bands I never knew existed. And laughter, love-making, long journeys with little money. But you've done it at least twice before with other women, Lawrence. It's addictive, the feeling that you would die for love. But what about the nights when I would be bound to cry for my children, or my craving to see my parents smile again with pride in me, or this unromantic desire I have to teach? In six months, wouldn't you be tired of all that and yearn for solitary travels again? What if I suggest we need sheets and saucepans to start up a new life? You'd leap away in terror.

Aloud she said suddenly, 'What I love most about you is that you are like a child.' How old was Lawrence? Perhaps forty-seven or forty-eight but his eyes still shone with the simple brilliance of a young boy.

'Why thank you, madam.' It was typical of Lawrence that he wasn't offended.

'The thing is, Lawrence, we have no right, either of us, to play this game. We both have children and other people who trust us.' But she felt sick with grief. Was that all her marriage had become, an altar upon which she must sacrifice love?

He seemed unaffected by her sanctimonious remark, which in any case she had made too late in the day, and she wondered if he would try and rescue her from it. She remembered sitting by the stream in the garden waiting for David to say something that would tip the scales and draw her away from the decision to part.

For God's sake make up your own mind, woman, she told herself. Jump one way or another, but do it whole-heartedly.

She now became aware that something in Lawrence had altered. He was like Matthew Illingworth who, when he felt he was being punished unjustly, switched off and put himself beyond reasoning. The little thread that had bound Lawrence to her since the night of Imogen's party had snapped. He had quite simply let her go because he was not prepared to waste any more time on her.

'I see,' he said at last, and looked directly at her. There it was, a blandness in his eyes where before there had been ardent enthusiasm. 'Well, look, can we at least meet up again before I go?'

'Yes, if you want to. Of course. You can stay now if you like, have supper.'

'No, no, I won't stay, no.' The sudden coldness was shattering. He stood fully upright and became somehow smaller, a middle-aged man in jeans. 'I suppose there's no chance of a lift to the station?'

'Yes, of course.' She picked up her bag again and they went outside.

What on earth has happened? she thought. How could he do that? One minute seem to ask me to give up everything, the next backtrack completely. Beside her in the car Lawrence spoke of a new job he hoped to take up in the States. His hands were relaxed on his lap as he looked out of a side window. There seemed to be no bitterness in him, he was not punishing her, merely waiting rather impatiently for the time when they could say goodbye. It was as if he had journeyed a long way to view a second-hand car, found it unsuitable, and as a result was trying not to resent the effort he had made to come and look it over.

In the station forecourt he kissed her cheek. 'Right then, see you, I'll keep in touch.'

She shook her head. 'I somehow don't think you will,

Lawrence,' and he smiled with something like pleasure that she should understand his whimsical unreliability.

Watching him go, Sarah managed to smile herself. Well, she thought. Well. So there goes Lawrence Taylor. But she was bereft of a dream that had haunted her for more than twenty years.

She began to drive towards Cedarview again, her eyes stinging with fatigue. But the car seemed to gain a momentum of its own so that soon she was heading west on the motorway instead, into a long trail of red brake lights.

It was Jamie she longed to see. She feared the impulse that hurried her towards him, but refused to resist it. Now Sarah, are you sure of this? she wondered. Do you really want to go to the one person you must not mess with? Don't visit him on a whim, don't destroy what little peace of mind he has. Are you sure you know what you're doing?

Yes. I'm sure.

The nurse in the hospital had said: *I've noticed kids pick up so quickly when they're valued by people.*

An hour later she reached Jamie's school. She spoke into the intercom in the wall. 'This is Sarah Beckett, I mean Parr. A parent. I wondered if I might call in to see my son. I was in the area.'

'Your son's name, Mrs Parr?'

'James. He's in Year ii.'

'Please close the gate behind you.'

The housemaster, Mr Williams, waited on the steps looking decidedly ruffled and red-faced as if disturbed from a doze. 'Why, Mrs Parr, what an unexpected pleasure. Did James know you might be calling? He never mentioned it.'

'No. No. I just wanted to see him as I was nearby, and thought on the off-chance . . .'

'Well, of course, I'll get him, but if you could notify us in future, Mrs Parr. It can be so unsettling for the boys to receive surprise visitors. And I know it's silly but whenever one hears that a parent is arriving out of the blue one always anticipates bad news. There isn't bad news, is there?' He pushed his lugubrious face nearer hers, suddenly troubled.

'No, no, nothing like that.' Her voice was high and foolish.

'Just step inside here, Mrs Parr, and I'll see what James is up to. You've just caught him. Bed at ten.'

Sarah was shown into a small interview room but did not sit down. How sad it was that she should feel so apprehensive about her son's possible response to news of her arrival.

There were reluctant footsteps in the corridor and Jamie's long figure appeared. Sarah's excitement was dampened by the sight of his white, unhealthy face and bloodshot eyes. He looked resentful.

'Jamie.' She went up and put her arms round his reluctant body. 'I'm sorry to burst in on you like this. I just wanted to see how you were.'

He hung back by the door, ready to escape. Perhaps he noticed that she was on the brink of tears.

'Please don't think I was checking up on you. It wasn't that. I just wanted to see you, that's all.' She had somehow expected that his surprise would turn to delight at seeing her. Instead, he was becoming more and more suspicious.

'Where's Dad?'

'In Malaysia, of course. Jamie, what I came to say was, please, please, if you want to, come and live at home next year. I'll be there. I'm so sick of being away from you and Lorna. There seems no point when you're the ones I really want to be with.'

He still had a boyish throat with a bulging Adam's apple. 'What about Dad?'

'I don't know, Jamie. It's not down to me. I've given him a very rough ride and I don't expect he knows what he wants himself. Dad is a separate issue. All I know is that I could never cut myself off from you and Lorna again.'

'I'd rather you were back with Dad,' he said.

She stood quite still, almost disbelieving the way she had forced this moment on herself. 'Is that what you really want, more than anything else?' Her cosy dream of a little house shared with her son and daughter was slipping away.

'Of course.'

'Jamie, I can't promise that. It makes it Dad's decision and he might not want it. Then you'd blame him.'

He shrugged.

He's manipulating me, she thought, playing on the weakness that brought me here to blackmail me back into my marriage.

'These things just aren't easy,' she said.

He was, for once, wide awake, and looked her in the eye. She saw David in him, weighing things up.

'Jamie, I will try and get it right for you,' she said.

Sarah drove home in a state of shock. The die was now cast. The conversation with Jamie had been terse but of enormous significance, like a contract.

It was midnight by the time she stumbled at last into the house and her muscles ached with fatigue. Hungry and over-wrought, she lay in a deep bath and ate soggy toast, thinking about the big house in Hampstead where Lawrence slept, with Mr Taylor in another room, and in yet another, Imogen. And here was Sarah, floating free at last from the potency of their magic, bobbing up and down among the fragments of her marriage.

Since Christmas David had phoned only three times a week. Their conversations had been crisp and clinical and it was Sarah who tried to prolong them, or add a touch of affection.

'I want you to put Cedarview on the market,' he told her the next evening.

'I think it's too soon. We haven't yet made up our minds what to do.'

'You hate the house and neither of us wants to live in it, I'm sure.'

'David, I think we should wait until we've talked some more.'
How could she tell him of the pledge she had made to Jamie?
'What I wondered, David, was shall I bring the children out
for Easter?' It was a measure of how far apart they had been
driven that her heart beat faster and her hands were clammy
on the receiver.

'I don't think that would be a good idea, do you?'

'They'd love to see where you work. And so would I.'

'The cost, Sarah.'

'I'll pay. I can afford it.'

'No. No. Don't come here. I might not be able to have time off.'

'What about the children? I could send them out on their
own, if you like?'

Sick at heart, she thought of herself at the airport, waving
goodbye, and then returning alone to Cedarview.

'I think not.'

'Well, will you come here?' Her breathing was rapid in the
ensuing silence. 'I'd like you to come here.'

No reply followed.

'All right, David, I'll spend the holidays in England with the
children. But you and I need to meet. Especially if you want
to sell this place. The children will be very unsettled.'

'Of course, of course. But at the moment I can't make any
dates for coming over. I'm terribly tied up with work.'

This was the David she had rejected last summer, the pragmatic businessman who always put work first, accepting that
things were perhaps not ideal but all right so long as the family
could get by. But who else was there? Was there any other
side of him left to love?

After this telephone conversation Sarah reviewed for the
hundredth time the decision she had made only twenty-four
hours previously.

It's what you decided, she told herself fiercely. You promised
Jamie you would start again if you could. And now you've
begun.

She sat in their bedroom preparing to go out again. Her hair had grown longer since September. It was as if her appearance had been allowed to unravel a little. Many of her expensive, tight jackets and skirts had been untouched for months. That night she felt as unprotected as a creature cracking out of its cocoon.

It had been intended to hold the meeting on the future of the rose garden in the Wyatt Hall but in the end attendance was so poor that it was quickly transferred to the Boulder Library. Apart from Laura Harding and a couple of her cronies, there were about twenty parents and a few governors. Otherwise current staff made up the numbers, as divided as ever on the issue. The art and history departments were firmly on the side of preservation and Robin Fenster had been particularly vocal on the subject. His ineptitude at sport was a standing joke among the staff and he represented the art department's view that the garden was an excellent resource for nature studies. There was an empty chair between Miss Stone and the head of art, presumably for him.

Other departments took a more pragmatic line, realizing that a substantial building project for the school might conceivably offer their subjects facilities beyond the sports hall. Sarah seated herself amongst the PE department, though they teased her for not being on their side. It was thought that she would support the garden on historical grounds whereas they canvassed strongly for better games facilities.

The local council was represented by a harassed-looking officer whose suit had obviously done service at many such events. The meeting was to be run by the rather weedy chair of governors under whose quavering jurisdiction it looked like being a long and unproductive evening. Behind him was the elegant stone fireplace, a relic of the past like the rose garden, with the plaque above it bearing the words:

*This library is dedicated to
the memory of Helen Boulder (1821–1860)
a dear and devoted servant of the school.*

Imogen was quite alone in the back row, dressed in black as usual, her posture relaxed and disinterested. When Sarah turned and caught her gaze there was no answering smile. Imogen's eyes were hostile, chips of ice.

Sarah began to sweat under the stolid glow of the electric lights. Lawrence must have admitted to their affair. It was the only possible explanation for such hatred. But why would he run to Imogen, except out of piqued pride and a desire to wound?

The shame of what she had done bowed Sarah's shoulders and made her cheeks burn. What must Imogen think of her?

The chair of governors was setting out the cases for and against the sale of the rose garden. 'Of course everyone here holds the memory of Miss Hardemon in the deepest respect . . .'

Sarah again swivelled round and faced Imogen. Look at me, Imogen, I want you to understand me. We are wounding each other by this animosity. But Imogen's gaze was fixed on the speaker.

'. . . the need for indoor basketball and netball courts. Not that I understand the rules of basketball. I only played it once and my team was massacred . . .' There was a mumble of laughter. Sarah turned back.

Her affair with Lawrence was nothing to do with Imogen. They were grown people. But in some ways Sarah was more dismayed about Imogen's reaction than David's. Imogen, then, was the benchmark against which she measured herself.

Laura Harding leapt up. In sixth-form debates she had always been self-righteous and excitable and at nearly forty her manner was even more hectoring and just as overbearing.

'It's all short term. Short-term aims. With all due respect

to Imogen, head-teachers come and go and they each have different priorities. But this garden really matters. I know Imogen thinks the sports hall is important, but to buy it you will be destroying something irreplaceable.'

Imogen said nothing in reply, though there was an expectant pause. Sarah glanced at her again and noted that she sat quite still, hand to her forehead, smiling a little, as if not a part of the proceedings.

I know exactly what you're going to do, Imogen Taylor, thought Sarah. You'll listen to all this and not bat an eyelid when the plans for the sports hall are shelved, but in your head you will have written it all off, not just the sports hall but the whole school. You don't want to trust anyone's motives so you've made this a test of how far people will support you and when they don't you'll walk away.

One of Laura's preservation society friends was talking about precious green spaces and the evils of huge supermarket chains swallowing up acres of land and damaging town-centre trade in the process.

Immediately he'd finished speaking Sarah put up her hand. The chair of governors blinked at her over the top of his irritating half-glasses.

'Imogen Taylor is head of the school. She's paid a lot of money to do her job, part of which is to discuss and identify priorities with the governors. Believe me, I think the rose garden is so important I'd have fought like mad for it a few months ago and I still would if there were other alternatives. But what's important about Priors Heath is that it aims to provide an excellent education for every child whatever his or her strength. A lot has been said about the rose garden being a symbol of the school and of Miss Hardemon's aspirations. Well, the rose garden isn't a symbol of Priors Heath. The pupils and their achievements are.'

'Blimey,' said a nearby PE teacher as she sat down. 'Spoken from the heart.' There was much applause and Sarah was conscious of her ability to influence. She dared not risk a glance at Laura Harding.

At the end of the meeting Sarah hovered in a distant corner of the library until everyone else had gone. Imogen stood at the door nodding abstractedly to parents as they left. It had been decided to support the case for the sports hall and now the governors and senior management team had to contend with the consequences. A working party would draw up a lottery application to include a bid for a drama studio and music room as well as the sports hall. Ha, thought Sarah, there you are, Imogen Taylor, pinned down, like it or not.

The caretaker waited in the passageway and Imogen offered to lock the outside door. There were things she had to collect from her office, she said. All this time she made no sign that she knew Sarah was behind her. The lights were clicked off, there was the clink of glass as Imogen helped herself to wine from the refreshment table, and then the sound of her departing feet.

Sarah followed. She'd become used to the feel of the school when the pupils had gone, the sense of a building that's waiting, with some fearfulness, for the next flood of students, as if too much was asked of it day after day. And it had been so well worn by the constant passage of young people that it had accommodated itself to their shape. Sarah felt the rush of feet on the old floorboards, the brushing of a thousand shoulders against the walls. Even, perhaps, she could hear the swish of a petticoat as one of Miss Hardemon's girls turned a corner, or a squeal of laughter from a war-time pupil with her scrubbed face and thick stockings.

In the entrance hall one light shone from the high ceiling, blackening the stained-glass window. Bess Hardemon's portrait was in shadow.

Imogen was halfway up the stairs, listening. She said, her face still turned away from Sarah, 'You're surely not expecting me to thank you.'

'Certainly not.'

'Look, I'm really tired. Whatever you have to say, can't it wait?' Sarah was being shut out by Imogen's formidable detachment.

'I don't think so.'

'No. You're Sarah Beckett. Whatever you want, you must have.'

'I'm not sure that's fair. I hope it isn't.'

Imogen sat down suddenly on the fifth stair. She had a bottle in one hand, a glass in the other. 'Then how may I help you, Sarah?'

'I noticed Robin Fenster wasn't here this evening. I spoke to Sonia Castelino yesterday and she's upset about her art project.'

'She's bloody lucky to be allowed on school premises.'

'I beg your pardon?'

'Oh for God's sake, Sarah. They were having an affair. At least she says they were. He's more ambivalent and tells me nothing was actually said or done to suggest a sexual relationship between them. Nevertheless, I've had to suspend him.'

Sarah had come close to the bottom step and her hand held the smooth curl of polished wood at the end of the banister. What had she stumbled into now? The world was a dirty and desolate place.

Imogen watched her. 'Not nice, is it?'

'Do you think it's true?'

'I think it's true she's obsessed by him. I suppose we should have spotted it earlier. He says she started to hang around all the time and when he realized it had got out of hand he tried to keep her at bay. Which of course made her even more persistent.'

Sarah remembered the rainy night of the sixth-form disco, when Sonia had stood dripping at the traffic lights and been picked up by Fenster's Metro.

'What a mess,' she said. 'How sad. You'd think someone as attractive and bright as Sonia would have more sense.'

'Oh yes, wouldn't you. Isn't it amazing, Sarah, how people screw up their own lives and other people's so regularly and so relentlessly.' She poured wine, lay back on an elbow so that her hair trailed on the cold stone, and regarded Sarah from hard eyes. 'By the way, I suppose I really should thank you for being on my side tonight. It's true I do want a sports hall, but perhaps you should also know I want rid of that garden. Too many hideous associations of people hunched in pools of their own blood.'

For the first time through Imogen's eyes, Sarah saw the figure of a girl crouched on cold grass, hair streaming across a face grey as ashes.

Imogen must have thought: So Sarah doesn't trust me enough to confide in me otherwise why would she make this terrible gesture of dismissal to all who love her?

'Imogen, I have to ask you, if the sight of me is so painful to you, why did you have me back at Priors Heath?'

Imogen lay full length on the white stairs, arms flung wide, a mark of her absolute authority over the place. 'Because I knew you'd be a bloody good teacher and the manager in me couldn't escape that. And I suppose, God help me, I thought I needed you. As it seems I did. Aren't you the knight in shining armour, galloping dramatically to the rescue tonight?'

She looked not at Sarah but at the high ceiling with its ornate moulding. Sarah perched beside her and took a long swig from the bottle. 'Has Lawrence left yet, or is it tomorrow?'

There was a long pause. At last Imogen sat up. 'Is there anything else of mine, Sarah, that you want?'

'I don't understand.'

'All through my school-days I ran wild with rage that I couldn't be you. Your lovely, lovely parents. Your little house with its funny pictures on the wall. And its garden, all organized and sweet-smelling and your dad's vegetables, so carefully grown. Your mother and the cakes she made. I associate her with the smell of baking and the way I used to creep over to the cooker in your kitchen and touch the warm oven door. Your brains, your beauty, even your bloody self-obsession. But there was one thing I did have which I thought precious, a brother. Now I find you took him too. And worst of all, you lied to me. When you slit your wrists, it was because of him, wasn't it? And you never said. Do you know, I even thought you did it because I'd been away and Laura had wounded you by poisoning our friendship. Now there's vanity for you.'

Sarah could scarcely take in this new perspective on her school-days. Her mind stumbled over the images Imogen had painted of her parents and her home. She saw herself suddenly as if through the wrong end of binoculars, tiny and sharply focused, moving through a fragrant and privileged childhood only slightly marred by teenage despair over the ending of a first love affair.

'Imogen, you sound as if I took Lawrence deliberately. I didn't. And I was too ashamed to tell you about it. I thought you would despise me even more. I was always afraid you thought me dull and silly. How could I tell you I'd fallen in love with your brother?'

'Why would I have bothered with you at all if I thought you dull? You didn't trust me, that's why you didn't tell me.'

'Imogen. Think. How would you have reacted?'

'God knows. But at least I would have understood what was going on.'

'And do you understand now?'

'I understand that there were two people who I always thought were on my side. Now I find they both had very different priorities.'

'We weren't betraying you. Besides, we're not your property, neither of us is. What's wrong with you? It's not like you to be possessive.'

'What's wrong, I suppose, is my honesty. I'm honest about how I feel, what I felt. I find your dishonesty hideous.'

'I knew Lawrence must have told you about us,' Sarah said at last.

'Oh, Sarah, Lawrence always tells me everything. Always. Except once, when I suspect he was too terrified of how I might react to him seducing my best friend.'

'I think one of the reasons I can't get Lawrence out of my head, why I was so in love with him, is that all the time he reminded me a little of you.'

Imogen raised her glass. 'Why thank you, Sarah, I am truly grateful.'

Into the dreadful stillness Sarah tried once more. 'Are you safe to drive, Imogen? Do you want a lift?'

Imogen laughed. 'Oh, no worries about me. If I'm not fit I'll take a cab. I always get home in the end. I have to because otherwise my father prowls about the house waiting for me.'

'You are very good to him,' Sarah murmured.

'No, Sarah, it isn't a matter of goodness. It's a matter of doing what I have to.'

'Would you have married, do you think, if it hadn't been for him?'

'Oh sure, yes. As you can imagine there's been a long queue of people wanting to be my partner.'

'I would think so, yes,' said Sarah defiantly.

'No one in my family has the foggiest idea how to love. Surely you know that. And anyway, you can't love where you can't trust, Sarah. And whom could I trust?'

Sarah traced the pattern in the wrought iron under the banister.

You can trust me. I love you, she thought. Can't you see?

She got up. 'My parents will be coming to stay after Easter. They always ask after you. Why don't you have lunch with us one day and meet them? And the children.'

Imogen's leg extended a fraction and she nudged Sarah's

calf with her toe. 'Get off home. You've got miles to drive. Go on, I'll be all right. But make sure you give the outside door a big slam when you leave.'

Sarah walked away across the polished floor, a tiny figure in a battered old house. She turned once and saw Imogen sitting alone on the stairs, not smiling.

16

January 1859

The first piece of news that greeted Bess on her return to Priors Heath after Christmas was that Mr Wyatt had decided to continue educating his daughters at home. All the outraged letters and petitions from parents had therefore been withdrawn and everyone was falling over themselves to conciliate Miss Hardemon.

In normal circumstances Bess would have vented her rage at once on fickle Mr Wyatt but for the time being she was tied up with too many other problems. Within a week of the start of term Faringford was hit by an outbreak of influenza. Class sizes were halved as some pupils were kept away because their parents feared infection. Teachers were also struck down so Bess, who had never taken a day's sick leave, was forced to teach three times her usual number of lessons. And there was a further blow. The male staff she employed for occasional lectures were on the whole less vulnerable to the illness but George Peachey didn't appear at all. After an unexplained absence of two weeks he sent a letter of resignation.

Bess, beside herself with disappointment and rage, was tormented by the memory of her hour by Little John's Pool with him. She had been so peaceful before his arrival and afterwards so wretched. It seemed a terrible indignity to have allowed him to stroke her hair. And now he had abandoned her completely. What crucial thing had she missed? What had she omitted to do or say that he felt the need to punish her in this way?

Her brother Gerald came to do some extra teaching and offered to make enquiries about Peachey.

'Certainly not,' she said. 'I have no further interest in Reverend Peachey. He's proved himself to be disloyal and unreliable. After two years' service I might have expected a little more dedication.'

'I've heard he has business in the north,' muttered Gerald, 'and that there have been difficulties in his domestic life.'

Bess raised her hand to prevent further argument. 'I was warned that he was untrustworthy and I wish I'd taken more notice. That is an end to the matter.'

Never again, she thought, will I put my faith in anyone, least of all any man. The fate of a school for girls matters so little to Peachey that he abandons us without explanation. Well, from now on I will have no more of it. Any relationship I embark upon will be strictly in the course of business.

At last, on the second Saturday in February, Bess had time to call on Mr Wyatt. Wrapping herself in her bonnet and cloak she set out along the Faringford Road heading for the High Street and Wyatt's Grocery Emporium.

It was early in the morning and the wintry sunshine was low and white, lighting the frozen puddles and dazzling Bess as she emerged from beneath the high wall of the brewery.

Faringford was growing rapidly. The railway, opened eight years previously, was bringing more and more trade to the town, the print works were expanding and the rows of terraced houses had multiplied. The High Street was an ants' nest of activity and Bess was greeted by several mothers and daughters who showed their usual amazement that Miss Hardemon could exist beyond the walls of Priors Heath.

The Wyatt stores had recently expanded into the adjacent shop-front, previously a drapery. Mr Wyatt was clearly prospering and Bess regretted the loss of the grateful donations

309

which would have poured into her school had his daughters been pupils there.

The family lived in airy rooms above the shop. Bess had met them regularly in church and knew them quite well but her unexpected arrival caused consternation. The maid was sent running down to the store to call Mr Wyatt and Mrs Wyatt left Bess alone in the parlour for several minutes after her first flustered greeting.

The family's main living room was crowded but not with the usual clutter of ornaments and draperies. A Beethoven Sonata lay open on the piano and the room overflowed with books. Every table was laden with periodicals and reference material. Alongside novels by Dickens, George Eliot and Charles Kingsley were books by Charles Darwin and John Stuart Mill. Bess was uncomfortably aware that she had not made time to read many of these modern authors and wondered what Lady Edgbaston would say to such a collection. It was doubtful whether any literature more substantial or controversial than a visiting card ever entered her drawing room.

When Mrs Wyatt came back she had taken off her apron. In her wake came her three daughters, faces scrubbed, hair combed. Bess judged that Mrs Wyatt, who had a broad nose and nervous brown eyes, must perhaps be the daughter of a craftsman or even a farm worker. She spoke in a low, nervous voice of her love of books and her lack of formal education. Her accent was local and she seemed slightly ill at ease in this comfortable room. Her daughters, seated in a row on the sofa, had much more poise.

There was a heavy footfall on the stairs and Mr Wyatt made his appearance. It seemed to Bess that the grocer had increased in girth by several inches since before Christmas. He had recently stood but failed to gain a seat on the Parish Council but he certainly now looked every inch the prosperous citizen, complete with round belly and fine wool frock coat.

He was obviously a little disconcerted by Bess's visit for he did much clapping together of his great hands and urging his wife to bring in refreshment, though Bess had refused tea several times. The two oldest girls were introduced again, the youngest being only about six and therefore not relevant to the occasion.

Bess was not deceived by the girls' self-effacing demeanour. All three had lively eyes and followed the conversation with great interest.

Mrs Wyatt again apologized for the untidy state of the room. 'It being Saturday, we rose a little late. I'm so sorry.'

But Mr Wyatt looked about him with pride. 'We're all avid readers, Miss Hardemon. Any ideas I have I owe to books. I hold book-learning in the greatest respect. As you know, I heard great things of your school and wanted my girls to attend. I have no boys, you see, so I thought, right then, we'll get these females educated so that they can be of some use.'

'And I am here, Mr Wyatt, because you wrote to me saying that you no longer wished the girls to come to my school. I had fully expected them to start this term.'

'Oh, we did wish them to attend your school,' put in Mrs Wyatt eagerly.

'The reason I changed my mind,' said Mr Wyatt, 'is that I don't want my girls ostracized by the town. I understand that your school does not admit the daughters of tradesmen. I am proud of my business but I won't have my girls suffer because I have overstepped myself.'

Bess, who felt minute and insignificant beside huge Mr Wyatt, gave little credence to this admission of humility. 'You hadn't overstepped yourself. Your daughters had all the entry requirements demanded by my school.'

Mrs Wyatt was by now looking very uncomfortable. 'Oh, it isn't easy, it hasn't been at all easy.'

'Mr Wyatt, your girls are likely to face all kinds of opposition in future. No woman's life is without conflict. Are you always going to encourage them to back down? I'm surprised that a successful businessman like yourself should adopt such a strategy.'

His blood-shot eyes fastened sternly on Bess. 'I won't have them used as guinea-pigs, Miss Hardemon. Until all girls of respectable, well-to-do parentage are accepted freely into your school, I will not be attempting to send them there as pupils. I don't wish to endanger either my family's reputation or that of your excellent school by pushing this matter any further.'

Well, Mr Wyatt, Bess thought, who's been talking to you? You might have thought of all this months ago and thereby saved me a great deal of difficulty. She detected the wily reasoning of Mrs Penhaligon behind his argument. Bess knew enough of small-town politics to guess that he had been promised a considerable favour in return for his acquiescence.

Rising, she smiled briefly at the girls and thanked Mrs Wyatt for her time.

Mr Wyatt took her hand and squeezed it comfortingly. 'My girls will bide their time, Miss Hardemon, and they will continue to have private tuition. I want them to be able to mix with the highest born in this town and they shall. It will come right, you'll see.'

Bess had been absent from Priors Heath for less than two hours but in that time a new crisis had arisen. Caroline Wentworth was waiting in the entrance hall, her elfin face crumpled with anxiety. An hour ago Miss Boulder had collapsed and been carried home to her bed and now a gentleman had arrived by carriage with an urgent note for Miss Hardemon.

'He won't talk to anyone but you, Miss Hardemon. I put him in the library which happened to be empty.'

Mary, agog with interest, was also hovering. 'You should have seen the state of his horses.'

'How typical of Helen Boulder to be sick when needed,'

remarked Bess unjustly. 'Soon I shall be running the entire school single-handed.' She thrust her cloak into Mary's hand and headed for the library. 'Perhaps you would wait in the schoolroom, Miss Wentworth, in case you're needed.' For some reason Caroline was looking decidedly aggrieved. I really can't take account of everyone's feelings all the time, thought Bess.

In the library was a man in a dark blue overcoat with a square, grey head and fleshy features. His top hat lay on the table and he had only removed one glove. He stood up when Bess walked in and looked at her with insolent blue eyes.

'I am Miss Hardemon. How may I help you?'

'My name is Buckleigh. I've brought a letter from my client, Mr Charles Lytton, who wants to see you at once.'

In an instant Bess knew that there was terrible trouble. 'Has something happened to Mrs Lytton?'

'I think you should read the letter, madam.' He was obviously enjoying the advantage given him by superior knowledge.

Some new commotion was taking place in the hall. As she opened the letter Bess heard the porch door opening and closing and Mary's breathless voice. It seemed to her that ever since Peachey had sat with her by the pond on the Longcross Estate things had been terribly out of kilter. Would nothing set them to rights?

> The Abbey House,
> Saturday
>
> Miss Hardemon,
>
> Two days ago my wife eloped. I have a great regard for you and therefore assume you had no hand in it. The man in question is a George Peachey, whom I believe Christina met at your school. I need hardly tell you that a savage blow has been dealt my household by this news.
>
> Christina is gone and there is no bringing her back, but I should like you to come here and tell me what you know of Peachey. I wouldn't normally put you to the trouble but I do not wish to leave my daughter alone in this house,

and in any case I hardly think a girls' school an appropriate place to discuss matters of this kind.

Your servant,
Charles Lytton

Bess first scanned the letter, then read it over several times. Though her mind resisted understanding she knew from the first minute that what it contained would change her life for ever.

Peachey. Christina.

No. No.

'I'll get my things,' she murmured.

At first the library door wouldn't open because her clammy hand slid on the knob. Outside Caroline Wentworth was holding an uneasy conversation with the unwelcome figure of Reverend Carnegie. Ah, thought Bess, so he's here already to pick over the bones.

'Miss Wentworth, I'd like a word with you in my office. I'm sorry, Reverend, a matter of some urgency has arisen. I can't speak to you today.'

But he followed her up the white staircase. 'Miss Hardemon.'

She loathed the dreadful heaviness in his voice. 'Yes, I know. I know,' she hissed. 'You need not have come.'

'Is there anything I can do?'

Leave me alone, she thought. Oh please, please. 'Nothing. I'm quite sure Miss Wentworth will manage in my brief absence.' Caroline Wentworth's feet were soundless on the stairs. She was like a little shadow in her grey dress, her hair braided neatly round her head. Bess halted suddenly and turned on Carnegie. 'Thank you, Reverend,' she said curtly.

He rarely looked her fully in the eye when she confronted him directly. Now he sank back a few steps. 'I'll call again tomorrow then,' he said.

*   *   *

An hour later she was in Lytton's carriage with Mary who was so excited by the outing she could scarcely sit still. If Helen Boulder had been well enough Bess would have brought her but there was no question of it and nobody else could be spared. Opposite sat Mr Buckleigh, Lytton's lawyer. He at least didn't bother to speak and so gave her the chance to pull herself together in time for the coming interview with Lytton. It was unlikely that they'd arrive at the Abbey House much before supper.

In her room at Priors Heath Bess had tied on her best grey silk drawn bonnet to shield herself from Buckleigh. She cut herself off from him beneath its brim and sank deep into the blackest, most godless chamber of her mind.

Christina and Peachey in the garden at Priors Heath, his dark form hanging over her as she dipped her paintbrush.

Christina framed by the high schoolroom window deep in conversation with Peachey, laughing aloud for the first time since coming back to the school.

Peachey's drawing room, and his long look across the room to the sofa where sat the odd trio from Priors Heath.

The elliptical conversation by the pond in Derbyshire.

And all the time Bess had assumed that it was she he loved, she whom he wished to impress, amuse and woo.

Dear God, she thought suddenly, what if I had accepted his sudden and meaningless offer of marriage? *I came because I want you to marry me.*

No, you don't want to marry me, she had replied at once. But if she'd said yes, might she have saved them all?

Now that there was no chance of ever holding a friendly conversation with Peachey again she grieved for him, her dear friend, her one possible lover. She felt grey and empty, a husk of a woman nobody could love, sexless and passionless. The long, long thread of her spinsterhood unravelled before her.

Then, of course, came anger. How dare they? How dare they sully the name of her school by using it as a trysting ground?

The sheer nerve. Their forbidden love affair had been conducted right under her nose. Christina had behaved unspeakably. She had drawn on all Bess's emotional resources and repaid her by this betrayal.

But how had it happened so fast, and why? Peachey seemed such an unlikely lover for Christina. In the first place there was a considerable age difference. At twenty-three Christina was probably twelve years Peachey's junior, although it was true that he, in turn, was several years younger than Charles Lytton. And Peachey was such a dapper, bright-eyed little man, somehow physically at odds with the slender, fair Christina.

What had he offered her? Was it the glimpse of his drawing room that had enchanted her, the modern paintings, the brilliant colours, the glamorous, decadent friends? Or was it a promise of freedom from a husband she didn't love? Or perhaps simply the chance to escape a life that had become a constant reminder of her failure to give birth to living children?

Slowly the implications for her school dawned on Bess. The dissent parents had expressed over the Wyatt girls would seem a mere whisper compared to their outrage that theology at Priors Heath had been taught by a dissolute and concupiscent clergyman. Did neither Peachey nor Christina think of me, Bess wondered, or the damage they might do me?

Buckleigh ordered the driver to stop for refreshment but Bess could only drink tea. She sat at the table in silence, thankful for the heavy skirts which concealed the shaking of her knees and for her years of practice at hiding her feelings. Not by a flicker of an eyelid would she betray her distress to a solicitor.

It was more than four years since Bess had called with Christina at the Abbey House just before her marriage. This time Charles wasn't waiting on the steps and Bess was shown in silence along the quiet passages to the study. She was struck immediately by how little impact Christina had made on the house. It was still meticulously maintained, precisely as well polished and well oiled as before. There was no suggestion in the maid's neat uniform, the gleaming silverware or the carefully brushed rugs that disaster had shaken the household.

Before Charles Lytton had risen to take her hand Bess had registered that his study was much too self-consciously sombre for her taste. She was still feeling light-headed and exposed after removing her bonnet and the sudden warmth of the room made her dizzy and faint. Charles was heavier-set and more florid than she remembered and did not smile. The hand that he offered her had known Christina intimately and been betrayed. Bess blushed as she returned his greeting. He ordered tea and gave her a seat by the fire.

'It is very good of you to come so promptly, Miss Hardemon. I know you must have many other demands on your time.'

She looked at him steadily and was aware that she had no knowledge of his character. In their previous meeting he had appeared to be a kindly and refined man but now his courtesy seemed forced and inappropriate. Of course he must be deeply angry and hurt, but she had anticipated the despair of a betrayed lover not the rage of a rich man who has been cheated. She also resented the scarcely concealed sarcasm in his voice. So, he thought little of her school and perhaps blamed her after all for what had happened.

She was silent.

'Miss Hardemon, I sent for you because this has all been so sudden I can scarcely take it in. Four days ago I returned from a business trip to Europe. The next afternoon I came back from work and found a note from Christina saying that she could no longer live with me because she loved someone else, a teacher at your school. She gave me his name because she didn't want it to be a mystery. I have met this man, Miss Hardemon. He called at the house before Christmas and even had lunch with us. I thought him amiable and clever, but by no means a threat. How did it happen? How much time did you give them alone at Priors Heath that such a relationship could have developed?'

The door opened and servants arrived with tea. Thank heavens, thought Bess who had not eaten since breakfast, that these rituals with food and drink must go on despite all the drama. The business of handing plates and napkins gave her time to soften her resentment at his rather bullying tones.

'There are over two hundred and thirty people in my school at any one time, Mr Lytton. You asked me to take Christina because you thought it would help her recovery. I did my best but I certainly didn't think it my duty to supervise her every waking moment. You can be quite sure that if I'd had any idea of impropriety I would have taken immediate action.'

His teacup was a fragile thimble in his solid hand and his lip curled on the rim. 'How could you have had any idea of what was going on? Of course, you wouldn't, would you?' She understood what he meant, and registered the insult.

Again she said nothing. Her appetite was gone.

'I do blame you, Miss Hardemon. Oh yes. What kind of judge of character are you that you allow such a man, a seducer, a clergyman for God's sake, into a school for girls?'

She folded her hands in her lap and gazed fiercely into the fire.

'We should lock up our daughters,' he said.

Her voice was cool and smooth as mercury. 'You're right, I had misjudged George Peachey. But also Christina. She went with him willingly, I suppose?'

He weighed her up and understood she was telling him he had failed as a husband. 'She is another product of your noble institution, Miss Hardemon.'

Her fury was a coiled spring. He is going to destroy me, she thought. He has been wounded and will now lash out at me like a wild beast.

'Mr Lytton, I think that every human being has the gift of

free will. It would be extremely arrogant to think that I, or any other teacher, had the power to mould a pupil's nature. I hope I have influence, but that is all.'

She was floundering. In her heart she knew that she did want to mould her girls. She wanted them to be independent, intelligent spirits, but with her own high principles, her sense of duty and responsibility.

'Oh, Miss Hardemon, make no mistake about it. You changed Christina's life. You were her ideal. The box of water-colours you once gave her is her most treasured possession. Indeed, it's one of the few things she's taken with her. I know that she found teaching Rebecca very tedious but I think she did it because you would have approved. She was restless and dissatisfied because she remembered you with all your energy and power. Nothing I did could really please her. I spent a fortune on drawing lessons for her, did you know that? For months at a time we had an art master here who worked alongside Christina. This house was full of her paintings. I took her half across Europe on our honeymoon because she wanted to go to Paris and Rome to look at pictures. I tolerated it all because I loved her. And now someone has come along with some other lure, and she's gone. You can be quite sure that her obsession with painting is behind this. Christina is cold at heart, and single-minded. She will do nothing for love.'

Was that true? Was Christina selfishly ambitious? Then you and I, Mr Lytton, have both been used, thought Bess.

'I was away for nearly a month after Christmas and of course that gave him his chance. I offered to take Christina but she refused because of Rebecca. Apparently Peachey was staying in the area most of that time so she must have told him I'd be away. Christina was constantly in the garden, painting the gatehouse, she said. She took the key of the upper room so that she could store her things there and shelter from the wind and rain. God knows it must have been pretty uncomfortable, if that's where they conducted their assignations. Sometimes the servants gave Peachey tea or lunch in the house. Rebecca was used as a chaperone.'

'I am very sorry, Mr Lytton.'

'Sorry, but not responsible, eh, Miss Hardemon?'

She hated him as she had once hated Carnegie. You men, she thought. How can I protect my girls from you? You are domineering, cruel and ruthless. Even when you smile, like Peachey, you are not to be trusted because what you want is something dark and hidden.

Carefully she placed her cup on the table, stood up and smoothed her skirts. 'You may take some small comfort that I have learnt a great deal from my experience of the past few hours,' she said. 'I know now that I must make my girls more alert to danger, more thoughtful, more conscious that we live in a self-seeking and predatory world. Now, if I may, I should like to speak to Rebecca.'

With impeccable manners he had risen and moved behind his chair. 'Of course. And I have had a room aired for you. I thought you would stay the night.'

It was already nearly six o'clock. There could be no question of going back to Priors Heath that evening so she would have to endure dinner in his company and a night in his house. A servant was called and she was taken upstairs. Though the portrait of the first Mrs Lytton was still in place there were spaces on the wall, presumably where Christina's paintings had been hurriedly removed. Bess was shown first to a comfortable room decorated with a luxurious, rose-patterned wallpaper, and then to Rebecca's schoolroom.

The child sat with her governess at a round table. Both were reading. The governess was sandy-haired and avid for more gossip. She was reluctant to leave the room but didn't quite dare defy Bess who wished to be alone with Rebecca.

The poor child was thinner than ever, her eyes like huge lamps in a pallid face. She was all joints and gawky limbs. Bess sat beside her and took her cold, big hand.

'I'm so sorry, Rebecca.'

'It's all right.'

'No, it's not all right. You'll miss your stepmother dreadfully. She's done you a terrible wrong by leaving you.'

'Oh, there was nothing for her here. She was much too talented and lovely. I knew that.'

'No. She had made vows to your father, and therefore to you. She should not have broken them.'

This child is much too composed for a twelve-year-old, thought Bess in alarm. Her life at the moment must be hell. Rebecca was terribly pale, her skin an opaque, greyish white.

'I don't mind,' she said.

Over the fireplace was a painting of a woman standing in the foreground of a scene where children picnicked among trees. The woman's back was half turned, she wore a dark dress and her arms were folded tightly across her chest as she watched the children. They were in sunshine, she was in shade. Bess knew little about art but she could tell by the detail of the grass and leaves, the way the light fell on the heads of the children and the texture of the woman's dress that this was a fine painting. She also knew from its title: 'The Childless Woman', that it was an unsuitable picture for Rebecca.

'Did your stepmother paint this?' she asked.

'Yes. My father has taken the others down. He wants to burn them. I rescued this. He doesn't come in here much and I don't think he'd take it away from me anyway.'

'I'm sure he wouldn't.'

They talked for a while about Rebecca's studies, but she wasn't forthcoming. The wonderful, luminous vivacity that Bess had seen on her last visit had been extinguished. This has been the worst crime of all, thought Bess, to put out the light in this child. Dear Lord, give me the wisdom to say something that will comfort her.

When she got up to leave she kissed Rebecca's cheek. 'Don't think that your stepmother didn't love you. I believe she did.

She talked of you often. I'm sure she will miss you dreadfully.'

Well, she thought, as she went back to her plush bedroom, it's not like me to be less than honest. Let's hope it helps.

At dinner she sat on Charles Lytton's right and managed to eat a little soup. He seemed to have realized that he'd been unjust to Bess because he was gentler with her and questioned her closely about Priors Heath. This time he was more reasonable when he spoke of Peachey.

'I could tell he had charm,' he admitted. 'He charmed me. He was interested in my work, and my reforms in the factory. Apparently he was writing an article about the most liberal practices in our new industries. God help me, I talked with him for hours. My wife never took an interest in my work, you see, so it was a novelty to find someone who could ask an intelligent question.'

Bess had a vivid image of Peachey seated at this very table, his fork waving with enthusiasm, his bright eyes darting from Lytton's face to Christina's.

She said quietly, perhaps made bold by a glass of wine: 'I suppose you wouldn't consider sending Rebecca to school. It's going to be terribly lonely for her here.'

He laughed bitterly and pushed aside his plate with such force that it almost slid off the table. 'Now I see why your school is so successful. I've never known such nerve. No, Miss Hardemon, I will not send my daughter to school. I shall guard her carefully and try to repair some of the damage done.'

'She'll miss Christina's company. She's a bright girl, and must be stimulated.'

'So that she too grows dissatisfied, I suppose.'

'No. So that she can be comforted, and directed. She is too isolated and therefore had become very dependent on Christina. I think she's a girl who would gain so much from contact with other children, and from a broad education. We must show her how to understand the world and develop her judgement so that she makes better choices than her stepmother.'

'I brought you here to blame you, Miss Hardemon, and I end up by struggling to keep my daughter. No. There is no question of her attending your school or anyone else's.'

But his manner was a little softer. Bess realized that he was very resilient and that once his pride was healed, he would recover from Christina's elopement. As she climbed the carpeted staircase to her bedroom she thought it likely that Lytton would sleep soundly while she was still reeling from shock.

Her bedroom was very warm and quiet. The embers spat softly and overhead a servant trod on an old floorboard. In the bed her cheek fell on laundered cotton, her body was snugly enfolded by a gossamer-light eiderdown.

George Peachey and Christina Lytton had galloped away into the night. Again and again in her imagination Bess pursued them until it was she who sat in the carriage beside Peachey. His bright eyes shone in the darkness with the old teasing affection. He would carry her far away from all the turmoil, all the hazard of Priors Heath where there were such incessant demands made on her, body and soul, into a future cluttered only by the love of a man. Her body contracted with grief and longing. His hand touched her hair again, but this time he was not resigned or regretful but tender. He pulled her close so that her head was tucked against his throat and his hand stroked her breast.

She leapt from the bed, marched to the window and threw up the sash. Cold air blew through the overheated room.

You would have sacrificed everything for the embrace of a worthless man, she told herself sternly, to spend hour after hour in the company of someone who obviously cares only for his own happiness. Oh, Peachey is a gifted teacher. He has charm. But in the end you would have been little more than a clergy wife, a bustling do-gooder whose absent husband whisked about the country collecting material for his essays and lectures. And who would run Priors Heath meanwhile, I wonder? Some feeble-minded woman with no vision. The fate of hundreds of girls depended on your decision not to snatch a few moments of selfish happiness.

She smiled at herself, and paced about until she grew less frantic. But when she lay down once more the dark interior of the carriage surrounded her and Peachey's breath fell on her mouth. Again she paced and grew cold by the open window, then knelt shivering to pray for strength. At last, curled in a tight knot under the eiderdown, she found sleep.

At six o'clock she got up, dressed, and packed ready to leave immediately after breakfast. A milky dawn bathed the garden in a grey, cold light, though it promised to be a bright and cloudless day. The gatehouse was an ancient presence among the trees.

Bess wrapped herself in her shawl, let herself out of the front door, and crept round to the garden. Her skirts trailed on the frosty grass and the hem of her gown quickly grew heavy with moisture. Moment by moment colour was returning to the garden, the browns of bare trees, the shiny green of holly, the honeyed stone of the gatehouse. Under the arch Bess found that the door which opened on to a steep flight of stairs had been left ajar, perhaps to banish any hint of secret meetings.

She climbed cautiously into the complete blackness of the stairs and came to a low door opening on to a gloomy room. The freezing chill of the night hung leaden in the still air and the oriel window at one end was so heavily latticed that there was very little light.

A thorough clearance had recently taken place. The floor was of bare, unpolished boards, a few old chairs and a round table had been pushed against the white-washed stone walls and in one corner stood a rolled carpet. There was an old cupboard but the doors had fallen open and it was completely empty. Its shelves smelt strongly of oil paint and turpentine.

She fingered the rough back of the carpet and its tangled

fringe. There was a fireplace but the hearth was empty and swept clean.

Suddenly Bess took hold of the rug and unrolled it so that it covered perhaps a quarter of the floor. It was very beautiful, diamond patterned and within each diamond a flower, fern or tree. Its pile was soft and velvety. She knelt and rested her palm on it, and then, in a slow, tentative movement, her cheek.

He was here. She felt him. His quick, sure feet climbed the little stone staircase and flung open the old door. His eyes shone. He was frightened and eager, intoxicated by what he was doing.

Perhaps they had stood together on this rug, Christina's head exactly level with his. He had folded her in his arms. His lips had kissed hers.

A shadow world lay in the glowing pattern of the rug. Bess lay curled with her hands pressed tightly to her breast, her face to the cold luxury of the silky pile, and cried for the first time in her adult life.

Having arrived back at her school in the late afternoon, Bess decided to make an unannounced call on Helen Boulder.

She had never visited Helen's small house before and was rather surprised to find the gleaming front door opened by a maid who stood in a neat, well-lit hall. If she'd ever bothered to imagine Helen at home Bess might have guessed at a couple of fussy, dark rooms. But of course Helen had an independent income and though the furnishings in her house were very plain they were quite elegant. With some reluctance on the part of the maid, Bess was shown upstairs to Miss Boulder's bedroom.

Helen looked dreadful, the scar on her cheek viciously prominent in her pale face. She was exhausted, and not very pleased to see Bess. She tried to lift her head but could not. Bess went up to the bed, quelling her irritation that Helen should be so inconveniently weak just when she was most needed.

'My dear Helen, I have come to tell you that you must get well at once.'

Helen gave a slight smile. Even Bess, who was inexperienced in the care of the sick, could tell that she was in great pain and very feverish. For want of any other purposeful activity she went to the hearth, seized the poker and urged more life into the fire. 'I hope that maid is looking after you properly. I shall have a word with her before I go. Ah, I see you're reading *Villette*. I wish I had time to keep up with modern novels.'

'It's about a schoolmistress,' murmured Helen, her voice thick with illness.

'Then I shall definitely avoid it at all costs.' She began adjusting the furniture and straightening cushions. Helen Boulder shifted restlessly in the bed. Her eyes had closed.

'Helen, do you know what's happened? Have you been told?'

'You mean about Mrs Lytton. Yes. Caroline Wentworth came earlier.'

'Then she had no business to. Fancy disturbing you when you're so sick.'

Again Helen smiled faintly.

Helen, thought Bess, you are the only one who can have an inkling of how I am suffering. You loved Christina and admired Peachey. I think you knew a little of how dear he was to me. Don't fail me now. 'I've taken down the sketch of the blossom trees she gave me from my office wall.'

Helen opened her eyes briefly. 'You haven't torn it up?'

'No. No, you can have it if you like. I thought you'd want it.' She sat down and began rearranging the brush and shovel on the fire dog. 'I'm hoping we shall weather the storm. Mr Lytton tells me there's bound to be a scandal. Peachey is well known in some circles, but Faringford is fortunately quite a backwater. I wonder, did they even think of the school when they went off?'

'I very much doubt it.'

'Helen, I can't understand them. Especially him. Why would he throw away everything like that? They'll never survive the scandal. It's so cruel. So many lives have been damaged. Rebecca, Charles Lytton, Peachey's sister.' She halted. Helen's eyes were now open and watchful. 'Why, Helen?'

'Love, perhaps.'

'Love. Nobody has the right to destroy so much because of love. Love.' Love in the cold room in the gatehouse.

'Oh, I don't know,' said Helen.

'Of course you do. Of course you know how wrong they've been, Helen.' Bess looked helplessly across at her and prayed for her early recovery. Helen was foolish and wrong-headed but her calm reception of the news was oddly soothing. 'I suppose you have no idea when you might be well again?'

'Perhaps the day after next.'

'Well, I suppose I must be content with that.' She couldn't help being affronted by Helen's illness. 'There is so much to do, Helen. Now that the question of the Wyatts has been settled, though not at all to my satisfaction, I'm hoping that the Board will give way on a number of issues. There is the question of tests for the girls. Of course they must be examined by some authority outside the school. A standard must be set. We must write again to Cambridge.' She took a pillow from behind Helen's head and gave it a severe beating. It occurred to her that her secretary's skin was a very poor colour and her breathing shallow.

Miss Boulder, perhaps made more courageous by the peculiarity of her situation, had something to say after all. 'Miss Hardemon, I have been thinking. At Priors Heath we work so much in isolation. This matter of examinations. Were we to join with other schools, if there was a general movement to have girls examined . . .'

'I know of no other schools that offer a serious education to girls. Our pupils would far outstrip any others.' She scarcely listened because there was one further matter she wanted to hurry past Helen which would perhaps exorcise the pain of Peachey's elopement. She would banish all reminders of him from the school and especially the one place she particularly associated with him. 'And there's something else I decided on my way back in Lytton's carriage this morning. I don't believe we'll have to buy any more land for the assembly hall after all. We shall build on the site of the rose garden. Gardens encourage idleness. In the hall the girls will have more space for callisthenics and team games, when I can finally persuade the Board to allow them, and that will provide plenty of exercise. If we use land already owned by the school costs will be considerably reduced. Good. And I've had some thoughts on nibs. I think we must get the girls to supply their own. If they have to pay for them out of their pocket money they will break fewer. What do you think?'

She reached down and knotted Helen's shawl more tightly about her neck. 'You must keep warm. I shall send the girl in with more coal. Rest now. You shouldn't excite yourself, or receive any visitors. We don't want to allow anyone to upset you.'

She hurried away. Already the strangeness of her morning collapse in the gatehouse after a sleepless night was a fading memory. Her talk with Helen had done her good. Life after all could go on quite successfully without Peachey. The affairs of the school were complicated and troublesome, but her way forward was clear. She must now work to protect her girls from the scandal and keep them so busy that they would have no time for the kind of emotional entanglements Christina Lytton had allowed to destroy her life.

17

Founder's Day, April 1996

The date of Founder's Day had been fixed since the war to fall at the end of the spring term, thereby avoiding interference with revision for public examinations.

This year, thanks to Imogen's decree, the usual service of thanksgiving in the Parish Church would be shorter and followed by lessons until lunch-time. Later in the afternoon fund-raising events were to take place in aid of the local hospice, the upper school providing amusements for the lower.

First the morning service must be endured. The Wyatt Hall was too small to accommodate the whole school so instead everyone had to be marched to St Matthew's Church, just as in the earliest days of Priors Heath the wan daughters of penniless clergyman had trudged through frost or rain to interminable Sunday acts of worship. It was not a pleasant walk. Traffic whisked by constantly and wind was funnelled along the high walls of the disused brewery.

A paved path went alongside Boots to the churchyard which was fenced by low iron palings. Opposite was a snug little close of almshouses. Under a shaggy yew lay the remains of Bess Hardemon, marked by a lichened headstone. A selected pupil from each year group placed a posy of white roses on her grave so that for this one day it was as if she had been dead only days, so fresh were the flowers.

ELIZABETH HARDEMON

1828—1901

To the Glory of God

There was no mention on the stone either of a grieving family or her work for the community of Faringford. Miss Hardemon had never retired and it was said that in eccentric old age she had defied anyone to make a fuss of her death. 'Let my school be my epitaph,' is how legend described her dying words. 'Like hell,' said Imogen.

The school was now so big that the church was crammed, sixth-formers in the chancel, eleven-year-olds at the front, the rest ranked by form in the rows behind. Next to the centre aisle, at judicial intervals, sat the staff. Sarah planted Matthew Illingworth by her side and he immediately folded his Order of Service into an origami battleship.

The church's gracious fifteenth-century architecture had been marred by Victorian worshippers with grandiose ideas. Lurid stained glass above the aisles told the life of doe-eyed Jesus, and the bulbous pulpit had been donated by the ubiquitous Wyatt clan. On the walls plaques eulogized the virtues of other prominent families, the Edgbastons and Godalmings, and over the south door was a modest brass plate in honour of Elizabeth Hardemon, for nearly fifty years the indomitable head-teacher of Priors Heath School. Nearby was another little plaque dedicated to the memory of Helen Boulder, who had given her name to the school library. The friendship between Miss Hardemon and Miss Boulder was legendary, as was Miss Hardemon's grief over Helen Boulder's untimely death.

Sonia had been selected to do a reading, a gesture designed to give her a grip on the present and to confront her with her role as a senior member of the school. She had a beautiful, low speaking voice and had rehearsed carefully. I wonder, thought Sarah, what actually went on? Surely Sonia wouldn't destroy Fenster's career with a lie bred of fantasy? Or had they really become involved in a destructive sexual affair? A school counsellor had been drafted in for Sonia, her 'A' level work was being monitored constantly by the head of the sixth form and a place awaited her at Birmingham to study the history of art. She, at least, might be saved.

The reading, the famous exhortation by Paul to the Corinthians, was the one chosen by Bess Hardemon for her own first celebration of the school's reopening:

'Though I speak with the tongues of men and of angels, and have not charity, I am become as sounding brass, or a tinkling cymbal.
    And though I have the gift of prophecy, and understand all mysteries, and all knowledge; and though I have all faith, so that I could remove mountains, and have not charity, I am nothing . . .'

Sonia read it with such reverence that the meaning was somewhat diminished but her dark beauty and holy intensity were impressive. As she stepped from the dais afterwards she caught Sarah's eye and smiled, a little self-conscious perhaps, and knowing.

Imogen now moved forward for the head-teacher's address. There was renewed attentiveness among the congregation and Matthew Illingworth stopped picking fluff from the pile of grey tissues he had extracted from his pocket.

But Sarah was suddenly restless. This was not her world but Imogen's and she yearned to be back at Cedarview with Jamie and Lorna who had broken up the previous Friday.

Imogen today wore a surprising red suit which added a slight warmth to her white skin but made her jaw and cheek-bones more angular than ever. Her hair was scooped into a large clip and she seemed entirely at ease. 'The quality I most admire about Miss Hardemon was her energy. I bet in many respects both pupils and staff thought her a nightmare . . .'

*   *   *

At the very suggestion that Cedarview should be sold, Lorna had conceived a perverse affection for it. 'Oh Mum, you can't. I love the house. I love my room and the garden. You can't sell it.' She had then embarked on the usual litany of accusations: 'That's typical. First of all you push my father away. Then you sell the house from under me.'

Whether the house was to be put on the market or not, Sarah had insisted during the first weekend of the children's holidays that they must embark on a great clearing operation. If the family was to live at Cedarview permanently the last vestiges of its life as rented accommodation must be banished, and if it was to be sold all the old debris must go in any case.

They were to begin with the two garden sheds and on Saturday afternoon Jamie and Lorna had followed Sarah reluctantly out on to the spring lawn.

The sheds, set among old trees, were disguised by ivy. Sarah, who couldn't walk in the copse without remembering Lawrence, glanced hurriedly at the children's faces but they were oblivious to her heightened consciousness. In the thick, creosoted gloom of the oldest shed were children's toys, a dolls' pram and a couple of bikes, squashed beach balls, muddy plastic spades and battered shuttlecocks. We have collected all the paraphernalia of a normal family, thought Sarah. It's just there are big gaps in our shared history when we've been away from each other.

Lorna discovered an undying affection for all the old toys. 'Mum, you can't give away that. I love that saddle bag. It's still fine.' But Sarah was ruthless and directed that everything they'd outgrown should go either to Oxfam or the tip.

The children weren't much help. Lorna found a rusty pogo stick and had to go and try it on a paved path somewhere and Jamie wandered off after a few more minutes, muttering about revision. Soon Sarah was working alone among the trees. The morning was the finest of the year so far and when she moved from shade to a patch of sunshine it was deliciously warm.

A brilliant blue and white sky drifted overhead among the branches.

Beyond birdsong came the scrunch of tyres on gravel and the soft thud of a car door closing. Lorna shouted twice.

Sarah straightened from sweeping up dry spiders and earth. She peered out across the lawn.

David was there. He had one arm around Lorna, and in his other hand he grasped the pogo stick. Sarah could imagine his expression, quizzical and affectionate, as he teased Lorna for bothering with such a ridiculous toy.

The newly brushed little shed provided a refuge and Sarah stepped back into it out of the light. She was breathing rapidly. He had given no inkling that he would come, though he had of course known that the children would be home that weekend.

Her inability to predict what might happen in the next few minutes paralysed Sarah. Had David come in the spirit of reconciliation or anger? Was the house really to be sold as a prelude to their separation, or would he make a renewed plea for her to travel abroad with him? In a moment of hot, white panic she realized that despite what she had told Jamie, she had no idea how she would respond to either of these demands. And the longer she stood alone in the copse the more difficult it was to emerge and be spontaneous, which might have allowed for something truthful to happen.

It was too late now. Her meeting with David must be calculated. To give herself time, she pretended that she hadn't seen him and began carefully replacing the few items that were to go back, deckchairs on one side, cricket bat, wooden tennis rackets, puncture repair outfit on the other. Meanwhile every nerve was tuned to his approach and her mind rehearsed a dozen likely conversations.

A cold David might stand at the shed door, watching her. 'Don't worry, Sarah. I haven't come back to claim you or to force you to do anything distasteful. We'll divorce and sell this house. The children will come to me in the summer holidays for as long as they want and you can do what the hell you like.'

The shed had three windows, each very dirty. One cracked.

Or: 'Sarah. Sarah.' He would have that whipped, pleading look in his eye. 'Please can we try again? I've come to terms with what happened with Lawrence. I still want to be married to you. Give it one more chance . . .'

And on one horizontal support a row of hooks had been nailed, ideal for hanging a snagged fishing net and a couple of buckets.

'Of course, Sarah, it's up to you. I shall never walk away from my responsibilities. We must resolve this one way or another because the cost is ridiculous. My flights, the loss of the rental on Cedarview and the children's school fees on top of everything! Tell me what you want and we'll just get on and do it.'

Lorna's voice wove its way among the trees, increasing in volume as she ran towards Sarah. 'Mum. Mum. You'll never guess what. You'll never guess who's come. Mum. Where are you?

The red of Imogen's suit blended well with the rich light from the stained glass in the chancel, one of the few original windows. Her long fingers clasped the edge of the lectern and her elbows were bent, so that her arms formed opposite sides of a diamond. Her face was infused with conviction. 'You see, what I think is that Bess Hardemon released in her pupils far more than she had intended. Her aims were in fact quite modest. She was a conservative little body, dead set against the suffragette movement and even university education for women. She was very religious, the daughter of a clergyman, and my guess is she had been more or less indoctrinated with the view that whatever her ability, a woman's duty was only to nurture. But so powerful were her abilities as an educator

334

that she wrenched open the minds of those Victorian young ladies, and then found she had hundreds of eager, bright individuals on her hands who could not be regulated beyond the classroom. The girls might do as Miss Hardemon said whilst in school but she couldn't stop their intellects and characters developing on and on well beyond what she had started.

'So before the nineteenth century was out Priors Heath girls were doing all kinds of things not approved by Miss Hardemon: they were scientists, doctors, explorers, secretaries, writers, artists, even revolutionaries, those who joined the women's movement. She had no moral jurisdiction over them. She might influence them, she might try and instil a sense of humanity and religious belief into them, but once they had begun to think for themselves her influence was rapidly outgrown. Look at Christina Lytton, one of her earliest pupils, and later one of the most despised women in Victorian polite society. You know it was Christina Lytton who designed the window in the Old House and inscribed the motto: "*Fiat Lux*", "Let there be light". She owed her freedom to Miss Hardemon, but abandoning her marriage to live with another man was hardly the kind of freedom Miss Hardemon had intended.'

'Oh,' said Sarah, stepping from the gloom of the shed to the dappled light in the copse. 'I don't believe it. Is Dad really home?'

'You must have heard him. Come on.' Lorna pranced off back towards her father who was standing on the little bridge with Jamie. He looked towards Sarah with a smile which simply said that he was pleased to have surprised them. In front of Lorna and Jamie, Sarah could do nothing but walk up to him and kiss his cheek. He rested his hand on her shoulder for a moment and then they moved apart.

'They tell me you've been spring cleaning. I'll get changed and come and join you.'

But Lorna, who had watched the kiss with frantic longing,

would not let them separate. 'No, no, you must be exhausted. Stay out here with Mum. Jamie and I will make you coffee. Won't we, Jamie? Come on.' Her brother hung back, watchful and silent. Then he backed away a few paces, turned, and allowed Lorna to take his arm.

Sarah and David laughed a little proudly at Lorna's assertive handling of the moment, and then David returned his hands to his pockets and Sarah watched him with the old detachment. What now?

He was rumpled from the long journey, his face was grey, his eyes obscured by weariness. 'So you've already made a start on things,' he said lightly, looking at the stream and the bank where he perhaps remembered her sitting the previous summer in her rain-drenched blouse.

'Yes. The children have been grumbling, of course. They hate disruption.'

'How's Jamie?'

Jamie, she thought, has put me in an impossible situation. How can I plead for our marriage to please him? She looked at David with a sense of rising panic. 'He seems less bothered about whether or not we sell the house than Lorna,' she said.

'Of course.' He walked across the bridge and into the trees. Sarah, in her coldly objective state, noticed that he was wearing a pair of grey casual trousers she had never seen before and she disliked them. They were too middle-aged. She ran to catch up with him and saw that he was blinking to relieve his sore eyes. He must still be adjusting to being home.

'I tell you what,' she said suddenly, surprising herself. 'I definitely shan't be staying at Priors Heath after the summer, even if I am in the country. I shall apply for other jobs. It's given me some invaluable experience and I'm grateful to it, but I'm ready to try a completely different school. It would be a retrograde step to work permanently at Priors Heath.' In fact she was offering him the information that she would be turning her back on the Taylor family, and on all the old associations.

'You'll need a job,' he said. 'We'll be short of money.' They walked carefully, side by side. 'I'm coming back to England, you see. It's no life for a married man on his own in Malaysia, or anywhere else abroad, I think. There's not much of a social life when you're alone but unavailable. People are wary of you.'

'I'm sorry,' said Sarah. 'I'm sorry I put you through that.'

He spoke like a financial adviser. 'So if I come home, which I shall after my contract expires in July, we'll be quite short of money. We're not getting the rental on this place any more as it is. And I'll lose all the other perks. Not to mention a hefty cut in salary – if I get a job at all.'

'Are you sure it's what you want?'

'Ah yes. Ah yes, Sarah, I did listen to what you said last summer and you were right. We took a certain route over the years and it was one that led us away from what we had once valued. I can't say I didn't enjoy it because I did. But when you didn't come back with me and I was left alone, I saw that it was a life without foundations. I was accumulating wealth for a future I no longer had and doing a job I didn't much enjoy for its own sake.'

She had no words for him, either of comfort or hope. He sounded lost and, she thought, weak. Suddenly he reached out and took her hand, not to hold it but to touch the wrist where an irregular scar was still marked as a pale, ribbed line. 'You were also right that I tried to protect you. I thought you were immensely fragile and that the life I gave you would keep you safe and happy without you having to confront the world too much. I did it out of love and I was wrong. On several counts. I see that you are tougher than I am.'

She looked at her thin wrist in his brown hand. 'So what shall we do?'

There was a long pause. 'Do you want to go on being married to me?' he asked.

Another pause, and then, on an exhalation of breath she said: 'Yes.'

Her grip on her wrist tightened as he closed his eyes and kissed her blindly, the pressure of his closed lips as familiar as the angle at which she must raise her head to meet him.

All the possibilities, all the loves, all the potential of a life without David blew away, alluring, glistening, departing and she realized how much she had wanted him to leave her. She looked into his brown, uncertain eyes and saw a man she had never properly valued, or bothered to cherish. She hated him for being the one with whom she had so carelessly offered to share her one adult life, and she loved him a little, as perhaps she had always loved him, for his willingness to take the risk.

Even Imogen could not hold her youthful audience for too long. Her glance flew across the upturned faces, capturing them for one more minute. 'Perhaps Miss Hardemon's greatest legacy was her creation of Priors Heath as a set of buildings where more than academic learning could happen. She made a library, the Wyatt Hall, and recreational facilities for the girls, including the rose garden which as some of you may know, we are to lose. She gave girls space to grow up away from the confines of their homes. And that's what I try to give you. I want the sports hall and maybe a drama studio because I want you to have the opportunity to exercise every part of your being, body and soul.

'I was a pupil at Priors Heath, as you well know. I kicked against everything, the rules, the teachers, the curriculum, the lot. But when I left I realized it had provided me with some invaluable practice for life. I had tried out ways of behaving, of conducting friendships and of rebellions in an environment that would contain me safely, unless I pushed it too far. That's what I want for you. I want you to leave Priors Heath confident, intolerant of under-achievement in yourselves and others, and above all not wasting time by wandering off in the wrong direction. Life is cruel to the don't knows, the easily led and the undecided. Miss Hardemon was none of those. Don't you be.'

After the service it was the tradition that every member of the school should file past the head-teacher, as they had once filed past Bess Hardemon, to shake her hand. Surprisingly Imogen had sustained this archaic custom and there was a long wait inside for row upon row of pupils to be dismissed. While the organist played a succession of rousing chorales a long crocodile formed outside the church and began the walk back to school.

Sarah was behind Matthew Illingworth, who made a pretence of wiping his hand on the seat of his trousers after contact with Imogen. Then Sarah took Imogen's hand herself. She was conscious of the cool grip of those long fingers and that Imogen's eyes held the merest hint of a mocking smile. But it was already time to move on. The pressure of bodies behind them was intense.

On the return trek to Priors Heath Sarah walked as if it was already her last day in the school. She was a participant in this ritual but in her head she had moved on. Priors Heath was about to undergo yet another transformation with its new buildings and its new neighbour, a supermarket. Imogen had shaken the school up and was now nudging her way into being fully accepted, as strong, as prickly and as irrepressible as ever.

And yet, thought Sarah, just for a moment it was good to be part of something timeless. Matthew Illingworth bobbed off the kerb and on to the road, out of habit removed a packet of cigarettes from his pocket, realized Sarah's eye was upon him and thought better of it. They came within sight of the school and Sarah saw with affection the familiar grace of the eighteenth-century façade and the way pupils poured through its open doors and round the side of the buildings as they were received back into the routine of the school day.

Sarah trod steadily and deliberately up the steps and into the entrance hall which milled with pupils on their way to the quad or the marble staircase. In this place people were always on their way to somewhere else.

18

Summer Festival, June 1859

The Summer Festival, held for the past two years at the beginning of June, was a celebration of the formal reopening of Priors Heath in May 1856.

In the morning the entire school was marched to St Matthew's Church for a service given by Reverend Rush. The grey frocks worn by the poor clergy daughters in the 1830s and '40s had been abolished by Bess but she did try to impose some degree of uniformity on the girls' clothes. For formal occasions such as this she insisted on plain, light dresses, preferably white, and straw bonnets. Each girl carried a white rose as a sign of hope and new, young life.

The long crocodile winding along the narrow pavements in the high street naturally attracted many stares and comments. Some ladies stood beneath fringed parasols to wave at their daughters who wisely ignored them. They had been ordered to walk in silence and warned of draconian punishment should anyone break the rule.

Bess marched behind her charges, on the alert for transgressors. In former years there had been a holiday spirit about this day, with girls allowed quiet conversation in the crocodile and even back at school. But absolute rules, Bess had now decided, were best. Talk led to giggles, disrespectful comment and an exchange of gossip.

There had been opposition to this new strictness from a surprising quarter. Miss Caroline Wentworth had actually protested that the girls were becoming resentful about the many regulations suddenly imposed on them without justification.

'They must learn obedience and self-discipline,' Bess had retorted. 'I'm preparing them for a lifetime of service to others. One day they'll thank me. Besides, they're free to do whatever they like in the garden.'

Helen Boulder had been present during the conversation, but had said nothing. She and Bess had already fallen out over this same question.

The crocodile wove its way into the little close and along the paved path to the church porch. Bess never forgot to seek out the tiny grey headstone marking Miss Porter's grave but today the sight of it made her fists clench. There had been so much cruelty and injustice in the past and yet Bess had the guilty sense that sometimes she craved the simplicity of those days. Then the way forward had seemed so clear. The fight for a proper diet, heat and kindness for the girls had taken all her energy.

Rush stood in his cassock at the church door like a butler welcoming a house party. Beside him, decked out in clerical plum silk, was Mrs Penhaligon, very much the lady of the house. The pair of them waylaid Bess.

'Excellent, excellent news, Miss Hardemon,' said Mrs Penhaligon in a confidential whisper. 'What do you think? The Wyatt family has moved into The Dower House in Loom Lane.'

'I fail to see . . .'

'So Lady Edgbaston and I both agree that now there can be no possible objection to the girls attending Priors Heath because of course the family won't be living over the shop any more. Now then, Miss Hardemon, I do hope you're not going to object. So many of our girls have fathers who work in business and have only recently bought property that if we allowed prejudice to get in the way of common sense we'd have to exclude half the school.'

Mrs Penhaligon's eyes were fixed on a point somewhere behind Bess's left ear, as if to say: I know you're going to be awkward about this but I won't listen to a word of protest.

'And of course,' added Rush, with a little cough, 'there is the matter of the donation. We must consider the donation.'

Mrs Penhaligon looked at him with exasperation. She obviously thought it indelicate to mention money at this stage, and especially in church.

Well good heavens, thought Bess, I wouldn't have thought it possible to embarrass Mrs Penhaligon. 'The donation?' she prompted.

'Mr Wyatt has offered us three hundred and fifty pounds as a down payment on the assembly hall,' announced Rush triumphantly, 'and more to follow, provided, of course, there is some dedication . . . possibly the naming of the hall. I had no idea Mr Wyatt's business was so prosperous. He's opened another shop in Westbury. Not a very big store, but thriving. And there are plans for a third, in North Faringford. So now, Miss Hardemon, your great scheme to build a hall can go ahead straight away.' He might have been a conjuror proudly producing a live white rabbit from his hat.

There was a brief pause. Bess knew she was cornered. Snobbery and greed had triumphed. She could hardly show her disapproval by refusing to admit either the girls or their father's money.

'It's a great pity the children weren't received into the school at Christmas. We might all have been spared a good deal of soul-searching.'

'I think Mr Wyatt was a little presumptuous to expect us to take them in January. But I suppose that's his nature. How can a businessman hope to succeed in the modern world if he's not just a little over-insistent?' murmured Mrs Penhaligon with a tolerant smile. 'He would be the first to agree that one of the many virtues of this school is its determination to take only the best type of girl. In his heart, I'm sure, he is glad

343

we didn't make an exception which might be an unfortunate precedent in the future.'

One of the main problems with holding the Summer Service in the church was that it gave the girls a rare chance for insubordination. The staff couldn't keep an eye on every pupil and Bess was expected to sit in the front row with the rest of the Board. Her shoulders grew more rigid each time there was a rustle or suppressed giggle from the pews behind.

Rush bumbled heavily to and fro across the chancel like a large beetle. His entourage of altar boys, released for the morning from the grammar school, whisked in and out of his path, intent on impressing the fluttering congregation of girls. Carnegie and Gerald Hardemon were allowed only a minor role in the proceedings.

The recent scandal over Peachey and Mrs Lytton had perhaps influenced Rush in his choice of sermon which was entitled: 'Our Future Mothers and Wives'. The general reaction among Faringford ladies had been to castigate the adulterous Christina Lytton rather than the charming, unmarried George Peachey and as she had no firm connection with the school a general outcry had been avoided after all.

Nevertheless, it would have been wiser for Rush to have chosen a much safer topic. Bess could imagine the nudges and smirks passing between the older girls in the back rows.

I can never fully banish the thought of George Peachey from my mind, she thought. I can only hope that time will be kind to me and dull the pain of missing him.

After a while she succeeded in turning her attention to the news she'd just heard about the Wyatts. The assembly hall was now a reality. Next year, if the building work went smoothly, this service might take place at Priors Heath. Then she would have complete control over proceedings and might even be able to restrict Rush to saying one or two short prayers.

'Our dear Headmistress, Miss Hardemon,' intoned Rush, who

had now embarked on a summary of the school's most recent achievements, 'has formed a liaison with other like-minded heads of school, in the hope that soon girls will be entered for public examinations. Furthermore rumours are afoot that there is to be a Schools Commission and Miss Hardemon herself might be asked to give evidence to it. Priors Heath, you see, is becoming an institution of national . . .'

Bess sat bolt upright, tense with frustration. It was a sheer waste of time to be pinned to a seat listening to Rush when there was so much to be done. From a few rows behind came a badly stifled snort of laughter.

No sunlight streamed through the long stained-glass windows above the chancel. Dear Lord, Bess prayed, don't let it rain this afternoon. Tea could be served in the garden on a fine day, thereby lessening the crush in the school. Ah, here was a new problem. If the assembly hall were to be built on the site of the rose garden, where would they hold future tea parties and fêtes, which, though disruptive, were great fund-raisers?

The congregation had risen to its feet and was singing: 'Lord of all Hopefulness, Lord of all Joy . . .' Bess joined in with her clear, tuneful voice. Certainly, she thought, she had now almost recovered from the blow dealt her by Christina and Peachey and was generally full of hopefulness again, but where was her joy?

Mrs Penhaligon pointed out that not even the sun would defy Miss Hardemon. By the afternoon there was enough blue sky for folding tables to be set up in the garden with some confidence. The girls were allowed to change after lunch and many compensated for their normal puritanical dress by adorning themselves in layer upon layer of ribbons and frills. Bess couldn't help being proud of them, even though she thought they looked ridiculous. They were so happy and excited, full of high spirits and a sense of occasion. It occurred to her that perhaps one of the greatest gifts Priors Heath had given them was a world of their own in which to shine.

Before tea parents were crammed into the schoolroom for a concert. Bess stood at the door to supervise proceedings while the performers lined up in the entrance hall under the watchful eye of Miss Wentworth.

Constance Edgbaston was to play a Mozart sonata and was third in line, decked out in a tiered pink frock with a puffy skirt and straining bodice. Flushed and unhappy she peered at her music as if she'd never seen it before.

'Constance, it will all be over in a few minutes,' said Miss Wentworth, 'you know the piece so well. There's no need to be afraid.'

'But I'm no good. I know it. They'll all think I'm terrible.'

'Music is perhaps not your greatest strength, Constance, but your mother will be so proud of you just for trying. You know that.'

'I'm useless at everything,' moaned Constance.

'That's untrue. You have some fine qualities. You always try, even though you do find things hard. You're brave, and that's a gift in itself, Constance.'

Bess, eavesdropping on this conversation, was ashamed. That girl's lack of confidence is probably my fault, she admitted. I belittle her because she's so slow and lumpy. My goodness, I really have lost my way. I had made it my mission to find only the good in each child and here am I deriding Constance for sweating in an unsuitable silk frock. I ought to be on her side.

She watched the girl take her seat at the piano stool and wipe her damp palms across her bodice. Constance played as if every phrase was a separate challenge but the applause at the end was extra loud in deference to Lady Edgbaston who beamed and nodded in the front row.

'Well done, Constance,' Bess murmured, touching the child's arm. 'I'm very proud of you.' She was repaid first by a look of cringing anxiety, then by dawning pleasure. It was probably

346

the first kind thing Bess had said to her for six months. I must stop judging them, Bess thought sadly, and learn to cherish them once more. This is Peachey's doing. He has made me bitter.

It occurred to her as she watched the slight figure of Caroline Wentworth move along the row of girls that as a headmistress she had lost a great deal over the last three years. Miss Wentworth had an affinity with her pupils. She loved to talk to them and nurture their talents. For Bess, on the other hand, the girls had become a source of endless worry. They fretted her. She wanted perfection from them and she watched them hawk-eyed for any signs of rebellion. Since the Lytton–Peachey affair the girls seemed to her exceptionally vulnerable.

And even Caroline Wentworth had begun to prove difficult. She was working alongside Bess on the scheme to prepare the girls for public examination, should they ever be allowed to enter, and had some hare-brained plan to sit the papers herself and possibly even go on to study for a degree. Caroline subscribed to all kinds of periodicals which filled her head with radical notions of higher education for women.

After the concert there was a shocking display of female vanity as the girls ran out into the garden with their mothers, exclaiming over each others' frocks whilst silently calculating whose was the most expensive. Bess stood in a corner by the wall and tried to visualize how the assembly hall would look in place of the rose-beds. Would such an imposing building perhaps make the nearby schoolroom very dark?

She was not left undisturbed for long. A succession of parents came up to shake her hand and express concerns about aspects of their daughters' learning. 'She has taken to sitting cross-legged, Miss Hardemon. What can I do?' 'Miss Hardemon, I've heard it suggested that the girls are to witness the dissection of a frog. Please ensure a female specimen is chosen.'

Mary had come rushing out of the house and was hopping about from one foot to the other.

'What is it, Mary?'

'Excuse me, Miss Hardemon. If you don't mind. Could I have a word?'

They withdrew out of earshot of nearby parents, who tried not to look too interested.

'What is it? Do calm down, Mary.'

'It's Mrs Lytton. She's in the carriage. She wants to see you.'

Bess could feel the drain of colour from her face. 'Of course I can't see her. What is she thinking of? Tell her I'm not available.'

'I did. She said please to let you know she was leaving the country. She was very anxious to speak with you.'

It was imperative to keep Christina's unexpected arrival from all these crowds of parents so Bess had no choice but to hurry out to the forecourt where a number of carriages were waiting and a playful breeze ruffled the tails and manes of the horses.

Near the gate a coachman was perched high on a hired carriage, whip in hand. The door was flung wide as Bess approached. She stopped in her tracks and looked with hostility towards Christina Lytton, whose face was hidden by the veil of her bonnet.

'Won't you sit inside with me?' Christina pleaded.

Nothing would induce Bess to climb into that dark interior. Christina lifted her veil and Bess saw that her beauty had changed again. Her eyes shone with health, her cheeks seemed rounder and her lips fuller. Though clearly nervous, she managed a tentative smile. 'We're catching the night train to Paris and we don't intend to come back to England for some time. I had to see you before I left. You've been constantly on my mind.'

She is probably the most selfish creature I have ever known, thought Bess.

'Miss Hardemon, I would not have hurt you for the world but I had to do what I did. It was my only chance. My decision to leave with George was very sudden, but even with more time it would have been wrong to write and warn you of it. I had no intention of being dissuaded, you see.'

George. Of course she called him George now. How audacious and proprietorial.

Christina's skirts of pale green lawn filled the carriage and the fringes of a lavender silk mantle hung over the seat. George Peachey and Christina were travelling to Paris by night and would sleep there in a shared bed. Bess's own closeness to this extraordinary experience, and her immeasurable distance from it sickened her.

'Miss Hardemon.' Christina actually reached out to touch Bess who stepped backwards to avoid contact. 'The truth is I love him. So much. Perhaps I ought not to have left but I don't regret it, even though I see now that the pain I have caused you is worse than I thought.'

Bess recoiled deeper and deeper into herself. Christina spoke of her stolen, immoral love so baldly, without shame.

'There is no other excuse than that,' continued Christina, her voice low and intense. 'I thought I could never be happy, and then I met George and I understood the joy of loving and being loved. Suddenly my life had value. It was an excitement I had only experienced once before, when I first met you. I realized then how much one person could nurture and inspire another, and I suppose I've been looking for that same exhilaration ever since.'

Bess spoke at last. 'You made your choice when you married your husband.'

'Ah yes, I deserve blame, not for leaving Charles but for marrying him at all. I was tempted by his kindness and by the chances he offered me to work on my paintings. These are not good enough reasons, I know. And I'm deeply ashamed of them. But I've paid heavily for being Charles's wife. You see I wasn't what he thought. He had few expectations of me except that I would be beautiful and look after his house and child and maybe become a mother, certainly be —' She broke off suddenly and looked away. 'He patronized my work. It was part of the ornament he displayed to his friends. But it got in his way. When he was at home I was to be entirely available to him and when he was absent all the housekeeping and teaching Rebecca had to be done so that on his return no one was busy with anything else except him. I think he very soon grew disenchanted with me, very soon he spent nights –'

Bess interrupted curtly. 'Marriage is sacred. Your duty was to support him. How you've disappointed him, Christina. Did you take any real interest in his business concerns or his family?'

'Miss Hardemon, he gave me no chance. He never took me seriously. The contrast with my life now makes me wonder how I survived so long in that house. George thinks I could be a great painter, Miss Hardemon. We're going abroad so we can work in peace. He'll write and I'll paint.'

Christina's eyes shone with enthusiasm. But Bess was relentless. Why did I never see before that she was just a butterfly? she thought. There is no depth to all this, she's as empty-headed as the worst of my junior girls.

'Did you consider Rebecca at all?' she asked.

At last Christina did look a little regretful. 'Yes. The hardest thing is to think of that child cooped up in the Abbey House. I had a sort of dream that Charles would agree to send her to you.'

'Not after you'd run away with one of my staff. I saw Rebecca in February. I think you have done her lasting damage. She lost one mother years ago and now you have deserted her. What a price, Mrs Lytton, for your pleasure.'

Bess paused for another moment to watch Christina's eyes cloud with sorrow, then she turned away.

But still Christina didn't give up. 'One last thing, Miss Hardemon. I have a gift for you. I wanted to thank you somehow, though you probably won't understand. All the happiness in my life has been due to you. I have designed a window, to go over the stairs in the entrance hall. I always think of you by that staircase, Miss Hardemon. I shall of course pay for its installation.' A roll of parchment was held out to Bess who kept her hands clasped together.

'Please, Miss Hardemon. Please.'

But Bess was walking away, dodging the carriages and their patient horses, skirting groups of parents in the entrance hall. Her heart was pounding.

She stood in the empty schoolroom for a moment and felt a flash of triumph. At least she had dented Christina's unbearable happiness a little. But already she was ashamed of her own harshness. She heard her father's slow, careful voice telling her that the desire for revenge was a slow poison.

But Christina has done a terrible thing, she thought. There can be no question of forgiveness.

Impulsively she hurried out of the hall and back to the forecourt, though conscious that the curious eyes of waiting servants were watching her. The horses pulling Christina's carriage had stepped daintily backwards to clear the gates and were now being whipped onwards.

Bess waved her hand. 'Excuse me. One moment.'

The window was thrust down and the door flung open. The carriage was still moving and Christina called to the driver. Her veil was clinging to her wet cheeks as she leaned out to Bess.

'I've been back inside the school and certainly the hall is very dark,' said Bess.

The parchment was placed in her hands. Bess, who had made this one concession at great personal cost, shut the door firmly and turned away.

The shade in the garden was soothing. Roses were in full bloom and their heady perfume blew softly across the paths as Bess walked slowly out among her pupils. She sent one of them off to fetch her a cup of tea and the girl skipped away with touching alacrity.

'Miss Hardemon.' Carnegie stood directly in the sunlight so that he overshadowed her completely. 'I have come to say goodbye.'

She looked up at him in utter confusion. Where had he sprung from so suddenly?

'Have you had tea already then?' she asked stupidly.

'I mean I am going overseas. To India.'

'I see.' Here at least is some good news, she thought. 'I hadn't realized. I had thought you intended to stay in this country for good. Weren't you unwell last time you went abroad?'

'I was going to stay here, yes.' He had fixed her with his unfathomable eyes. 'But I believe it is my duty now to work as a missionary again.'

'I'm sure there are plenty in India who will benefit from your charity.'

'Miss Hardemon, I have a request to make before I go. I've heard that you might intend to have the new assembly hall built on the site of this rose garden. I think it would be a pity.'

They both stared about them a moment at the luxurious flowers and the flounced dresses of the girls. Still shaken by her interview with Christina, Bess scarcely knew where she was. It was surely not possible that Carnegie, of all people, was asking her to preserve the garden.

'Why, Reverend. It's an ideal situation for a large hall. Don't you agree? So easily reached on a wet day under a short, covered way. The other possibility, of purchasing the site beside the boarding house, would be both more expensive and very inconvenient.'

'But to lose the garden . . .'

Bess couldn't help smiling at the irony of her situation. But looking up at him she remembered that he had lost his one, dear sister and decided to be kind. 'Some of it would be preserved. I believe there will be space for several beds and perhaps a hedged walk around the hall.'

'No. No. To leave so little would be a great shame. A shame.' Carnegie seemed more than ever at a loss for words and could only repeat 'a shame'. He turned and looked again at the brightness of the garden. 'I have many memories of this garden. Many memories, Miss Hardemon.'

For the first time Bess felt a little sympathy for Carnegie who was close to admitting that the earlier destruction of the blossom trees had been a great sin. He looked away from her, vaguely following the progress of the girl in pale blue who approached with Bess's tea. Did he too remember the clusters of freezing, underfed children who still haunted this garden?

'I know that this school means a great deal to you, Reverend,' she said at last. 'We've had our differences, you and I, but from the very first I have been aware that you've always had the school's best interests at heart. I will bear in mind what you have said.'

By a twitch of his shoulder and a straightening of his spine, he drew himself even more upright. His voice in reply was as toneless as ever. 'Yes, I believe you will. Then I hope the garden will be saved.' He made no move to leave her side even though the conversation had obviously reached an end.

Suddenly she put out her hand. 'I shall miss you,' she said.

His great fist closed over her small fingers. When he spoke his voice was so low that she wondered afterwards if she had heard him correctly. 'It would give me great comfort to know that were true.'

Lady Edgbaston hove within calling distance and Bess withdrew her hand.

'Miss Hardemon. A word. Constance tells me you have been explaining the theories of Charles Darwin. Do you really think that's wise? I have discussed the matter at length with dear Reverend Rush and he suggested I speak to you in person.'

Later, when the garden was cleared, the tables folded and the girls dismissed, Bess began a meticulous patrol of her school, closing windows and picking up a discarded programme.

At the bottom of the white staircase she paused and peered through the gloom of the entrance hall which seemed a melancholy place once it had been abandoned by the girls who brought it life. A stained-glass window was certainly a good idea. But Christina would always be a presence on these steps now, with her disturbing beauty and rare talent for twining herself into the consciousness of others.

It occurred to Bess that what she had told Carnegie was true. She would miss him. For years he had been her whetstone. Her energy and indignation had been generated in part by her hostility to him so that he had become a part of what she was. She shook her head in an effort to dismiss him from her mind.

Helen Boulder was waiting in her office, her face drawn with exhaustion. The day had been taxing for all the staff, and Helen was still not fully recovered from her attack of influenza which had left her with a rasping cough. They had taken to drinking tea together late in the afternoon, to mull over the events of the day and to discuss any outstanding correspondence. Bess settled herself in her usual chair and accepted a cup. Helen, sensitive to her mood, sat opposite and waited.

'I am very tired tonight, Helen. Is there anything urgent remaining to be done?'

'Nothing urgent.'

There followed a long pause.

'Of course you know Mrs Lytton was here.'

'Oh yes. Dear Mrs Lytton.' Helen was actually smiling rather fondly. Ridiculous woman, thought Bess.

'She has given us a window, of all things, to be installed above the stairs. What do you think of that?'

They peered at Christina's design which seemed extraordinarily modern in its simplicity and brilliant colours. 'Artistic licence, I presume,' said Helen, 'none of the girls has her hair tied back.'

'Hardly Constance Edgbaston,' said Bess, tracing the flowing robes of one of the maidens in the design. 'You see the space in the scroll, for a motto. Mrs Lytton, in her directions, suggests: "*Fiat Lux*". A little pretentious for a humble girls' school, don't you think?' She caught Helen's eye and both smiled at her use of the word 'humble'.

Helen was reading Christina's suggestions that the window be crafted by hand. 'She has been more than generous,' she murmured.

Both women were silent for a while. Helen coughed, and a spoon rattled against her teacup.

For how many more years will I sit here night after night with Helen Boulder? Bess wondered.

After a while she roused herself. 'Tomorrow we'll call in the architects to draw up plans for the assembly hall. I shall take advice on where to put it. With the Wyatt money we can be more flexible. Dr Ford recommends the firm of Manners and Henderson so we certainly shan't choose them.'

'I have the addresses of three local companies. And I think you should visit other schools to be certain of what you want.'

'There must be plenty of light. I'm sure of that. And I'd like the girls to be able to recite and perform on a proper stage. Shall we draw up a few proposals?'

Helen picked up paper and pencil.

Outside a fine evening closed over the garden. Girls' voices could be heard at supper in the boarding house. The maid Mary slammed a door downstairs.

19

Founder's Day, April 1996

In the art room at the end of the day dust floated through thick orange sunshine.

Sonia Castelino and a couple of other students were stationed there, guarding a display of 'A' level work. Sarah stepped slowly through the warm light to examine the portfolio on Christina Lytton.

A copy of Bess Hardemon's portrait had been pinned to a board and surrounded by Sonia's own drawings. Ms Sarah Beckett had been caught from ten different angles, head down reading, animated in conversation or in moments of repose. Sonia had attempted to show how Lytton might have built up her portrait of Bess Hardemon from a similar set of rapid sketches.

So that's me, thought Sarah. I wonder, what do I think of this woman? In some of the portraits she looked surprisingly sharp-eyed but there was occasionally an amused, affectionate smile that Sarah found rather pleasing. She moved hurriedly on, not wishing to be seen admiring herself.

'This picture of "The Childless Woman" was one of the few Lytton's husband didn't destroy after her elopement,' Sonia told her. 'Her stepdaughter bequeathed it to Birmingham City Art Gallery. But you see the contrast between it and the next paintings. From here on her brush strokes are much freer and her paintings are infused with colour and light.'

Suddenly the peace of the room was disturbed by the arrival

of Imogen with a party of governors. Sonia hurried forward eagerly to meet them and there was a buzz and press of bodies in the room.

The last paintings were the most famous. Sonia had researched Lytton's influences in the years between 1859 when she had fallen in love with Reverend George Peachey and her death in childbirth in 1867. Her painting of 'Desdemona and the handkerchief' had been deconstructed alongside Burne-Jones's 'The Backgammon Players'. Lytton's preoccupation with texture and colour relationships were, according to Sonia, exceptionally sophisticated.

In Lytton's finest work, 'The Gatehouse', all the usual Pre-Raphaelite fascination for the natural world was evident in the way ivy and ferns seemed to cling to and caress the old brickwork, while clear daylight filtered through the trees. But Lytton had branched out sufficiently to invest her characters with such feeling that it was an intensely intimate painting. A man and a woman were pressed cheek to cheek under the arch of the gatehouse, his face turned away completely, hers in grey half-light as she looked towards a third figure, that of a woman in a blue dress who stood as if suddenly arrested by the sight of the embracing couple. Only her smooth head and high cheek-bone were visible but the tension between the two women, rivals in love presumably, was a remarkable achievement.

Sarah had been conscious for some moments that Imogen had come up behind her. She could feel her heat and smell her faint, musky perfume.

Imogen's long finger with its smooth, oval nail pointed to the woman in blue. 'Bess Hardemon. In every painting. Idealized here in "Desdemona". And even in "The Childless Woman". It's her, time after time.'

'Surely not. No. How can you tell?'

'I've talked about it to Sonia. It's possible. Artists did reuse material all the time. There's something to do with her posture and the way she holds her head that gives away the fact that it's the same woman. Don't you see it?'

'But why?' Sarah murmured.

'Fascination, I suppose. Or obsession. Or guilt.'

Sonia was on the other side of the room, talking eagerly to the chair of governors.

'Is she all right?' asked Sarah quietly.

'Oh, she's fine now. But Robin will have to go. There's no doubt he was well out of order. Look at her.'

Sonia had certainly changed. She had lost her former softness and become watchful and self-conscious. Aware of her power, she smiled up at the chairman and touched his arm to direct his attention to another painting.

Sarah and Imogen were perched side by side on the edge of a table, their hands inches apart. In a moment or two Imogen would spring away, cat-like, and lead the governors back to her office. She had never hung about in her life.

Suddenly a sharp elbow was pressed into Sarah's upper arm. 'Do you remember the bowl of fruit?' Imogen said, and laughed. 'I have never in my life seen anyone as horrified as you. It was worth it for the expression on your face. Poor Sarah.'

Their heads went down and their shoulders shook with laughter, as in the old days they had struggled to regain composure in time to avoid a telling off.

'I tell you what,' said Sarah, 'if I had the chance again, this time I'd go for the peach.'

Hughes